About

Ann Lethbridge studie[...] always loved the glamorous, if rather risky, Georgians and in particular the Regency era as drawn by Georgette Heyer. It was that love that prompted her to write her first Regency novel in 2000. She found she enjoyed it so much she just couldn't stop! Ann gave up a career in university administration to focus on her first love, writing novels, and lives in Canada with her family. Visit her website at annlethbridge.com

Regency Secrets

Regency Secrets:

The Widows
of Westram

ANN LETHBRIDGE

MILLS & BOON

First Published in Great Britain 2023
By Mills & Boon, an imprint of HarperCollins*Publishers* Ltd,
1 London Bridge Street, London, SE1 9GF

www.harpercollins.co.uk

HarperCollins*Publishers*
Macken House, 39/40 Mayor Street Upper,
Dublin 1, D01 C9W8, Ireland

ISBN: 978-0-263-31902-6

A LORD FOR THE
WALLFLOWER
WIDOW

This book is dedicated to Lilly, a very special young lady who recently came into our lives. Lilly, you may never read Grannie's stories, but provided you grow up a strong, sensible woman like your mother you will make me very proud.

Prologue

April 1812

Redford Greystoke, Earl of Westram, forced himself not to look away from the three black-clad, heavily veiled ladies arraigned before his desk. It broke his heart to see them. Beneath those veils hid three beautiful young women. Two were his sisters, the other his sister-in-law. All of them widowed on the same day, at the same hour. Their husbands had been absolute idiots. Their loss left him numb.

From being an earl with a brother as heir and a spare hopefully in the offing, he'd become the last male member of his family with three destitute women to support. The very reason for their presence here and the reason for the animosity filling the air.

'You *will* remain under my roof,' Red repeated firmly. 'There is no more to be said on the matter.'

'Redford.' Lady Marguerite, his sister older than him by two years, had taken the role of spokesperson. She spoke quietly enough, but nevertheless with underlying heat. 'You cannot tell us where we shall reside.'

The trouble with widows was that they thought of themselves as independent women.

'I can, if I am to foot the bill.' Damn. Now he sounded like a truculent schoolboy. 'Let us be clear, ladies. I do not have the funds to set you up in your own establishments, whether I might wish to do so or not. You will reside with me in Gloucestershire until your period of mourning is over. At which time, I will be more than happy to open the London town house from where we will set out to mingle with our fellow peers.'

Lady Petra, his other sister, glared at him. Despite the veil hiding her face, he knew exactly the look directed his way when she was crossed. Petra was a master of glares. 'If you think I could ever marry anyone else...' A handkerchief in a black gloved hand disappeared beneath her veil. She sniffled.

He mentally cursed. 'No one is forcing you to do anything. If next year you do not wish to attend the Season, or go to balls, you may stay at home.' But knowing women as he did, he had no doubt they'd be bored within a few months of isolation in the country and begging to attend a ball or Almack's.

His sister-in-law, Carrie, the woman he hoped like the very devil was carrying his brother's heir, put an arm around Petra's drooping shoulder. 'It is all right, lass,' she said softly.

He liked Carrie Greystoke. A great deal. She was a practical no-nonsense woman, though she must have had a momentary loss of reason when she'd agreed to wed his harum-scarum brother. Fortunately, since her husband's death, she had been a rock of good sense in the eddying currents of grief and shock.

Sometimes he thought she was almost too calm. The

kind of calm that he suspected hid quiet desperation. He forced the thought aside. All three women were baulking at his proposal and he needed to marshal all his faculties if he was to prevail.

'Pluck up your courage, Petra,' Marguerite said. 'No need for tears because a bunch of idiots went off and got themselves killed.'

Marguerite had also wept on his shoulder when the news had been delivered. The fact that she now had her emotions under control was a very good thing. He hoped.

Petra, who had lost not only her husband and lover but her very best friend in the world, buried her head on Carrie's shoulder and sobbed.

Red wanted to bury his head in his hands and weep, too. For a few short weeks, he'd thought he was finally able to see his way clear of the debt left him by his father. Until the earth crumbled from beneath his feet, leaving this gaping abyss. He still didn't know what had sent these women's husbands off to join Wellington's army. Some sort of wager was the only explanation he'd been able to glean from their friends. Whatever it was, it had been the most nonsensical ridiculous prank— He cut the thought off. There was nothing he could do about the past. The future was his concern now.

The thing that had shocked him the most was the extent of Jonathan's debts. They had eaten up every penny and more of the wealth brought into the family by his marriage to Carrie. Red still could not believe he had not known that his brother had dipped so deeply in the River Tick.

And what his father had been about, letting Red's two sisters marry men without prospects, he could not imagine. Except that his father had been overindulgent where his daughters were concerned, giving them whatever their hearts desired. Which was why they were being so dashed difficult now.

'I think it would be best if you would let us at least try to manage on our own,' Carrie said, over his sobbing sister's head. 'We won't be a burden on you, Westram. I promise you that.'

If Carrie supported his sisters' mad scheme, then he was lost. Sensible and down to earth and as stubborn as they came, she would never give in. Perhaps it would be best if they learned first-hand that they were like babes in the woods when it came to the real world. Then they would listen to reason. His reason.

He threw his hands in the air. 'As you wish. I will give you the period of your mourning to try this experiment. I can afford very little in the way of allowances.' He shot Carrie a look of apology. 'I am so sorry, but all the money you brought to the marriage has gone to pay Jonathan's debts.' Jonathan had also charmed her father into handing over what should have been her widow's portion to invest in what his brother had called a sure thing on the 'Change. If her father had talked to Red beforehand, he would have disabused him of the notion. And maybe Jonathan would still be alive today. 'I would replace what my brother misappropriated, if I had it. I do not. Perhaps in time...' He tailed off, sick at heart. His sisters were no better off. He was appalled that their husbands had left their affairs in such disarray. He sighed. 'I will give you the use of Westram Cottage in Kent provided you can keep yourselves on that property within your allowances.' He glared at them. It was the only way he could maintain his dignity. 'I will be checking.'

They'd be back knocking on his door within a month.

Marguerite rose. Carrie did likewise, helping his younger sister to her feet. As always, he was taken aback by the woman's height compared to that of his sisters. His family tended to be on the short side.

'Thank you, Red,' Marguerite said, her voice warmer than it had been since this discussion had started. 'You will not regret it.'

Oh, yes, he would. Of that he had no doubt.

The ladies filed out.

Red poured himself a brandy and swallowed it in one gulp.

Chapter One

April 1813

Carrie Greystoke carefully dusted each shelf, as she had done every morning since the little shop had opened three days before. She replaced what she considered the shop's *pièce de résistance*, a sumptuous leghorn bonnet decorated with handmade flowers and cherry-coloured ribbons, in the window and took up her position behind the counter. Hope however, was beginning to fade.

In the three days since the doors of First Stare Millinery had opened not one customer had entered the little shop. If she didn't sell something soon, they would likely have to admit defeat. The thought of going to the landlord to admit her error in thinking she and her sisters-in-law could sell the product of the hard work they had put into the bonnets these last few months was humiliating.

Mr Thrumby, a friend of her dead father's, had taken a chance in renting her the shop. For her father's sake. Perhaps if it had been located on Bond Street rather than the less fashionable Cork Street... But then it would have been far too expensive. As it was, they'd had to pool all of their meagre resources to pay the first month's rent on this narrow little establishment. Shelves lined one wall, displaying bonnets on little stands. The glass-topped counter behind which she stood had been an extravagance, but was an absolute necessity to display the painted fans, lacy gloves and embroidered slippers also made by her sisters-in-law.

After an hour, she slumped on to the stool. Perhaps she should rearrange the window again? What on earth was she to tell Petra and Marguerite? They would be so disappointed when she returned home in two days' time with nothing to show for their efforts.

A shadow fell over the window display.

Carrie straightened and pinned a smile on her lips.

The shadow passed on. Her heart sank.

'I be back, missus.'

Jeb, their young ruddy-faced lad of all work at Westram Cottage, had brought her up to town the day before the shop opened. It was he who had built the shelves and carried in the counter she had purchased in a down-at-heel shop in the Seven Dials. He'd also helped her furnish the room she used as lodgings at the back of the shop, since it was too far for her to travel home to Kent each evening.

Marguerite had not been happy about this last arrangement, but had given in when Carrie agreed to come home to Kent with Jeb as her escort every Saturday night in order to attend church with them in the morning. They planned that she would return on Monday afternoons with new stock for the shop.

Not that they would be needing any new stock. They still had all the old stock left.

'Did you deliver all of the flyers to the addresses I gave you, Jeb?'

'Yes, mum.'

The flyers had been another costly idea they could ill afford, but she had to get the word out about their offerings somehow. An advertisement in the newspaper would have reached more people, but was horribly expensive.

Unfortunately, she had no way of knowing if the flyers had got into the right hands. Perhaps she should go and stand at the entrance to Hyde Park and hand them out herself to passers-by. Not just any passers-by, but ladies of quality with good fashion sense.

It might work.

She would go about five this afternoon. Fortunately, she was still largely unknown to society as she had not been introduced to very many people of the *ton* before her hasty marriage to Jonathan. In addition, their wedding had been a tiny family affair, because her father had been at death's door. Why Jonathan had even singled her out… She squashed the thought and the accompanying pang.

Face it, Carrie. He'd chosen her because he'd been looking for a way out of his money troubles. Somehow Father must have learned of this circumstance and, worried about her future once he passed away, had made Jonathan an offer he couldn't refuse. Carrie had known none of this when she'd arrived in London before the Season began. Jonathan had been pointed out to her by her aunt when she went on her first carriage ride in London. He'd bowed to her and she'd agreed with her aunt that he really was a most handsome gentleman. The next day he'd arrived at her door on a morning call and a few days later had proposed.

Everyone had said it was love at first sight. She'd been a complete fool to believe such nonsense.

In hindsight, it was as plain as the nose on her very plain face—he'd only married her to get himself out of debt. If she had known, she would never have agreed. Not even to please her dying father, who had been thrilled to see his daughter become one of the nobs. She certainly hadn't expected her bridegroom to take to his heels the morning after the ceremony. No doubt he couldn't stand the thought of living with his plain, middle-class, gruff wife. That had hurt dreadfully. Worse yet, he'd not even done her the courtesy of coming to her bed on their wedding night.

That particular rejection had hurt to the core of her soul. And still did, when she listened to her sisters-in-law giggle about the joys of the marriage bed during the long winter evenings at Westram Cottage when they'd been working on fabricating the hats and bonnets they now hoped to sell. Not that she'd ever told them the truth about her wedding night.

'Put what is left on the counter, Jeb, please. It is time for you to return to the cottage. I am sure the other ladies have all manner of things for you to do.'

Jeb scratched at his unshaven chin. The poor fellow had been required to bed down with the horse in a stables some distance from the shop, since there was no place for him to rest his head here.

'Are you sure, mum? I don't like leaving you here alone. A bed of iniquity Lunnon is. Me ma said so.'

'I will be perfectly fine. The locks you have added to the doors and the bars on the windows will keep me quite safe. And Mr Thrumby's man is more than a match for any intruder.' Mr Thrumby's man guarded the back entrance at night.

Jeb's expression remained doubtful, but she kept hers firm and unyielding.

'As you wish, Mrs Greystoke.' His formal use of her married name was his way of administering an admonition. But it was worse than that. It was a lie. She never really had been Mrs Greystoke. Not properly. Little did anyone know the use of her married name made her resentment of her husband burn like acid.

She forced her mind back to more mundane topics. 'I will see you back here on Saturday afternoon.'

He touched his forelock and left.

Now she really was on her own.

She slid open the top drawer of the counter, removed three of the lacy embroidered handkerchiefs and put them in the front window. Handkerchiefs were not as expensive as bonnets. A cheaper purchase might lure someone in. She shifted the bonnet to present a more intriguing angle and returned to her stool.

One sale. Then she would be sure she was on the right path.

Lord Avery Gilmore, younger son of the Duke of Belmane, stepped out into the street and blinked in the light of mid-morning. The porter of the gaming hell where he'd spent the last many hours slammed the door behind him. Avery grinned. His night had been reasonably successful. His pockets were plump enough to ensure not only that there would be food on his sister's table for a few more days, there would plenty left over for coal for his fireplace and a bottle of really fine brandy.

He never came home empty handed. After his father had thrown him out of the family for refusing to marry the woman Papa had chosen, he'd had years of living by his wits on several continents to hone his skills at the gambling tables. Last night and into this morning had been more successful than usual. Perhaps Lady Luck had turned her smile his way.

Which was a good thing. All these years of living abroad, he'd become adept at supporting himself, but having learned of his sister's struggles from his older brother, he now felt financially responsible her, too. At least until her husband could earn enough to support his family as a barrister, which would hopefully be soon, since he had recently been called to the bar and accepted for a pupillage in chambers.

Finally, after last night, Avery could truthfully tell Laura not to worry about money, at least for a while.

Blithely, he strode for his lodgings, but halted at the sight of a very pretty bonnet in a window polished to a mirror-like shine. A cleanliness one didn't often find in the backstreets leading off Bond Street. He crossed the street to take a closer look, avoiding the dollops of horse manure and the vagabond lounging in a doorway. Fellows like that would cut your purse in the blink of an eye if you weren't careful.

Avery knew all about cutpurses and their ilk. The owner of the Ragged Staff, the establishment he'd just left, had accused him of being a fraudster, because he had so easily seen through the house's ploy to trick him out of his winnings. For a moment, it had looked as if he might have to fight his way out of the hell, but for the interference of some of the other customers, who were only too happy to see someone win for a change.

Pigeons for the plucking they might be, green as grass, too, but *they* were also gentlemen.

Avery wavered a little on his feet as he stared at the bonnet displayed in the window. He shook his head to clear it. Too much cheap brandy, though he was nowhere close to foxed. His unsteadiness was more from lack of sleep, though he had no doubt he would have the devil of a headache later. He squinted at the hat. The violets and primroses decorating the crown were not real, as he'd thought at first, but silk. He didn't want the hat, but he did want a posy to offer to Mrs Luttrell later. The poor little pet pined for such marks of attention. Would silk flowers raise her spirits?

The confection blurred. Dash it. He was a little more in the bag than he had thought. He really needed to go home to bed. But he also needed a gift...

Silk flowers lasted longer.

No doubt they would also cost a great deal more. Still, Mimi Luttrell would be more compliant with such a mark of attention. And for once he had blunt in his pocket.

He entered the narrow shop.

A tall, remarkably tall, young woman rose to her feet behind the counter. Her face was not pretty exactly, but handsome, with fine grey eyes and a mouth that begged to be kissed even as she frowned. Why was she frowning?

Gad, she really was tall. Not quite his height, but close to it.

'Good day, sir,' she said, her voice pleasantly deep. 'How may I be of service?'

He stared at her in surprise. Outwardly, she looked like a shop girl in her dun-coloured gown and prim cap, but she sounded like a lady, for all that there was a trace of the north in her accent.

Plush full lips pursed in disapproval. 'Is something wrong?'

He dragged his gaze from her mouth to her face. Brought his mind back to the task at hand. He gave her his most charming smile. 'Nothing wrong at all. I simply had not expected to find such a lovely lady brightening my morning.'

The frown reappeared. 'It is after midday, sir, and this is a ladies' millinery shop. Perhaps you mistake where you are?'

He swayed on his feet, surprised by her lack of response to his smile. He had smiled, he was sure of it. 'I beg your pardon, but I certainly do know where I am. Your shop has a remarkable array of very fine bonnets.' That compliment ought to cheer her up. 'And you, I notice, have remarkably beautiful eyes.'

Astonishment filled her face. 'Sir—'

Clearly, he was not up to snuff this morning, or else the lady was not of a flirtatious bent. 'How much for the violets, madam?'

The floor shifted uneasily beneath his feet and he propped a hip against the counter.

Warily she backed up, her expression puzzled. 'Violets?'

'Yes, violets. In the window.'

'There are no— Oh, you mean the ones on the bonnet. They are not for sale.'

Everything was for sale for the right price. 'I'll give you sixpence.'

Her eyes widened. A hint of desperation lurked in

their depths. Grey depths. Grey depths, encircled by a smoky line around the edge.

He waited for her acceptance.

She shook her head. 'I am afraid it would ruin the look of the bonnet.'

He blinked. Had she really turned him down? Well, there was a surprise.

'You can soon make a new trimming.' He waved at the other bonnets. 'Put one of those in the window in the meantime.' He peered at one festooned with rosebuds. 'This is just as pretty as the one in the window.' A wave of dizziness hit him and he rested one hand on the counter for support, hoping she wouldn't notice.

A hand sporting a wedding ring flattened on the counter as if to steady it against his weight. He felt a surge of disappointment at the sight of that ring. Really? No. He was just disappointed that she wouldn't sell him the posy.

'All right. I'll give you a shilling.'

Now who was desperate? And why? He could just as easily buy a posy from a flower girl. There was one on every corner. Except that something told him that this silk posy would be received with a great deal more pleasure. And he never ignored his well-honed instincts of a veteran gambler. Yes, he relied on his skill and never played foolish games of chance, but there was also that certain something that told him when to bet high and when to hold back. And right now, it had a feeling about those flowers.

Another frown shot his way. 'I will not take advantage of a man obviously in his cups. There are plenty of fresh violets for sale on the street at this time of year.' She made a shooing gesture with her arms.

Why the devil was she being so intractable? 'Fresh?' he scoffed. 'I'll be lucky if they last until this afternoon.' He leaned forward, giving her his best friendly smile. 'I need to make a good impression. Those flowers are better than real ones.'

She eyed him askance. 'If you want to make a good impression, you will need to sober up first, I should think.'

'Rather direct and to the point for a shop girl, aren't you?'

She coloured faintly. 'If there is nothing else...'

'I am not leaving until you sell me those flowers.'

'Then you must buy the bonnet.'

Aha! So that was the game she was playing. 'I can't imagine you get many customers stuck away here on this side street. Isn't it better to have a shilling in your hand than no sale at all?'

She closed her eyes briefly. He felt uncomfortable as desperation won out over what had been a very ethical response to his demand. Sadly, he'd been right. Everything did have a price.

'Very well. I will sell you the violets.' She came around the counter. He moved back to allow her to pass in the narrow confines of the shop. Once more he was struck by her height and now got a look at what could only be described as a sumptuous figure. As she leaned over to remove the hat from the window, he ogled the swell of her derrière, its curves beautifully outlined by the dark fabric of her narrow skirts. Surprisingly, for all the fabric's drab colour, it was of the finest quality of cotton.

Which was strange for a shop girl.

He squeezed back against the shelves as she returned to the counter with her prize.

She took down another bonnet to place in the window, not the one he had suggested, he noted, but a summer hat with gauzy yellow ribbons and a cluster of cherries adorning the upturned brim.

Once she was satisfied, she returned and removed the violets from the bonnet and wrapped them in tissue paper. 'I hope your lady is suitably impressed.' She held out her hand. 'One shilling, please.'

The dryness in her voice struck him on the raw. Clearly, she thought the gift paltry. He glanced down at the wares on display in the glass case. 'How much is that handkerchief? The one embroidered with violets.'

'Thruppence.' She smiled for the first time since he had walked into the shop. It changed her whole face from plain to lovely. Not pretty, exactly. But...lovely. He blinked.

She pulled the drawer towards her, withdrew the delicate square from the case and laid it on the counter.

Another wave of exhaustion washed through him. He forced his spine straight. Besides, he'd already spent quite enough. Silk violets for a shilling? He must be more foxed than he'd thought.

'I'll take it, Mrs...'

Again, a wash of colour rose up her face. 'Greystoke.'

Greystoke. The name sounded familiar. Propped against the counter, he watched her fumble in the drawer. She pulled out a calling card which she wrapped inside the tissue paper along with the handkerchief. 'In case you should know of anyone who might be interested in one of our bonnets. They are of the finest workmanship. Perhaps your wife...' She smiled encouragingly.

Once more he found himself staring at her in a bemused fashion. 'I am not married.'

She glanced at the neatly wrapped package. 'I see.'

'Those are for a special lady of my acquaintance.' Hell, why had he felt the need to say such a thing? The recipient of his purchases was none of her business. 'A very special lady.'

'Of course.' Her voice held not a scrap of interest. She tied the package with a ribbon.

He bowed and hand over his calling card. 'It has been a pleasure doing business with you, Mrs Greystoke.'

Out in the street he glanced through the window to see Mrs Greystoke rearranging her display of handkerchiefs and watching him from the corner of her eye. Making sure he departed post-haste, no doubt.

He clapped his hat on his head and marched off.

A spray of silk violets for a shilling. He hoped like hell Mimi Luttrell appreciated the sacrifice.

But he would tell her about the bonnets. Because Mrs Greystoke was right. Even in his inebriated state, he could tell they were of the finest quality.

Whatever hopes Carrie had harboured that Lord Avery's purchase would result in a swarm of ladies interested in hats had died over the following two days. He hadn't bought a hat, he'd merely pillaged its decoration. The hat, *sans* violets, now resided on the highest shelf, there to languish until her return to Kent.

There it remained, a constant reminder of his wheedling smile and beautiful brown eyes rimmed with the longest eyelashes she had ever seen. Disastrously beautiful brown eyes with gold flecks scattered like sunbeams across them. Not to mention how he towered over her, which so few men did. Dash it all, she did not want to think about Lord Avery, the younger son of a duke, she'd realised later, having properly read his calling card. A wealthy young man she should have tried to convince to buy a dozen embroidered handkerchiefs instead getting flustered and wrapping up one. She'd made a proper mull of it, as her father would have said.

The idea of returning to the ladies at Westram with nothing but the grand sum of one shilling and thruppence and a ruined bonnet had given her nightmares. Her handbills had not brought in a single customer and she dared not use any of these meagre funds to print more. All in all, the shop in which she had placed such high hopes was a failure.

They would be able to afford one more week's rent from what little funds they had saved over the winter before she had to close the doors. It was so frustrating. If the ladies of the *ton* saw these bonnets, their original design, their craftsmanship, she had no doubt they would snap them up. But how was she to accomplish it?

For the third time that morning she rearranged the items beneath the glass counter top, putting lacy gloves beside the chicken-skin fan Marguerite had painted with a pastoral scene. The bell above the door tinkled. She straightened. Her jaw dropped. 'Lord Avery?'

He bowed. 'Mrs Greystoke.'

She glanced behind him. There was no sign of the very special lady he had mentioned. 'How may I help you?'

'I have need of another of your fripperies.' He scanned the hats.

Blankly she stared at him. 'This is a millinery shop, my lord. You bought the one and only violet nosegay in the shop and I have no intention of demolishing any more of my stock for a whim. However, I would be more than pleased to sell you a hat in its entirety. What you do with it afterwards would be your prerogative.'

Oh, dear, that was not the way to treat a customer. Especially the younger son of a duke. But really!

'It is hardly demolished.' He gave her that heart-stopping crooked smile that had flustered her the first time he'd gazed at her. He looked even more handsome this morning than he had the other day. His lovely brown eyes were clear and bright, his jacket unrumpled, his dark brown hair carefully ordered. And that smile... It was doing devastating things to her insides. 'And besides,' he continued, 'a hat is far too personal item for a gentleman to purchase. In my experience, a lady needs to try on several bonnets before she can decide on one. Do you let your husband buy your hats?'

'My husband is dead.' She clamped her jaw shut. Now why had she told him that? And in such a blunt manner, too. He might think she was interested in him and before she knew it he'd be taking advantage. That was the sort of thing men did. It had been drummed into her at Mrs Thacker's Academy for the Daughters of Gentlemen.

His expression changed to one of sympathy. 'I am sorry.'

Why should he be sorry? She meant nothing to him. But he was right about him buying his lady a hat. Most women did prefer to choose their own. There was something very intimate about the purchase of a hat and it was decidedly perspicacious of him to realise that particular fact. Clearly the man knew women.

A suggestion was in order. She gave him a tight little smile, wishing she knew how to be a little more charming. 'Perhaps you could bring her with you and let her choose.'

He gave a low chuckle, a deep rich sound that seemed to stir things up low in her belly. 'Perhaps one day. In the meantime...'

'Well, I doubt any lady would be pleased to receive the same gift, even if it is in a different colour and form.'

His brow clouded. 'No. You are right.'

'What about a pair of gloves?' She brought out a pair and set them on the counter.

'Too practical.'

'An embroidered pair of slippers.' She laid several before him.

'Too mundane.'

'Not these. The workmanship is the finest you will see anywhere.'

He shook his head. 'I would prefer something more...'

'Romantic?' She smiled sweetly.

'Unique.'

'What about a fan?' She spread two hand-painted silk fans, showing off the delicate paintings, one of a ballroom scene and the other of the countryside.

He picked one up, opening and closing it and inspecting the painted sticks. 'Very nice. Are they imported from the East?'

'No, my sister-in-law makes them.'

'She is a talented woman.'

Carrie smiled. She loved to hear her sisters-in-law complimented. She'd been an only child and the idea of having sisters thrilled her.

He stood there, staring at her mouth as if he had never seen a woman smile before. Her body flushed warm. Goodness, but the man was a flirt.

'Your special lady will love using it,' she said firmly. 'It is sure to be admired by all her acquaintances.'

He gave her a sharp look. 'And put me in her good graces?'

She nodded encouragingly. 'Of course.'

'How much?'

'Half a crown.'

His lips thinned. 'That's a little steep, don't you think?'

'Is the lady not worth it, my lord?' She flicked it open. 'Nevertheless, because you are a repeat customer, I am willing to sell it to you for two shillings.' That was six-pence more than the price she and the others had agreed upon, but the man's need seemed urgent. And her own needs were pressing in.

'Very well. Two shillings it is. Though I feel I am getting the worst of this bargain.'

It was not good for a customer to feel that way. 'You will not see another fan like this one anywhere, I assure you.'

'I see another right there.' He pointed to a third fan.

She spread it open. On this one, the leaf was a pale blue silk and showed a scene of the ocean at sunset. 'It is not at all the same.'

He grinned. 'You have me there, Mrs Greystoke. Very well, I will take this fan for two shillings.'

He dug out his money pouch. 'I hope you will rec-ommend my shop to your lady,' she said as calmly as possible despite the rapid beating of her heart. Was it him making it beat so fast? Or merely the idea of finally making a sale? She wrapped the fan in tissue. 'When she is next in need of a hat.'

'I most certainly will. Indeed, I will mention your shop to every one of my acquaintances.'

He bowed and left with the little package tucked under his arm.

Carrie could not help admiring his lithe male figure as he disappeared through her shop door. He was so masculine. Despite his elegant tailoring, he looked athletic and fit. He'd no doubt be an excellent lover. She blushed at the unbidden thought. It was his flirting that had made such a wicked thought about a man she scarcely knew occur to her.

She was a woman, wasn't she? And her thoughts were her own. As long as they remained merely thoughts, she was doing nobody any harm.

What would it be like to have such a handsome gentleman paying attention to one?

Lord Avery would no doubt be a master of the art of flirtation. And she had never been the object of a gentleman's attentions. Not even her husband's.

A sigh escaped her. She was such a fool. No doubt Lord Avery would never even think of her again, let alone mention her little shop to anyone.

She looked in the tin cash box. The grand sum of three shillings and thruppence stared back at her.

The Westram ladies were going to be so disappointed.

Chapter Two

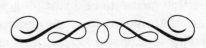

'What do you think?' Mimi Luttrell batted her lashes at Avery, her pale blue eyes soulful, her lips pouting provocatively.

He stifled the urge to yawn. Mimi would run a mile if he so much as hinted at anything sensual between them. She had agreed to this little outing in his company because her husband preferred the hunting field to escorting her to shops and balls. She wanted to feel appreciated, that was all. And perhaps wake her errant husband up to the fact that she was a desirable woman.

It was strange how differently the English husband regarded the position of cicisbeo to those on the Continent. In Italy a man would see it as a compliment that his wife garnered the attention of a young attractive gentleman. He would even participate in funding said gentleman, provided the *affaire* was conducted according to the rules. In England, such financial arrangements were despised by noblemen who liked to guard their wives, pulling up their drawbridges as if they were castles.

It had certainly worked that way with Lady Passmore, the first lady whom Avery had endeavoured to charm on his recent return from the Continent. Her neglectful husband had hot-footed it all the way back from Scotland to stake his claim on his wife and hadn't been far from her side ever since.

To Avery's surprise, the whole thing had also been financially rewarding, both in terms of her eternal gratitude expressed in her effusive thank-you note accompanied by a parting memento he'd sold for a goodly sum and with the commissions from the merchants where he had taken her to shop, the latter being the same sort of arrangement he had entered into in Italy where he'd been living until recently.

There, in Venice, he'd fallen into the role of cicisbeo quite by chance, having at first been attracted to the lady in question, only to discover there were financial benefits to be reaped from what could only be described as a platonic relationship, and all with the approval of the lady's husband.

Here in London, he was walking a much finer line between husband and wife, but Lady Passmore had been so delighted with the results of her innocent flirtation with Avery that she'd advised Mimi to contact him about a similar 'arrangement' to see if it worked on her dilettante husband, too.

And he was happy to oblige, as long as Mimi shopped in the places he recommended and did not expect him to come to her bed, since socially that would put him beyond the pale.

'I prefer the blue.' He'd picked out the fabric because he had known that it suited her perfectly.

Mimi frowned at herself draped in the material in the looking glass. 'Why?'

He gazed at her silently.

She glanced over at him and gave a trill of laughter. 'Really, Ave, darling. Please explain.' Again, she fluttered her lashes.

Unfortunately, Mimi's girlish tricks were a little too cloying for his taste. He much preferred the stern looks he encountered in a certain millinery shop. And the very rare smile he was able to coax from its owner.

Madame Grace, the dressmaker, pursed her lips as if trying to hold back words.

Avery had no trouble interpreting that look of disapproval. Madame Grace knew that this lady was married to someone else. The dressmaker likely thought he was a libertine, if not something worse, but that was because she did not understand that his goal was to bring the lady's errant husband home to her side, not drive a wedge between the couple. If Mimi's husband did not show up in a day or two, the man didn't deserve his wife. But he would since he did not yet have his heir and his spare. He certainly would not want another man poaching on his turf, at least until that duty was completed. And knowing the minds of men, it would be a long time before her husband strayed again.

While Madame Grace might pout about giving him his cut of what Mimi spent in her shop, she knew where her best interests lay. Why should he not be paid for the extra business he brought her way?

Not that these arrangements brought him a huge income. They merely helped augment his winnings at the table.

Avery leaned back in his chair in the fitting room at the back of Grace's shop and smiled lazily at the woman staring at her image. 'Because that blue shade brings out the colour of your eyes, my dear, and the lustre of your skin. The rose colour you have there does not complement, rather it shouts your best features down.'

Her lips formed an O of surprise. Again, she peered into the mirror and turned this way and that. 'How clever you are, Ave.' She turned to the dressmaker. 'Let me see the first one again?'

Madame Grace swathed her in the pale blue fabric, pleating it artfully so it displayed well.

Mimi nodded slowly. 'I see what you mean. I'll take it.'

Behind her, the dressmaker heaved a sigh of relief and Avery knew exactly how she felt. Sometimes ladies spent hours looking in the mirror and bought nothing. But Madame Grace should know better than to worry about one of Avery's ladies. They never left her establishment without placing an order.

Oddly, he used to enjoy accompanying a woman shopping, but more recently it had simply become a chore. He gave Mimi a broad grin of approval. 'Where do you want to go next, Puss? Slippers?'

Ladies loved their shoes and the cobbler made a healthy profit that he was more than happy to share with Avery.

Mimi stroked the pale blue fabric. 'Which bonnet would I wear with this?'

He stilled. An array of exquisite bonnets popped into his mind. But he did not have an arrangement with Mrs Greystoke. Indeed, he'd been doing his best to ignore the fact that he had ever met the woman, because he found her far too intriguing. A distraction. Yet, despite his best efforts, he kept thinking about her smile.

Why hadn't he offered her the same arrangement he

had with other merchants? Was he concerned about what she would think about him? Why would he even care?

'Ave?'

Mimi's peevish tone brought him back from the recollection of a tall stern-faced woman to the dressmaker's shop. He gritted his teeth. He hated it when Mimi called him Ave. It was presumptuous and demeaning, but she was his sister's bread and butter and as such her irritating little foibles had to be tolerated.

'Yes, Sweetling?'

'I don't have a bonnet that will go with this fabric.' She touched the rose fabric, now discarded on the counter. 'I do have one with pink ribbons.'

The lady did love pink. He recalled that particular hat with an inner shudder. It was hideous. Not in the first stare of fashion either. 'You wish to drive out in a brand new carriage dress wearing a bonnet you must have worn at least five times?'

Mimi winced. 'You think people would notice?'

'Other ladies would certainly notice. The gentlemen would not give a fig, I suppose.'

She grimaced. 'But the ladies will mention it to the gentlemen and they will rib George about not providing for his wife. I won't have them belittling George.'

Mimi was really fond of her husband in the strange way of the *ton*.

'A bonnet it is then,' he said. 'I know just the place.' He winced inwardly. He really was going to do this, then? Take her to visit Mrs Greystoke? Where he wouldn't make a penny in commission. He must have porridge for brains. Except he wasn't thinking with his brain if the surge of warmth in his veins at the thought of seeing her again was anything to go by. 'Afterwards,

we will see new half-boots to complete the ensemble.'
And put a few coins in his purse.

Mimi put her arm through his. 'Perfect.'

Trailed by Mimi's maid, they strolled down Bond
Street, looking in shop windows until they passed a milliner's shop. Mimi pointed at a jaunty hat with a huge
feather. 'What do you think of that one?'

'It really isn't you.'

'It is all the crack. It might look better on.'

'We can come back if we don't find anything else.'

For a moment, he thought she would refuse, but she
shrugged. 'Very well.'

When he turned off Bond Street, she frowned. 'Really, Avery? Where are we going?'

'Not far. This shop has the best hats for really decent
prices and if you purchase one, you won't see another
hat like it anywhere.'

Her face lit up.

Finding something unique but not outrageously priced
was always the trick. There was nothing worse than arriving at a ball or a drum and discovering another lady in
the exact same gown or riding Rotten Row and meeting
a lady wearing the same carriage dress or hat.

Ladies set great store by such things. Whereas most
men were happy wearing black coats and buff pantaloons with the occasional idiosyncrasy of a fanciful
waistcoat.

He opened the door to Mrs Greystone's establishment
and ushered Mimi in.

As far as he could tell not a single bonnet had been
sold since his last visit two days ago.

'Good morning,' she said, eyeing him askance.

'Good morning,' Mimi said.

A strange look passed across Mrs Greystoke's face as she took in his companion. An expression she quickly masked with a bright smile.

'This is Mrs Luttrell,' Lord Avery said.

Mrs Greystoke dipped a curtsy. 'How may I be of service, madam.'

'I need a hat.'

Amusement danced in Mrs Greystoke's dove-grey eyes. 'Then you have come to the right place.'

Avery felt a surge of gladness that he had brought Mimi here. He'd recognised the shadows in Mrs Greystoke's eyes the last time he was here. Desperation. He just hadn't wanted to acknowledge he didn't like it. He had enough responsibilities as it was.

Nevertheless, the idea that she was desperate had weighed on his shoulders. And he was glad he had the means to do something about it, even if it did leave him a bit short of funds.

Mimi pulled forth the scrap of blue fabric Madame Grace had cut off the bolt. 'This is the fabric for a new carriage dress. What do you suggest?'

Avery wedged himself in a corner by the counter and let the two women have at it. His part would come later, when a decision was to be made. In the meantime, he could not help but compare the two women. Mimi, a sweet English rose at first glance, but with all the experience of a married woman, and Mrs Greystoke, not exactly pretty, but striking and strangely innocent.

Greystoke. Now why did he keep thinking that name sounded familiar?

Lord Avery's special lady was older than Carrie had expected and apparently a widow to boot, but pretty as a picture, nonetheless. The sort of woman she would have expected to attract him, if she was honest. Carrie helped the lady remove her hat and brought down three bonnets that she thought would suit the lady's face and complement the fabric.

A maid eased in through the door. Mrs Luttrell frowned. 'Boggs, I am sorry, but you need to wait outside. There really isn't room in here for another person.'

The maid, who was all of eighteen, looked worried. 'Yes, mum.' Her accent came from the north. She started to back out.

The sound of someone from her home county gave Carrie an odd feeling in her stomach. A bit of the same feeling of homesickness she'd experienced when she'd first arrived in London to go to school at around the same age as the maid. She'd been sent to a young ladies' academy to acquire a bit of polish, as her father put it.

'Your maid can wait in the back room,' Carrie said. 'This is not the best of streets for a young girl to linger on.'

'Thank you, mum,' the maid said with a look of relief.

Mrs Luttrell gave Carrie a sharp look. 'That is very kind of you, Mrs Greystoke. I can certainly vouch for Boggs's honesty.'

'Indeed.' Carrie smiled kindly at the girl. 'Perhaps you could make us all a cup of tea while you are waiting.'

The girl beamed. 'That I can, mum.' She glanced at her mistress. 'That is, if you agree, madam.'

'It is a wonderful idea.' Mrs Luttrell picked up a bonnet Carrie hadn't suggested. 'What about this one?'

Carrie tried not to frown at the choice. 'If you wish to try it on, you may, but I think you will find it hides your face and, with a pretty face like yours it would be a shame.'

'Do you think so?' She turned to Lord Avery. 'What do you think, Ave?'

He gave her an indulgent smile and for a moment Carrie wondered what it would be like to have a man smile at her in that warm lazy way.

'I think Mrs Greystoke knows what she is about, Pet,' he said. 'Trust in her judgement.'

Mrs Luttrell put the bonnet aside and picked up one of Carrie's suggestions. 'May I try this one first.'

Carrie helped her put it on. She tied a neat bow and directed Mrs Luttrell's attention to the looking glass.

Mrs Luttrell viewed herself from various angles with pursed lips.

Carrie held her breath. This was it. This was her chance to get this shop found by ladies of the *beau monde*. Oh, she could tell that Mrs Luttrell was not a diamond of the first water, or a member of any of the first families of the *ton*, but she wore her clothes well and other ladies would admire her, if she wore the right hat.

After a couple of minutes, Mrs Luttrell turned to Lord Avery. 'What do you think, Ave.'

'I think you should try them all, before making up your mind. I like that one very much, but another might suit better.'

How very odd. Most men hated shopping.

So the lady tried on all three. When she reached the last one, Lord Avery straightened. 'I like them all,' he said. 'The last two looked equally good on you, Mimi. Whichever one you pick you cannot go wrong.'

Carrie did not agree with him. She preferred the one Mrs Luttrell had chosen to put on last. 'The one you have on now suits you particularly well,' she said, not wishing to argue with his lordship, but wanting the lady to make the right choice.

Lord Avery picked up his cup and sipped at his tea. He'd put a great deal of sugar in it, Carrie had noticed.

Mrs Luttrell turned this way and that and then also took a sip of tea. 'I am sure I cannot decide between this one and that one.' She pointed to the first one she had tried on.

'Take them both,' Lord Avery suggested.

Carrie stared at him. Surely, he was jesting?

Mrs Luttrell frowned.

Dash it! She was going to refuse them both now. 'Truly, the one you have on suits you best, madam. It is perfect for this time of year. I am sure you will be doing a great deal of driving out now the weather is changing for the better.'

'You are right,' the lady said.

Carrie breathed a sigh of relief.

'But if I am doing a great deal of driving out...' she turned towards Lord Avery and batted her lashes '...then I *will* need more than one bonnet.'

Lord Avery nodded. 'I should say so.'

'Then I will take them both.'

Carrie snapped her mouth shut. Showing her surprise was not the way to do business. 'Let me wrap them for you, while you finish your tea.'

In short order, she had both bonnets wrapped in tissue paper and in their boxes, while Mrs Luttrell drank her tea and chatted with her companion.

Carrie waited for them to finish their conversation. 'Where would you like me to send the bill, Mrs Luttrell?'

She hated the idea that she was not to be paid right

away for the purchase, but it was the way the *beau monde* did their business. Hopefully, Lord Avery could afford such extravagance.

'Send it to my husband,' Mrs Luttrell said and handed over her card.

Shocked, Carrie could only stare at her for a second or two.

Mrs Luttrell didn't seem to notice her surprise, but Lord Avery had a naughty twinkle in his eye. The wretch. He knew Carrie was shocked all the way to her toes. Her back had gone stiff and her smile had frozen solid on her lips.

Glancing at the address, she put it in a drawer for safe keeping. As soon as they were gone she would write up the bill and have it sent round to Carlin Place. She could only hope that Mr Luttrell approved of his wife's purchases while in the company of another man.

More to the point, what did that make Lord Avery? Her lover? How very shocking. And disappointing...

'Oh, look, Ave, darling, there is another of those pretty fans. It is similar to the one you bought for me.'

'Each one is unique,' Carrie said, aware her voice was terser than she would have liked. Was she really such a prude? It wouldn't be the first time she had heard of a man taking an interest in another man's wife. She had just thought it happened behind closed doors, not flaunted in the faces of respectable people.

'I have received a great many compliments on it, you know.' Mrs Luttrell stared down into the cabinet. 'Now I can tell everyone who asks where it was bought.' She gave Carrie a sharp look. 'As long as there are no more exactly the same as mine.'

'I will guarantee there is not, Mrs Luttrell,' Carrie said. 'Or I will gladly refund your money.'

The woman nodded in approval. 'Boggs,' she called out.

The maid materialised from behind the curtain. 'Yes, mum.'

'Pick up the boxes. We are leaving.'

'It is all right, Mimi, dearest,' Lord Avery said. 'They are two bulky for Boggs. I'll carry them.' He bowed to Carrie. 'Thank you, Mrs Greystoke. I wish you good day.'

Mrs Luttrell waved a hand. 'Yes. Thank you. You can be sure I shall let everyone know where I purchased my hats.' She frowned. 'Though it would be better if you had a more fashionable address.'

They left the shop, making it feel suddenly very empty. Carrie herself felt empty. Surely it was nothing to do with the knowledge she'd gained about Lord Avery? It must be to do with the excitement she'd experienced in making her first real sale.

Now she had good news to take home. It was such a relief.

'How did we do?' Petra's voice rose to a squeak.

Carrie removed her bonnet and gloves in the hall. It must be so hard for the other two waiting at home, wondering if all their hard work had been appreciated. 'Not too badly for our first week.' Much to Carrie's astonishment. 'We have covered next week's rent with a little left over for supplies.'

It was almost four in the afternoon, her back ached from the long drive home and yet she could not help feeling proud.

Marguerite popped her head around the drawing room door. 'I thought I heard the cart. Petra, for heaven's sake let her pass. Carrie, come and sit down and have a cup of tea. You must be worn to the bone.'

She was, but she was also exhilarated by their success.

She hung up her spencer, then joined her sisters-in-law in the drawing room. She sank into the most comfortable chair in the room beside the hearth. Bless them, they had saved it for her. She loved having sisters.

Petra brought her a cup of tea and somehow managed to hold back her questions until Carrie had taken a sip.

'Well?' Petra exploded.

'We sold two bonnets, a fan, a handkerchief and a posy.

Petra frowned. 'Only two bonnets.'

'Two bonnets are better than none,' Marguerite said, in prosaic tones. Clearly, she was also disappointed. Some of Carrie's excitement dissipated.

She forced herself to sound cheerful. 'I am sure the lady who purchased them will tell her friends and then we will have trouble keeping up with the demand.'

'It is a wonderful start,' Petra said, clearly trying to hide her doubts. She gazed at the tea tray. 'Are those shortbread biscuits, Marguerite. Isn't that a bit extravagant?'

Her older sister looked embarrassed. 'I only made a few. We need a treat now and then. And see, I was right. We have good news to celebrate.'

Petra pointed to the hat box. 'What is in there.'

'A hat. I removed the decoration for a gentleman who wanted it for a posy.'

'A posy? How very odd,' Petra said, giving her a sharp look.

Carrie felt the heat rise to her cheeks. Why would

talking about Lord Avery make her blush? 'I thought so, too. Actually, I think he was intoxicated.' She'd seen her father and uncle in their cups often enough to recognise when a man was more than a trifle warm. She put up a hand at their shocked expression. 'He was never impolite, simply a little slurred in his speech.' As well as wavering on his feet. 'He said he wanted it for a special lady. At that point, I had sold nothing. Better to sell a bit of trim than nothing at all.'

'Very wise, I should say,' Marguerite said. She opened the box and drew out the hat. 'It is easy enough to replace the...' She raised an eyebrow in question.

'Violets,' Carrie said. Violets for a special lady indeed. Mrs Luttrell was a very pretty woman. Dainty and delicate, not unlike Carrie's sisters-in-law. The sort of woman Carrie had always envied. And while Carrie could not approve of Mrs Luttrell's closeness with Lord Avery, she could certainly understand why she would attract a handsome lord. Perhaps it was difficult for a woman to ignore such a charming man's attentions and hard for him to ignore such a pretty lady if she was lonely.

Carrie, being plain and gruff and unattractive, would never catch the eye of a man like Lord Avery. She would be far better to focus her thoughts on making a go of this venture instead of indulging in stupid flights of fancy about a handsome gentleman. Such dreams would only lead to further humiliation.

'Which hats did you sell?' Petra asked.

'The chip straw and the blue shako,' Carrie said. 'Unfortunately, the shop is a little bit further from Bond Street than I realised. There is not much passing traffic. It is going to take a while to build our clientele.'

'But you think it will build?' Petra asked.

'I hope so.'

The ladies fell silent, thinking about the consequences of failure, no doubt.

'What we need is something really different,' Carrie said, thinking about the lovely Mrs Luttrell again and how she'd seized upon the idea that no one would ever carry the same fan as the one Lord Avery had given her.

'What sort of something?' Marguerite asked.

'Lots of places sell bonnets, though ours are unique and beautifully styled,' Carrie hastened to add. 'But we need an item ladies cannot purchase elsewhere.'

'I have no idea what you are talking about.' Marguerite looked thoroughly puzzled.

Petra looked intrigued.

'Perhaps something a little risqué,' Carrie said, her face immediately fiery.

'Risqué?' Marguerite pursed her lips in disapproval. 'We don't want to attract the wrong sort of customer.'

They already had. Carrie bit her tongue to stop the words from forming.

'Don't be prudish, Marguerite.' Petra said. 'We don't care who buys the hats, do we? If we can't make a go of this, we'll all be shipped back to London to live with Westram. And all he wants to do is marry us off. The thought of another marriage...' She shuddered.

Carrie frowned. She'd always thought Petra's reaction to marrying again quite odd when her first marriage had been so happy. Perhaps when one found true love, one could never face the prospect of another man.

Still, they had *all* agreed that none of them wanted to marry again.

So they needed to make a success of their shop. Carrie swallowed. 'I was thinking perhaps of something for the boudoir. Something feminine and alluring.' Something a gentleman like Lord Avery might want to buy for a special lady. 'Something a wife might buy to rekindle her marriage?'

The other ladies' eyes widened.

'That sounds...wicked,' Marguerite said, looking worried. 'I am not sure Westram would approve.'

'He won't know unless someone tells him,' Petra said sharply.

Marguerite stiffened at the less-than-subtle implication that she would go to their brother and tell tales.

'Well, let us put our heads together and see what we can come up with,' Carrie said quickly. 'We will do nothing unless we all agree.'

'You know,' Petra said, turning to Marguerite, 'Carrie knows far more about running a shop than we do. We should follow her advice.'

'You are right,' Marguerite said. 'Carrie, you must do whatever you think is best to make the shop a success. We will help you all we can.'

Their vote of confidence made her heart swell with pride. 'It is a joint venture, ladies. Together we can do anything.'

They toasted each other with their teacups.

Leaning back, Carrie sipped at her tea. She had no doubt that, between them, they could come up with something unique that would appeal to the likes of Mrs Luttrell.

'How is the garden coming along?' she asked Petra. The cottage had both a kitchen garden at the back and a large front garden full of roses. Petra had agreed to take on the task of providing vegetables and herbs for their table. She actually liked grubbing around in the dirt.

'Really well,' Petra said. 'It is too bad we have so little ground. I could do so much more.'

'I don't think you would have time,' Marguerite said. 'You already work your fingers to the bone on the hats.'

Carrie handed Marguerite the cash box. 'I sent the bill for the bonnets to the lady's husband.'

Marguerite looked inside. 'You will need some of this for change. The rest can go towards our household bills.' She rose to her feet. 'It is time to start on cooking dinner. After that we will see what we can come up with to bring more custom to the shop.'

'I've been working on hats all day,' Petra said. 'I need some fresh air. I'll go and do a bit of weeding.'

It seemed wrong that these ladies who had grown up with every privilege should be required to work so hard now and all because her husband had led their husbands astray. Or at least she thought he must have. She could not think of any other reason they had left with him to join Wellington's army.

She was determined to do her share to make up for it. 'I will fix the hat,' Carrie said picking up the hat box. 'After all, it is my fault it is spoiled.'

'We have two more finished for you to take back with you,' Petra said. She frowned. 'And I'll make a couple of extra posies in case that gentleman should return.'

Carrie's tummy gave a funny little hop. It had been doing that every time she as much as thought of Lord Avery. 'I doubt if he will,' she said and followed Petra from the room.

Chapter Three

Avery opened the door for Lady Fontly to pass into the milliner's shop. It had been two weeks since his last visit. He had forced himself to stay away, though he had encouraged Mimi to recommend the shop if anyone should admire her new hat.

As he entered, he was taken aback by the changes.

Rose-filled vases graced every open space not occupied by a bonnet or a lacy cap. There were two women in the narrow space between the door and the counter, a lady and her maid, being helped by Mrs Greystoke, and there were giggles coming from behind the curtain leading to the shopkeeper's private quarters. Maids having cups of tea, he assumed.

He turned to his companion. 'I apologise, Elizabeth, I did not expect it to be this busy.'

Lady Fontly, green-eyed and auburn-haired, beamed. 'How clever of you, Avery. I heard whispers about this place, but was unable to discover its location.'

He kept his expression blank. Whispers? About Mrs Greystoke? 'Then it is my pleasure to bring you here.'

The customer at the counter turned at the sound of his voice.

'Lord Avery?' Mrs Baxter-Smythe's eyebrows shot up and Avery inwardly groaned. 'And Lady Fontly,' she said with a sly smile. 'How very…surprising to meet you *both* here.' The widow cast him an arch look and her innuendo was perfectly clear.

Mrs Baxter-Smythe had made more than one attempt to begin a flirtation with him, but she was a widow. Avery had no truck with widows. They usually had brothers or fathers or distant cousins, who would see their role as protectors of virtue. And no matter how merry the widow, they were unlikely to pass up the chance to marry off a single relative to the son of a duke.

Avery bowed. 'Likewise, I am sure, Mrs Baxter-Smythe.'

The widow turned her gaze on his companion. 'I understand Lord Fontly is out of town at the moment?'

Elizabeth's cheekbones coloured. 'He has gone to the races in Newmarket.' She sounded a little too defensive.

'How you must miss him,' Mrs Baxter-Smythe cooed. 'And you only recently married.'

'Lord Fontly has a horse entered in a race,' Avery put in cheerfully. 'Not something even a newly wed husband should miss.'

Elizabeth recovered her composure. 'And he recommended Lord Avery take me shopping, since it is something he hates to do.'

Avery gave her arm a little squeeze of approval. Elizabeth had been hurt by her husband's departure so soon after their marriage, so he had suggested that a new hat might be just the thing to make her feel better.

He became aware of a pair of grave grey eyes watching the interchange between him and the ladies. It was the sort of considering look one might get from a tutor who realised you were not going to live up to your potential. Her eyes held curiosity along with a dawning understanding.

What did she understand? That he served as an escort when a lady's husband was absent? Did she think it was more than that? Let her think what she wished. Everyone else did. And naturally his special ladies never discussed him with others. They were married, after all.

'It seems everyone has discovered this place,' Mrs Baxter-Smythe said. 'Does Mrs Greystoke not carry the most beautiful hats you have ever seen?'

'I have not yet had a chance to look.' Elizabeth glanced around. 'But I must say at first sight they appear to be most attractive.'

'Each and every one is stunning,' the widow said. 'And do ask her about the other unique items she has for sale.' She pinned her eyes on Avery. 'I am having an open house next Monday. Afternoon tea. I would love to see you there.' She moved her focus to Elizabeth. 'If you are free, I would love you to come also, Lady Fontly.' The afterthought was a deliberate snub.

Mrs Baxter-Smythe was a denizen of the *ton*. For Elizabeth not to accept would put her on the fringes of society. Flirting with him was one thing, but declining to attend one of Mrs Baxter-Smythe's at homes was quite another.'

'I shall be delighted to escort you,' Avery said, smiling at Elizabeth, who dipped a little curtsy. 'If Lord Fontly is not back in time.'

'Oh, but of course,' the widow said. 'Your husband is welcome also, should he be home, if he does not think it a terrible bore.' She gave them a sickly sweet smile, squeezed past him and Elizabeth and left the shop with her maid trailing behind her.

A young woman he recognised as the wife of a prominent banker appeared from behind the curtain. Her eyes were dancing and her cheeks were bright pink.

A shop assistant appeared right behind her with a tissue-wrapped package.

At the counter, Mrs Greystoke smiled calmly and wrote up a bill.

Avery frowned. Why on earth would anyone go behind a curtain to try on a hat?

Mrs Greystoke gave Elizabeth a cool smile. 'How may I help you, madam? Is there something you would like to try on?'

'Elizabeth, may I introduce Mrs Greystoke, the owner of this establishment. Lady Fontly is looking for a bonnet.'

Lizzie pursed her lips. 'I am looking for a something summery. Something to wear on a picnic.' The picnic she'd planned for her husband's return. Avery had suggested it as a way to engage the twit's attention. The man had to be an idiot if he left such a pretty wife at a loose end during the Season.

'What about this one?' Mrs Greystoke lifted down a becoming wide-brimmed straw bonnet trimmed with strawberry leaves, flowers and berries. 'It is our latest arrival. It will see a lady through the hottest part of the summer and is ideal for both town and country.' She tilted one side of the brim upwards. 'It can be worn one of two ways and comes with three different colours of ribbon.'

Liz hesitated. 'It is lovely.'

Why the hesitation? 'Try it on,' he urged.

Mrs Greystoke tilted her head on one side and looked at her shrewdly. 'Or perhaps you were seeking something a little more intimate?'

Elizabeth blushed.

Lady Fontley was not as sophisticated as some of the other ladies he had taken under his wing, those like Mimi Luttrell whose husband had arrived home more than a week ago and made it plain his wife no longer needed an escort, much to Mimi's satisfaction.

He took Elizabeth's hand and raised it to his lips. 'What is it, Pet?' he asked in a low voice. 'I thought we wanted something that would make your husband look at you anew? Is the bonnet not to your liking?'

'It is beautiful, but—'

'I think Lady Fontly would like to inspect our other wares.' Mrs Greystoke gestured to the counter.

The last time Avery had looked at the items on display there had been neatly ordered fans and gloves and handkerchiefs. Now there were froths of lace and silk.

'Tansy, fetch his lordship a cup of tea,' Mrs Greystoke said. 'Unless you would prefer something stronger?'

Another change. An assistant. He found he did not like it for some reason he could not name.

'Nothing for me, thank you.'

Mrs Greystoke went back behind her counter and brought forth a flimsy robe of scarlet, edged in lace. 'This is a very popular style of *robe de chambre*, my lady.'

When she spread the garment out on the counter and put her hand between the layers of fabric, Avery almost swallowed his tongue. The robe was so sheer as to be almost invisible and there were strategically placed openings that were revealed as the lace trim fell to one side.

What the devil was Mrs Greystoke doing, showing garments like that to a respectable woman? All right, so Elizabeth had accepted his offer of escort in a fit of pique when her husband left town to go on yet another spree with his friends for the fourth time in a month. The poor dear was feeling neglected, but she was still a modestly brought up girl—

'What do you think, Lord Avery. Will Roger like it?' she whispered in his ear.

A man would have to be dying, or at the very least dead from the waist down, not to like the idea of the curvy Lady Fontly in such a shockingly revealing negligee. Unfortunately, all Avery could think about was seeing Mrs Greystoke in the gown. She was so lusciously tall, it would look far better on her than the petite Lady Fontly.

'Yes,' he said a little more tersely than he intended. 'It is deliciously wicked,' he added a little more warmly.

'Would you like to try it on, Lady Fontly?' Mrs Greystoke asked.

'May I?' Lizzie asked.

Mrs Greystoke smiled. 'You can use my private quarters at the rear of the shop. Tansy will be happy to help you.' She looked back at him. 'Gentlemen are not permitted.'

Liz looked relieved. 'Do you have it in any other colours?'

'We do. One for every day of the week.'

Liz giggled. 'Good lord. Really?'

Mrs Greystoke inclined her head. 'Really.'

Avery inhaled a breath. His forte was helping ladies choose outer garments that showed them off to advantage. Things such as this were best left to the women themselves. Or their husbands. He didn't want to be facing pistols at dawn over such a trifle. 'The colour you have there would suit you very well,' he said, smiling. 'Try it on. You can always try a different colour if you decide you do not like it.'

Elizabeth took the whisper of fabric and lace and followed the shop assistant into the back of the shop.

'And how are you, Lord Avery?' Mrs Greystoke asked.

Since there was now no one else in the shop he gave her his best charming smile. 'A little surprised, I must say.'

'At our new venture?'

Our? Who were the others? She had said her husband was dead. 'Yes. I thought you were a milliner.'

'Oh, we discovered a demand for something no one else was offering. We thought it a suitable addition to our inventory, since most of our customers are ladies.' She gave him a considering look and lowered her voice. 'How is Mrs Luttrell?'

'She is well, so far as I am aware.'

A crease appeared in her forehead as she considered the implications of his remark. He had the decided urge to kiss that little frown. To taste it with his tongue. To smooth it away with his thumb.

'If you should see her,' Mrs Greystoke continued, 'give her my thanks for sending her friends along. If there is ever anything I can do for her, I would be most happy to return the favour.'

Good old Mimi. She had kept her word, then. Was that the reason he had hesitated about returning here? Because he feared she might have not done so and that he would discover Mrs Greystoke more desperate than before?

'I will let her know, but I believe she is away at the moment. At a country house party in Sussex.'

'Oh, I see.'

What did she see? Ah. Did she think he was doing something underhanded with Lady Fontly in the other lady's absence? 'Yes. We parted on the most agreeable terms.' He emphasised the word 'parted'.

Her frown deepened and the disapproval in her expression said she had drawn some conclusions she did not like. He quelled a faint sense of hurt and the urge to explain. It was none of her business how he chose to support members of his family.

A moment later, Elizabeth emerged with a neatly wrapped package in her hand. She looked ready to explode with excitement. 'I love it.'

'Did you wish to purchase a hat also?' Mrs Greystoke asked.

'Yes. Yes, I do.'

They agreed on the summer bonnet Mrs Greystoke had already recommended and when she wrote up the bills, she wrote one to Lord Fontly. The other she wrote to Lady Fontly. 'In case you wish to keep it as a surprise,' she explained.

Or in case she wanted to wear it for Avery, he thought, feeling a little bitter at her misjudgement, despite knowing how it looked.

Mrs Greystoke handed him the hatbox. 'Enjoy your purchase.'

When she said those last words, she was looking at him. Oh, yes, she really thought him some sort of Lothario.

Fortunately, Elizabeth did not notice her misunderstanding.

Annoyed at Mrs Greystoke and feeling slightly ashamed of himself, he left the shop.

The next morning as Carrie swept the front step and the narrow path in front of her window, she could not help wishing the shop had a better location. Mr Thrumby had warned her more than once to keep her door locked and bolted at night and not to linger in the street during the day. Fortunately for her, he and his wife occupied the upstairs rooms, the stairs to which were reached by way of a hallway that passed her back door. He kept a porter on duty at that back entrance, both day and night, so there was always someone nearby who would come at her call.

Hearing the sharp tap of footsteps on the pavement, she lifted her gaze from her broom to glance up the street. A familiar figure strolled towards her. Lord Avery. Behind him a door slammed. The gambling hell Mr Thrumby had warned her about no doubt. There could be nowhere else he was coming from at this time in the morning.

Why *did* men gamble away their fortunes in such places? It was so utterly irresponsible. They ruined themselves and they ruined their families. They also gambled away their lives for the sake of some foolish bet. As her husband had. Furiously, she brushed at the paving slabs, as if she could sweep away the memory of her wedding night along with the news of his death in some terrible battle in Spain a few weeks later. She wanted no truck with any man who gambled.

As if she could sweep away Lord Avery along with the memories. Even if he was the most handsome, most charming fellow she had ever met.

He removed his hat and bowed. 'Good day, Mrs Greystoke.'

Blast. She had meant to whisk herself inside before he reached her shop. Hadn't she? She straightened and met his gaze. She couldn't believe how haggard he looked, how tired and drawn, and yet his usual charming smile curved his lips and his eyes warmed as they rested upon her face.

An answering warmth trickled through her veins. 'Lord Avery.' She couldn't believe how breathless she sounded. It must be all that vigorous sweeping.

'Up and about early this morning, aren't you?' he said.

She folded her arms across her chest and narrowed her gaze. The first time he'd visited her shop he'd been quite bosky. This morning he simply looked tired. 'As are you. *I* have to make ready for my customers.'

His smile broadened. 'Indeed. And here I am.'

She frowned. 'The shop is not yet open.'

His smile changed from charming to wheedling. 'Surely you will not make me come back later.'

'What did you want?'

'Another of your delightful posies, naturally.'

She sighed, but inside her chest her traitorous heart was galloping like a runaway horse. 'Come in, then.'

He followed her into the shop and she went behind her counter. She felt more comfortable, more in control when there was a solid piece of furniture between them. She spread out several little sprigs on the counter. 'These are all I have at the moment.'

He stared at the array 'Did you make any of these?'

What an odd question. 'I helped make the pink roses and the yellow sweet peas.'

'I'll take the roses.'

'I really would not recommend those for Lady Fontly. The yellow would be better for her colouring.'

He grinned. 'It is not for Lady Fontly.' He tucked the spray of flowers into his buttonhole. 'It is for me.'

'Oh,' she gasped. 'That was why...' Surely not.

He raised a brow. 'That was why what?'

Heat raced up her face to her hairline. 'Nothing.'

He chuckled. The deep rich sound sent a shiver down her spine and made her want to giggle like a girl not yet out of the schoolroom.

'It was why I asked if you had made any of them,' he said. 'I wanted something to remind me of you. I need cheering up today.'

He was flirting with her. She felt uncomfortable. Awkward. What was she supposed to do? Should she be flattered or annoyed? Better to ignore the whole thing than make a fool of herself. 'Will there be anything else, Lord Avery?'

He gave a little grimace. 'No. That will be all, thank you, Mrs Greystoke.'

She wrote up her bill. 'Why do you do it?' Oh, there went her brusque tongue again, asking questions regarding things that were none of her concern.

He leaned a hip against the counter. 'Do what?'

'Gamble. You must have been up all night, you look so dreadful.'

'That bad, hmmm?'

She nodded. She forestalled the urge to ask if he had won or lost, but he seemed so weary, she guessed it was the latter.

'I do it to keep the wolf from the door, Mrs Greystoke. To put food on the table. Coal in the hearth. To keep body and soul together.' He sounded bitter.

The son of a duke needing to earn a living? 'Surely…'

'Surely what?' His tone was suddenly dark, even a little dangerous.

She handed him the bill. 'I beg your pardon. It is none of my business.'

He glanced down at the paper in his hand and back at her face. 'You were going to ask why a man in my position, the son of a duke, needed to earn his living in such a manner.'

'Oh, please. I have no wish to pry.'

'My papa is a man with high expectations of his sons. I have disappointed him and therefore I am to make my own way in life.'

She knew all about parental disappointment. 'Why not engage in some sort of gainful employment?' She winced. Dash it, she sounded disapproving.

His lip curled and his smile became mocking. 'You sound just like my father.'

Mortified, she began to put the rest of the nosegays back in their places in the drawer. 'I beg your pardon. It is not my place to judge.'

The kettle on the hob began to sing. She raised her gaze to meet his. 'Would you like a cup of tea?'

He looked surprised. And then pleased. 'That is the best offer I have had in the last twenty-four hours. But I would hate to interrupt your morning.'

'It is no interruption. I went to sweep the step while I waited for the kettle to boil. Would you throw the bolt on the shop door for me? No lady goes shopping at this early hour.'

He did as she asked and then followed her behind the curtain into her private quarters. Very small quarters, she realised as his large form seemed to take up most of the space in the little kitchen-cum-sitting room-cum-dining room. And more recently a place for ladies to try on naughty night attire.

She winced. And then there was the alcove curtained off, where she slept. Perhaps he wouldn't notice.

'Please, sit down,' she said.

He took one of the two chairs at the small kitchen table while she busied herself with the pot and tea leaves.

'This is where you live?' he asked, his voice full of curiosity. 'All alone?'

'This is where I stay during the week while the shop is open. I go home at week's end to collect more stock.' She glanced over her shoulder to discover he was frowning.

'London is not a safe city for a woman on her own,' he said.

'I am perfectly safe. My landlord, Mr Thrumby, lives upstairs and his man keeps an eye on my safety.'

He looked less than satisfied. She hadn't expected him to care about her well-being. It surprised her and warmed her in odd ways. Something inside her chest seemed to soften.

She brought two cups of tea to the table along with milk and sugar on a small tray. 'Please, help yourself.' It was hardly the sort of elegant tea a lady would serve in a drawing room, but she was pleased to see him adding cream and sugar to his cup and sipping the tea appreciatively.

She felt bad for him. While he had not said in so many words that he had been disinherited by his father, clearly it must be the case. A gentleman such as he would have no trade, no skills, to fall back on, so it was no wonder he gambled. And then there were his special ladies. Mrs Baxter-Smythe's sly words returned to her mind.

A terrible idea entered her head. Terrible and exciting and awful. Terrifying.

So awful, yet so awfully tempting. She struggled to think of a way to phrase her question. Her request.

He leaned back in his chair with a boyish smile. A smile quite different from his usual practised charm. It made him seem more endearing. 'That is the best cup of tea I have had in a long time.'

As a general rule men like him, charming handsome men, made her feel uncomfortable. She always felt awkward, as if her arms were too long and her feet too big. Lord Avery, on the other hand, made her feel…womanly. Even attractive. She could not help beaming back at him. 'Thank you.' She took a sip of her own tea.

A friendly silence descended. It felt companionable. As if they had known each other for years.

She put down her cup. 'I wanted to ask you…'

He tilted his head in question. 'What?'

'I am not sure how to put it?'

'Ask away.'

'Do you also earn money from the ladies you escort to my shop?' The words were too blunt when she had meant to be tactful.

He stiffened. 'What makes you ask?' he said. His voice was calm, but his eyes were cold. Shuttered.

She repressed a shiver. Oh, dear, why hadn't she left well enough alone. 'Something Mrs Baxter-Smythe said.' Dash it, she should never have opened her mouth. She had spoiled everything.

His lips thinned. 'Mrs Baxter-Smythe is jealous because I do not count her as one of my special ladies.'

'Ladies you escort while their husbands are out of town.'

'Exactly.' He put down his cup. 'And, yes, they do pay for my services.' He picked up his hat.

He was going to leave and she still hadn't asked her awful question. 'Can any lady hire your...services?'

His eyes widened, then narrowed. 'Are you asking for yourself?'

Heat rushed all the way up her face to her hairline, but she was not one to hide behind a lie. 'I am.'

He put his hat down and shook his head. 'I am not sure I fully understand what it is you are asking me. The ladies I escort are all wealthy and married. Single ladies present too many complications since I am single myself.'

She twirled her cup on its saucer. Did he think she was looking for a husband? 'I am not seeking anything permanent, I assure you. I would prefer something...' She frowned and set the handle of the cup at the proper angle.

'Something?' he prompted. His voice held a distinct chill.

She glanced up. His lips were still a thin straight line. 'Brief,' she blurted. In for a penny in for a pound her father always used to say. 'One night. I am willing to pay, of course. Whatever the other ladies pay.' She still had a little of her personal allowance for the month left over.

His eyebrow lifted. 'Let me get this clear. You wish to pay me to bed you.' His tone was grim.

Embarrassment rushed through her in a hot tide. Oh, why had she said anything at all? But having done so, she pressed on, her cheeks hotter than fire. 'As you can imagine, there are particular disadvantages to being alone. I simply thought that...' She gave an awkward laugh.

'I do not bed my special ladies for money, Mrs Greystoke.' His tone was as dry as dust. 'I merely serve as their escort in their husband's absences. And since you do not have a husband, the arrangement would not work.'

He was trying to let her down gently, to couch his rejection in kinder terms. She didn't believe him for a moment. She had seen the looks that had passed between him and Mrs Luttrell. And Lady Fontly. She wasn't such a fool as to think the ladies merely wanted him to take them shopping.

Resentment spurted through her and a healthy dose of disappointment. She should have known all his flirting with her was nothing but a hum. 'You don't have to lie, Lord Avery. You can simply say no thank you.'

'You may, of course, think what you wish, Mrs Greystoke, but I would advise you not to listen to gossip.' He clapped his hat on his head and strode out of her shop.

Clearly, he viewed her offer as an insult. Something in her chest shrivelled.

'I win!'
The men around the table groaned as the young fellow opposite Avery laid down his cards and scooped up the guineas in the centre of the table. 'Waiter, more wine here.'

Astonishment broke Avery broke free of his reverie. He glared at the rapidly disappearing gold. Money he needed for Laura and her family.

'I've no luck tonight,' one of the other men said.

Another threw his cards down in disgust. 'I need a drink.'

The whist table broke up.

Avery stared at his hand. He should have won. His skill was legendary among London's gamers, which was why he had been reduced to gambling in hells like this one, where he would meet men who were not aware of his reputation. Amend that, he thought bitterly. His skill had been legendary. These past few days he'd been unable to concentrate. Not only was he losing at the tables, he'd been avoiding all of his social engagements, including a request from Lady Fontly to suggest a new hairdresser. He knew just the fellow who would have put a considerable sum of money in his pockets.

And now this.

The conclusion he'd been avoiding for the past few days became unavoidable. He needed to see Mrs Greystoke and get the dashed woman out of his head. He could not stop remembering the way she had looked at him when he had refused her offer. It wasn't the hurt in her eyes that haunted him, it was the acceptance.

She had expected his rejection.

He rose from his seat.

'What? Giving up already?' His opponent, Giles Formby, a young gentleman from Surrey, frowned. 'Don't you want a chance to recoup your losses?'

Avery shook his head. He wasn't such a fool as that. 'Another day.'

Craddock, the hell's owner, sidled up to Formby. 'You won't beat me so easily.'

Giles's opponents perked up.

'If you'll take a bit of advice from someone who knows gaming,' Avery said to the younger man, 'leave now, while your dibs are in tune. Come, I'll find you a hackney outside.'

Formby hesitated, then nodded. 'You are right. It is getting late.'

Craddock shot Avery a hard look. 'The night's young yet, gents.' His smile became oily as he turned it on Formby. 'Surely you ain't leaving yet, young sir? Not when lady luck is looking kindly upon ye.'

The young man glanced at Avery, who raised a brow. He didn't want to alienate Craddock, but nor did he want to leave a wet-behind-the-ears boy to the cardsharp's tender mercies. Avery won by skill, Craddock would use any means at his disposal to relieve the young man of the money he had won.

No one who did not pay for the privilege was supposed to win in this place. Including Avery, who paid a percentage of his winnings for a place at Craddock's tables. Avery had contributed a considerable sum of money over the past couple of months. He hoped Craddock would let him get away with leading the mark out of trouble, at least this once.

He leaned close to the young fellow's ear. 'I know a place where the wine flows free and a man can find himself cosy between the sheets.'

Giles swallowed. 'A brothel?'

Damn, but the boy was a fool. Had Avery ever been that innocent? 'A very exclusive place I know. Want to go?'

Giles nodded eagerly.

Craddock frowned, but let them leave without another word. No doubt he assumed that Avery had another plan to get his fingers on the boy's money, so he would be receiving his share later.

Outside in the brisk evening air, Avery pushed Giles into a hackney. 'Where do you live.'

Giles looked puzzled. 'I am lodging in Golden Square. Number three. Why?'

Avery gave the address to the driver.

'I thought we were going to a brothel?'

'You are going to a place where you don't have to pay for wine and you have clean sheets waiting. You will thank me tomorrow. And so will your parents.'

The boy looked chagrined at the reminder of his parents and then grinned broadly. 'Won't Pater be proud when I tell him I won. After all his warnings about gambling hells, too.'

'Only if you refrain from going to another,' Avery said drily. 'You were lucky tonight.'

'I know. And besides, tonight was my last night here. I am due home tomorrow. I'm on my way down from Oxford. I can't delay any longer or Papa will worry. He's not a bad old chap, but he does fuss so.'

Very lucky indeed. Avery wished he had a papa who cared enough to fuss over him.

'Buy a nice gift for your mama and buy a new waist-coat for yourself and go home.'

The boy sank back against the squabs, his expression thoughtful. 'Thank you, sir. I will.'

The boy might be naive, but he wasn't stupid. Avery wondered if he would have been so sensible at that age. He stepped back and the hackney coach clattered off into the night.

He strode down the street and turned into the alley that ran behind Mrs Greystoke's shop. There was an odd feeling in his gut. A sense he might be making the worst mistake of his life. The gold plate on the door identified the residence of a Mr Arnold Thrumby. He hesitated. Did he really want to do this?

Her expression, the instant acceptance of his rejection, swam before his eyes once again. If nothing else, he could not allow her to continue to believe she was not worthy of his attentions. Damnation and how the hell was he to do that? He'd just have to play it by ear. The way he always did.

He knocked.

After a few long moments, the peephole opened. 'Who be knocking at respectable folks' door at this time of the night?' a deep voice grumbled.

'A visitor for Mrs Greystoke. Lord Avery. I am expected.'

Hopefully the lady would not give him the lie. Though he would not put it past her to deny him entry. She was not like any other woman he had ever known. Which accounted for some of his fascination.

Footsteps retreated and a little later returned. 'She says you best come in.'

The elderly porter opened the door and stood back. 'At the end of the hall there.' He indicated with his thumb. He locked and bolted the door and sat back down at his post.

So much for her safety. The porter needed a swift kick somewhere it would hurt for letting a man visit the lady in the middle of the night.

The door to Mrs Greystoke's apartment stood ajar, allowing a small bar of light to escape into the corridor. He pushed it open and stepped inside.

She was sitting at the kitchen table facing the door, wearing an old brown woollen dressing gown pulled tight around her form. A heavy rope of brown hair curled over her shoulder and rested on her generous right breast. At her throat, a fragment of lace peeped out from the enveloping gown and skimmed the hollow of her throat. The scrap of frill was a nod to her femininity. And it was the most erotic sight he had ever beheld.

Slowly he raised his gaze to her face. 'Mrs Greystoke. Good of you to see me at this late hour.'

'Lord Avery?'

Her voice held a question, though her face was perfectly calm. A calmness she wore like armour to hide her worry. But the tremble in the hand that clutched her robe close gave her away.

He shouldn't have come. 'I don't suppose you would offer me a cup of tea?'

She stared at him for a long moment.

He really should not have come.

She rose from her chair, tall, magnificent, composed. 'Very well.'

Chapter Four

He wanted a cup of tea at this late hour? What did he think this was? A tea house? To calm her thundering heart, she busied herself with stirring up the coals and filling the kettle of water. To her mortification, she realised he was still standing with his back against the door. Watching her. And taking up far too much space in her little kitchen.

'Please,' she said. 'Sit down.'

He moved with cat-like grace across the small space and took the chair against the wall beside the kitchen table. It didn't help. His watchful presence unnerved her. She should have told the porter to send him away. Of course she should. But then she never did anything she was supposed to do. Except for marry Greystoke. And look what a mistake that had turned out to be.

He said nothing. Why didn't he say anything?

She was hopeless at small talk.

She kept her back firmly pointed in his direction, until finally there was no more excuse to avoid his gaze. She carried the tea tray to the table and set it down. She sat opposite and poured his tea. She recalled he liked lots of sugar and cream and put plenty in before handing him his cup.

'Thank you.' His deep voice resonated around the room.

'I—I don't have any biscuits, I'm afraid. I gave them all to Jeb. For his journey. To Kent. I haven't had time to bake more.'

He stirred his tea, took a sip. 'Excellent.'

She blushed like a schoolgirl at the compliment.

He leaned against the chairback. Relaxed. Confident. Elegant. Whereas she felt as if her hands were too large for her arms, like an ungainly colt.

'Was there something you wanted?' she blurted. So awkward. And her blush went from warm to scalding.

He put down his cup. 'I have been considering your proposal.'

The blood drained from her head. 'No. I mean I made a mistake. I wish you to forget it.'

A brow lifted. He tilted his head. 'I wish you would hear me out.'

She turned her face away. Embarrassed. Mortified. Angry at her stupid impulse. 'I beg you will say no more on the matter. You were clearly insulted by what I asked.'

'Mrs Greystoke, I apologise if I was rude. I ought to be used to the gossips by now.'

She drew in a shuddery breath. 'But I think ladies do not generally ask for your services so bluntly.' She tried a smile. It felt weak. She straightened her shoulders. 'Let us say I have changed my mind.'

'Have you?' His voice sounded wistful. Almost regretful.

Again the horrible blush. She'd done nothing but dream about the what ifs all day. What if she had flirted with him? What if she had enticed him? What if she had been someone other than Carrie Greystoke, daughter of a merchant and as blunt as a darning needle?

He reached across the table and took her hand, gently, lightly, his thumb brushing across the back of her fingers. Tingles shot all the way up her arm. She drew in a quick breath. Never had she felt anything so startlingly sensual. Her inner muscles clenched.

'Please listen to my proposition before saying any more,' he said gently. 'I am simply suggesting we get to know each other a little better over the next two weeks and see where the attraction between us leads. That way neither of us will be uncomfortable.'

Attraction. Between them? Had he really said that?

And two weeks? She had imagined a single night in his arms and a whole host of delicious regrets the morning afterwards. Two weeks? Goodness. Her heart picked up speed at the idea of a minute in his company, let alone fourteen days. 'How much would you charge?' Oh, stupid, *stupid* thing to say. So lacking in refinement. So horribly crass.

His lips tightened.

She waited for him to storm out again. Good. It was what she wanted. Dread hollowed her stomach. Against every particle of common sense drummed into her since childhood, she opened her mouth to apologise.

'Actually, that is not the way it works. My rewards are more indirect.'

She flushed as much at the innuendo as at the deepening of his voice and the intensity of his gaze on her face. If only he would come right out and say what he wanted. Instead of hinting vaguely and leaving her in the dark feeling awkward. 'As I said, I changed—'

He held up a hand, the one that was not still holding hers. She snatched that hand back and closed her fingers around the residual warmth as if she could somehow save it.

'Let me finish,' he said and amusement danced in his eyes. Not mocking, simply amused.

'Then please stop beating about the bush and tell me.'

His eyelashes lowered a fraction, hiding his thoughts. A small smile curved his lips. 'That is what I like about you, Mrs Greystoke. Your unfailing honesty.'

He liked her honesty, whereas she was ready to melt into a puddle every time he looked at her. This was clearly not a good idea, but she would let him have his say before she asked him to leave.

'Continue, then, but please recall the hour is late and I have an early start in the morning.'

His grin was cheeky. 'Very well. In a nutshell. This is my proposition. Since being seen in my company will increase your business, I will escort you around town in your lovely bonnets and you will pay me fifteen percent of any additional profits. Think of it as a fee for bringing new business to your shop. This is similar to the arrangement I have with other shopkeepers around town.'

Her jaw dropped. This was how he made money from his special ladies? Not from… Oh, heavens, he must think her terrible for asking him to… Oh, dear. 'So shopkeepers give you a commission on what the ladies in your company buy from them.'

'Yes.'

She frowned. 'But what you are proposing to me is different. You could make the same arrangement with me as you have with the other tradespeople.'

He inclined his head. 'I could. But it would be nowhere near as enjoyable as what I am suggesting. It allows us to kill two birds with one stone, as it were. We will explore the very obvious attraction between us, while introducing your product to ladies of the *ton* in a way that will spark their curiosity.' He shrugged. 'And if we discover we do not wish to deepen our acquaintance, at the end of two weeks we will go our separate ways, each of us better off financially.'

'Won't you being seen in the company of a mere shopkeeper be detrimental to your reputation?' Not to mention what Westram would say, were he to hear about it. Marguerite had decided it would be best not to tell him about them opening the shop. Or at least not until they knew it was successful. Once they were financially independent, there would be nothing he could do. They hoped. She also knew from his letters that Westram was currently out of town, busy on his Gloucestershire estate, so there was little danger of meeting him unexpectedly whilst out and about with Avery.

A cynical smile curved his lips. 'One thing I have learned with regard to being the spare to a dukedom is that one can do anything one wishes, except perhaps murder, and no one will say a word. Besides, there is no doubt in anyone's mind that you are a lady, despite your occupation.'

It was almost as if he *really* wanted her to accept his offer. A little flutter of anticipation stirred low in her belly. She was so very tempted to agree. And if it led nowhere, she would be no worse off than she was right now.

The lonely woman inside her longed to say yes. The shopkeeper immediately saw the flaw in his proposal. Honesty required her to speak. 'I would not know which sales resulted from such an arrangement and which did not.' At the moment, she wasn't making much profit at all. Just enough to cover Tansy's wages and the cost of further supplies. This could be the opportunity they needed to really catch the notice of ladies of the *ton*. What would her sisters-in-law want her to do?

She recalled Petra's words of faith in her abilities to make the shop a success. This would be a way of proving her right.

She forced herself to meet his gaze.

The corners of his eyes crinkled with silent laughter, as if he knew exactly what she was thinking. 'I trust you completely to do what is fair.' He smiled. A warm genuine smile that sparkled gold in his eyes.

She swallowed. It felt too intimate. She in her dressing gown, he with the shadow of a day's growth of beard on his chin. She had the urge to touch the stubble. To discover how it felt against her skin. And if she agreed to this, then she might just have the chance to do so.

He leaned forward, gazing into her eyes. 'Nothing else will happen unless you want it to.'

Her heart tumbled over. She was lost and did not care if she was never found. 'All right.' Her voice came out in a hoarse sort of croak.

He held out his hand. 'Then we have a bargain.'

To her immense surprise, she shook it. 'We do.'

Inside her stomach butterflies took wing. What on earth had she agree to?

He rose. 'I will pick you up tomorrow afternoon and we will go for a drive. Wear one of your bonnets.'

'Tomorrow?'

'It is your half-day closing, is it not?'

Breathless at how quickly things had moved, she nodded.

He picked up his hat and gloves. He gazed down at her. 'Do not look so worried, Mrs Greystoke. It will be fun.' He leaned forward and brushed his lips against her cheek and strode out of her kitchen.

Longing filled her. She wanted this. She touched her cheek where his silky lips had left a warm glow. It was the first time a man, other than her father, had kissed her. Small thrills chased along her veins, making her tremble.

She must have gone mad.

She wanted to run away and hide. She wanted to go with him, have him kiss her again.

Standing on the edge of a precipice must feel like this. Longing to leap, to fly into the void, but knowing that in the end all you would do was fall and get hurt.

Calm down, Carrie. This was first and foremost a business arrangement. An exchange of one thing for another, with additional possibilities. Surely she understood commerce well enough not to falter having shaken hands upon their bargain.

And besides, after getting to know her better, he might decide he no longer found her attractive.

Her heart sank. Her husband had certainly discovered her to be so unbearable as to prefer risking his life to marriage to her.

And if she did not take this chance, she would never forgive herself if another opportunity never materialised.

Every morsel of sense she had said she was treading on dangerous ground. Taking unknown risks, the way her father had. But she had opted for safety when she married Jonathan, only to discover she'd stepped into a quagmire of worry. How could this be any worse?

For heaven's sake, she was the one who had made the

proposal in the first place—was she now going to back away from the challenge?

She got up and began to clear away the tea tray. If she was going to go out and about with a nobleman in order to show off her bonnets, she would need something very different to wear. Fortunately, she had a whole trousseau of clothes bought before her wedding and never taken out of their wrappings, packed away in a trunk at her aunt's house. She would send for it first thing in the morning.

While it would likely all come to nothing, since it was unlikely such a handsome engaging man would truly find her attractive, she would endeavour to look her best for him and for the shop.

Avery wended his way through the traffic towards Mrs Greystoke's emporium the next day. Greystoke. He *had* heard that name before. It niggled at him. Surely if recalling the name was important, he would remember where he had heard it. And besides, it was a fairly common name, his memory might have nothing to do with her at all. He shrugged off his doubts as he pulled up at the end of the lane leading to the back door of her shop.

He tossed a coin to a lad loitering nearby. 'You know Thrumby?'

The lad nodded.

'Knock on his door and have the porter escort Mrs Greystoke out to me. Understand?'

The boy nodded and dashed up the alley.

A few minutes later, Thrumby's porter marched out with Mrs Greystoke. She looked more magnificent than usual. She had discarded her drab workaday gown in favour of an emerald-green carriage dress trimmed in black velvet and cut low over her generous bosom. Her hat, a spectacular confection trimmed with a pheasant feather tilted jauntily to one side. He could not have chosen anything better to show off her looks. He grinned and jumped down as she approached.

He took her hand and bowed. 'Good day, Mrs Greystoke.'

'Lord Avery.' She sounded a little breathless.

'I am not too early, I hope?'

'Not at all.' She was gazing wide-eyed at his vehicle, which was a very dashing high-perch phaeton.

'Will the height trouble you?' he asked, wondering if he should have borrowed his brother's brougham instead.

'Not at all,' she said. 'I begged Papa to buy me one just like yours, but he thought it far too frivolous.'

'You like to drive?'

'I do. Not that there have been very many opportunities.'

'Then you must drive this one.' Bart probably wouldn't mind, as long as they didn't overturn it.

She smiled and seemed to relax. 'I would like that, but not today. These gloves would not survive.' She held out her lace-clad hands for inspection.

A sensible answer. 'Very well. But next time wear your driving gloves.'

Her expression said there might not be a next time. What? Did she plan to give him his *congé* before they had as much as driven out once? Was it possible his charm had deserted him? Or had he somehow made a bad impression? Clearly, it was something he needed to rectify.

And not because he needed her money. Her shop was likely barely surviving. Any profit from their arrangement would be minimal. No. This was about making her see him, as a person, someone she would want to spend time with because of *who* he was and not just what he could do for her.

Though why he cared, he wasn't sure. He never had before. At least not much. Being the second son of a duke had quickly taught him that most people were interested in getting to know his father or his older brother and thought to use him as a stepping stone in that direction. Even the woman he'd loved had stepped on his heart when she'd accepted his father's bribe to marry someone else.

He pushed the thought aside. It was so long ago now, he scarcely remembered her face. Later, much later, he'd heard that she had died in childbirth, and he'd felt sad, but not as devastated as he would have expected. And Bart was hinting that, now Avery had returned to England, the Duke would like him to settle down and find a wife. More likely that was Bart's hope, since he was baulking at the idea of wedded bliss with the woman their father had chosen to be the next Duchess, poor fellow.

Well the Duke was going to be disappointed with regards to Avery. As soon as he was sure Laura's husband was financially able to support his family—and according to Laura that would be any day now—Avery would be off on his travels again. His brother would just have to do his duty. After all, he was the heir.

In the meantime, Mrs Greystoke required his full attention, because he was determined to fulfil the terms of their agreement and to bed her into the bargain, provided she remained willing.

Determined? The idea took him aback. With most of his ladies, he simply ensured they were happy doing what he wanted them to do. What was it about this woman that made him want to please her? Perhaps it was because she so rarely smiled.

As if she had some inner sadness.

He helped her up into the carriage. Her long legs made an easy task of the climb and afforded him a glimpse of a very finely turned ankle. He stifled the urge to curl his hand around the delicious curve of her lower calf. It was far too early for such intimate play. And while many of the ladies he escorted would laugh and take it as their due, this skittish woman would likely run for the hills.

He liked that. Her mix of modesty and boldness. After all, it was a bold woman who propositioned a man the way she had and all the while maintaining her dignity.

He returned to his seat and set his horses in a steady trot.

'They are beautiful steppers,' she said after a few moments.

'Yes. I made an excellent purchase five years ago.' When his dibs had been in tune. If Father learned that his brother Bart was now paying to keep Avery's horses in fine fettle, there would be hell to pay. And no doubt the horses would have to go.

They made their way through the usual rush of London traffic and out on to the open road.

'Where are we going?' she asked after a few minutes of watching the road.

'Hampstead Heath. There is a nice little tea house there.'

She tensed. 'Oh.'

He frowned at the doubt in her voice. 'I can assure you it is quite respectable. I thought you might feel more comfortable this first time, if we went somewhere quiet.

Somewhere we can talk and get to know each other better in comfort before we face the *ton* head on.'

Her shoulders relaxed. 'I see. Yes, I suppose it is for the best.'

Dash it all, what did she mean by that? He knew better than to ask, though. Females were notoriously fickle, but she seemed content to go along with his plan so he would leave it at that. No sense in forcing her to speak her mind. Hopefully today's outing would set all of her fears at rest.

'Where do you call home?' he asked, to divert her thoughts. 'I can tell you originate from somewhere in the north, but not exactly where.'

'I was born and raised in Nottinghamshire, but when I am not keeping shop I reside in a small village near Sevenoaks with my sisters-in-law. I have grown to like the south of England.'

An evasive answer if ever he'd heard one. 'My family hales from Wiltshire, near Salisbury. We have more than a few bishops in the family. Have you ever visited the cathedral there?'

'I have never been to Wiltshire.'

'It is devilishly flat in more ways than one.'

'I would love to visit Stonehenge.'

So, the lady knew her history and her geography. Unlike many of her peers. 'I would like to show you around. It is one of the strangest sights I have ever seen in the world.'

'Have you seen a great many sights in the world?'

'Yes, indeed.' He noticed that her tension diminished even more. The lady clearly did not like to talk about herself, but was delighted to talk about him. Another thing that made her unusual. Well he certainly didn't mind talking about his experiences, if that was what she wanted. At least for now. Eventually he would learn all her secrets. 'I have been to several of the great continents—Europe, India, Africa—but there are many places I have still to visit.'

'Where will you go next?' she asked.

'The Americas.'

'Oh. Is it your intention to go soon?' Her voice lacked any emotion, as if she didn't care one way or the other.

Her lack of interest stung. He kept his voice equally expressionless. 'As soon as I may.'

'What holds you back?'

He hesitated. Was there more behind that question than mere curiosity? Well, there was no need to hide the truth. His sister's runaway marriage had caused a lot of gossip just over two years ago—her husband, John, was so much beneath her—but these days hardly anyone remembered her existence. Not that Laura had ever had a come out, so while her name had been on everyone's lips, her face had been unknown. It was only their father who refused to let go of the past. After all, while Laura's marriage straight out of the schoolroom might have been impetuous, John came from a decent family, despite the fact that they had no money, and would make a fine barrister some day soon. It had taken him far longer to get established than it should have because of the Duke's interference, which was why Avery had returned to England to help. It still made him go cold when he recalled Father's threats against John. 'Family responsibilities mostly.'

Carrie swallowed a gasp. She thought he had assured her that he was a single gentleman, not one with a family to support. She had looked him up in *Debrett's Peerage* and it had said nothing about him being wed. Not him or his older brother. It had mentioned a married sister. To a commoner. Perhaps it was not the most recent edition.

Oh, dear, it seemed she had made a very bad error in judgement. 'Really.' Her tone sounded repressive. Disapproving. It expressed her feelings exactly.

He glanced her way. 'It surprises you that I would care about my family?'

'I—I didn't know you had a family.'

'Not much of a one. A brother and a married sister, whose situation was somewhat dire, although it has been improving lately.'

She frowned. 'You do not have a wife?'

'Heavens, no. I already told you I did not. I am not the marrying sort, I'm afraid.'

Oh! It was his sister he meant. Not a wife and children. The relief left her feeling weak. 'It is good of you to care about your sibling.'

He raised an eyebrow. 'Why would I not?'

'Oh, no, I didn't mean that. Of course you would. I was a little confused.'

He negotiated around a carter travelling at a snail's pace and cast her a smile. 'Come now, Mrs Greystoke, it is not like you to beat around the bush. What is going on behind that lovely face of yours.'

Lovely? She almost swallowed her tongue. She didn't know whether to be pleased by the compliment or annoyed by his analysis of her character. In the end, she chuckled and decided to tell him the truth. 'Well, when you said you had family responsibilities I suddenly imagined a wife and children squirrelled away deep in the country while you enjoyed yourself in town.'

He laughed outright. 'You really do not have a very good opinion of the gentlemen of the *ton*, do you?'

'Oh, I do not paint them all with the same brush, but you have to admit, it is not an unheard-of situation. I was warned about it very carefully at the seminary for young ladies I attended. Sadly, I have found it to be mostly true.'

He stared at her for a second, then turned his attention back to his horses as they came up on another lumbering trade vehicle. A coal dray this time. Once they were safely past the obstruction he shifted slightly as if wanting to see her face better. To look her in the eye, as her father would have said. 'Who are your family, Mrs Greystoke? Your name has a familiar ring, but I have not been back in England long and I never did take much notice of such things before I left.'

'I told you, my family are merchants in Nottinghamshire.'

'And your husband's family. Why are they not caring for you, instead of sending you out into the world to earn a living?'

'My husband's family helps as much as they are able.'

Why she did not want to tell him about Westram, Petra and Marguerite, she was not sure. Perhaps it was because she feared Avery would be shocked to know she had dragged Westram's sisters into trade when the nobility frowned so much on that sort of thing. She did not like the idea of the *ton* ridiculing the Earl either. The poor man was doing his best in the face of such a terrible family tragedy.

He glanced up at the sky. 'It seems we are to be lucky with the weather today, Mrs Greystoke.'

Carrie winced. How she hated the sound of her husband's name on his lips. 'Do you think…would you mind calling me Carrie? All my friends do.'

'Carrie,' he repeated. 'Short for Carolyn or Caroline, I assume.'

She gave a short laugh. 'I wish it was. No. My name is Carrington. My father wanted a son. He picked out the name before I was born and refused to countenance another when he discovered I was a girl. It was his mother's maiden name.'

His smile held commiseration. 'I am named for some long-lost ancestor, too.'

'I like the name Avery.'

He grinned. 'Good, then that is what you shall call me and we will forget all about the Lord thing and the Mrs thing.'

'In private,' she warned. There was no doubt her association with a well-known rake was going to get back to Westram eventually. She should not have agreed to these outings, but on the other hand, how was she ever to become a woman instead of a spinster?. Fortunately, she did not have to worry about pleasing Avery, the way she would have to please a husband, and could just be herself. Blunt brusque Carrie. After all, in a roundabout way she was footing the bill for his time.

An odd sense of disappointment filled her. A feeling that she would have been just a little bit happier if he was escorting her, not for financial gain, but simply because it pleased him to do so.

Such foolishness. Yet he had said he found her attractive. He had also called her face lovely.

Had he said those things because she was his business associate? Or because he flirted without thinking?

Whatever it was, she was going to enjoy it while it

lasted. If Westram decided to put his oar in…well, she would deal with that when it happened.

No sense in crossing bridges before you came to them.

For the rest of the drive they talked about things he had seen on his travels abroad. The sights of Rome and Florence. The ruins in Greece. Some of his adventures involved avoiding the ongoing war between Britain and France. The time passed quickly and pleasantly and they were soon drawing up at a tea house on the edge of the heath near the village of Hampstead.

'What a lovely spot,' she remarked as he helped her down.

He looked pleased. 'I am glad you like it.'

There were other carriages outside the shop. Carrie braced herself for the scrutiny of strangers, while hoping like mad there was no one either of them knew.

This was it, then. Her first clandestine meeting with a man. *So what?* a little voice whispered in her ear. *You are a widow. You can do whatever you wish.*

She straightened her shoulders.

He smiled and offered his arm. 'Shall we?'

They entered to the tinkle of a little bell above the door.

A lady in a prim cap and apron bustled forward. 'Lord Avery. How lovely to see you again. Your usual table?'

'Yes, please,' Avery said.

His usual table. Again, there was that unaccountable feeling of disappointment that he had brought other women to this spot. She squashed it flat. His other ladies were why she had chosen him in the first place. She'd known from the first what sort of charming flirt he was. Why would she expect anything different? In truth, she did not know what to expect at all, so she should just put aside her worries and enjoy the experience. It wouldn't likely happen again.

An older couple seated in an alcove off to one side looked up as they entered a parlour scattered about with round tables covered in white cloths, some with seated guests. Each table bore a little vase containing a single rose.

Strangely, the older couple glanced at them with curiosity in their gazes, but not, thank goodness, recognition, before returning to their tea and quiet conversation. Carrie breathed a sigh of relief. There was no one here either of them knew and even if some of them recognised Avery, it would not mean anything.

She gave herself a mental shake. What was she thinking? The whole idea was for people to recognise them, to admire her bonnets and to come to the shop. Indeed, that was why she had worn this very fetching hat.

The woman led them to the table in the centre of the bow window. It looked out over a small garden full of flowers and gave way to the distant view of London's spires.

'What do you think?' Avery asked, once they were seated.

'It is charming.'

Avery smiled. 'Not to mention that they have the best cream cakes in all of London.'

'That we do,' their waitress said, beaming. 'Shall I bring you the usual assortment, my lord?'

Avery glanced at Carrie, clearly asking for her opinion.

'Whatever you think,' she replied.

'Yes, the usual assortment,' he said to the woman.

'What sort of tea would you like?' the woman asked.

This time he gestured to Carrie. 'You choose.'

He really was a lovely man. While she might not know what sort of cakes were on offer, she did know her tea. 'I would like Oolong,' she said.

'Good choice,' Avery approved.

The waitress bustled off.

Avery smiled at her. 'Tell me about your family.'

'I am an only child. I mentioned before that my father wanted me to be a son, but my mother never had any other children after me. It was a great disappointment to them both. They would have liked a large family. Is your family large?'

'There are three direct descendants of the Duke. My older brother, then me, then my sister. But there are hundreds of relatives scattered across Britain and France.' His mouth twisted wryly. 'At least it seems so. Every time I go anywhere someone claims kinship. I would like you to meet my sister, Laura. We are very close.'

'I don't believe that would be appropriate. Do you?'

'Why not?' He lowered his voice. 'I think she'd like you. She married against my father's wishes, so he cut her off. She's just as *de trop* as me in polite circles.'

'How very cruel.' Her own father had been the opposite. Far too doting. Suffocating, almost.

The waitress appeared with a tea tray.

She set it in front of Carrie and scurried away. Carrie inhaled the fragrant steam. 'This is very good tea.'

'Not once have I been disappointed.'

Carrie poured.

The woman returned with a tiered plate piled high with confections. They looked delicious.

'I put extra of your favourites on there, my lord,' she said with an indulgent smile.

He grinned like a small boy given a treat. 'You are a wonder, Mrs Bentlock.' He looked at Carrie. 'Let us hope we have the same taste in cakes.'

'Personally, I never met a cream cake I didn't like,' Carrie said laughing at his eagerness.

Mrs Bentlock dipped a small curtsy.

'I can see I will have to watch you,' Avery said, his eyes twinkling. 'Or you'll be eating all the best ones.'

She laughed. It took her by surprise. It seemed he was one of the few people who could surprise a laugh out of her. She wasn't used to his sort of teasing. But she liked it.

Using the silver server, he carefully lifted a confection on to her plate, cream and strawberry jam layered between flaky pastry. 'Try this one.'

She took a bite. It melted in her mouth. She closed her eyes for a moment as she savoured the burst of strawberries and cream, and the explosion of buttery pastry. She swallowed. 'Oh, so delicious.'

She became aware of his gaze watching her mouth with an intensity that caused her insides to tighten. He brought his gaze up to meet hers and the desire in them took her breath away. Heat rushed up from her chest all the way to her hairline.

His lips curved in a sensual smile. 'I am glad you like it. It is my favourite of them all.'

He picked the same kind and took a large bite with white even teeth before it got anywhere near his plate. He managed it without creating a single crumb on the pristine white tablecloth, whereas she had managed a veritable avalanche of pastry flakes on and around her plate.

'I can see you are an expert.'

'I am. My mother used to bring us here when we were children as a special treat. The Duchess did not approve of crumbs. The secret is to inhale, just a little, as you bite.'

'I would be more likely to choke,' she said, eyeing the last mouthful on her plate.

'Mother did not approve of choking either.'

He spoke with such seriousness, she had a feeling there was more to his words than he was saying, yet he looked perfectly cheerful. Perhaps he was making a joke? Unsure how to respond, she sipped her tea.

He put a different sort of cake on her plate. A scone with more of that lovely jam and cream in the middle. 'Wait,' she said, smiling at him. 'I haven't finished the first one yet.'

He grinned. 'You have to keep up or I'll be hogging them all to myself.'

'Aha, a challenge. I can tell what you must have been like as a boy.'

'I had to be quick. My brother is three years older than me. He could make short work of a plate of cakes. Laura and I had to guard our plates, too, or he'd filch from them as well.'

'It must have been fun.'

His gaze shadowed. 'We did have fun upon occasion, though being the heir and spare to a duke is a serious business.'

'I would imagine so.' Since it seemed like a bit of a painful topic she decided to change it. 'You mentioned that you visited India. What was it like?'

'Like?'

'Well, I do know that it is hot and that the people are exotic and different, since I have read about it in books, but I have never met anyone who has actually been there.'

'It is exotic and different.' He squinted as if looking into the distance. 'The heat is extraordinary.'

'Like a hot summer day?'

'Not even close. The air is like a wall of steam pushing against you in the middle of the day. And it smells different. The spices used in their foods lingers in every breath. It is crowded and noisy and since everything is in the local dialect, one is confused and awed. I spent a lot of time simply watching it all.'

'Did you see any elephants?'

'Elephants? Yes. They are everywhere. They are used the way we use horses, more or less. For farming, pulling heavy loads, carrying people.'

She ate the scone. 'Oh, my goodness, that is so good, I don't know which I prefer now.'

'Then try this one.'

He plopped a jam tart with a blob of cream right in the middle on to her plate.

She took a bite. Again, the pastry melted on her tongue. 'Oh, my.' She sighed. 'Are elephants as big as they appear in books?'

'A book cannot do justice to the size of them, I'm afraid. Such a massive body, so much strength, all carefully controlled by their mahout.'

'Mahout.' She liked the taste of the word on her tongue. 'I would like to see that. Did you ever ride one?'

'I did. Several times. The local Sultan was most insistent on showing the son of a duke every courtesy.' He sounded a little bitter.

'Was it uncomfortable?' she asked, trying to understand his sudden change of mood.

He seemed to relax at her question. 'It took a bit of getting used to, I must say. One is an awfully long way from the ground. And, my Lord, how it sways. Like a ship in a heavy swell. The stomach takes a while to settle down. Although I must say I prefer an elephant to a camel any day of the week.'

She laughed. 'Don't tell me you have ridden on a camel, too?'

'All right. I won't.'

He was teasing her again. She tapped his foot with the toe of her slipper and gave him a mock frown. 'Tell me.'

His eyebrows shot up. 'Eat the last cake and I will.' He placed it on her plate. This was a little round sponge cake with its top cut to look like little wings sprouting from a dollop of cream.

She poured them both another cup of tea and dutifully ate the cake. It was so light, it was like eating fresh air. 'Absolute heaven,' she declared. 'Now tell me.'

'Very well,' he said, chuckling. He covered her hand with his where it rested on the table. The warmth of his skin was a delicious shock. Her toes curled inside her slippers. Never had a man touched her so intimately. She had the strange urge to lift his hand to her mouth, to brush her lips against the hairs on the back of his knuckle, to feel the weight of it in her palm. She swallowed a gasp of surprise and looked up to again find that intensity in his gaze that made her breathless and sent little thrills running along her veins.

'Yes, what?' she managed to say, more or less in a normal voice.

'I did ride a camel. But they are unpleasant beasts, constantly grunting and moaning their displeasure. They also spit.'

She grimaced. 'They spit at people?'

'It is a form of aggression or defence, I believe. Their owners take great delight in putting the unwary traveller in the line of fire.'

He looked so disgruntled, she couldn't help laughing. 'One spit at you?'

'He caught me right in the eye. It stung like the blazes.'

She shuddered. 'I think I will avoid them, then. Though I'm hardly likely to meet one in London.'

Out of the corner of her eye, she noticed that the other couple, were leaving. The woman was looking at them. It seemed as if she intended to approach. She said something in a low voice to her companion and he shook his head as he responded, not looking their way at all, since all his attention was focused on the woman at his side. He gave her a look so full of warmth and affection, it made Carrie's heart stumble. It seemed to envelop the woman like an aura. Like some warrior of old offering his lady protection. It was…beautiful.

The woman gave a light laugh and as she passed their table she offered Carrie a smile of encouragement. Carrie blushed and dropped her gaze. No doubt the woman thought they were married, or at the very least betrothed. If she knew the truth, she would likely be horrified. Assuming she and her companion were married.

If they were married, they were certainly happy and that made her feel strangely glad.

'More tea?' she asked Avery.

He shook his head, eyeing the empty cake plate.

'You were right, these are the best cream cakes I have ever tasted.'

'I'm glad you enjoyed them.' He sounded very pleased with himself.

She could not help wondering how many other women he had brought to this spot. The owner certainly seemed to know him very well. Something unpleasant twisted in her chest, causing a pang. Really? She was feeling jealous? Or possessive? When she knew this was nothing more than a temporary arrangement cooked up between them?

The pang became a sharp ache behind her breastbone. Ridiculous. She'd had her chance at marriage. Look what a failure she had been. She would do better to devote herself to helping her new family. They had welcomed her with open arms and they deserved her full attention. This thing with Avery was merely a fling, if it turned out to be anything at all. A brief one at that.

He gave her a smile, as if he sensed her unease. His usual charming smile. The one that made her toes curl in her slippers and stole her breath. It was warm and lovely, and touched her heart in unexpected ways. How could it do that?

She had been letting the longings she'd tried so hard to suppress sneak out into the light. She really must not do that. Not with this man. Or any other. She would only get hurt.

He tilted his head. 'Tell me about the most interesting thing you did as a child?'

'Interesting?'

'Yes. Some adventure that stays in your mind as a fond memory.'

Most of her childhood had been a rather serious affair. But... 'I remember going to Goose Fair with Father and Mother. It is held every year in Nottingham Town Square in September.' She smiled at the recollection. 'We went because we needed a new gardener and a supply of cheese for the winter. Father said it was the only place all the best local cheeses were to be had. I was more interested in the fairings on the stalls and the entertainers. I remember, we bought bunches of ribbons from a tinker for me and Mother. There were jugglers and mimes and you had to keep your hand on your reticule because of all the pickpockets. And then there were the geese. Hundreds of them. They made such a racket.'

'Oh, yes,' Avery agreed. 'Fairs are great fun. It was grand mingling with all the locals. Bart and I used to go to one near our estate every year. And when we were older we used to sneak off from our tutor to watch the boxing matches. I won quite a bit of money off him betting on the outcome.' He smiled fondly.

She wasn't sure if his smile was for the memory of the fair, or the recollection of the money he had won. She wanted to think it was the former. 'I only went that once.' Mother had died not long afterwards. Father had never been so jolly again.

Avery grinned at her. 'I sometimes forget the fun parts of growing up. I haven't thought about those fairs for years, and though I have attended many a boxing match they were all between professional fighters. In those days it was local lads, most of whom we knew.'

She had not thought about that day in years. It was a good memory and she could not help smiling at him. 'Well, I think that was my most adventurous afternoon. It certainly doesn't come anywhere close to elephants and camels.'

'Have you ever been sailing?'

'No.'

'Fishing?'

'No. I grew up in the middle of Nottingham. There was no opportunity for such things.'

He laughed. 'I suppose not. Perhaps one day I could—' He broke off.

There would never be a one day for them. To fill the awkward pause, she glanced around the table. 'I could not eat another bite or drink another mouthful of tea, could you?'

'No, indeed.' He gestured to Mrs Bentlock to bring the bill and after he had paid her, he helped Carrie to rise. It was not long before they were tooling back along the road towards London.

Chapter Five

Avery felt unusually contented. Perhaps it was the good weather. But more likely it was the company of the woman at his side. There was something about her calm air of contentment that settled his constant urge to be on the move.

'Do you think they were married?' Carrie asked. 'The older couple in the alcove?'

Startled by the wistful note in Carrie's voice, Avery glanced at her face and caught a look of such longing it shook him to the core.

'Probably not,' he said rather more brusquely than he had intended. 'They looked too happy.'

The light in her face went out. Damn. He had not meant to be so forthright, but he certainly didn't want her getting romantic notions of a long and happy life together.

He didn't want a wife. A family tied one down. Look at how he was forced to kick his heels here in London for Laura's sake. And perhaps just a very little for Father's, though the old man would never acknowledge his presence in town. Not unless Avery gave in to his ducal demands and married a woman of the Duke's choosing.

Which went full circle around to the disappointment on Carrie's face.

She shifted in her seat, putting distance between them, and he instantly regretted the loss of intimacy that had been growing between them. He should have been a little gentler, but he could not afford to give her the wrong idea. Then another reason for her interest in the couple occurred to him and he felt worse.

'Do you miss your husband?'

Her expression changed. Stiffened. Becoming more remote.

Hell, why had he asked her that? His usual easy manner around the ladies seemed to have deserted him entirely.

'We were not married very long,' she said coolly. 'He—died a very few weeks after we were wed.'

He frowned. 'You did not know him beforehand? It was not a love match?'

'It was arranged very quickly.'

'His death must have come as quite a shock, then?'

She nodded.

Damn. It was like pulling teeth trying to get any information from this woman. Perhaps he should leave well enough alone, but something drove him on. The need to understand what made her so sad beneath her outward appearance of complacency. At least his talk of his travels had made her forget her unhappiness for a while, for her laughter had been genuine. And then she'd had to start on about marriage.

Resentment filled him. Resentment that even if he wanted to, he could not afford to marry. Not that he did. The very thought appalled him. He liked his freedom. No, the real resentment was against his father for forcing the issue. He shoved his feelings away, they were not worth the bother, and focused on Carrie. On her sadness.

'May I ask how he died?'

She hesitated as if trying to find a way to express what ought to have been a simple answer. 'He died in battle. At Badajoz. Shortly after we married.'

The mists in his brain dissipated in a flash. Now he recalled where he had heard the name Greystoke. It had been a huge on dit a week or so before he came home. Laura had told him all about the three noblemen who had gone off to war and been killed in Spain, leaving the house of Westram in complete disarray.

An abyss seemed to open up at Avery's feet. 'You are Westram's sister-in-law.' He could not help the note of accusation in his voice. This was bad news indeed.

She tensed. 'I am.'

'Why in heaven's name did you not tell me?'

Her spine straightened. 'I do not see how it is relevant.'

'And what the hell is Westram about, letting you keep a shop like some common merchant's wife?' Leaving her around for men like him, or worse, to prey on, for heaven's sake. Or leaving her around to trap some unsuspecting nobleman into marriage. God help him, had he really fallen into such a trap?

'I am some common merchant's *daughter*,' she said icily.

'You are related to a peer.' He could not help his fury. 'The settlements—'

'Are hardly any of your business.' She stared ahead of them. 'What a wonderful view.'

So, she was not prepared to discuss her husband with

him. That was fine. He had no wish to become embroiled in her personal circumstances.

The sister-in-law of an earl. This was why he never pursued single ladies, even if they were widows. He'd certainly jumped in with both feet in this instance. What the hell was he to do? End it, right here and now, would be the most sensible course of action.

Dammit it, he didn't want to. Not yet.

He was surprised by his reluctance. Normally, he would have no such qualms. But then, it was a matter of honour. A gentleman never went back on his word. He'd just have to find a way to handle it so he did not find himself leg shackled.

Carrie didn't know whether to feel miserable that he had discovered who she was, or relieved. She should have told him right at the beginning. Guilt gnawed at her stomach. Guilt that she hadn't been honest when she prided herself on speaking the truth, along with disappointment that he was clearly going to end their association before it had properly begun.

Nor could she imagine going through this again, asking another gentleman to be her lover, only to be rejected. She shuddered inside; the thought of asking another gentleman made her feel ill. Positively humiliated. She should not have asked Avery either. At least he had been a gentleman about it. Instead of turning her down flat or leaping into her bed for some exorbitant sum, he'd proposed a different sort of arrangement, with the possibility of more being left in the hands of fate. But what the 'more' might entail she wasn't quite sure and hadn't liked to ask.

But she had offered him money and since he was a

gambler, like Jonathan, he no doubt would expect to be paid, just as he expected her to pay him for helping her sell her hats.

She pinned a calm expression on her face and observed the passing view as they drew closer and closer to the fringes of the city. Once they reached her little shop, they would never have to see each other again. A sense of loss filled her chest. It was surely only because she knew she would never attempt anything like this again. It was all just too demeaning.

The silence between them became oppressive. Nothing she thought of to say sounded right in her own ears. How did one put an end to such a contract anyway? It was highly embarrassing. For them both.

'I'm sorry I was sharp with you,' he said quietly as they passed the first smattering of houses at the edge of the city.

'Not at all,' she said, trying to sound as if she didn't care. 'I never should have approached you in the first place. I doubt it will make the slightest difference to the success of the shop.'

His eyes widened. 'You are giving me my marching orders?'

Oh, dear, was it not permitted to end such an arrangement? Not even one that had been vague in the extreme?

'I thought that now you know who I am, you would not wish to be seen with me. I quite understand.'

His eyebrows crashed down. 'Why would you think such a thing?'

She took a deep breath. 'I know what the gossips say about me. That after one night with me, my husband found me so unappealing, he left for the battlefields of Spain.'

He stared at her. 'Who on earth told you that?'

She shrugged, trying to hide her hurt. 'It is common knowledge.'

He glared. 'I've certainly never heard it said.' Damn. He hadn't been in London at the time. And Laura would never have been so unkind as to pass along such malicious gossip.

'Well, if you must know, it was my aunt-in-law. She had been against the marriage, the moment she heard of it, and refused to attend the ceremony. She visited Westram as soon as she learnt the news of Jonathan's death. She was not reticent in speaking her opinion. Poor Westram did not know where to look.'

'He should have looked her in the eye and told her to mind her own business.'

Avery sounded strangely furious.

'She was only repeating what she had heard. And you mustn't blame Westram. He is a good man.'

'Then what is he about letting you and his sisters set up a shop in town?'

'We are widows and Westram has nothing to say in anything we do.'

Avery turned on to Bond Street, his face set in grim lines, but he seemed to accept what she said about her brother-in-law.

No doubt Lord Avery would now want to end their agreement. And his vague offer to see where their attraction led had probably simply been a way not to hurt her feelings. She really wasn't cut out for this sort of thing. She knew nothing about flirting or enticing a man. She always managed to put her foot in her mouth. 'I think it best if we do not see each other again,' she said flatly, anxious to have an end to her shame and embarrassment as soon as possible.

'Do you, now?'

'Yes. I do. I am finding the whole thing terribly uncomfortable to say the least. I must ask that you never speak of what I asked of you to anyone else. It was all a foolish mistake.'

He stiffened, his hands tightening on the reins so much one of his horses tossed its head.

He pulled up at the spot where he had picked her up. 'I don't have time to discuss this right now. I have another appointment. Nor can I leave the horses to take you inside.'

'I can manage to walk a few steps to my door,' she said calmly, while her nose and eyes burned as if they wanted to cry. How very stupid.

'I will visit you later this evening.'

She took her courage in both hands and glanced at his face, which was still set in grim lines. It was exactly the same sort of face she had seen on her husband on the day of their wedding. 'No,' she said firmly. 'I will not be at home this evening.'

'You are out?' he said. 'Or just not at home to me?'

'I don't see what difference either one makes.' She jumped down on to the pavement.

Her dress caught on the carriage door. His gaze widened as it landed on a good deal of her exposed leg. Snatching it free, she shot him a glare. 'Thank you for a wonderful afternoon.' She marched up the alley.

And that was that. The sound of his horses' hoofs gradually receded. When she could hear them no more, she knocked on the door to let the porter know she had returned.

* * *

The next morning passed for Carrie as if the clock's hands were weighted. For some reason, though the shop was busy, time seemed to hang heavy. Likely because sleep had evaded her the previous night. Too many images of Lord Avery escorting one of his special ladies to some ball or another. Which was ridiculous. She had hated the two balls she had attended, so why should he not go with someone else?

Balls were the worst form of torture for a girl on the outskirts of society, unless she was really pretty or good at flirting and making herself noticed. She had only attended a couple in London before her father became seriously ill and not one young man had invited her to dance. Another reason she had accepted Jonathan's proposal so quickly. Marrying him had been a way to escape the humiliating rituals of the marriage mart. If only she'd known that her father had more or less bribed him to come up to scratch, maybe she would not have been so quick to accept it as a way out.

No, she was much better off staying home. And besides, she wasn't ever going to see Avery again, was she? She had ended things very handily. It was far better being the one to bring things to a conclusion than to be the recipient of rejection. And she couldn't imagine that *his* feelings would be hurt.

At least she'd had the courage to speak her mind.

Then why didn't she feel the slightest bit courageous? Indeed, it felt more like she had run away. Dash it all, she wished she'd never met the man.

She sighed.

'Is everything all right, missus?' her assistant Tansy asked, looking up from where she was tying a bow on one of the bonnets. The girl was turning out to be a treasure. She had a flair for arranging things.

'Why would it not be?' Carrie asked.

'That is the second time you have sighed in as many minutes,' Tansy said, looking worried. 'Perhaps you need a cup of tea. We've been so busy this morning and I don't think you even had breakfast.'

She hadn't. She'd felt too miserable for food.

But she could not be presenting a long face to her customers. That was the surest way to get a reputation as a sourpuss. Shopping was supposed to be a pleasant experience.

She forced a smile. 'You are right. A cup of tea is in order for both of us. I'll go put the kettle on the hob.'

She left Tansy in charge of things and went through the curtain. A cup of tea would cheer her up. And she would not let herself think about Lord Avery ever again. Or at least not enough to make her sigh.

She stopped abruptly and blinked as she found him ensconced at her kitchen table, his hat and gloves set in the middle like a centrepiece, his long legs sprawled out into the middle of the floor.

Her heart hit a gallop in a second flat. 'Lord Avery. What are you doing here?'

'Waiting for you.'

'How did you get in?'

'The porter. He knows I'm a regular visitor. I simply needed to cross his palm with a bit of silver.' He offered her a wheedling smile. 'I thought you might prefer it, to my entering by the front door.'

She took a deep breath. Had she smiled back? Oh, surely not. 'As I said yesterday—'

'We had a good time yesterday did we not? I enjoyed

it immensely and I thought of somewhere you might like to go today.'

'I cannot go anywhere today. The shop—'

'Your Miss Tansy can manage perfectly well for an hour or two.'

'An hour or two?' Her voice rose. 'Certainly not.'

'I also came to apologise.'

She stiffened. She did not want him to apologise. She did not want any of this.

Chapter Six

Avery had thought it would be a simple thing. Show up. Smile. Tell her he was sorry for yesterday's argument and they could move on. It was how it had gone with other women in the past. Clearly not with this one.

'Carrie, I truly am sorry. Being the son of a duke, I am a prime target for women on the marriage mart.' That was what his father had said about Alexandra, the woman he'd thought he'd loved. Back then he hadn't wanted to believe it. Now he wasn't so sure. 'When you...' He hesitated. She had not lied about who she was, but she had certainly been evasive. 'When you did not reveal your relationship to Westram immediately, I jumped to the wrong conclusion. I should have known better.'

Her expression eased. A fraction. 'I still do not think this...' she waved vaguely between them '...is a good idea. I should never have brought it up. And I would appreciate if you would forget all about it.'

Damn. Much as he did not want to, he gathered himself to rise and leave. A wicked thought entered his mind 'You are actually going to break our contract?'

She stared at him blankly. 'Our contract? I made you an offer. I am withdrawing from it.'

'Oh, no. I offered you a contract. We shook hands on it. In this very room.'

'I brought the matter up first.'

'I rejected your offer. You took mine. Is that the sort of dealings the members of the *ton* can expect from the owner of this shop?' Blast. That really wasn't so very kind, was it, making it sound as if he might ruin her reputation? He wouldn't, of course, but he could see from the doubt in her face she wasn't sure. That hurt.

But needs must. He did not disabuse her of the notion. Instead of backing down, as he ought, he maintained an implacable expression.

'If I recall correctly,' she said, 'we were to decide whether we found each other *mutually* attractive. I—'

He jumped in before she could say something delightfully blunt that could not be got over. 'We agreed to give it two weeks while we see if we can increase your sales.'

She pressed her lips together.

He pushed ahead. 'I am asking you to come with me for an hour or two, that is all. So I can prove I am serious about my apology. It is only fair.'

'Fair?' An unwilling smile curved her lips. 'Who are you to talk about fair? You simply want your own way.'

Relieved, he grinned. 'Comes of being the younger son of a duke, I'm afraid.'

'Then being the younger son of a duke is bad for one's character,' she pronounced grimly.

He stood up and bowed. 'I will not argue that point. Shall we go?'

She glanced down at herself. 'I cannot possibly go out with you like this.'

'What you are wearing is perfect for this expedition of ours. This time it is not about showing off your hat and we will not see anyone who knows either of us.'

She frowned. 'What on earth can you mean?'

'You will see.'

Curiosity won out over caution, as he had hoped it would. Guessed it would, actually, given her lively turn of mind. 'You should probably wear a shawl, though. The wind is a little cool and while it is not far to walk, I do not want you catching a chill.'

'We are walking?'

'It will not take long.'

She stuck her head back into the shop area. 'Tansy, I am going out for a short while.'

She then took down a shawl from the peg on the back of the kitchen door and shook her head as if admonishing herself. 'Very well, then. Let us be off.'

A slight doubt niggled somewhere in the centre of his chest. If he was wrong about this, no doubt it would be the very last he would see of her. But he was not wrong.

He escorted her to the Strand by way of Piccadilly. He was pleased to discover that she did not dawdle and that it was very easy to match his long stride to her steps, because she was also tall. Of course, he knew why she was striding out—she planned to have this expedition of theirs over as quickly as possible.

The Strand was busy with traffic and pedestrians, both fashionable and common folk, but as they neared his objective, she glanced his way. 'Where are you taking me?'

'Just a few more steps.'

He drew them to a halt outside the Exeter Exchange.

She wrinkled her nose at the strong smell of animals. 'You are bringing me to a menagerie?'

'Yes.' He paid at the wicket and ushered her in and up the stairs. 'There is someone I want you to meet.'

The stiffness disappeared. 'I have heard of this place,' she said. 'They have all sorts of exotic creatures, I am told. How did you know I had never been here?'

He smiled. He really liked how she used her brain. He led her through a doorway into a vast room. 'Because of this.'

The vast room contained cages down its length, a tiger in one, a lion in another, other beasts that she would have lingered in front of if he had not hurried her along. It was the cage at the far end to which he directed her attention.

'An elephant!' she exclaimed.

An attendant came up to them as they reached it. 'Chunee his name is, ma'am...sir. An Indian elephant. He weighs seven tons, if you were wondering.'

Carrie looked at the creature with an expression of awe. 'He is enormous. This is the sort of elephant you rode in India?'

'Yes, though they were draped in scarlet and gold cloth and had a *houda* on their backs. A sort of seat with a canopy.'

She frowned. 'Is he dangerous?'

'Not a bit,' the keeper said. He grinned, exposing brown teeth. 'Though you do have to watch out for his tusks. And I am very careful to keep me feet out of his way when I clean out his stall. Wouldn't harm a soul, he wouldn't. Got a sixpence, sir?'

Avery handed over a coin.

'Remove your glove and hold out your hand, flat like, ma'am.'

Carrie looked a little worried.

'It will be fine,' Avery said. He'd done this himself, but was not going to spoil her surprise.

Carrie took off her glove and reached out, palm up. The keeper put the sixpence on it. 'Now stand very still.'

The animal uncurled its trunk and it glided out from between the bars.

Avery held his breath.

Carrie didn't dare breathe as the sinuous grey nose waved in front of her. She risked a quick peek upwards into the beast's eyes and was surprised how small they seemed in such a large head. There was a glint of amusement in those dark orbs and suddenly the fear went away. No creature who could smile in quite that way could possibly mean her harm.

She steadied her hand and watched in awe and delight at the tip of his snout, no trunk, found her fingers. A blast of wet warm air across her skin made her jump, then a sort of suction and the trunk retreated. The sixpence was gone.

'Did he eat it?' she asked in surprise, watching the animal curl up the proboscis and put it in his gaping red mouth.

'Ah, not he,' the keeper said smugly. 'He's no fool. Hold out your hand again.'

Once more, the trunk came through the bars. This time it dropped the wet sticky coin in her palm. She closed her fingers around it. The elephant's nose didn't retreat as it had before, but reached out to touched her cheek. Again, she felt that strange sense of suction.

She froze.

'It's all right, ma'am. Just his way of smelling you. Much like a dog does.'

'Can I touch him?' she whispered.

'If you wants,' the man said.

'Don't be afraid,' Avery said. 'He won't hurt you.'

She raised a hand and patted the grey wrinkly skin. It was rough to the touch and warmer than she expected. The trunk curled around her hand in the oddest way.

'He likes you,' the keeper proclaimed. 'There's not many that's brave enough to touch him.'

The animal shifted on its enormous feet and that's when she became aware of the chain around one of his ankles. 'Why is he chained?'

'A precaution, ma'am. That's a big beast.'

Chunee flapped his ears as if listening to their words. He released her hand and the tip of his trunk wandered down her length all the way to her toes. He blew out a breath and she once more felt heat and moisture against her ankles through her stockings.

A small boy escaped his nursemaid and ran up beside them. He had a sixpence in his hand, but when the elephant reached out to take it, the lad threw it and hared off.

Carrie watched, fascinated, as Chunee used his trunk to search through the straw until he located the coin. The sensitive tip of his trunk curled around it. Once more, she held out her hand and he dropped it in her palm.

'It is amazing, isn't it,' Avery said, 'that such a large animal can be so delicate. I have seen them pick up logs ten men would be hard pressed to lift and push over a tree as if it was kindling. And heaven help you if you make one angry. They can run faster than we can. And their charge is ten times worse than that of a bull.'

Carrie swallowed. The very thought of him getting loose... 'Does he ever come out?' she asked the keeper.

'He does, when he's performing in the circus. We keeps him here between times.'

A strangely sad feeling came over her. 'Do you think he's happy?' she asked Avery.

He looked surprised and frowned. 'He's well fed. He is well cared for. I don't see why not.'

She wanted to believe him. She really did.

He blew out a breath. 'You are right, Carrie. I doubt if he is truly happy. But, then, are horses truly happy? Or cows? He is very well cared for as you can see. Better cared for than some of those I saw in India, in fact.'

She reached out and rubbed the elephant's nose. It made a strange rumbling sound down its trunk. She jumped, but did not move away, just kept rubbing and the volume of the sound reduced.

'It sounds like the purr of a very large cat,' she said.

'I heard them make that sound in India when they greeted each other. He sees you as a kindred spirit.'

She liked that idea. She rubbed her hand higher up his trunk and he blew out a loud breath. Kindred spirit to an elephant.

'He makes that noise when I washes him,' the keeper said. He grinned. 'He really likes his bath. So he must really like you.'

'How long do elephants live?'

'A very long time. Fifty or sixty years, I'm told,' Avery said.

'Extraordinary.'

They walked back along the cages and a pacing tiger

snarled. She leapt back. Avery put his arm around her waist. 'Steady on. It can't get out.'

She laughed self-consciously. 'I know. He startled me, that is all.'

'Well, now you have seen an elephant, I suppose I should return you to your shop.'

She had forgotten all about the shop.

'Thank you for bringing me. It was a lovely surprise.' In fact, when she thought about it, no one had ever given her such a lovely gift. Avery was not only charming and attractive, he was thoughtful, too.

Avery guided Carrie out into the street. He had thought she would be delighted to see a real-life elephant. He still wasn't sure if he was completely forgiven, however. It would now be up to her to make the first move. He certainly wasn't going to force the issue. If he really did not want to have any more to do with him, then so be it. It was her decision. The fact that he enjoyed her company, that he liked her, was neither here nor there.

They walked in silence for a while.

'I'm sorry—'

'I'm sorry—'

They both spoke at once and they both laughed.

'You go first,' he said.

'I am sorry I got angry yesterday. You were right. I should have told you who my family is. It is just that Westram would not like the idea of his sisters as shopkeepers and milliners and I did not want to further antagonise him should he discover it. He would not be pleased were he to learn of our...association either. He is really quite stuffy about things.'

Avery would be stuffy about such things, too, were

Laura to enter into such an arrangement with a man like him. Damn it.

'And that is why you decided we should not see each other again.'

She nodded.

'I was going to apologise for my harsh words regarding your chosen profession. There is nothing wrong with it at all, I was simply surprised Westram allowed it. And apparently he does not, if you are keeping it a secret from him.'

'In our opinion, Westram has enough troubles without being burdened with the care and feeding of three widows. I must tell you that he was perfectly willing to do so until we married again. But since none of us wishes to ever be wed again, we could hardly impose on him to be responsible for us the rest of our lives. The bonnets, the shop, provide us with a means to be independent.'

'You wish never to marry again? Not ever?'

'Never.'

He ought to be dancing a jig at the news. Instead, he felt some sort of strange regret. He pushed it aside, focused on what was important. 'So my concerns of yesterday are completely without foundation.'

'Yes.'

They turned on to Piccadilly. 'Then there is no reason why we cannot continue as we agreed.'

'To share in the profits, if business increases.'

He frowned. 'And to see where our mutual attraction leads. I can assure you my attraction to you has not lessened these past few days.'

She flushed scarlet. 'But—'

'Has your attraction to me dwindled?' He might as well get to the heart of her hesitation. A lady had a right to change her mind about a fellow. In his experience, they also often said yes when they really meant no, or they pretended one thing was wrong when it was really something else. Yet he did not think Carrie was that sort. Up to now, she had always been brutally honest.

She made a funny little sound.

He peeked around the brim of her bonnet to see her face as red as a peony. 'Carrie?'

'No,' she said. And walked faster. 'Much as I do not want to, I still find you attractive.'

He forced himself not to laugh. 'Well, I will take that as a compliment.'

She snorted.

At that he laughed out loud.

She rounded on him. 'What is so funny.'

He touched the tip of her nose with a finger. 'You are, my sweet. And I adore you for making me laugh.'

A smile touched her lips. 'You are impossible. You know that.'

'I am. But in the meantime, all is forgiven and we will continue where we left off.'

'How can I say no? Clearly, a man who is able to conjure up an elephant in the middle of London is worth a second chance.'

He had the feeling there would not be a third. For a brief moment, he wished he had not made a bargain with her to do with profits and money, but then he remembered Laura's anxiety about next month's rent and he shrugged off the sentimental notion. But he did hope the attraction between them would blossom and they could find something more than simple financial gain.

And that was a shock.

But why not? She did not want to marry any more

than he did. He believed she had spoken the truth on that matter, she had been so vehement. So why should they not enjoy each other to the full?

He delivered her to her back door and kissed her hand before knocking. 'Drive out with me tomorrow, in Hyde Park?'

She looked anxious. 'Are you sure that is a good idea?'

'If we are to promote your wares to the *ton*, it is.'

She swallowed. 'You really are wishing to continue with our arrangement?'

'I am.' Her obvious reticence puzzled him. After all, even if he had changed the terms somewhat, this had been her idea. Unless... 'Are you saying you are ashamed to be seen with me?' The idea gave him a strange feeling in the pit of his stomach.

She looked horrified and he felt a sudden surge of relief. 'Of course not.' She straightened her shoulders. 'I worry that potential customers might not approve of my driving out with you, me being a shopkeeper.'

He frowned. 'You are Westram's sister-in-law.'

She shook her head. 'I have been in mourning most of the time since I married until just before opening the shop. My father died within days of the wedding and then my husband... No one really knows me as anything but a milliner. Even though they must all know the story of my husband's death, I doubt anyone would associate a mere milliner with the Earl of Westram and he is also currently out of town, so we will not meet him either.'

He had a feeling there were things she was not telling him, but he did believe she thought members of the *ton* would look down on her and he didn't like it. 'Well then, they need to know you are the best milliner in town and to do that we need to flaunt a few of those hats of yours.'

She shook her head at him, but one of her rare smiles graced her lips. 'Well, since it seems you will not take no for an answer, I will drive with you in the Park tomorrow.

He grinned. 'Wonderful. I will come for you at four.' He banged on the door.

The porter opened it and once Avery saw she was safely inside, he strolled off. To his surprise he realised he was whistling.

What was he thinking? He stopped at the end of the alley and glanced back. Great heavens, was he actually looking forward to showing her off to the *ton*? Hmm. It might be a little of that, but surely it was more about winning. It was not in his nature to simply give up on something he wanted.

Though he had given up on his father, had he not?

That was different. It was his father who had given up on him. And when the old man heard Avery was squiring a shopkeeper around town, he hoped it would give the old curmudgeon a few sleepless nights.

He glanced at his watch. It was early yet. Time enough to visit with Laura and her husband, before going to the new hell that had opened in St James's. The stakes were said to be the highest in London.

Chapter Seven

Ensconced beside the dashing Lord Avery and tooling through the streets of Mayfair, Carrie felt as if she looked down upon the world. It was the very first time she had been driven by a gentleman in Hyde Park and it felt wonderful. She felt wonderful. Feminine and somehow cherished.

Of course, she knew it was only his excellent manners that made her feel that way. Theirs was for the most part a business arrangement, after all, but he played his part to perfection and she was determined not to put him to shame. Hopefully the carriage gown she had chosen to wear today was suitable for the occasion.

He grinned at her. 'You look lovely.'

Good heavens, could the man read her mind, or was the fact that she had butterflies dancing in her stomach showing on her face? 'Thank you.' She hoped she sounded confident, instead of grateful for every crumb of kindness sent her way.

'That bonnet should draw a few eyes,' he said approvingly.

Oh, he was talking about their plan, not actually complimenting her looks. 'It is one of Petra's best efforts yet, it is called a *chapeau à la Salamanca.*'

'Clever, naming it after a battle and the military style is all the rage right now. It suits you.'

They turned through the gates into the park. Carrie was immediately struck by the vast numbers of people jostling for position. Not only were members of the *ton* in their elegant equipages vying for attention, but there were hawkers selling everything from roasted chestnuts to violets. She tried not to stare wide-eyed like some country bumpkin.

'Is this your first foray into the fashionable hour?' Avery asked, amusement in his voice.

Hmmm. Clearly, she had failed to look suitably bored. 'It is.' Now she sounded rather grim, as if he had asked her if it was the first time she had been tortured.

There had been a number of firsts coming her way ever since she'd met Lord Avery. Her first assignation at a tea house. Her first glimpse of India through the eyes of someone who had been there. Her first look at an elephant and now her very first drive in Hyde Park.

Then there was also the first she was anticipating with a mix of excitement and terror. Although that one was not yet a certainty. Her mouth dried at the thought of making love with Avery. She really wasn't sure she would be able to drum up the courage to go through with it, either, should the opportunity appear on her horizon.

A carriage drew up beside them going in the opposite direction.

Mrs Baxter-Smythe and a young girl. 'Why, how delightful, Lord Avery.' She glanced at Carrie and her eyes widened in shock, her mouth opening and closing like a landed fish. 'Mrs Greystoke,' she finally managed to say. 'Imagine meeting you.'

Carrie imagined hundreds of eyes suddenly focused on her sitting beside Lord Avery. A man known for libertine tendencies with other men's wives.

Lord Avery leaned forward and gave the girl beside Mrs Baxter-Smythe an easy smile. He held out a hand. 'I don't believe we have met. May I say how delightful you look in that hat.'

It was one of the ones the Mrs Baxter-Smythe had purchased in Carrie's shop. How clever of him to notice.

The girl blushed and looked adorably confused.

Mrs Baxter-Smyth looked horrified. 'Sukie, this is Lord Avery. Belmane's younger son. And his companion is Mrs Greystoke. Alfred, drive on!' The coach lurched forward.

'How...rude,' Carrie said looking back over her shoulder at the stiff-backed Mrs Baxter-Smythe, who was clearly lecturing her daughter.

Lord Avery chuckled softly. 'It is well known that I have no intention of taking a wife. Therefore, Sukie's mama is being suitably protective of a daughter barely out of the schoolroom.'

'You did that on purpose,' Carrie said and she could not prevent herself from smiling at the mischievous twinkle in his eyes. 'Poor girl. She'll be dreaming of you when she goes to bed tonight.'

'And her mama will remember that I liked the hat.' He gave her a quizzical look. 'Will you be dreaming of me, I wonder?' he asked with a teasing note in his voice.

'Certainly not.' Heat rushed to the roots of her hair. She hadn't meant to sound so brusque, but his question had touch her on the raw. She had been seeing his face in her dreams since the first day they met.

He laughed, sounding not at all put out, and manoeuvred around a couple of carriages whose owners had stopped to chat. 'I shall dream about you.'

'What a bouncer,' she scoffed.

He cocked an eyebrow. 'My dear Mrs Greystoke, you clearly underestimate your allure to the poor male of the species. Look at the way that fellow is staring at you.'

Indeed, another gentleman walking along the grass beside the carriage path was eyeing her through his quizzing glass. His female companion elbowed him in the ribs.

'I hope,' she said, a little more stiffly than she had intended, 'that he was admiring my hat.'

'I doubt it. Most gentlemen do not notice such things except in the most general of ways. They notice the lovely face beneath the brim. The slender neck supporting the confection. The luxurious curls framing the enchanting expression.'

The heat in her face said she must be positively scarlet at such fulsome compliments. 'I assume you are talking about the young lady by his side,' she said repressively.

'He wasn't looking at that young lady through his quizzing glass.'

'Foolish man,' she muttered.

'Do you mean him, or me?'

'You. You dolt.'

He laughed out loud, a deep, rich, happy sound that sent the butterflies in her stomach racing along her veins to dance in the tips of her fingers. How did he make her feel so utterly weak at the knees with a laugh? It wasn't right.

They reached the end of the Row and he expertly turned the carriage around without coming afoul of any of the many vehicles around them making the same difficult turn. Others weren't so fortunate. A landau and a barouche had their wheels locked, much to the amusement of a couple of children.

As they started back down the Row, they came face to face with the lady and gentlemen whom they had seen at the tea shop on Hampstead Heath.

The lady recognised them instantly and smiled and waved before leaning over to point them out to her escort.

Without thinking, Carrie waved back.

'Who the devil is that?' Avery asked.

'It is the couple we saw out at Hampstead. Surely you recognise them.'

'I didn't look that closely. I was too busy looking at you.'

Carrie's mouth dropped open.

'I was,' he said with a shrug.

'You, sir, are a terrible flirt.'

The admonishment seemed to cheer him. 'That I am.'

He drew up beside a carriage containing three very pretty young ladies, all blonde and all dressed in the height of fashion, with a woman who was either their companion or their mother.

'Mrs Greystoke, meet Miss Gideon and her sisters Lydia and Evelyn.' Miss Gideon stared intently at Carrie and she felt prickles dart down her back the way she always did when other daintier women took in her size. 'What a beautiful bonnet,' the girl exclaimed. 'Where did you buy it?'

Oh. The merchant in Carrie bustled to the fore. 'From a shop on Cork Street, First Stare Millinery.'

'It is stunning,' one of the other girls said. She frowned. 'Mrs Luttrell mentioned that shop to Mama, I believe.'

The chaperon looked up. 'She did, Miss Evelyn. A day or so ago.'

'Mother thought the address a little out of the way,' the oldest girl said. 'I think it would be worth it, if it sells hats like that one.'

Her own headgear was not nearly as nice as the one Carrie wore. 'We have lots of styles suitable for all events and weather,' she said and could not keep the pride from her voice.

Avery bowed. 'Excuse us, ladies, we are causing a traffic jam.' He set his horses in motion.

Carrie bit her lip. 'Did I press too hard? Do you think they will come to the shop?'

'Of course, they will. Everyone in London knows that my ladies wear only the most elegant of creations.'

'Then this drive has been worth it,' she said, relaxing.

He made a sound like a cross between a laugh and a groan. 'Then let us go home.' He turned on to Park Lane and set off at a spanking trot. 'I do hope you gained some personal pleasure from our drive,' he said, his eyes twinkling as he glanced her way. 'I know I did.'

Oh, yes, the man was a terrible flirt. And a man who did not take anything or anyone very seriously.

A good thing, surely. She certainly did not want to take him too seriously either. Once their time was up, they would likely never meet again. A pang squeezed her heart. A sense of loss. Apparently, she was becoming attached to him. That really would not do.

'I was wondering if you would like to come with me to the theatre tomorrow night?' he said. 'A chance to wear another of your elegant hats.'

The theatre. Another first. Longing filled Carrie, but obligation made her shake her head. 'I go home tomorrow afternoon.'

Something inside her warmed when he looked disappointed. Something she tried to douse with cold water and cold logic.

Laura looked tired Avery thought as she greeted him with a hug. 'Where is that disgraceful husband of yours?' he asked cheerfully, but perhaps a little too pointedly. It was gone nine at night.

'Working. As usual.' She sighed. 'Lannie, bring tea to the parlour, would you?'

The elderly maid took his coat and hat and disappeared into the back of the house. A very tiny house in Golders Green.

He handed over his previous night's winnings.

'You shouldn't,' Laura said, looking torn. 'John doesn't like it.'

He liked his brother-in-law, mostly, but John did not like him passing along his winnings at the tables. The man found it hard to accept that he was not yet providing a good enough income to support a wife and child.

'Don't tell him, then.'

Laura shook her head. 'We do not keep secrets from each other.'

They had married for love. Their father, his Dukeliness, had not approved the match, but Laura and John had gone ahead anyway. Once John built his practice up now that he had passed the bar, his income would increase substantially. Until then Avery would continue to do what he could for his sister and to hell with what John thought.

'I promise you, I won this honestly and no one was left destitute upon the parish.'

She smiled. 'I hope you kept enough for yourself this time.'

Laura had come to his lodgings unexpectedly and found it freezing cold. She had been most indignant that he had given all of his winnings to her and left himself without sufficient funds to heat his room. He had promised he would never do such a thing again.

'I did. And how is my nephew, the estimable Derek?' Derek was nearly two years old and the reason Laura had been required to wed so precipitously, despite her father's insistence that she could marry as he dictated and pass the child off as her husband's. Or not. He had said no one would care as long as they became part of the ducal family.

Sadly, he was right.

But despite the bullying and threats from her father, Laura had run off with John. And was now cut off from any financial support from that quarter. But John was getting more and more clients and soon would be on his feet, according to Laura.

Avery could not wait for that day to come. Then he would be free to return to his travels. His wanderings, as Laura called them. And yet, unexpectedly, at least for the moment, he was in no hurry to leave London. A certain Mrs Greystoke continued to hold his interest, though he could not figure out why. Perhaps it was the thought of that magnificent figure unclothed and beneath him. No doubt once he had had his wicked way with her, he could move on to pastures green. If the war continued the way it was going, soon all of Europe would be open to travel.

The thought left him feeling hollow. Almost home-sick. He pushed the sensation aside. He had no home here in England.

'Derek is asleep, bless him,' Laura said, her face lighting up.

The maid brought the tea tray and some shortbread biscuits which Avery wolfed down.

'Haven't you had dinner?' Laura said disapprovingly.

'Not yet. I thought I'd go to the chop house when I left here.'

'You will not.' She rang the bell and the maid returned. 'Set the table for one and bring Lord Avery some stew.'

'I can't eat John's supper,' Avery protested.

'You can and you will. Besides, there is plenty enough for two.'

Avery grinned. 'Bossy.'

'Stupid.'

Once he'd eaten and was leaning back in his chair, thoroughly replete, Laura gazed at him over the top of her knitting. 'I gather you have a new lady friend?'

His heart stilled. He kept his face bland. 'I have several friends who are ladies.'

'Don't be obtuse, Avery. I'm your sister. A statuesque brunette has been seen on your arm on more than one occasion. I still have contacts among the *ton*, you know. Who is she?'

Laura had always been popular among her peers because she never put on airs. Her closest friends hadn't abandoned her, despite her fall from grace, either.

'One of my shopkeepers fits your description. Perhaps

it is she of whom you have heard.' Laura knew about his other form of income in the vaguest of ways.

Laura frowned. 'You don't usually parade shopkeepers in Hyde Park. You really are intent on getting your revenge on Papa.'

Good Lord, the visit to the park had been only yesterday. News travelled fast. 'Heard about that, did you? She is a lovely woman. Runs a milliner's shop in Cork Street. You should look in on her. Her hats are true works of art.'

'Harriet's godmother said she's seen you with her twice now. She said the lady was strikingly handsome.'

Good lord. It was a small world. Harriet was Laura's oldest and dearest friend. Her family had gone against the tide of opinion by supporting Laura's decision to marry a mere lawyer, despite the ducal fury. And Harriet's godmother was right, Carrie was striking and quite lovely when she smiled, though the lady herself did not seem to think so. Indeed, he often had the feeling Carrie felt that she was some sort of antidote.

'I don't believe I know who Harriet's godmother is. What is her name?'

'Countess Longacre. She and her husband are leaving town tomorrow, so Harriet said. They were passing through London on the way to their property in the north and stopped for a few days to visit friends.'

He had forgotten how small London really was, or at least the London of the *ton*. Everyone was connected to everyone else.

He missed that about England. Until now, he hadn't realised just how alone he had been these past few years. How lacking in companionship. Being with Carrie had somehow brought it to the fore.

An odd pang pierced his chest. 'Well, believe me, it is nothing but a business arrangement.'

Despite being settled beside the hearth with her sisters-in-law around her, Carrie could not stop her mind from wandering back to Avery. Had he gone to the theatre alone, or with someone else? She couldn't help hoping it was the former.

Petra peered at her over the hat she was decorating. 'There is something different about you, Carrie. What has happened?'

Marguerite put down the book she was reading out loud and glanced from one to the other. 'Different how?'

Oh, dear, she might have guessed Petra would suspect something; the girl was just too perceptive for her own good. 'Yes,' she said, hoping she did not sound defensive. 'Different how?'

Petra pursed her lips. 'You look…happier. There is a glow about you that was not there before.'

A glow? 'I am just pleased that things are going well with the shop, I suppose.'

Marguerite set the book aside. 'It is wonderful,' she said, thoughtfully. 'I am astonished, to be honest, given how many established milliners there are in London.'

'None of them have a flair for uniqueness the way you do,' Petra said. 'I am not at all surprised.'

Marguerite had the most amazing ideas, but it was Petra who was able to bring them bring them to life. She was an excellent needlewoman.

'It is not only the hats,' Carrie said. 'The lingerie is very popular too. We are nearly sold out.' Glad that Petra had accepted her explanation, she forced her mind to turn to business. 'I am guessing we will need double the number of nightgowns next week. Or more.'

'Oh, dear,' Petra said. She looked at Marguerite. 'I don't see how we can possibly double our output *and* produce more hats if they are also selling as well as you say.'

The hats were more expensive and ladies usually only purchased one or two per Season, but they were purchasing the nightgowns by the half-dozen. 'We will need to employ some women from the village to help.'

'Oh,' Marguerite said dubiously. 'So we are to start a factory? I am not sure Westram would approve.'

'Pooh,' Petra said dismissively. 'He never comes near the place. He won't know anything about it. Besides, they don't have to come here to work. We can provide them with the materials and the instructions and they can make them in their own homes.'

Carrie nodded. 'And I cannot see why Westram would object should it ever come to his attention. The additional income to the families will encourage his farm labourers to remain in the village, instead of them departing to work in the factories up north.' The cotton and wool mills were gobbling up workers across the country, leaving farms with fewer and fewer men to tend to the land.

'I can also limit the number of gowns sold to each lady,' Carrie suggested.

Marguerite frowned. 'Why would we want to do that?'

'Because then they will pay a higher price for them,' Carrie said.

'Or they will go elsewhere,' Petra warned.

'No one else will provide what we provide,' Carrie said with a certainty that caused the other two ladies stared at her.

'Quality and uniqueness.'

'The two things that are important to the *ton*,' Petra agreed. 'And for that they will pay outrageous sums, too. We will have to keep coming up with new ideas, though, Marguerite.'

Marguerite opened her sketchbook. 'I will see what I can do.' She glanced over at Carrie. 'I agree with Petra, though. There is something different about you.' Her expression changed. 'Do not tell me you have met a man?'

Carrie felt her face heat. 'I—'

'You have,' Petra squealed. 'I knew it! When are we going to meet him? What is his name? Are you—'

'Stop!' Marguerite said, staring at Carrie intently. 'Can you not see you are embarrassing the poor girl? If she doesn't want to tell us, that is her business.' She bit her bottom lip. 'You will be careful, won't you, Carrie? Men are such fickle creatures.'

And you couldn't get more fickle than Lord Avery. Which was why she had picked him. She groaned out loud. 'I have entered into an agreement with a gentleman. He is part of the reason our business has improved so rapidly. But—'

'Are you lovers?' Petra asked.

Carrie's face burned. 'No!'

'But you would like to be.' Petra's face lit up. 'Oh, Carrie, how wonderful. The first of us to have a gentleman caller. I am proud of you.'

Surprisingly, although Petra had seemed so devastated by the loss of her husband, she had been the one to suggest that they might entertain gentlemen once they were out of mourning, should they so desire. She seemed almost anxious for her sisters to enjoy the delights of the marriage bed, as she had called them when they had discussed the matter.

'I am not sure I am quite ready for that sort of thing,' Carrie said awkwardly, unwilling to say too much about Avery in case it should all come to naught.

Petra sighed. 'I can understand that. I am certainly not ready for it myself, but you had so little time with Jonathan. It doesn't seem right that your youth should be wasted just because—' She bit her lip and waved a hand. Oh, dear, was she going to cry again?

Marguerite pressed her lips together. She had been more reticent about the whole idea of them being merry widows, but then she was the oldest sister and had very strict notions of propriety. On the other hand, it had been her idea to convince Westram to let them live quietly in the countryside as independent women. And she had agreed that as such they should be able to do whatever took their fancy. Provided they were discreet.

'Marguerite, tell Carrie about the local squire,' Petra said. 'He is a bachelor.'

'A most disreputable one, too.' She visibly straightened. 'I would sooner hear about this man of yours, Carrie.'

Hers. The thought carried a lovely warmth with it. Well, he was hers, for the moment, she supposed. Carrie shared as much as she dared, but said nothing about him being the son of a duke, leaving them with the idea that he was some sort of merchant.

She felt a little uncomfortable about doing so, but they would never meet him and in a few days their little affair would be over. Indeed, it might never amount to much of anything at all.

Carrie collapsed, exhausted, in her little sitting room. Avery had been right, their brief foray into society together had brought curious ladies to her shop. There had been a constant stream of customers since midday and not one of them had complained about the prices. Indeed, it seemed the more exclusive and expensive the shop, the better they liked the wares. She really hoped Petra's idea of employing women to help with making the nightgowns worked, or soon they would completely run out of items to sell.

She pushed to her feet, filling her kettle with water and putting it on the hob. Something else unexpected was the way she had looked up with hope in her heart at every tinkle of the shop door bell. And the way her heart had dropped each time when the jaunty figure of Lord Avery had not been the one stepping through her door.

She just wished she had told her sisters-in-law the truth about him. That she had offered him money to become her lover. But how was she to explain that, while he'd been kind enough to pretend take her out to tea and to visit an elephant, somehow she had the feeling he was doing it because he was reluctant to take matters between them any further? He was simply being kind.

One thing was certain, whatever happened in the end, being seen in his company had definitely helped the business. He had certainly earned his finder's fee and for that she would be eternally grateful.

Tired to the bone, she removed her cap and pulled the pins from her hair, while she waited for the kettle to boil. She removed her shoes and put on the slippers Marguerite had embroidered for her as a Christmas gift.

A knock sounded on the door.

A breath left her in a rush. She bolted upright. Heavens above, was he here now? She glanced in the mirror, realising that her hair was a tangled mess hanging down her back, and her face was pale. She pinched her cheeks to bring a bit of colour to them.

'Mrs Greystoke? I have your supper here.'

Supper. How on earth could she have forgotten? Mrs Spate cooked her dinner at the same time as she cooked for the Thrumbys. Carrie felt so tired, she simply hadn't been hungry enough to tell the woman she was ready for dinner. She got up and unlocked her door. The middle-aged cook brought in a tray and put it on the table. She was so thin and angular, no one would ever guess she was an excellent cook, except perhaps the redness in her cheeks from bending over a hot stove might give her away.

'There you go, ma'am,' the woman said with a smile. She put her hands on her hips and eyed Carrie up and down. 'And mind you eat it all. Mrs Thrumby's orders.'

Her landlord's wife was a motherly sort and seemed to see it as her duty to keep an eye on Carrie.

Carrie inhaled. 'It smells delicious. I am starving.' She was, too. She just hadn't noticed.

'I'll send the girl down for the tray later.'

'Thank you.'

The woman bustled out and Carrie pulled up her chair to the table. It did smell delicious. There was a juicy pork chop with apple sauce, a bowl of clear soup, fresh baked bread, and buttered carrots and parsnips. And a little bowl of rice pudding for dessert. A meal fit for a queen.

She tucked in heartily. She had never been one to pick at her food. Finally, full to bursting, she put all the dishes back on the tray, leaned back in her chair and closed her eyes. She simply needed a minute or two, then she would put the tray outside the door.

A soft knock startled her awake.

Her gaze took in the tray of empty dishes. Darn. She had not yet put it outside. 'Coming,' she called.

The door opened instead.

There, looking elegant if a little damp, was Lord Avery. He grinned.

She gasped and put a hand to her hair. 'I thought you were the maid from upstairs come to collect the tray.'

'Sorry. No.'

'I— Oh,' She blinked to clear her head.

'May I come in? Your porter recognised me and let me find my own way.'

'Of course.' She got up and picked up the tray.

He took it from her hands. 'Where do you want it?'

Finally, her brain started to work instead of wanting to drink in his sartorial elegance. 'Outside the door.' She certainly didn't want the maid coming inside to fetch it while he was here.

While he put it outside the door, she ran frantic fingers through her hair, trying to coax it into some sort of order.

He closed the door and gave her another of his beautiful smiles. 'I am sorry, I should have sent around a note telling you I would call in, but it wasn't until I found myself close by that I thought of it.'

She was ridiculously pleased to see him, though she wished she had changed into something nicer. She gestured to a chair. 'May I offer you tea?'

He hesitated, his gaze searching her face.

The bottom dropped out of her stomach. One look at her in disarray and he was wishing he had stayed away.

Then he crossed the room and took the chair. 'A cup of tea would be lovely.'

Relieved, she stirred up the fire to heat the water

more quickly. 'I am sorry I do not have anything stronger to offer.' She ought to get something in. Wine or port. Brandy?

'Tea is most welcome.'

He had such lovely manners, she turned to face him with a smile.

'I cannot stop long,' he said, looking slightly uncomfortable.

What? Oh, he had said he was close by. He had not intended to stay. He must have seen from her face how pleased she was to see him and was simply pandering to the gruff widow who had to pay for a man's company. A pang squeezed her heart. She turned back to making the tea, determined not to show she was in the slightest bit hurt.

'I have some biscuits if you would like some,' she said over her shoulder, as she poured the water over the tea leaves.

'No, thank you. I have a dinner engagement.'

'Oh, I hope this won't make you late?' she said cheerily.

'Not at all.'

She brought the tray to the table and set it down between them.

'You look tired,' he said.

A polite way of saying she looked as if she'd been pulled through a hedge backwards. If only she hadn't pulled all the pins out of her hair. 'The shop was extremely busy today. You are going to be very pleased with our increase in profits.' She hoped she sounded businesslike and not hurt. Fortunately, he was not looking at her, he was stirring the sugar she had put in his tea.

'I am glad it is going well.' He looked up, smiling. 'But you must be careful not to run yourself ragged.'

The hedge turned into a shipwreck. 'Oh, I am used to hard work.'

He nodded. 'Still, do not overdo it.'

'I won't.' The man was unusually solicitous. It was part of his charm. No doubt his special ladies really appreciated how attentive he was. She pushed back the jealous thought. She had no right to be jealous.

She wanted to ask him where he planned to go for dinner, but resisted the urge. It was none of her business. Even a wife would hesitate to ask her husband such questions, at least according to her aunt who, on the morning of Carrie's wedding, had tried to give her some advice about the sort of things a wife might expect from a husband. Leaving the next day for Portugal had not been on the list.

'I did have a reason for coming here this evening.' His jaw flickered. He looked a little less sure of himself than usual.

Oh, this was it, he was going to end their arrangement. She steeled herself. 'What is that?' She made herself smile, a thing of carelessness, though her lips felt stiff and her chest tight.

'I wanted to ask if you will you drive out again with me on Wednesday afternoon.'

Wednesday would be the second half-day closing day he had asked her to do something with him. The pain of thinking of saying goodbye was replaced by a lightness out of proportion to the invitation. 'You think we should go to Hyde Park again?'

'No. I think we have accomplished all we set out to do. This will be purely pleasure.'

She tried not to let his words sound like more than they were. He was being kind, that was all. He did say he wanted them to get to know each other better. This was part of it. 'Where will we go? Back to the tea shop?'

He shook his head. 'It is a surprise.'

She didn't always like surprises. Sometime they were not very pleasant. But... 'Very well. Wednesday afternoon. What time?'

'Noon, if you can manage it?'

'I can. Tansy can manage for the hour or so before the shop closes.'

'Good. I'll be off now, then.'

To her surprise he leaned in and kissed her cheek.

She was still touching the spot his lips had caressed when the door to the street closed behind him.

Chapter Eight

Avery found himself whistling as he knocked at Carrie's door on Wednesday afternoon. He was a few minutes late. He hoped Carrie wouldn't give him a bear-garden jaw, but he'd had a little more trouble borrowing the carriage than usual. His brother had caught him in the carriage house and had futilely wasted precious minutes trying to persuade him to visit with their father.

Avery had been very tempted, but when he asked if the old fellow actually wanted to see him, Bart had looked more than a little tense. 'Somebody has to make the first move towards a reconciliation,' he had mumbled.

'That's all very well,' Avery had replied. 'The question is whether he will throw me out on my ear when I tell him I still have no intention of marrying to please him.'

'Dammit, Avery, you don't have to say that, you could just say you simply are not ready yet. Give him some hope of winning, at least. You know what a stubborn, prideful man he is.'

'I am not going to lie to him.'

Bart had looked ready to throttle him. 'If you don't act soon, you might never get the chance to make things right with him.'

A cold shiver had run down his spine. 'Is he that ill?'

'I don't know. The doctors will tell me nothing. On his orders.'

'I'll think about it.'

Bart sighed. 'Please do.'

'Now, may I borrow your carriage? I have an appointment.'

For a moment, Avery had thought his brother was going to say no, perhaps as a way to try to bring him to heel, but then he merely waved a hand, a gesture of assent.

'You usually take the curricle.'

'I need the town carriage today.' He wanted a bit of privacy. 'I'll have it back by seven at the latest.'

'Do not rush on my account,' his brother said. His voice sounded a little thin. 'I'm too busy for gallivanting.'

'All work and no play made Jack a dull boy,' Avery quipped, but his brother was already out of the stable doors and heading for the house. He wasn't sure whether he'd heard him or not.

Perhaps he should have followed Bart in and tried to make his peace with his father. But he knew Papa very well. An apology would not suffice. Only obeying the ducal edict would make the old autocrat happy.

Thrumby's porter was used to Avery coming and going and did no more than touch his hat and nod when he admitted Avery.

Carrie opened her door the moment he knocked. She looked delightful in a rich burgundy-and-black-striped carriage gown with a shako-styled hat set at an angle and sporting a net veil that skimmed the bridge of her nose and made her look mysterious, and elegant. Only a tall woman could carry off such a look.

'You look…magnificent.'

She looked surprised. 'Why, thank you, my lord.' She tipped her head to one side. 'Since you didn't say where we were going I was not sure what to wear.'

'That outfit is perfect for our destination.' He frowned at it. 'Or it will be if…' He checked the hem and smiled. 'Good, there is a loop to hold up your hems. I wouldn't like your gown to become soiled.'

'So, we are walking, then?'

'We will be, once we get there.'

She laughed and shook her head. 'No use trying to tease it out of you, I see.'

He laughed. 'None at all. Shall we?'

He escorted her out to the carriage and they climbed aboard.

Laughter was still bright in her eyes. 'Shall I try to guess?'

He crossed the small space between them and sat at her side, put one arm around her shoulders and gave her a grin. 'Now that would be a waste of your breath.'

She gazed up at him, her grey eyes questioning, her full lips parted, tempting him to discover their softness and plumb the sweetness of her mouth. He lowered his head a fraction, holding her gaze, seeking her permission. Heat rushed through his veins. His body tingled.

Her breathing quickened as if the air within the carriage had become too thin, her full bosom rose and fell in the most delectable way, yet there were shadows in her eyes. A slight furrow in her brow. She was worried. Unsure.

He did not want her anxious or afraid. He wanted her joyful and happy. Desiring him as much as he desired her. But it was far too soon for that. Knowing women as he did, he was not entirely surprised at her reticence. They had met each other only recently, but even in that short time he had learned she was not the careless sort.

Kissing her now, as much as he wanted to, might well have her fleeing for the safety of her family. He took a deep breath and, ignoring his body's demands for more, he gave her shoulders a light squeeze, careful not to crush her pretty hat. How marvellously well she fit into the crook of his arm.

The tension in her body eased and they gazed out of the window in companionable silence for a time. Something else he liked about her. The lack of incessant chatter. The aura of calm that surrounded her, now she wasn't fearing his intentions.

'Are you ever going to tell me where we are going?' she asked when they had left the outskirts of town. 'This is certainly not the way to Hampstead.'

'You are right. But you will see where we are going when we get there. I really want it to be a surprise.'

'A nice one, I hope.'

'It is certainly intended to be. It isn't too far, I promise.'

Soon they entered the village of Paddington and drew up near a village green crowded with people and stalls as he had been promised. He breathed a sigh of relief.

Carrie sat up straight, then turned in her seat to face him. 'It is a fair!'

'A rather small one, I'm afraid. Would you like to take in the sights?'

She shook her head at him. 'You are a very surprising man, Lord Avery.'

'I simply aim to please. It is nowhere near as grand as the Goose Fair in Nottingham, but I thought it might amuse you for a while this afternoon.'

He climbed down and helped her out. She hooked her arm through his and gazed about her with bright eyes and a smile on her lips. At the sight of her pleasure, his heart swelled in the stupidest of ways. 'What would you like to do first: visit the stalls, ride on the merry-go-round, or watch one of the side shows?'

She laughed with delight. 'You mean us to actually ride on the merry-go-round?'

'Naturally.'

'Then let us do that first.'

It was what he would have chosen, too. He guided her across the green to the far side where the merry-go-round held the place of honour in amongst a milling crowd.

Now she was faced with the whirling structure, Carrie's heart picked up speed. Would she dare? But with Avery's gentle pressure at the base of her spine, it seemed she had little choice. After her bold words, she certainly wasn't going to back down.

Avery paid for their tickets and they waited in line for their turn. As she looked about her, she realised there were very few people present whom she would call gentry. The patrons looked like shop girls on their afternoon off, or labourers, plus an assortment of very rough characters who looked like they would cut your purse or your throat with equal enthusiasm. She shifted closer to Avery, who put an arm around her waist.

A tall, skinny, middle-aged man in an old-fashioned frock coat and a top hat wandered over to the line in which they stood. He removed his hat and beamed. He opened his arms wide as if he was meeting a group of old friends. 'Ladies and gents, lassies and lads, I offer you a wonder of nature not to be missed. Did you ever wonder what the future held? Did you ever want to improve your fortune at the tables, or know which horse to bet on in a race? Madame Rose can tell you all this and more. All you need to do is cross her palm with a bit of silver and you will gaze into the future.'

'Can she tell me where to find a handsome husband?' a young woman further up the line called out. Her friend giggled and nudged her with her elbow.

'She will answer whatever you ask her,' the barker said, drawing closer to the two girls. 'She'll give you a love potion if you wants.'

''Ow do we know she's not a fraud?' the other girl said. 'She's a gypsy, isn't she?'

The barker smile widened. 'She tells you things about you no one else knows. You'll see.'

The girls whispered to each other and checked their meagre store of coins. The queue shuffled forward. Soon it would be her and Avery's turn for the merry-go-round.

Carrie's stomach lurched when the barker's toothy grin focused on her next. Avery gave her a little squeeze. 'We will visit you a little later, friend.' Avery had a certain presence about him, a confidence that brooked no argument.

The man's friendly grin wavered a bit, but he bowed and moved on.

Carrie let go a sigh of relief.

'Would you like to have your fortune told?' Avery asked.

Did she really want to know her future? What if she didn't like what was in store? 'Would you?'

'I wouldn't mind knowing the outcome of the New-market cup,' he said. 'I'd be set up for life.'

Gambling. Her stomach churned. He might think a wager on a horse race was harmless enough, but she knew better. Jonathan had gambled away a huge amount of money Westram could ill afford and then married her to help pay off his debts. He'd ruined not only his own life, but impoverished his sisters and his unwanted wife. And then he'd had the gall to take his own life by flinging himself into battle because he'd never wanted to marry her in the first place.

In trying to explain what had happened to all her father's money, Westram had said that in his opinion some people got so caught up in the excitement of winning, they could not stop even when they lost. It was some sort of compulsion. A compulsion that had hurt too many people in Carrie's opinion.

One man of that sort in her life was one man too many, if they did not care whom they hurt.

'I would far sooner let the future be a surprise,' she said quietly.

He laughed. 'Don't be such a stick in the mud.'

'You don't really expect her to tell you the outcome of a horse race, do you?' Heaven forefend he risked his money based on such things.

'Her guess is as good as mine. Come on, Carrie, it is only a bit of fun.'

He seemed so cavalier about the whole idea. It didn't

sit well in her stomach, but who was she to spoil the day? 'All right. We'll go after this.'

They shuffled forward again and watched the two shop girls whirling around, their giggles rising to shrieks the faster the two men in the centre of the contraption pushed against the spokes. And then it was their turn.

They sat side by side on the seats of a replica of an open carriage, while another couple mounted a goose and a gander and a mother and child mounted a couple of gaily painted horses. It turned slowly at first. Avery put his arm around her waist to steady her and the world around them passed by in a blur. Carrie closed her eyes.

Beside her Avery laughed, clearly enjoying the sensation that made her stomach feel queasy. She forced her eyes open and gradually managed to pick out things as they rushed by. A girl selling ribbons. A donkey giving rides to children. The colourful awnings of the stalls. She grinned at Avery and then giggled, resting her head on his shoulder and enjoying the sensation of closeness in the rush of movement.

The roundabout slowed and came to a stop. Avery helped her down. Strangely the earth beneath her feet seemed to keep moving. She staggered a few steps while he held her tight. Finally, the world stopped spinning and everything was back to normal.

'Are you all right?' he asked.

He sounded concerned. She gave her head a little shake. 'Yes, I think so. That was fun.' She glanced back over her shoulder. 'Thank you. I would never have dared to get on there by myself.'

'You look a little pale.'

She put her palms to her face. 'Do I? How odd. My

stomach was a little queasy at first, but I did become used to it.'

He took her hand. 'What would you like to do next? Look at the fairings?'

Glad he hadn't suggested the fortune teller, she nodded. 'I need some ribbons for the shop. Perhaps they will have something suitable.'

They walked along the row of carts and barrows some of which were set beneath striped awnings. There were all sorts of things for sale. Lucky hares' feet, ribbons of every colour, trinkets made of china, bunches of heather, bits of lace, pipe stems. But the ribbons were mostly not new and Carrie decided they would not do for the quality of hats in her shop.

Avery bought her a sprig of heather to pin on her coat for luck while she bought him a handkerchief that likely had been stolen. They laughed about their purchases, vowing they would keep them as mementoes of the day. A baker ringing a bell caught Avery's attention. He had a tray of delicious-smelling meat pies balanced on his head.

'Are you hungry?' Avery asked.

'I am,' she said. 'It must be all the fresh air.'

The baker lifted the tray down so they could make their choices.

'I am not sure I can eat a whole one,' Carrie said. Her stomach gave a little grumble as if to deny her words and they collapsed laughing.

The baker looked at them as if they had run mad.

'Two pies, please,' Avery said, handing over some coins, and they wandered along side by side eating their treat. A small dog appeared and danced along beside them. It leaped up and down all around them, begging.

A small boy charged over as if to claim the animal and stumbled into Avery, who caught him by the arm and gave him a little shake. 'Go play off your tricks somewhere else, lad,' he growled.

The boy gave him a cheeky grin and dashed away, calling the dog as he went.

Carrie blinked. 'What was that about.'

'He was trying to pick my pocket.'

Avery didn't seem angry.

'Is he not a little young to be involved in crime?' Carrie asked.

'Not these days. Most of the crime committed in London is committed by children.' His voice was grim.

'Something ought to be done about it.'

'There are things being done, but not nearly enough. Wipe your hands on this.' He passed her his handkerchief, not the one she had given him, but another. 'It is clean.'

She chuckled, did as he suggested and handed it back. 'I suppose he was trying to steal this.'

'Likely. And that lace you were looking at earlier was likely cut from the bottom of some poor unsuspecting lady's petticoat, so you had better watch out for yours.'

'This way, lady and gentleman,' a greasy-looking man called out to them. 'In here you will see the most amazing sight of your life. Take a peep at the bearded lady. It is as real as the hair on your face, sir. Pull it if you don't believe it.'

Carrie grimaced. 'I don't think I really—'

'Nor me,' Avery said. 'I am much more interested in the fortune teller.'

Carrie's heart sank. She had been hoping to avoid that too. But it seemed that it was inevitable. They wove their way between the people flocking around the stalls and avoided the flocks of geese and the man offering to box anyone who would like to try to win a shilling and found the little red-and-white-striped tent on the outskirts of green.

There was no evidence of the barker, but a sign pinned to one of the flaps proclaimed that Madame Rosie was in and willing to read palms, tea leaves or look in her crystal ball for a variety of prices.

'Come in,' a hollow-sounding, foreign-accented voice said.

'There are two of us,' Avery said.

'That is fine,' Madame Rose replied from the dark inside of the tent. 'Come in, my lord.'

Avery winked. 'It seems the lady knows her business.'

Avery held back the canvas for Carrie to enter. Perhaps this wasn't such a good idea after all. He'd been teasing her when he suggested they have their fortunes told, but he had a sense that Carrie, while she had agreed, was apprehensive.

He leaned close and lowered his voice. 'Don't take anything she says seriously. It is all a hum.'

Once the tent flap closed, it took a moment or two for his eyes to adjust to the dim light inside. To his surprise, the woman sitting at the table on the other side of the room was not some old crone, but a rather attractive girl with dark brown eyes and black hair pulled severely back under a kerchief. She seemed to be draped in brightly coloured scarves. Her idea of a gypsy costume, no doubt.

She waved towards the chair placed on the other side of the table. 'Sit, please.'

Her heavily accented voice made the hairs on the back of his neck stand up for some reason. Ignoring the strange sensation, he led Carrie to the chair and stood behind her.

Madame Rose held out her hand palm up.

Carrie glanced over her shoulder at him. 'She wants her money.'

Avery handed over a coin. The woman looked at it closely, then it seemed to disappear, no doubt up her sleeve. She must think him a Johnny Raw if she expected him to fall for those sorts of tricks. He realised she was staring at him. When she saw that she had his attention she jerked her chin. 'Stand over there. I wish to be private with the lady.'

'I'm not leaving.'

'I did not say leave.' She glared at him. 'Move over there.'

There was another chair in the corner adjacent to the opening into the tent. Carrie nodded. 'I'll be quite safe with you there.'

Safer than she likely knew. His travels had taught him to be alert for danger and to always be prepared. He therefore never went anywhere without a knife in his pocket. If the woman was really some sort of seer, she would know that already. More likely she would have guessed he would not come to a fairground completely unarmed. He didn't believe in her nonsense, but he had no doubt she would be skilled at judging people. He retired to his corner and kept a close eye on the woman as well as the entrance.

After a moment's discussion, it seemed that Carrie had decided to have her palm read. As the gypsy's voice dropped into a low mutter, Avery discovered he could not make out a single word. There was some chatter back and forth as if the woman was asking Carrie questions. The woman bent over Carrie's palm, turning it this way and that to catch the light and muttering in a low monotone. He felt his eyelids droop. Damn, it was warm in here.

Carrie gasped at something the woman said.

Avery straightened, his gaze flying to her face, but while she had pulled back a little, she did not seem to be in any danger. Madame Rose said something that sounded comforting and non-threatening and Carrie leaned forward again, peering intently at the finger tracing the lines on her palm. The muttering began again.

A few moments later it was over and Carrie was getting up.

Avery rose and strode forward. 'Is everything all right?' he asked Carrie. She looked shaken, but not exactly scared.

'Yes. Everything is fine.'

'What did she tell you?'

She laughed. 'Not to tell anyone what she said. Really, it is nothing but a lot of nonsense.'

The girl grinned. 'You wait and see, my lady. You will know I am right and you will thank me.'

'She will never see you again,' Avery said firmly.

The girl shook with silent laughter and the bangles hanging from her ears and festooning her wrists jingled. 'Take your seat, sir.'

Carrie started to move away.

'You may stay, my lady,' the girl said. 'There is nothing for him to know that he does not already know. Bring her the chair, if you would, sir?'

These people always talked in riddles. It was part of

their stock in trade, but he carried the chair over, then sat in the one vacated by Carrie and held out his palm.

'No, no, my lord. It is the cards for you, I think.'

More mumbo jumbo. He shrugged. 'As you please.'

She began laying out a deck of large cards with a strange design on their backs. Once she had them set out in rows, she began turning them over one by one and muttering. After she turned the last card over, she gave him an odd look. 'Your fortune intertwines with this lady's, but the path is not straight.'

She sat back.

'That's it?' he asked. 'That tells me nothing. Clearly, this lady and I are friends. Anyone could tell me that. What about the first race of the Season at Newmarket? Do you have a prediction?'

She wrinkled her nose and peered at the cards. 'A black horse with a white flash on its nose.'

'What about it?'

She stared at it again. 'It will change your fortune.'

'How? Good or bad?'

She shrugged. 'It depends on what path you choose before then.'

He laughed. 'You really are a charlatan, aren't you? Hedging your bets very well, my dear.'

Carrie shifted uncomfortably. He took her hand in his. He didn't know what the woman had told her, but he didn't want her taking it too seriously.

The gypsy girl gave him a cold stare. 'I can only tell you what I see, but estrangement from someone important in your life is a key turning point. Only by swallowing your pride will you ever know true happiness.'

His pride? He was not the one who was proud. If it wasn't impossible, he would have said his father had paid her to tell him this nonsense. He laughed. 'You know who I am, don't you?'

'I have no idea. I am only telling you what I see.'

'Rubbish. Anyone who knows me would have said just what you said. Your barker discovered who I was and told you, so you could pretend to know what you are talking about. I have met your sort before. Many times.'

'The cards tell me that it was once your dearest wish to be a soldier when you were a lad. But you chose a darker path.'

His stomach fell away. No one knew of his youthful dream. Absolutely no one. Apart from his father, who had refused to allow it. He swallowed the sudden dryness in his throat. 'A lucky guess. Every boy wants to be a soldier.' Why did he sound unconvinced?

The woman touched one of the cards. 'You are coming to a fork in the road of life, my lord. Choose wisely. At the moment, you appear poised to head in the wrong direction.'

'What are these choices you speak of?'

Her voice changed to an odd sort of monotone. 'The cards have spoken.' She shook her head as if to clear it. She gathered up her cards.

'I hardly call that speaking. I have more questions than answers.'

'It is in your hands.' The woman got to her feet and Avery stood, too, out of politeness, though he hardly felt polite. He felt irritated.

The tent flap drew back, letting in daylight. He turned to see the barker gesturing them out 'This way out, ma'am, my lord. Madame Rose has spoken.'

When he turned back Madame Rose had gone.

Damn it all. Of all the ideas he'd had, this one was

likely one of the worst. He hadn't thought about his father's refusal to buy him a commission in the army in years.

He escorted Carrie out of the tent and into a day that had turned from reasonably bright to overcast. 'Where to now?'

Carrie glanced up at the sky. 'Do you think it is going to rain?'

'It is hard to tell, but it seems likely. Shall I take you home?'

'I certainly think we should head back in the direction of the carriage, don't you? We can look at the rest of the stalls on the way.'

They sauntered between the stalls. 'Don't take anything Madame Rose told you too seriously,' he advised. 'There is nothing of the occult in what they do. It is all trickery and clever guesses.'

She glanced at him, her eyes troubled. 'I suppose so.'

'No, truly. I know these—oh, will you look at that. Have you ever seen a sword swallower?'

'A—? No, what is that?'

Pleased to have found something to take her mind off the fortune teller, he grabbed her hand and hurried her through the gathering crowd around a man with several swords laid out on a bench at his side.

Carrie's eyes widened. 'You are not going to tell me he is going to swallow those swords.'

'He is. In a manner of speaking.'

'I suppose you are going to tell me this is another trick.'

'There is certainly a trick to it,' he agreed.

Carrie stared in horror at the young man who stood in the middle of the circle of curious people. Beneath a black cape, he wore his shirt open at the throat and tucked into a wide belt studded with shiny metal. A bandana encircled his forehead, giving him a piratical look.

Another man moved through the crowd, holding out a hat. 'Famous throughout Europe for his daring and skill, the Spanish Count will astonish and delight. Never will you see his like again,' the man shouted as he passed through the gathering.

Avery tossed some coins in the hat. The man bowed and winked. 'Thank you, sir.' He continued on, shouting his words of encouragement until he must have decided he had received enough donations.

Meanwhile, the performer stood, arms folded, looking imperiously down his nose is if all commercial transactions were beneath him. He reminded her of Westram.

She giggled.

'What?'

'He looks like my brother-in-law.'

Avery narrowed his eyes. 'That much of a tartar, is he?'

Oh, she really should not give him that impression of her beleaguered brother-in-law. 'He can be, when pressed.'

The barker returned to the performer's side and muttered something in his ear, then turned to the crowd. 'Ladies and gentlemen, I present the Count of Barcelona.'

The young man bowed and removed his cape with a flourish.

The crowd shuffled closer. Avery put his arm around her shoulders, holding her close and serving as a barricade against the press of people. She felt protected. Cared for. It was such a lovely feeling.

A feeling the fortune teller had warned her against, before she'd said her odd rhyme.

Trusting your head will ensure your safety, I confess.
Trusting your heart is taking a chance when.
Only one path leads to true happiness.

But oh, feeling protected was such a lovely sensation. It seemed to warm her all the way to her toes.

The young man picked up one of the blades and waved it around. 'I 'ave 'ere an ordinary sword.' He held it out so members of the audience could touch it, feel its sharpness and strength.

'It is all a trick,' a man behind them shouted. 'It folds up.'

The Count held the blade towards him and shrugged. 'You are welcome to make it fold up, if you can.'

The man stepped into the middle of the circle and pushed and pulled at the blade and twisted and pressed at the hilt. When he had finished he gazed out at the surrounding people. 'By Gad, it is real.'

'A plant,' Avery murmured in her ear.

'You mean he is part of the show. That it is all a hum.'

'Yes. But he is not lying. The blade is real enough.'

The man disappeared back into the crowd and the sword swallower lifted the blade point first high above his tipped-back face.

Carrie's mouth dried. She pressed tighter against Avery's side.

The sword slowly disappeared into the young man's mouth and down his throat.

The crowd cheered and clapped.

'One sword, ladies and gentlemen. Do I hear you call for two?' the man who had collected the money shouted. He began passing his hat again and people added more coins.

The young man slowly took down the second sword, but it seemed much more difficult and he had to pull it up and then push it down more than once. Finally, he turned in a circle with head back and two swords hilts projecting from his wide open mouth.

There was another sword remaining on the chair.

'Go on then,' someone in the crowd shouted. 'Let's see you do the other one.'

'No, no,' his partner cried, looking anxious. 'That is merely a spare. Three is far too dangerous. It has never been done.'

The crowd began chanting 'Three. Three. Three.'

'Surely he won't,' Carrie said, appalled. 'What if he cuts himself?'

'If he cuts himself, he will die,' Avery said drily.

'He can't do it,' a man behind them said. Carrie turned to see a big belligerent-looking fellow glaring at Avery.

'I wager he can,' Avery answered, grinning.

At his side, Carrie made a strange sound. A sob of protest.

''Ow much?' the fellow said.

'A shilling.'

'I don't want to watch this,' Carrie said.

Avery laughed at the horror on her face. 'There is nothing to fear. He can do it.'

She glanced over at the couple in the centre of the circle of people, where the barker was speaking to the Count with a worried expression. Whatever the Count said in response was not clear, but once more his helper passed round the hat. 'You want to see a man risk his life, you needs to show me your coin, ladies and gents. The man has a wife and children to support.'

Avery tossed another coin in the passing hat.

Carrie began to turn away. Avery held her tighter. 'You will never get through that crowd and I cannot run out on a bet. It will cause all kinds of trouble.'

'Give me your shilling now and you can run wherever you wants,' the big man said. 'Can't he, Jim?' Jim proved to be an equally large fellow with a broken nose.

Avery glanced around. Even if they wanted to leave, it would be impossible while everyone was crowding in so close. 'Close your eyes and don't look,' he said to Carrie.

When the barker held the third sword out to the Count, she buried her face against Avery's coat. The crowd fell silent.

He liked the feeling that she had turned to him for protection, even if he knew the so-called Count was perfectly safe. He gave her a comforting little squeeze.

The man slowly slid the third sword home. A cheer went up.

'I told you he could do it,' Avery said to the man who had taken his bet.

The man grumbled.

Carrie made a sound of disgust. 'That was horrible.' She started to push her way through the crowd, while Avery accepted his winnings.

He quickly caught her up. 'Hey! What is the matter? I've seen that trick hundreds of times. The man is simply trying to earn a living.'

'Are you telling me, no one ever dies?'

He winced. 'Once in a while maybe…but—'

'Once in a while is once too often for me.' She glanced up at the sky. 'Dash it. It is raining.'

He muttered something under his breath and then raised his voice. 'It would have been helpful if Madame Rose could have forecast a shower. Then we would not have got wet.'

The heavens opened and the rain began in earnest.

Sitting next to a damp and clearly unhappy lady was not exactly the way Avery had planned the afternoon to end. He still wasn't exactly sure why she was fuming.

'What did Madame Rose tell you?' he asked.

She turned away from the window and shivered. 'It was all very vague.'

Clearly, she didn't wish to tell him. He didn't like it that she was upset. He had expected her to see through all the nonsense at the fair.

He put his arm around her. 'Don't let her ramblings upset you. It really is all a sham. I bet she asked you some pretty pointed questions before she got around to telling you anything.'

'Not really questions. She said she saw that I was an only child and, when I agreed, she said my parents had wanted a son, which was true.'

'She is a clever one. The first is a guess and if she'd been wrong she would have seen it in your face and changed it. The second an assumption based on your reaction to the answer and her knowledge of human nature.'

Carrie looked unconvinced. 'She also said I had been married, but not to you.'

'Well, everyone knows I am not married and she had to know who I was.' He grimaced. 'Her man only had to have seen us getting out of this carriage. It has our coat of arms on it. He might have thought I was my brother, but since neither of us is married, it makes no difference. They make a point of knowing who is who.'

'Surely no one would have expected you to visit such a little place?'

He offered her a comforting smile and a squeeze. 'Please. It was intended to be a bit of fun. I really don't want you upset.'

'I am not upset about the fortune teller.'

He pulled her close and she leaned against him with a sigh. 'Well, I suppose it all ended well, but…' She took a deep breath and he thought she was going to say something, something important, but she didn't say a word. He thought it best to let the topic drop.

'Will you accompany me to the theatre tomorrow?' he asked to divert her mind to more pleasant topics.

Mouth agape, she stared at him.

Hurt by her astonishment, he shrugged. 'I had the feeling that if you hadn't been going home to Kent last week, you would have accepted my offer to escort you. So, I thought to ask you again. Mrs Siddons is playing in *Measure for Measure*.'

She hesitated. Damn it. Was she still fussing about the sword swallower? If he had thought there was the least danger the man would be injured, he would not have encouraged her to watch. Didn't she understand that? 'I bought the tickets thinking you would like to go.' Dammit, now he sounded sulky when he had intended to sound offhand. 'It will be very good for business,' he hastened to add. 'It will give you a chance to wear one of those evening headdresses.'

'May I think about it?'

What was there to think about? He gritted his teeth. 'By all means. Send a note round to my lodgings with your decision.' He handed her his calling card with a bow.

'Thank you.'

He wanted to press her to agree. He opened his mouth to do so. He also wanted her to decide to go, because it was what she wanted.

Damn it, when had he ever been so confused?

Chapter Nine

Avery had never enjoyed going to the theatre as much as he had this evening. Fortunately, he'd won the use of the box at the tables the previous night, something he'd deliberately set out to do. Not that he was going to mention that to Carrie, who had been delightful company. She didn't chatter during the performance, but instead watched and listened intently. In fact, she rarely chattered about anything. Something he really liked about her. Something else.

He gazed at her sitting opposite him in the carriage. There were a great many things he liked about Carrie Greystoke. If he hadn't sworn off marriage altogether, she was just the sort of woman he might have liked for a wife.

He recalled, with discomfort, the note he had received earlier in the day. A request from his father that he visit. When he had asked his brother what it might be about, Bart had looked grim. 'He's heard about your widow.'

'She is not *my* anything.' Even if he wished she was. A cold sensation had filled the pit of his stomach. 'Is the old fellow getting worse?'

Bart had sighed. 'Not really, but he did have a letter from a distant relative earlier in the week. Seems you've been seen all over the place with this woman.'

He gritted his teeth. And the gossips would have a field day with this evening's outing. He was going to have to bring his association with Carrie to a close before he ruined her reputation instead of helping her business.

'Is something wrong?' Carrie asked.

Damn. He'd let his thoughts show on his face. Since when did he let down his guard around one of his ladies? But that was the whole point. Carrie was not *one of his ladies*. She was different. Better. More important somehow.

'I had a bit of bad news today.'

'Oh, I am sorry to hear it.'

'I am sorry to let it spoil our evening. I don't have to ask if you enjoyed the play, I could see from your face during the performance that you did.'

'Mrs Siddons was really quite wonderful, I must say. She lived up to her reputation.' A lantern on the street caught her smiling and he tried to capture that expression in his mind. A memory to treasure. Bah, what nonsense.

'I have never been to the theatre before. I enjoyed it immensely, though I suppose it is terribly gauche of me to say so.'

'Not at all. It delights me that you are pleased.'

She laughed as if she did not quite believe him, but that the compliment was welcome all the same.

'I mean it,' he said, moving from his side of the carriage to sit beside her.

The atmosphere in the carriage seemed to change. It grew warmer and crackled with tension. The attraction between them had not diminished in the slightest. Indeed, it seemed to have flourished.

He took her gloved hand in his, stroking the cotton-covered palm with his thumb.

A little sound like a quick indrawn breath reached his ears. He smiled. 'You like that.'

'I do.' She sounded shy, her voice trembling a little.

'Palms are very sensitive, right here,' he said, circling his thumb in the centre of her palm slowly. 'Even with two layers of fabric between us.'

She let out a shaky breath. 'Apparently so.' She did not pull away. He took it as a sign that he should continue.

He shifted towards her, bringing his other hand up to cup her cheek and jaw, turning her face towards him. 'You look stunning tonight.'

Her laugh sounded embarrassed. 'It is kind of you to say so.'

He frowned. 'I mean it, Carrie. You drew a great many eyes.'

'I have Marguerite's creation to blame for that.'

'Not at all. It simply did you justice.'

'You are such a flirt.' The pleasure in her voice lightened his heart. While she clearly did not believe his compliment, it had nevertheless pleased her femininity. Somehow, he would convince her, he was speaking the truth. He dipped his head towards her.

She put a tentative hand on his shoulder, not pushing him away, but not encouraging him closer, either.

Good heavens, his bold widow was also shy. The idea made him smile. And since Carrie seemed incapable of subterfuge, he was positive it was a genuine emotion.

When was the last time he had actually flirted with a truly shy woman? He did not think he ever had.

He lowered his head, his mouth coming closer to hers, hovering where he could feel her rapid breaths on his cheek and mouth. He could feel the warmth rising up from her body, as if she was blushing.

He moved his hand so his fingers curled around her nape, but his thumb pushed gently upwards on her chin. 'Carrie, if you do not want me to kiss you, you had better say so now.'

She swallowed. 'I do.'

He stilled. Shook off the strange sensation that those two little words had given him and chuckled. To his own ears it sounded a little forced, but fortunately she did not seem to notice.

'I do want you to kiss me,' she said. The longing in her voice was shocking.

What was a gentleman to do except satisfy a lady's wishes?

He started with the briefest brush across her lips, felt them part under the gentle fleeting pressure. The pulse below her ear thrummed beneath his fingers. She was not lying when she said she wanted him to kiss her.

How nice when a woman, no matter how shy, knew what she wanted and told a man. A great asset to lovemaking. His body hardened.

The strength of his reaction startled him for a moment. Oh, he had no trouble getting aroused by a beautiful woman, but it was early in the game. He certainly did not want to rush her because he lacked control.

He brushed her lips again and felt her breathing quicken and she shifted, turning towards him, giving him better access, leaning into him. A completely unconscious gesture of interest.

He pressed his lips to hers, feeling their soft plushness give beneath his mouth. He savoured their ripe fullness, nuzzling gently. A small sigh escaped her and she relaxed into him. He raised his head, gazing down at her, unable to see her expression in the darkness inside the carriage.

He put an arm around her shoulders and pulled her closer. The magnificent plumpness of her bosom pressed against his chest. Once more he took her lips, tenderly moving his mouth against hers, until he felt her soften, a slight yielding of her body to his touch.

She was not a woman to easily give up control. She had an inner strength he could not help but admire.

He stroked the seam of her lips with his tongue.

A little promise of the taste of things to come.

Carrie couldn't actually believe she was kissing a man in a carriage, as bold as brass. Until Avery had come into her life, the only kiss she had ever received in her life had been a peck on the cheek or a fleeting brush of lips on the back of her hand by some overbold friend of her father's.

Her husband had not even done that. His salutation on the day of their wedding had been to the air beside her cheek.

This was extraordinarily delicious. Naughty, too. Her insides tightened at the thought of the wickedness of sitting in a carriage kissing a single gentleman. A man she had no intention of marrying, but had every intention of taking to her bed. Hopefully.

His tongue played along her lips, sending shivers

down her spine and making her squirm on the seat at the tightness deep within her. A pleasurable but somehow irritating sensation that made her seek something more. She gave herself up to the storm of desire running though her veins and leaned into him, slipping her hands around his neck and into his hair. Her gloves foiled her need to feel the silkiness of his hair and the warmth of his skin, but she was too entranced by the glorious feeling of his mouth on hers to break the contact and remove them.

She could scarcely breathe for the pounding of her heart in her chest as if it had grown too large to be contained within the space behind her ribs. This was not what she had expected to feel while being kissed. Not at all. It felt wonderful, but somehow not quite enough. The tips of her fingers tingled as if they needed the sensation of touch. Heat raced along her veins. It was as if someone had stoked a furnace deep inside her.

His tongue swept inside her mouth.

Her body went up in flames. She gasped with the shock of it.

He broke the kiss. 'Are you all right?'

An unsteady breath gave her the power of speech. 'I—I should think so.'

He chuckled huskily. 'We are almost at your street.'

Oh, no! This lovely deliciousness was going to come to an end far too soon. 'Would you like to come in for a cup of tea?'

Inside she groaned. Men didn't want cups of tea. They wanted wine or spirit.

'I would love a cup of tea.'

Why, when he said it with that growl in his voice, did he make it sound like so much more than tea? She shivered.

He gently withdrew his arm from around her as the carriage slowed and stopped. He jumped down and helped her out. 'No need to wait,' he called up to the coachman.

A little thrill curled up in her stomach. Excitement mingled with fear. What if it was really only tea he wanted? Why on earth would she think so after that kiss? He seemed to enjoy it as much as she had and they were already into the second of their agreed-upon two weeks.

The porter let them in without comment, though he did give her a rather narrowed-eye stare. No doubt he was reporting on her movements to Mr Thrumby. Dash it. She was a widow. If she wanted to discreetly entertain a gentleman caller, it was no one's business but her own.

She let them in to her apartment, removed her shawl and gloves, but when she went to fill the kettle he caught her around the waist and turned her to face him.

His expression held hunger and heat.

The slow burn in her veins flared to life in the face of such desire. She gasped.

'Hush,' he said softly, cradling her in his arms. 'Do not worry. I won't do anything you don't wish to do.'

She realised her spine was as stiff as a board. So stupid. She relaxed against him, forcing fear to the back of her mind. This was what she wanted. Had asked for. She trailed her palm down his cheek, felt the faint haze of stubble graze her palm. Prickles ran across her shoulders and down her spine.

Fear rose up once more to hold her in thrall. Fear of rejection. Of humiliation. 'So,' she said softly, bravely, 'have you decided where this attraction between us leads?' She winced. Why could she not sound flirtatious and sweet instead of blunt and matter of fact.

He grinned at her. He was one of the few men she did have to look up at. Her insides melted. Not only because he was so very handsome, but because he made her feel small and feminine. And the warmth in his eyes bolstered her confidence.

'I think we both know where this is leading,' he said, his voice a low deep murmur full of sensual undertones. He hooked a chair leg with his foot to bring it clear of the table and sat down, bringing her with him to perch on his knee. 'Now, where were we when we were so rudely interrupted?'

On our way to heaven, a voice inside her whispered. A foolish voice, but one she could not ignore, none the less. She yielded to the pressure of his arms enfolding her in his embrace and relaxed against him. She gazed up into his face and returned his smile. His gaze fixed on her mouth.

Yes, she wanted to say.

He needed no encouragement, or verbal permission. The next moment his mouth covered hers and was teasing and wooing with pliant expertise until she thought she might die of the pleasure. Her extremities tingled, her heart pounded loud in her ears and low in her belly her muscles tightened, causing pleasurable little thrills to ripple along her veins through her body.

When his tongue stroked the seam of her mouth, she parted her lips. And when he explored her mouth with gentle touches, what had gone before seemed innocuous, innocent. This was a sensual wickedness that set her body on fire.

Avery couldn't recall when he had enjoyed kissing a woman more. Carrie seemed so untutored, almost innocent in her hesitant enthusiasm. He could not quite put his finger on what made her so tantalising, but the desire to make love to her was beyond anything he had ever experienced. The fact that he was sitting on a chair with her delicious derrière squirming in his lap was not helping his control.

He broke the kiss and took a breath.

She stilled, gazing at him with concern in her eyes. The heat of lust was not making it easy to process what her expression meant, but instinctively he sensed she needed reassurance. He smiled at her and ran one hand down her arm and stroked her back. 'You kiss divinely, my sweet. I am almost undone.'

Worry changed to confusion. She swallowed. 'Should I make tea?'

He swallowed a laugh and managed a gentle smile instead. 'Tea is not going to ease my predicament.'

The blank stare left him wondering what sort of pillock her husband must have been. Was he one of those chaps who did his duty as fast as possible and left his wife unfulfilled and in the dark, figuratively and literally? If so, it was no bad thing the fellow had gone off to meet his maker.

She stared. 'Is something wrong?'

Damn. His thoughts must be showing on his face again. He stroked the shell of her ear with a fingertip and down her jawline to rest at the tip of her determined little chin. He traced her lips. 'Nothing could possibly be wrong, apart from my need to catch my breath for a moment.' To regain a little control, for surely she could feel how hard he was beneath her luscious bottom.

She took a couple of quick breaths. 'Oh, yes.'

Her lips were so plump. How would they feel on his

pulsing shaft? And…that was not helping in the least. Sensual she might be, and bold, but those sorts of intimacies would have to wait until later in their relationship. If there was a later. Occasionally, he had the sense she was not quite as bold as she had originally made out. If it turned out she was having second thoughts about wanting him to be her lover, he would have to find a way make a graceful exit. Ultimately, it was her decision.

'Let down your hair for me, love.'

Her eyes widened. 'My hair?'

'Mmm… I love your hair down around your shoulders. It makes you look even more desirable.' And wanton. He'd been hard pressed to leave the other night when she looked as if she'd just risen from her bed after a good tumbling. He'd wanted to be the one to make her look that way.

He spread his legs wider apart, which put her more firmly on to his crotch, but would also balance her while he began the task of pulling pins from her hair. With both of them at it, it did not take long for the beautiful mass of wild curls to fall down around her shoulders. He sifted his fingers through the silky strands and massaged her scalp.

Eyes closed, she sighed with pleasure. 'That feels so good.'

'I don't know how you ladies can stand all that ironmongery in your head.'

She opened one eye and looked at him askance. 'Fashion before comfort. Besides, who wants to see a woman going around with a bird's nest on her head?'

I do. 'It looks lovely like this.'

She didn't look convinced.

So he kissed her. Immediately, she melted into him,

kissing him back. This time her little tongue licked at his and he withdrew it slowly, giving her time to follow where it led. His groin tightened unbearably when she began a slow exploration of the inside of his mouth. The pleasurable pain of it had him lifting his hips, seeking friction against that plump little bottom that was moving to a gentle rhythm in his lap.

She wanted him just as much as he desired her.

He let her take charge of the kiss, responding to her touches, to her little sounds of pleasure and shifts of her body, bringing her closer, stroking her hair back from her face, touching her everywhere.

The bed in the alcove behind the so-discreet curtain called with a siren's song. As did her passion, the sighs and moans deep in her throat. He had thought perhaps to wait to fulfil his part of the bargain, to draw it out a little longer, for both their sakes, but now he found he could not, would not. It would not be fair to either of them.

Would it?

He pushed aside the question asked by his conscience, and, with her clinging to him, he rose to his feet.

'Oh,' she murmured, clinging tighter, then once again looking uncertain. She slid down his body to her feet and pulled back. That would not do.

With fingers that were skilled from lots of practice, he began unlacing her gown. 'We should make you a little more comfortable,' he said. 'You seem to be having trouble breathing. Perhaps your stays are too tight?'

She nodded, though she looked none too sure.

He eased the gown over her shoulders. Thank heavens for the fashion for tiny bodices and low necklines. A little push and it slipped down her arms and fell to the floor. She stepped out of it and he shoved it aside with his foot. He took her by the forearms and took a step back, letting his gaze wander over her lovely hourglass shape beneath her shift and stays. Her legs were long and, while not slender, they were beautifully proportioned and lightly muscled.

He smiled at her. 'My word, you are lovely. Now it is time for those stays. Turn around, sweetheart.'

Her breath gave a little hitch and she turned her back towards him. He leaned forward, peering around that gorgeous mass of hair to see her face. He feared he might have been too forward, but the expression on her face said otherwise. There was a dreamy distant look on her face and in her eyes.

A cold fist clutched at his heart. She looked as if she was recalling something from her past. Perhaps her husband? Perhaps the man hadn't been a completely idiot after all. He quelled the urge to ask. If she was thinking of her dead husband, he absolutely did not want to know. He undid the bow at the bottom of her stays and swiftly pulled the tapes free of the holes. The garment fell free and he tossed it aside.

He glanced down at the way the featherlight fabric of her shift skimmed the rounded globes of her bottom and fell just shy of her knees, leaving her pretty shaped calves in their delicate stockings exposed for him to enjoy.

She was better than any picture he had ever seen.

He caught her around the waist a handspan below her fabulous heavy breasts and stroked over the magnificent swell of her hips and down her thighs to the hem of her chemise.

She swallowed.

He smiled at her shyness. It was a delight to find a

woman who retained a little of her innocence after her marriage, despite his very real puzzlement over it. Most married women, in his experience, became bold and often assertive in a way that left a man trying to catch up. Not that he often had that problem, but he could see how some men might have trouble.

He spun her around to face him. She looked so adorable, so pink-cheeked, something welled in his heart. A need to bring her great pleasure and see her smile.

He caught her under her thighs, lifted her, while she clung on for dear life, the soft hazy look in her eyes, fading away. He managed to sweep back the drapery and expose a narrow cot. He almost groaned out loud, whether because it was so small or because it was a bed—finally.

It did not matter which. He lowered her to the pristine white cover and when she was sprawled there, looking up at him with eyes large and anxious, he knelt beside her on the floor and plundered her mouth.

Chapter Ten

Despite that she still retained her shift, the way Avery looked at her made her feel naked. Vulnerable. Exposed. What did he see when he looked at her like that? A large woman, who men did not usually find attractive? A chore he had contracted for that he would like over and done with as soon as possible so he could be on his way?

Her breathing, shallow and fast from their kiss, began to slow. Her heart that had been beating with excited anticipation only a few moments ago was now pounding with fear that he would walk away. That once more she'd be left, embarrassed, humiliated and alone.

There was nothing she could do except lie there and wait for his rejection.

'My word, but you are beautiful,' he murmured, his voice deep and husky. His gaze ran down her body, clearly seeing right through the filmy fabric that now was drawn tight across her breasts and draped over her hips.

She glanced down along her length, aware that her breasts rose like twin peaks in a mountain range and that the nipples were as hard as beads. They lifted the fabric in a most unseemly way. Instinctively she raised her hand to cover her lack of modesty, but he caught them in his. He kissed each of her fingers in turn, make her insides melt and those little nubs on her breasts tingle with anticipation that he might kiss her there, too.

Never had she had such an unseemly thought in her life.

'Carrie,' he said softly.

She forced herself to look into his face, braced herself to see the distaste, but found nothing but heat and sensual pleasure. It shocked her to the core. Her body tightened unbearably.

'Yes,' she managed, though her throat was dry and her voice sounded raspy.

'Darling,' he murmured. 'I want you so badly.'

A ripple of pleasure moved out from her core.

'I—' She cleared her throat. 'I want you, too.'

There, it was out in the open for him to do with as he willed. At least with her husband she hadn't said anything quite so foolish. She'd simply nodded when he'd said he was leaving. He'd apologised, for he had been a gentleman, but that hadn't made her grief any less painful.

The horrible thing was that she had been unable to grieve when she'd heard the news of his death, for she had already been dead inside. But now, it seemed as if this moment had washed all of that bitterness away and her body had finally come to life.

He rose to his feet, his gaze never leaving her face, and undid the buttons of his coat.

Oh, good lord, she was going to do this. She really was.

Her body began to shake, to quake as if the bed was

rocking beneath her. She gripped the covers to hold herself steady. To stop herself from fleeing.

Fortunately, Avery didn't notice her panic as he was stripping off his jacket and moving with an efficiency that brooked no turning back.

Carrie took a deep breath.

The bed might be small, but the woman laid out before him like a banquet was the most sumptuous morsel Avery had ever set eyes on. He could not wait to taste her delights. About to pull his shirt over his head, he suddenly became aware of her terror.

It chilled him to the bone, like a dip in a frozen pond.

What the hell had her husband done to her? Instead of leaping on her and devouring her, as he had been inclined to do, he sat on the edge of the bed and removed his shoes, stockings and after a quick glance in her direction, his breeches. Oh, she was definitely nervous. Leaving his shirt on, he stretched alongside her on the narrow bed. She shifted over to give him room.

Or to give herself space.

He rolled on his side. Clearly, for all her boldness, her willingness to say what she wanted, she needed careful handling. Something had happened in her past that made her skittish.

He cradled her face in his hands and kissed her lips, tasting her sweetness, feeling the rise of her passion as she gave herself up to pleasure. Against his mouth, her full lush lips felt like heaven. The way her tongue responded to his invasion of her mouth, dancing in perfect harmony with his, fuelled his desire.

She rolled towards him, wrapping her arms around him, a soft hum of pleasure vibrating against his chest, where they touched. He eased his thigh between hers and, a moment later, her leg was wrapped high against his hip, the heat of her centre scorching his skin, making him dizzy with lust as if he was some sort of schoolboy, not a man who had bedded some of the most beautiful women every country had to offer.

He had thought himself somewhat jaded. Instead, here he was panting after this woman as if she was his first venture into bed sport. Madness. And utterly delightful.

Slowly he broke their kiss and, gazing into her face, he saw the haziness of desire and longing, along with the signs of arousal. Flushed skin, parted rosy lips and heavy-lidded eyes. A beautiful passionate woman. Why any man would leave such a wife and go off to war he could not imagine. He ran his hand down her spine, coming to rest on the swell of her hip. Slowly he caressed every inch of her back, her bottom, her upper thigh, while nuzzling at her neck, learning the places that made her shiver and those that made her gasp, and those that caused that delightful little hum of pleasure in the back of her throat.

When his thumb touched the underside of her breast, her breath hitched, but it was not fear this time, or not really. It was more like nervous curiosity. He took his time stroking her creamy flesh, while he dropped kisses on her throat, the pulse point in the hollow of her throat, upper chest and finally at the top of the magnificent rise of her breasts. She shuddered with pleasure.

He palmed the luscious fullness, gently kneading the bounteous flesh until her hips undulated against his groin. He bit back a groan, but held himself still, leaving it to her to discover just how hard he was, while he finally achieved his goal with his mouth. He licked the hardened nub of her breast through the fine lawn fabric of her shift.

'Oh…' She sighed against his shoulder, her hands sifting through the hair at his nape and sending shivers all the way to his shaft.

He was going to…

Shocked, he took a deep breath, regained control and eased her on to her back the better to pay attention to her other breast, massaging and kissing to the music of her sighs and moans. Her hands wandered his back in light stroking circles. Her thighs parted and he nestled into the cradle of her hips. A perfect fit for once. Because of her height, they were groin to groin. A most pleasurable sensation. Intensified when she wrapped both legs around his hips. She wanted him closer.

But first there was the issue of their clothing. He stroked one hand down her thigh, until he found the hem of her chemise, easing it upwards until it would go no further. He knelt up.

Her eyes fluttered open, anxiety filling her expression as if…she expected him to leave? Or was she fearful of being seen in all her glory? Far more likely, she was simply a particularly modest woman. He let his gaze roam her body. 'Beautiful,' he said. 'Gorgeous.'

A hesitant smile curved her lips.

'Will you let me see all of you?' he asked, twitching the bottom of her shift.

A blush suffused her face, but she nodded and lifted her hips and then her shoulders to help him pull it over her head. Now all she had on were stockings that ended just above the knee, tied with little blue garters. The curls at the apex to her thighs were light brown and her rosy nether lips beckoned seductively. Her breasts were full and bouncy with rosy nipples. So erotic.

'That is the loveliest sight I have ever seen,' he said, glancing up at her face, but her gaze was focused on his torso, on the place with his shirt tented over his erection.

She licked her lips and his shaft jerked in response.

She started and her gaze shot to his face.

'He likes that you are interested,' he said. 'Do you want to see?'

A little jerk of her head he guessed was a nod of agreement. How very nervous she was, like a bride on her wedding night.

The thought shocked him. He was a man without illusions. He knew women liked to act innocent, but usually he could see right through their wiles. With Carrie, though, he never quite felt sure if it was an act or not. Mostly because she was always so brutally honest. Pushing the nonsensical thought aside, he grabbed the back of his shirt and leaned forward to pull it off over his head.

Then down his arms, exposing his chest.

He almost laughed at her disappointed glance at where the shirt lay in his lap. That pouting look he could certainly interpret. A woman deprived of a treat she had expected.

He bundled up the shirt and fired it off at the kitchen chair.

She came up on her elbows to look at his erection, providing him with a perfect view of her bounteous breasts. He reached out and gently cupped them from the sides, feeling their soft weight in his palms. A touch on his shaft had him hissing in a breath, but she was too intent on shaping the crown of it to notice. She traced a fingertip down his length and gave his balls a little poke. She frowned.

It all became as clear as day. Her husband had been one of those men who took his pleasure without thought for that of his partner. Which meant Avery would have to make up for the lack.

Carrie knew what men looked like—how could she not when there were naked statues all over the place? She just hadn't expected to be so entranced by the sight of him fully aroused. To find herself gazing at him in awe and wonder at the contradictions. His member was so much darker than the rest of him and jutted towards her in a most intriguing way, while the other parts were surprisingly soft and silky.

Now some of the things her aunt had said to her before her wedding made a lot more sense. But she really didn't see how there would be enough room for him inside her body. Or he was bigger than a normal man. Certainly, she'd never seen one on a statue that looked as if it could possibly grow to that size.

He reached down and took her hand in his, cupping her hand around the soft part below the...penis, she remembered it was called. He used his hand to stroke her palm against him and it felt like marbles inside a velvety sack. He released her hand and she continued to gently massage, feeling the rough hair against her skin with the silky softness beneath. She smiled shyly up at him. 'I love the way it feels. Do you like this?'

He was watching her with hooded eyes, his expression dark yet somehow soft. 'Yes, it is exceedingly arousing. I like this, too.' He grasped the shaft in his fist, stroking up and down.

She followed his example and he threw his head back with a groan of pleasure.

Then his fingers burrowed into her nether curls and parted her cleft. And suddenly she was melting from the inside out. She collapsed back on the pillows, unable to support herself. Something inside her tightened, then flew apart. Like magic. Blissful. Amazing. Otherworldly. Her legs and arms felt like lead. She gasped for breath.

A soft curse caused her eyes to open. His expression was ruefully amused. 'You came faster than I expected,' he said. He looked pleased.

The words made no sense to her.

He leaned over her, one hand beside her head, the other between them. For a moment, she thought he was going to work that amazing magic again, but he was pushing something into her and then, yes, that lovely sensation again, as he thrust his hips forward.

The part of him she thought too big.

A pinch of pain. She winced with a little cry of protest and opened her eyes. She'd been right.

Hanging over her, he was frowning like a demon. His expression gave the impression he was in pain.

'Does it hurt you, too?' she asked, though her mouth felt dry and the words seemed difficult to form, she was still breathing so hard.

He shook his head. 'It is not possible.'

Her heart missed a beat. Was this why her husband had left her? 'It doesn't fit?' Disappointment filled her.

He made a choking sound. 'Oh, it will, but we will have to take it slowly. Tell me if I hurt you.'

She lay frozen, rigid, waiting for pain, but then he started to move, slowly inching forward and back with a kind of rocking motion of his hips and it felt…nice. More than nice. And then he used his hand in that other place and the tension she had felt before started to build again. Higher, this time, with the stimulation on his hand and his member inside her.

She closed her eyes.

'Carrie, look at me,' he said.

She forced her eyelids open. The intensity on his face was almost scary. The tendons in his neck stood out under his skin, his shoulders blocked the light from the room and he continued to move, until she did not think she could stand it any longer.

Again, that feeling of shattering some sort of barrier, so much more intense than before, and she was flying apart into a thousand tiny pieces. Sinking into some sort of abyss where all she could hear was her breathing. And his. He made a soft sound and withdrew from her body, rocking hard against her hip for a moment or two and then sank down on to his side to lay beside her.

He drew her into his arms and kissed her forehead. 'Lovely, lovely girl,' he murmured into her hair. 'Oh, my sweet child. Why didn't you tell me?'

Tell him?

His breathing deepened. He seemed to have fallen asleep. She lay in the circle of his arms, her head on his chest, her heart still racing as if she had run a mile. Why hadn't she told him what?

Chapter Eleven

Avery slowly came to. Replete. Content. Blissful.

And then he remembered. Damn it all.

What an idiot he'd been not to recognise the signs. But honestly, when would any man expect a widow to be a virgin? It was almost beyond the realm of possibility. But apparently not entirely, since the evidence was right before him. And perversely he was pleased.

When he ought to be furious.

He glanced down at where she lay nestled against his chest. Her eyes were closed and she was breathing evenly, but she wasn't asleep.

'Well?' he asked.

'Well, what?' she responded in a very small voice.

'Why did your husband not do the deed?' Dash it, that didn't sound exactly right. He gentled his voice. 'I do not understand why a married woman would still be a maid.' That really wasn't much better. Hell, how did he ever end up in this situation?

A small sound struck him through the heart. Dear God, was she crying? He'd made her cry? He wanted to leap out of bed and run a mile. Instead, he drew back, lifted her face until she had no option but to look at him and wiped her eyes on the corner of the sheet. 'What is it, Carrie?'

She sniffled.

He didn't even have a handkerchief to give her. She pulled something out from the tangle of sheets and wiped her nose. Her shift, he realised. He gently stroked her arm. 'Hush. It is all right. It doesn't matter. I was surprised, that was all.' Shocked, more like it. Such a mess. 'I would have been a lot more careful had I known. I hope I didn't hurt you too badly?'

'Oh, no,' she said, her voice sounding watery and full of sadness. 'It was lovely.'

Then why did she sound so miserable? True, he could have done a whole lot better if he had not been blindsided, but it wasn't that awful surely?

She sniffled again and mopped up her tears with the scrap of fabric.

What else could he say? Perhaps her husband had been unable. Hell, that would send a man off to get killed in the war, wouldn't it? And he could just imagine that scene playing out. A man's worst nightmare that.

'He left me the moment the ceremony was done,' she said softly.

He frowned. 'Right after?'

'He escorted me to the suite of rooms he had booked for us at the hotel, where I was to change before the wedding breakfast, and I never saw him again. Our few guests were waiting for us to make our appearance, but he never returned. The next day, I learned that he had gone to join Wellington's army.'

The forlornness in her voice nigh on broke his heart. Something that should not be happening. Hadn't he heard enough sad stories from the ladies he escorted about to harden him to the vagaries of his fellow man? Of all the tales he'd been told, though…

'The man was an idiot.'

'I thought so, too,' she said with a wry little laugh.

He let go a sigh of relief. Brave to a fault. He gave her a squeeze. 'That's my girl.' His? He winced. Those sorts of statements would get him into more trouble than he already was. Yet he could not help offering comfort. 'May I say how honoured I am that you chose me to be your first lover.'

A little silence met his words and then came a beautiful smile. His heart gave an odd little lurch. Oh, yes. He was really in trouble. 'Um…' she said.

He clenched his jaw, waiting for the admonition he so rightly deserved. 'What is it, Carrie?' He sounded terse. What was it about her that drove his easy charm into hiding? He turned to face her. 'Was there something I can do for you?' Something else.

'I was wondering if you would like to dine with me tomorrow evening? Here.'

Oh. Instead of a bear-garden jaw she was inviting him to dine. Desire flooded his body at the thought of being alone with her again.

Now he had slept with her as she'd wanted, he really ought to say farewell and get back to his life, because since he'd become involved with Carrie and her business he had not been to one ball to find someone to replace Elizabeth or escorted one lady on a shopping expedition. He hadn't even spent much time at the tables either. His income was suffering badly and that meant Laura would also suffer.

He really should call a halt to this right now. 'Yes. I would like that very much.' The words were out before he could think them through. But then, she had just given him the most amazing gift of his life, one he would likely never receive again. Not to mention he enjoyed her company.

The glorious smile he adored broke out again. 'I shall look forward to it.'

And dammit, so would he.

He reached for his waistcoat in the heap of clothes by the bed, grabbed his watch and peered at the time. 'Oh, Lord.'

'What is it?' she asked sitting up, the sheets pulled tight across her mouthwatering breasts.

He forced his gaze away. That was not the direction his thoughts needed to go, and besides, since this was her very first time, she would likely be sore for a few days so he should keep that in mind when he came for dinner the next day.

'I promised to meet someone and I am already late.' He slid out of bed and pulled on his clothes. He glanced over at her, watching him and wanted to slide right back under the sheets. Grimly he forced himself to continue dressing. He glanced her way and saw her watching him, her gaze oddly pained.

'What is it?' he asked, despite knowing he shouldn't.

'Are you going gaming?'

The question was laced with disapproval and it hurt when usually he didn't care what people thought, but he wasn't going to lie like some naughty boy caught teasing the family pet. Gaming was how he made his living. 'I am.' He buttoned his waistcoat and turned to face her.

'Oh.' There was a world of dismay in her voice.

'Is there a problem?'

She flinched at his tone and he felt like some sort of ogre.

What the devil? 'What is it, Carrie?' He did not mean to sound impatient, but really? He didn't answer to her any more than he answered to his father. Why was it people were always wanting to control his life when they really knew nothing about him?

She shook her head, her hair moving like a waterfall about her creamy shoulders. 'I don't see why it is enjoyable for gentlemen to risk everything on the toss of a dice or...something equally foolish.' Sadness reverberated in her voice.

His jaw dropped. What? Did she think he routinely fleeced green boys of their fortune or ruined men down on their luck? Looking at him as if he was some sort of Captain Sharp, no less.

He never cared what people thought of him or said of him. So why would he care now? A chill entered his veins. He picked up his hat and gloves.

'It is how I make my living, madam. I bid you goodnight.'

The next evening, while tidying up from yet another extraordinarily busy day, Carrie caught a strange look from her assistant. 'Is something wrong?'

'No, ma'am, but...well, you are humming. You didn't do that when I first came here and I wondered what has made you so happy.'

Humming? Oh, goodness. Heat crept up her face. 'I suppose I am happy because the shop is doing so well.' Certainly not because she was expecting Lord Avery later this evening. She had half-expected him to cry off on their dinner after they had parted on such bad terms, but since she had not received a note cancelling their engagement, she could only assume he would arrive as promised. And, yes, that was making her happy. She shouldn't have said anything about his gambling. Gentlemen gambled. It was a fact of life. And they did not like to be criticised. Certainly, Carrie Greystoke was not going to change those facts of life.

'Yes, ma'am.' The girl sounded none too convinced.

Surely she could not have an inkling that Carrie was entertaining a gentleman in her rooms later that evening. No, it wasn't possible. She frowned. 'Why would I not be pleased that the shop is doing well?'

'Oh, I didn't mean it that way, ma'am. It is just that you work so hard and it seems to get busier every day. If this keeps up, we won't have enough stock to satisfy our customers. I expected you to be worried.'

It was true, there were a great many gaps on the shelves. 'I will bring more stock back with me when I return from Kent on Monday.'

A note she had received from Marguerite indicated that they had managed to gain the services of several women in the village, but that until they were fully trained, she and Petra were working long hours to meet the demand. Hopefully they would have enough stock on hand for the following week at least. And in a few more weeks it would be the height of summer and the *ton* would be departing the city for cooler climes and they would have enough of a hiatus to prepare for the Little Season. They would also need new autumn designs if they were to maintain the interest of their customers. After all, while many of the ladies had come to take a look at the shopkeeper who had caught Lord Avery's eye, they had fallen in love with the hats. And it was the hats, and the naughty nightwear, that would keep them coming back.

The girl finished tidying the drawers and glanced around. 'I think that is everything.'

'It is indeed. Off you go home and I will see you first thing in the morning.'

The girl smiled. 'Yes, Mrs Greystoke. If there is anything else I can do to help, please let me know. I love working here. It is so much nicer than being a housemaid. It means I can go home and help my mum with the little ones while she gets dinner, but if you needs me to stay late or to do anything at all, I will be happy to help out.'

'Thank you. I will be sure to let you know.' But please right now...just go. 'My goodness, is that the time? You don't want to be late, or your mother will worry.'

The girl shrugged into her coat and with a cheery wave was gone. Carrie locked the door behind her and leaned against it in relief. At last. Now she could bathe and get ready for Avery. This must be their last night together. Since the shop was doing so well, it would not be fair to her sisters-in-law to continue with their arrangement when it was no longer needed. He'd helped her get started and that should be an end to it.

While she had honestly not expected him to make love to her once he'd explained he did not do that sort of thing for money, the fact that he had, made her want to make this evening as special for him as he had made this time with him special for her.

But first she needed to get ready.

Excitement rippled through her belly. She had decided on a very wicked plan. She hugged her arms around her waist, but did she dare follow through on it?

Yes, she had to do this. Avery had taught her she was not a complete failure as a woman. He had called her lovely. He had made her feel utterly feminine. A feeling she would treasure for the rest of her life. And this was one thing she could do for him and bring him some measure of pleasure.

On his way to visit Carrie, Avery dropped in at Laura's lodgings. Having let himself in as usual, he stopped short at the sight of his older brother seated in the armchair by the fire. He almost turned tail, but that would be cowardly.

'Bart,' he said warily. 'What are you doing here?'

Laura put her needlework aside and rushed forward to greet him. 'Now, now, Avery. No need to sound so unfriendly.' She gave him a peck on the cheek. 'Bart came to see how we did and to report on Father's health.

Avery set his hat on the table and shook hands with his older brother. 'Good of you, Bart. How is the old fellow?' He tried to keep the bitterness out of his voice, but clearly had not succeeded when his brother gave him a narrow-eyed stare, then shrugged. Only Avery could solve the bad blood between him and his father.

And to be fair on his brother, the Duke kept his heir so short of funds there was little he could do to help either of his siblings. The best he could do for Avery was loan him his carriages on the odd occasion. And for his sister? Laura never said anything, but no doubt he did what he could. Unfortunately, most of the care for Laura fell on Avery's shoulders. Or it would until her husband was able to earn a decent income.

Bart glanced at Laura and back to Avery. He heaved a sigh. 'Sometimes he is the way he always was and sometimes I am amazed he is still with us he is so fragile.

Quite honestly, I don't see how he keeps going. Strength of will, I suppose.'

Avery's stomach dipped. The longer time went on the less likely he would ever be reconciled with the Duke. And, despite everything, that did not sit well in his gut. 'I am sorry you have to bear the brunt of it.'

His brother looked grim. 'It is truly pitiful to see.' He took a deep breath. 'Which brings me to the reason I called here today.' Again, a look passed between him and Laura.

What the hell? He glared at them both. 'What are you two plotting?'

'Nothing,' Laura said, sounding anxious. 'It is just that...'

'Father is extremely agitated about the female you now appear to be...courting.'

Avery froze. 'I am not *courting* anyone.'

'Damn it, Avery—' His brother's cheeks coloured. 'I beg your pardon, Laura, but devil take it, Avery, a widowed shopkeeper?'

'She is a business associate,' Avery snapped. 'Nothing more.'

'Well, whatever she is, Father's not pleased you are still seeing her.' His mouth tightened. 'He nigh on had an apoplexy thinking you'd be trapped in marriage to such a one when you can have your pick of half the nobility in England.'

'I have no intention of marrying anyone and so you may tell our father.'

His brother snorted. 'Driving in Hyde Park? Taking her to the theatre. Smelling of April and May is how he has heard it.'

Laura frowned. 'Avery, surely you are not toying with

the lady's affections? I told you before that Harriet's godmother saw you in Hyde Park, too, but apparently she reported to Harriet that she had never seen a lady so much in love.'

Avery's jaw dropped. *In love?* 'Nonsense. We are simply good friends.'

'I'll wager you are,' his brother said morosely.

Avery shot him a grin, because he knew it would annoy his brother. 'You are just jealous.'

'Avery—' his brother growled.

'But what of the lady's reputation?' Laura asked. 'You know how people talk.'

After running off with a man society considered beneath her, Laura had suffered her share of gossip.

'She doesn't care about such things. She is a milliner.' Avery mentally crossed his fingers that no one had discovered her relationship to Westram. If that ever came to his father's ears he might be singing a different tune about her suitability as a bride. Maybe it was just as well their *association* was due to end shortly. The thought scoured a hole in his gut. He forced himself to ignore it. 'I take a commission on sales resulting from my recommendations to her shop. That is all there is to it.' On a financial level, anyway.

Laura frowned. 'That might be all it is to you, but are you sure she feels the same way?'

Now they brought it to his attention, he wasn't at all sure, given her actions. He inhaled a deep breath. 'Whatever the case, I am not marrying her or anyone else. Besides, why is Father so concerned about me? You are the heir, Bart. It is your *duty* to marry and provide the next heir. I suggest you get on with it post haste.'

His brother's face hardened. 'I am doing my duty. As you well know, I am betrothed.'

'You've been betrothed for nigh on five years. Why haven't you married the girl?'

'That is why, you idiot. She's barely out of the school-room.'

Avery winced. Their father had chosen a girl from an excellent family for his brother. Unfortunately, she'd been fourteen to his brother's twenty-five at the time. Her family had signed the settlements, but had insisted the wedding not take place until after she'd had her come out. Thank God.

For Laura, the Duke had chosen a man in his fifties. Of the three of them, the woman chosen for Avery had seemed on the surface the most acceptable in terms of age. Except that Avery had been in love with some-one else, Alexandra. Or had thought so anyway. All the young bucks new on the town had been in love with Lady Alexandra Wellford. She'd been the most beauti-ful of all the debutantes that year, although her family's pockets were largely to let.

Avery had thought she loved him in return, until his father bought her and her family off. When Avery had discovered what the Duke had done, they had had the most awful row. It was then that he'd told his father he was never going to marry and they hadn't seen each other from that day to this.

'I'm sorry. I forgot she was so young. How much lon-ger do you have to wait?'

'Until next year.'

'I hope she is worth it. I really do.'

His brother's expression became blank. 'I will do my duty.'

Avery frowned. 'Surely—'

'I am not going to discuss my intended with you, Avery. I merely came to ask Laura if she knew anything of this shopkeeper before I approached you about it.'

'You don't need to worry about me, I can assure you.'

'You know, if you would just settle down with someone reasonable, Father would reinstate your allowance. He has mellowed considerably over the past few years.' Bart looked so damned hopeful, Avery almost weakened. But he knew his father. It would never be enough. He'd want to rule his life completely. First the wedding, then he'd be relegated to managing one of the family estates and answering to his father for every aspect of his life. He'd tried to appease his father all through his boyhood until he'd almost lost sight of himself as a person. He was not going to subjugate himself again.

'Thank you, but, no.' He pulled his purse from his pocket and emptied the contents on to the table. 'Laura, this should keep you going for a few days. I will bring more in a week or so.'

Bart curled his lip. 'I suppose that is payment from your widow for services rendered?'

'And?' Avery said icily.

His brother grimaced.

Avery punched him lightly on the shoulder. 'What a stuffed shirt you are becoming. It is actually my ill-gotten gains from the tables.'

'Hardly any better.'

Laura looked upset. 'Please, both of you, do not fight. You are the only family I have left. I hate to see you so at odds.'

Inwardly Avery winced. He hated it, too, but he wasn't going to buckle to his brother's pressure. 'We would not be at odds if he didn't think he had the right to tell me what to do.'

'I am trying to save you from yourself, Brother. And if you think gaming is a good way to make a living, it is not. Sooner or later it will lead you into trouble.'

Why did everyone want to run his life? He bowed. 'Please excuse me, Laura, I cannot stay. I have another engagement.' He stalked out.

He wasn't feeling exactly good about things. He hadn't lied to his brother, but he hadn't been truthful either. Damn it, the man was almost as bad as their father. He didn't deserve to be told the truth about Carrie.

Outside in the street, Avery let go a breath. It wasn't true. His brother was a good man. Too good.

Chapter Twelve

Carrie glanced at her clock for about the fifth time and ran her hands down the front of her gown. Even with the addition of the negligee it was so sheer… What if he took one look at her trying to be seductive and laughed? Oh, this was such a stupid idea.

She ran to the clothes press. She still had a few minutes before he was due to arrive. The gown she had worn to the theatre would be better than this, surely?

A creak behind her. She jerked around. Too late. He was here and looking so handsome and well dressed. She swallowed. She really should have worn something more appropriate.

His eyes widened as they ran down her length. The smile on his face broadened. 'My word, you look good enough to eat. Was this what you meant by dinner?'

Her nervousness fled. She smiled back, though she knew from the heat in her cheeks she was also blushing. 'No. I promise I do intend to feed you.'

He closed the door behind you. 'You know, that doorman let me in without a word. I am sorry if I surprised you.'

She let out a breathless laugh. 'I told him to send you straight back here.'

A brow tilted up. He glanced at the evening gown she had pulled from the clothes chest, still gripped in nervous fingers. 'Am I too early? Shall I come back? Though I must say what you are wearing is absolutely enchanting. No wonder the ladies of the *ton* can't get enough of them.'

He knew just the right thing to say to set her at ease. She dropped the gown back into the chest and closed the lid. 'I was putting it away.' As lies went, it was fairly white. It certainly wasn't going to do anyone any harm and it was certainly better than admitting she had started to panic. She had wanted to wear this outrageous robe for him. After all, she'd bought it and would certainly wear it again.

'Ah, I see,' he said. He hung up his hat and tucked his gloves inside it. He raised his chin and gave a sniff. 'Something smells good? And not only your perfume.'

The man knew just how to make her feel at ease. He was lovely and kind and generous to a woman most men considered as plain as a pikestaff and not worth their time. She just wished she had more to offer. Her heart ached a little, knowing he could never be hers, but she had intended this evening to be for him and pushed such thoughts aside. There would be time enough later for regrets.

'Mrs Thrumby's cook kindly prepared enough for two.' She gestured to the armchair beside the hearth. 'Please, sit. May I offer you some sherry?'

'Will you join me?'

'I will.' She smiled.

'Then, yes, please.'

She poured them both a glass of the sherry she had bought earlier in the day and, having given him his, she took the small stool opposite.

He raised his glass. 'Your health.'

'And yours.' They sipped.

'Very nice,' he remarked.

Relief filled her. She had spent rather more on it she should have. She rose. 'No, please. Do not get up. Finish your drink while I put the first course on the table. Soup to start.'

She ladled the soup into bowls and placed them on the table. 'Whenever you are ready.'

He came to the table at once. 'Pea soup. How did you know it is one of my favourites?'

She laughed. He would have said that about any soup, she was sure, but she wasn't going to spoil things by being practical. She was determined she would not. 'A lucky guess.' They took the seats opposite each other.

He tucked in with obvious relish. 'How was your day?' he asked. 'Was the shop very busy?'

How normal it sounded. How like family. Her heart gave a little squeeze. This sort of family would never be hers.

How could she let such regrets enter her mind, when she had her sisters-in-law? It was wrong of her. Terribly. But she could not seem to help it.

'Extremely.' She hoped she sounded more cheerful than she felt.

'I am glad to hear it.'

Good, he had noticed nothing of her longings in her voice. 'Me, too. Mrs Buxton-Smythe came in today and she brought Lady Carstairs with her. I think our reputation is assured among the ladies of the *ton*.'

He paused in his eating to look at her. 'Then you no longer need my assistance even though our two weeks are not quite up.' His face was grave.

She managed a smile, even if it did feel false. 'I believe you are right. But I really must thank you for your help in putting us on the road to success.'

'You would have got there by yourselves eventually,' he said cheerfully.

'It would have taken a great deal longer and…and we might not have been able to survive long enough, to be honest.' She had his share of the profits ready for him, of course, but she did want him to understand how very much she appreciated his help, though he seemed determined to brush it off.

She cleared away the soup bowls and took two plates out of the oven where she had put them to keep warm. The roast beef didn't look as if it had dried out. Not too much, anyway. And the vegetables looked fine, too. Mrs Thrumby's woman had explained how to keep the meals warm for half an hour.

Once they were both served she sat down again.

'My compliments to the cook,' he said after a couple of mouthfuls and a sigh.

She frowned. It was almost as if he did not usually eat proper meals. 'I am glad you are enjoying it.' Oh, heavens, she had forgotten the wine. She shot up from her chair.

He rose, too, looking worried.

'Oh, sit, please.' She ran to the pantry and fetched out the decanter of red wine she had put there to keep cool. 'I nearly forgot this.'

He took the decanter from her. 'Allow me.' He poured them both a glass.

He raised his. 'To the most beautiful woman I know.'

She tried hard not to show disbelief on her face or in her laugh. 'To my most favourite gentleman caller.'

He frowned fiercely. 'Your only gentleman caller, I hope?'

Her jaw dropped. 'I was jesting. The only other men who call here are Jeb and Mr Thrumby.'

'Hmmph. I am glad to hear it.'

Oh, even his pretence at jealousy made her heart beat faster and her skin feel warm. 'Eat,' she urged, hoping that such thoughts did not show on her face. She did not want him to realise his departure would hurt her terribly. Far more than she'd been hurt when her husband left. Because her heart hadn't been involved. Only her pride.

She stilled. Every nerve in her body tingling with awareness. Her heart? Surely not. The man made his living from ladies who paid him for his services and, worse, from gambling. He lived on the edge of ruin and seemed to enjoy the risk. Look at the way he had wagered money he could ill afford on the life of the sword swallower.

It all left her feeling terrified. And fascinated at the same time. She could not help staring at the way his throat moved when he swallowed, at the even white teeth when he bit into his meat, at the way his fingers curled around the stem of his glass when he lifted his glass to drink. Such long clever fingers.

He glanced up and caught her watching him. She dropped her gaze to her plate and forced herself not to hide her heated cheeks beneath her palms. Why on earth had she acted like a schoolgirl? It was perfectly ridiculous. 'I hope the beef is not too dry,' she said. 'It was in the oven a bit longer than it should have been.'

'I thought I was right on time,' he said.

When she glanced up at him, she saw that his eyes were alive with amusement. At her. Oh, she was so hopelessly gauche when it came to this flirting stuff. 'Is it?' she asked. 'Too dry?'

He carved another piece from the slice on his place and gravely chewed. 'It is perfect.' A flash of those lovely white teeth as he smiled. 'Just like you.'

'Hardly,' she said, attacking the slice of meat on her plate. Did he think she was a fool? That she did not look in the mirror and see the truth?

'And that gown of yours is enough to drive any redblooded male insane.'

She could agree about the gown, but not what it covered. 'I am glad you like it. My sister-in-law Marguerite came up with the design.'

He leaned back and gave her what she could only describe as a rakish stare. 'With you in it, the gown quite takes my breath away. Though I expect that was your intention.'

Inside she cringed. 'I thought you might want to recommend them to your special ladies.'

His expression darkened. 'There is only ever one special lady at a time, you know.'

Was he saying…? 'Are you classifying me as one of your special ladies?' Her heart gave an odd little thump. She put down her knife and fork and took a fortifying sip of wine.

'You are very special.'

'That was not my question.'

He straightened his knife and fork on his plate, then lifted his gaze to meet hers. 'You are not one of my special ladies, you are my only special lady.'

She blinked. 'You do not sound happy about that.'

He gave a little grimace and a sigh. 'It is somewhat bad for business.'

'Oh.' What had she been thinking? 'I have your money.' She leapt to her feet.

He caught her wrist. 'I do not want your money.'

Something inside her shrivelled. He meant he did not want her. 'Oh.' She glanced around the kitchen, sifting through her mind for something to say that would not sound like he'd hurt her feelings. 'I do not expect anything more from you,' she said. At his look of shock, she continued on quickly. 'You have fulfilled the terms of our arrangement to the full.' Oh, that didn't sound quite right. 'I mean the increase in trade is quite remarkable and it is all down to you.'

'Is that what you mean?' he said drily.

'I—yes, of course. What else would I mean?'

He pushed back his chair.

An ache filled her chest. He was going to leave and he hadn't even had dessert.

He tugged on her wrist. She hadn't realised he was still holding it. Off balance, she lurched towards him and, a moment later, she found herself perched once again on his knee. He tipped her face up to meet his gaze. 'Carrie,' he murmured. 'I find myself quite at a loss. It is not your money I want, it is you.'

'Oh,' she gasped.

'And that, my dear, is very bad for business.'

She wasn't sure whether to laugh or cry at the way his words made her feel inside. 'But we have decided to bring our arrangement to an end,' she said, deciding it was better to feel nothing at all, because if this was really the end of their association, she did not want him to leave with the recollection of her crying all over him. Instead, she would prefer him to recall her with a smile on her lips. 'So, should we not make the most of it?' Oh, goodness, where on earth had that come from? 'But first you must let me serve you dessert.'

His arm tightened around her waist. 'Dessert? I thought *you* were dessert.' He pulled her close and nuzzled in her neck. Shivers coursed down her spine. Her brain turned to mush.

'Oh, no. There's…' What had he said? She was dessert? Goodness '…um…trifle,' she finished saying. Oh, how wretched! Once more she had missed the opportunity to meet his seductive flirtation with some witty response. No doubt Mimi Luttrell would have known exactly what to say. Bother.

He laughed and let her go. 'Trifle, hmmm. That reminds me of something my sister said.'

She popped to her feet and cleared away the dirty dishes to hide her discomfort. 'Really? What did she say?'

'She wanted to know if I was trifling with your affections.'

When she glanced up, he was watching her intently, waiting for her reaction, despite that he'd asked so nonchalantly.

She served the trifle and smiled. 'I think we both know that is not possible.'

'I told her that was so, but people are talking and—'

Her heart seemed to still. 'And we have reached the end of this venture.'

'Indeed.' There was an odd note in his voice. She wasn't sure if it was relief, or something else. His expression gave nothing away, however. It had to be relief. What else could it be?

Her poor heart felt bruised and sore. She managed to breathe around the pain. 'It makes perfect sense.' She shot him what she hoped was an arch look. 'And then people will wonder what happened, so curiosity will continue to bring them to my shop.'

He gave her a faint smile. 'Smart girl. Naturally, I will continue to advise the ladies of my acquaintance to patronise your shop. Why would I not? You have the very best bonnets in London.'

'Then everything is just as it should be.' She smiled while inside she felt as if she was dying. 'Now eat your dessert and tell me if that is the most delicious trifle you have ever tasted.'

He gave her an odd look, but picked up his spoon.

Avery ate as he had been ordered. 'It is excellent.'

Everything was going exactly to plan. The civilised ending to their arrangement by way of a delicious companionable meal served by a woman so gorgeous he would certainly never forget his first sight of her in that filmy robe as long as he lived. He'd been fighting his arousal since the moment he'd walked in her door.

Everything about this evening was perfect.

Then why was he feeling so damned discontented?

Surely it wasn't because she was accepting his departure from her life with such equanimity? He usually hated scenes and female tears when it came to a parting. Another reason he preferred his dealings with females to be strictly business.

No, he should be delighted with the way the evening was going, but despite everything he had said, he felt uneasy, as if he was making some sort of mistake.

The spoon part way to his lips he stilled, glanced

across the table at her, where she was watching him, her chin cupped in her palm. She looked lovely. Alluring and not simply because of the extraordinarily sensual gown draping her luscious curves. She was lovely inside and out. Honest yet sweet, self-sufficient yet completely feminine. Undemanding. So different to any other woman he'd ever met.

She'd make any man a wonderful wife.

Any man but him.

He couldn't afford a wife. While he did well at the tables, nothing was ever certain about gambling. He'd sometimes had weeks of poor luck which was why he had set up his arrangements with various shopkeepers. And that was not something he would continue if he was married. And while Carrie was Westram's sister-in-law, she was still a merchant's daughter and completely unsuitable so there would be no help from his father. His gut clenched. If the old fellow decided to buy her off, the way he had with Alexandra, or tried to do her professional damage as he had with John, well, Avery might just end up committing patricide and that would help no one.

'You don't like the trifle?' she asked.

He started, realising he'd been staring at her instead of eating. 'It is nearly as delicious as you.'

As usual she gave a self-conscious little grimace as if she didn't believe him. He wanted her to believe him. He wanted her to realise her self-worth, to feel confident in her femininity. If he could give her nothing else, surely he could give her that?

He took her hand across the table. 'If this is to be our last night together, it seems a shame to waste it speaking half-truths. You are a very desirable woman and I want you more than I could ever want dessert.'

She blushed prettily and met his gaze head on. 'Thank you.'

Yes, that was what he had wanted, her acceptance of his compliment. Still holding her hand, he got up from the table and brought her to her feet. 'And while I love looking at you, Carrie, I would much rather be holding you in my arms.' He suited the action to the words, drawing her close, feeling the gorgeous soft wells of her generous figure flush with his body. 'I'd much rather be tasting you.'

He kissed her, gently at first, a merest brush of their lips, but as she melted into him, he deepened the kiss, making it firmer and more insistent.

Her lips parted and he tasted the sweetness of custard and the tartness of raspberry, but most of all he tasted Carrie. A far more exotic flavour to him than any confection. The way she yielded beneath his touch made him almost dizzy with desire.

His hands wandered over her familiar swells and hollows, stroking her in ways that made her press closer into him, while her hands trailed up from his chest to work their way around his neck and winnow through his hair.

The pleasure of her gentle touch aroused him more than the sight of her in the clinging gown had done. The scent of her filled his nostrils. Something spicy and clean. A scent he never wanted to forget. He kissed her, until they were both breathless and trembling with pent-up need and he was forced to stop before his legs gave out.

He rested his forehead against hers, breathing hard. 'I want you.'

'I want you, too,' she said.

He nodded and shrugged out of his coat. She attacked

the buttons on his falls while he undid his waistcoat. He toed off his shoes and tore off his waistcoat. She sank to her knees, pulling down his pantaloons until he could step out of them. She flung them over a chair and sank back on her heels with a smile, waiting for him to remove his shirt.

'I think it is your turn to remove an article of clothing,' he said, raising her to her feet and tugging at the pretty red ribbon that held her robe closed at the neck.

She swallowed as the delicate fabric fell to her feet, revealing the nightgown beneath. If one could call it that. It was the sauciest garment he had ever seen. It tied at the back of her neck and dipped all the way to below her navel. The fabric barely covered her nipples and only stayed in place because of the narrow plaited belt around her waist. The skirts fell to the floor, but a slit up the sides revealed her glorious long legs and her feet encased in high-heeled slippers.

She peeped up at him from slightly lowered lashes. 'Is it—?'

'You are the most sensual sight I have ever seen.' His voice rasped in his dry throat. His erection jutting upwards, tenting his shirt, should be proof enough of his words, but in case she had not noticed, he whipped off his shirt and flung it aside. 'I want you. I need you.'

He swept her up and deposited her on the bed. 'And right now I am going to have you.'

Her delighted smile filled his vision.

Held in his arms, her head resting on his shoulder as he carried her to the bed, Carrie realised that, despite everything she knew about him, she was head-over-heels in love with him. Not because he was handsome and charismatic, though he was all of that and more. And not because he had proved himself a wonderful lover and was about to do so again, but because underneath all that swaggering bravado he was one of the kindest people she had ever met.

It was going to be so very hard to let him go.

Never in her life had she felt the pull of her heart. She'd never been in love, not once, so it wasn't surprising that she would fall for him. It was what he did. He made women fall for him. She knew it meant nothing. So then why did she feel so wonderful and so wretched at the same time?

She knew he didn't love her back and he had never lied about it, but she did think he liked her and she wanted to make this evening memorable. Their last time together.

She smiled when he paused at the little alcove containing her bed. With his arms full of her, he did not have a free hand to draw back the curtain. She reached out and pulled it back and he gently deposited her on the bed, gazing down at her, his body gloriously displayed to her wandering gaze.

For a man who spent his days escorting women around town and his nights at the gambling tables, he really was amazingly fit. His chest was broad, his shoulders deeply muscled, his waist and flanks narrow and firm. And his erection was proud and aggressive.

She licked her lips.

His member jerked.

Pleased, she glanced up at his face.

He grinned at her, his teeth a flash of white. 'Yes, he wants you also.'

She swallowed. Hopefully she wasn't going to spoil

this by doing something stupid. She wanted this evening to be perfect, something she could remember all her life, for there would never be another man in her life. She would not dare do this again. Besides, no man could ever live up to Avery, not in her mind or in her foolish heart.

A heart that must be ignored. *Trusting your heart is taking a chance.*

She leaned back on her elbows, sprawling, so the gown would leave her legs bare to his gaze. When she had tried the pose earlier, she had thought it looked inviting. When he didn't move, she thought perhaps it was too much. Too eager, too demanding.

She shifted, trying to make herself less…less something.

'No,' he rasped. 'I just want a moment to remember the way you look right now.'

Oh. A smile pulled at her lips. A surge of happiness swelled her heart. He always said the most lovely things. As she had planned earlier, she pulled free the strategically placed comb and her hair tumbled down around her shoulders.

'You little minx,' he said approvingly. 'You planned that.'

He looked pleased.

As she had hoped. She tossed him a saucy glance. 'I'm glad you liked it.'

A serious expression flitted across his face. 'I like everything about you.'

And she adored him. Loved him. Stunned at the admission, she took a deep breath, forcing the words back where they belonged in the deepest reaches of her heart where she would treasure the memory of having loved and been loved, if only for a brief time.

She held out a hand to him. 'Are you going to stand there all night, or are we going to make some more memories together?'

In a moment, he was on the bed, kneeling astride her, leaning down and kissing her lips, his tongue delving deep into her mouth, sending tingling sensations out to her fingertips and in the deepest regions of her body. Breathless and trembling, she lay back against the cushions and twined her arms around his neck, pulling him down with her, feeling his weight on her body, pressing down on her breasts, his erection hard against her belly. Yes, this was what she had been missing, the feeling of belonging, of sharing, of being close.

When he broke the kiss and gazed down into her eyes, she stroked his hair back from his face with her palms. She would not say the words, they were buried and his rejection of them would hurt far too much, but she could fill her gaze with that love and give him the gift of her body, and bring him pleasure.

His hand came to her breast and swept the scrap of fabric aside. His gaze left her face and dropped to where his thumb was slowly circling her nipple.

Her nipples hardened to stiff little points, one bare, the other hidden, but obvious beneath the fabric of the nightgown.

'It seems they are ready for you,' she said softly, tilting her hips at the pleasure of his touch.

'It would seem so,' he said. His eyelids drooped a fraction as he gazed down at the tight little nub. He swooped down and licked it.

She gasped.

He looked up at her with a piratical grin. Then he lowered his head slowly. She waited for the lick that held such shocking sensations. It never came. He opened his mouth and took in the peak of her breast. Heat rushed to her core where little pulses sent waves of heat through her body. She moaned at the sheer overwhelming deliciousness of the sensations rippling along her veins.

And then he sucked.

The painful pleasure blanked her mind to everything except the tight drawing sensation on her breast and all the way down to the apex of her thighs. Her hips ground against him, seeking to ease the pleasurable ache. This time she knew what it was she wanted, what he would bring her. She tried to part her thighs, to encourage him closer, to bring him into the cradle of her hips, but he ignored her attempts, continuing to kneel astride her, his erection brushing her belly, but not going where she wanted it.

Indeed, if anything, he lifted himself up, further away.

She made a sound of protest.

He released her nipple on a hard little suck and pressed a brief kiss on her lips. 'Patience, little one. Let us not rush this.'

Little one? Was he talking to her?

But when he loomed over her like that, when his shoulders blocked her view of everything but him, yes, she did feel a whole lot smaller and vulnerable. And he was right, much as her body protested, she did want to savour every second of this last time.

She sighed. It was so lovely. She never wanted it to end. And yet she wanted him to bring her the release her body craved.

Chapter Thirteen

Never had Avery had so much trouble controlling the animal urges roaring through his blood. It might be knowing this would be the last time they would ever make love. Or it might be her inexperience exciting him more than it should, but the only way to stop himself from racing to the finish was by keep physical distance between them. For a while longer, at least.

If she would let him. Her legs came up around his waist, her heels digging into his buttocks as she lifted her hips to rub her sex against his groin, while she pulled his head down to kiss his lips and dance her tongue around his. Delicious. Seductive, yet innocent. He didn't know what aroused him the most, her hesitant touch or her boldness in demanding what she wanted.

Once he'd learned the way of it as a youth, he'd always been the one in charge in bed. Always set the pace, controlled the flow. Carrie set things end over end, leaving him running to catch up. As he was now. Breathless, bordering on driving into her and losing himself in her slick heat and to the devil with the consequences.

That was not going to happen.

Breaking off the kiss, her pushed backwards, breaking her hold around his neck and his hips. He pressed first one knee then the other between her thighs and, smiling her approval, she parted her legs to accommodate him. She reached out to pull him back to her.

He ignored the invitation and sat back on his heels, letting his gaze wander over the salacious sight of her white smooth thighs, the damp curls at their apex that gave him a little peek of her feminine rosiness. He skimmed upwards to her waist with the plaited belt and the rumpled fabric of her nightgown hiding her belly. He undid the tie and pulled it free, sweeping the scrap of material aside to view her slightly rounded belly and the magnificent globes of her breasts with their hard-tipped peaks.

His mouth watered at the utterly scrumptious sight she made. He pressed a kiss to her navel, swirling his tongue around it, enjoying the way she squirmed at the pleasure of his touch. Her hands roamed across his shoulders, her fingers combed through his hair, her moans of encouragement filled his ears. Slowly he worked his way up to tease and lick each nipple, moving from one to the other in quick successions, taking her sensual defences by storm, until her hands lay limp on his shoulders and he could see the rapid beat of her pulse in the hollow of her throat and feel her hips stirring restlessly beneath him.

Once more, he sat back. Her heavy eyelids lifted a fraction or two.

'Is something wrong?' she whispered hoarsely.

'Everything is perfect.'

She frowned at his erection as he scooted backwards, looking lost and confused. Then gasped as he lowered his head to her sex. He swept his tongue up the sweet little cleft, tasting her essence, feeling the heat of her desire.

She made a noise in the back of her throat that he was sure was a denial and he lifted his head, looking past her beautiful breasts to take in her shocked expression.

'No?' he asked. 'You don't like it.'

'I don't—'

He pulled away.

'No! I mean, I have never felt anything so—'

He waited. He had known this would be a shock to her, but he wanted her to know the pleasure of this. She deserved to know the pleasure of this. But he would not force it on her. She was too new to the art of lovemaking. But he did hope her boldness would not let her down. 'So?' he questioned, pressing her, intrigued, wanting to hear what she thought.

'So wicked,' she gasped. She rubbed her hands up and down his forearms where he braced himself beside her hips. 'I—' She cast him a shy smile. 'I liked it.'

'There is more,' he said.

She hissed in a breath and the little sound caused his groin to tighten. He was in trouble all right. 'Show me,' she whispered.

Big trouble.

He dipped his head and swirled his tongue around, flicking it back and forth across her most pleasurable spot. She cried out and shuddered. 'Avery,' she murmured. 'Oh.'

She lay lax beneath him.

He should have expected her swift response. She was a very sensual female aroused quickly by touch. He leaned over her and kissed her lips. She flicked out her tongue, licking at him, tasting herself on his mouth and looking surprised and very pleased.

'That was so nice.'

'Only nice?' he teased, grinning down at her.

'Amazing. Wonderful.'

'Better.'

'Out of this world.'

He nodded his approval and took her lips in a long heart-stoppingly lovely kiss.

When it was over and he rose above her, holding himself up on his hands, she looked worried.

He gave her a questioning look.

She blushed. 'What about you? Are you not going to take your pleasure?'

'Giving you pleasure is my pleasure.'

That did not seem to please her. 'But I want to give you the same kind of pleasure you gave me.'

His shaft jerked in response to her words. 'Are you sure?'

She glanced down between their bodies, her gaze seeking out his erection, and licked her lips.

'You don't have to, you know.'

He certainly didn't expect it, given her inexperience. 'Do you like it?'

She sounded so serious, he wanted to smile. 'I most certainly do.'

'Then I would like to.'

Who was he to argue with a lady, especially when she wanted to give him such an incredible gift? Except—

'Well?' she said, sounding almost cross.

Too delighted for words, he stifled a grin and rolled over on to his back. 'Have at it.'

She gazed at him as if what she was looking at was

the most wonderful thing she had ever seen and licked her lips. He almost came apart.

A small secret smile curved her lips. 'I don't think I have ever seen anything so tempting as this.'

He groaned as her delicate hand curled around the base, squeezing ever so lightly. He forced himself not to push into her hand, holding himself still by gritting his teeth until they hurt. As she leaned over him, her hair fell forward, hiding her and what she was doing from view. All he could do was feel the heat and wetness of her tongue as she gave an experimental lick at the head of his shaft.

He bit back a groan of frustration. He did not want anything to call a halt to these proceedings.

Then she took him fully into his mouth and his vision blanked. He swallowed hard, reaching for a scrap of control, while she used her mouth and tongue to explore his shape and size.

Finally, she gave an experimental suck and he almost came apart.

Quickly, before he succumbed to her teasing, he reached down and gently lifted her up towards him and kissed her senseless.

When he broke the kiss, she smiled with a little cat-like smile. 'You liked that.'

'More than I can say,' he managed to gasp hoarsely.

He rolled her on her back and came over her, gazing down into her lovely face. 'But we do this together, this time.'

Carefully, he pressed the blunt head of his shaft into her body, circling his hips while he watched her face, probing for the spot that would bring her the most pleasure.

She moaned, her hips writhing, her body tensing as if pulled as tight as a bowstring. He rocked, moving against that spot until her head was thrashing and her heels were trying to press him deeper into her body.

The base of his shaft tingled with the urge to drive deeper. He slid deeper into her and withdrew. She groaned her pleasure. Lifted her hips, sought to bring him deeper still.

And then there was no more waiting or teasing, he could do nothing but thrust into her, pound against her, while caressing her breast with one hand and kissing her lips, sucking her tongue into his mouth.

Her inner muscles seized around his shaft, tightening so hard, it was like being held in a hot hard fist. His vision filled with white light and he exploded into darkness as he felt her shudder with the force of her own climax. His body pulsed his seed into hers.

Only when the shattering ceased and the pieces of him came back together did he realise that he had not withdrawn from her body as he had intended.

Damn it all. Not for years had he made such a foolish mistake.

Wrapped in Avery's arms, Carrie had never felt quite so…treasured. It was more than the lovely sated feeling after their lovemaking. It was a feeling of belonging. As if she had found her true home. She snuggled closer and he tightened his arm around her, stroking her back. She cracked an eyelid and peered at his face. He was still asleep. The caress had been instinctual, rather than deliberate, and that pleased her more than it probably should.

The man certainly knew how to make a woman feel precious, even in his sleep.

The haze of pleasure slowly drifted away and she put her thoughts in order, instead of letting her heart rule her head. Yes, the lovemaking was amazing, but tonight was their last night together. It had to be. The longer he remained as her lover, the harder it was going to be to let him go.

There was no future for them. He was a reprobate, a charming one, but a reprobate none the less. He made his living as a ladies' escort and, worse yet in her eyes, by gambling.

Besides, while her sisters-in-law would happily close their eyes to a love affair, as they had all agreed that they would, that was all it could ever be. They had agreed to stick together, to help each other through thick and thin. None of them was ever going to marry again. As wonderful as this was with Avery she could not see herself being a man's permanent mistress. She only had to imagine how horrified her father would be, were he alive, to have guilt and shame making her go hot and cold by turns.

No. This would definitely not continue after tonight.

Avery rolled over on to his back and put his arm over his eyes. She raised up on her elbow. 'Are you awake?'

He sat up, his bare torso reminding her again just how young and virile he was. He placed his elbows on his bent knees and scrubbed his hands through his hair.

She frowned. He seemed…unhappy about something. The wonderful warmth she'd been feeling, even though it had been tinged with loss, dissipated and left her feeling cold. 'What is it?'

'I fear I got a bit carried away,' he said. He rubbed at the back of his neck. 'I didn't take proper precautions.'

What?

'I could have got you with child.' He looked at her, his face thoughtful. 'When did you say your husband died?'

Oh. He was worried about her having a baby. Oh my word, that would certainly complicate matters. 'Over a year ago. Surely it isn't possible? Not so quickly.' Everyone said it was not. Couples often tried for many years before the wife fell for a child.

'Anything is possible.' He sounded rather off-hand. 'We can hope not, I suppose. But I will do right by you, Carrie, should we be unlucky.'

Oh, dear, he was not happy about the idea at all.

There was a scuffling sound outside the door.

Avery's head came up. With a sudden premonition, Carrie clutched the sheets to her chest. Had she locked her door after—?

The door slammed open. Westram stood framed in the doorway staring into the room. His gaze found the bed. His expression went from angry to furious.

'Well, madam?' he snapped.

Avery glanced at her, eyes wide. His surprised expression disappeared in an instant and was replaced by dawning understanding and then a bored smile as he turned his attention to Westram. 'Someone you know, Carrie?' he drawled.

'I am her brother-in-law, sir. Westram,' the Earl said, his voice full of menace.

'Lord Avery Gilmore, Second son of Belmane at your service,' Avery replied.

Carrie had never heard him sound so regal.

He spoiled the effect by flashing an insolent smile. 'You will forgive me if I do not get up?'

Was he trying to make Westram more annoyed than he was already?

But Westram's demeanour changed in an instant. He looked—pleased. 'I see.'

What? 'Why are you here, Westram?' Carrie asked.

'I received a letter from an interested party about what was called your goings on.' Westram looked down his nose. 'You said nothing to me about opening a shop, Carrie Greystoke. But that is only part of it, isn't it?' He glared at Avery. 'If you don't care for your own reputation, you could give some thought to those of my sisters.'

Avery made a sound like a growl.

Westram glared at him. 'And as for you, sir, what are your intentions towards my sister-in-law?'

Beside her, Avery shifted uneasily.

Oh, no. Westram was not going to do this. 'How dare you, Westram?' Carrie cried. 'What I do is none of your business. I am an independent—'

'You live under my roof, madam. I feed you and clothe you and you are my brother's widow. Therefore you are my responsibility. If I had gleaned any idea you planned to drag my sisters down to the level of—'

'Enough, sir,' Avery thundered. 'Mrs Greystoke has done me the honour of agreeing to become my wife and if you say one more disparaging word about her, I shall be forced to thrust them down your throat where they belong.'

Carrie froze. At the words. At the fury in Avery's voice. At the longing filling her heart.

Westram's demeanour changed in a moment. 'Your wife, you say?'

'I do,' Avery bit out, putting a hand over hers to still her protest.

Westram scanned her living quarters and his lip curled. 'I hope you intend to keep her in better circumstances than this?'

'Now look here, Westram,' Carrie said. 'There is no need to ridicule what we have done here. Our shop—'

'We, madam?' Westram said. 'You turned my sisters into shopkeepers?' He shook his head. 'And I thought you were the sensible one.' His gaze returned to Avery and spoke harshly. 'You, sir, will be expected at my lodgings tomorrow morning to speak of the settlements. I assume eleven of the clock will suit you? In the meantime, allow me to use my carriage to deposit you at your lodgings, forthwith.'

'No need,' Avery said, equally tersely. 'I will walk.'

'Then I will see you off the premises.' Westram turned his gaze on Carrie and there was a coldness in his eyes Carrie had never seen there before. 'I will send my carriage round in the morning to return you, madam, to Kent. When you arrive, you may inform my sisters that I will be calling on them in a day or so. You may also inform them that you are to be married within the fortnight.' He smiled at Avery. 'I assume that will suit, Lord Avery.'

It was not a question.

Avery inclined his head.

'Very well. I will wait outside for you, my lord.' He turned and stalked out.

As he left, Carrie got a glimpse of Mr Thrumby hopping from foot to foot. She buried her face in her hands. 'Everything is ruined.'

She should never have let herself be entranced by

Avery. Never let the desires of her heart overcome the sense of her mind. Her sisters-in-law were going to be so unhappy at this outcome.

The moment the door closed, Avery shot out of bed and, grim-faced, began dressing. Despite everything, she could not stop admiring his lean narrow flanks and firm buttocks or the breadth of his shoulders, or the feeling of disappointment when all that glorious male disappeared beneath his clothes.

'Avery,' she said her voice catching, 'I am so sorry.'

He left off buttoning his falls to give her a hard smile. 'Never mind. We shall manage, my dear.'

She didn't want to manage. 'Surely you don't intend to go through with this plan of Westram's? Let me talk to him in the morning. I am sure I can smooth things over.'

He shot her a look of such incredulity, she recoiled. 'Are you sure this is not exactly what you wanted?' he asked.

'I—I beg your pardon?'

He let go a breath. 'Never mind.' He shrugged into his coat and picked up his hat.

'I do mind.'

'Let it go, Carrie. We will discuss this some other time, when Westram isn't pacing the hallway outside the door. It isn't the first time I have been thrown out of somewhere and I'll wager it likely it won't be the last.' His chuckle sounded hollow. 'Care to bet on the odds?'

Carrie froze. Here they were in the direst of circumstances and he was making one of his awful bets. Exactly the sort of bet her husband had made before departing for the Peninsula.

'I don't care to bet,' she said stiffly.

'Good thing, too. You would lose.'

He walked out of the door and closed it behind him.

Carrie leaped out of bed and turned the key. She gazed around her, seeking some sort of divine inspiration. The only thing that occurred to her was that she had messed it all up. Dash it all. The shop she might have been able to explain to Westram, but Avery had added a whole level of complication she could not explain away. If only… If only she hadn't been so curious.

It was all Jonathan's fault. If he had done his husbandly duty… *Argh*. She could not place the blame anywhere else. It was her fault. She had ruined everything.

Westram was right, she was not good enough to remain with his sisters. And what was she to do about Avery and his talk of marriage? She didn't want another marriage of convenience. Another man forced to the altar.

Her heart squeezed in longing. Her throat felt as if she had swallowed something large and dry. The backs of her eyes burned.

Oh, no. She was not going to cry over something she never intended and had no wish for. No wish at all.

Tomorrow she would have to find a way to sort out this whole blasted mess. Hopefully Westram's temper would have cooled somewhat and Avery could be brought to see sense.

Avery, at his lodgings and still in his dressing gown the next morning, gazed into the maelstrom within his cup as he stirred his tea. Engaged to be married, by God. There was absolutely no way around it. Carrie had been wrong when she said Westram took no interest in what his sisters did. He also should have known better than to believe it. Perhaps it had been wishful thinking on his part, damn it. Not that there was anything Westram could do to him if he did not come up to scratch. His reputation was already as black as it could be and he had not a penny to his name.

He should have stuck to his principles. Never got involved with a single lady. And if for one moment he thought Carrie had actually engineered that scene last night, if he for one moment thought that she had either written to Westram or had her landlord do it, he'd be on the next boat travelling to India, or China. But upon reflection, he realised Carrie was incapable of such deceit and felt awful for having suggested as much. No. It wouldn't be Carrie. She wasn't like that. It had to be the Duke. And while he wasn't quite sure what the old man might be trying to achieve, Avery should have expected something of the sort after his conversation with Bart and taken the necessary precautions.

But Westram insisting on marriage was likely not the outcome the Duke hoped for, surely? More likely he'd be hoping Westram would set Avery to the right about. Papa certainly wouldn't want him marrying the daughter of a merchant. Would he? Perhaps he didn't know Carrie's exact circumstances.

But despite what Avery had said to Carrie the previous evening, when his temper had been high, he wasn't even all that displeased about Westram's demand. He hadn't wanted to say goodbye to her after their lovemaking last night. He wasn't ready to bid her farewell. And Westram wasn't wrong to sneer at the way she was living in that little shop. She deserved so much more.

His gut tightened. And just how was *he* going to provide more?

He closed his eyes and leaned back. He'd have to play for higher stakes, which increased the risk of higher losses. With luck, John would soon start earning enough to support his family so Avery could leave Laura to him. Avery certainly wouldn't be playing escort to anyone else's wife. He hadn't done so since meeting Carrie and he could not see himself ever doing so again. And while he had no problem with his wife being a shopkeeper, a husband should be the breadwinner.

A scratch at his door brought him upright. Had Bart heard the news? It wouldn't surprise him. His brother had an amazing network of suppliers of intelligence. It was the only way he managed to keep the Duke from committing some new folly.

'Come.'

The door opened and Carrie stepped in. 'Lord Avery, I have come to thank you for your kind proposal, but I am afraid I cannot accept.'

Shooting to his feet, he stared at her blankly. As the words made sense, a sharp pain pierced his heart. 'Why?' It was the only thing he could think of to say. His mind went back to that day when he'd been twenty-two and still green about the gills and another lady had said almost the same thing to him. Had Father bought this one off, too? But then why bring Westram into it at all? None of this made any sense. He was missing something.

Carrie lifted her chin. 'I do not think we should suit. You never wanted to be married and nor did I. I value my independence.

Last night, Westram had indicated he had no intention of allowing her to maintain that independence. Had something changed? He gestured to the chair on the opposite side of the little table. 'Please, sit down. Have you breakfasted? Would you like tea?'

'I—' She gazed longingly at the toast rack.

'Help yourself.' He went to the cupboard beside the hearth and brought back a fresh cup and saucer. He sat down and proceeded to pour tea while she buttered a slice of toast. 'I don't have any jam, I am afraid.' It was a luxury he could do without.

She nibbled at the toast, then put it down on the plate and clasped her hands in her lap. 'I came early so I could catch you before you went to your appointment with Westram.'

There were shadows around her eyes. She'd clearly spent a sleepless night worrying. Dash it all. 'Carrie, I told Westram we were affianced. There is no way I could in all honour go back on my word now.'

She drew in a deep breath. 'I did not give my word.'

'You did not deny it.'

When she opened her mouth to object, he shook his head. 'Think about it. Would it be so very bad?'

She glanced around his lodgings. 'I don't think I can keep the business going. Thrumby was most distressed when he came to see me this morning. He said if he had known Westram had not approved of the venture he would never have allowed me to rent the shop. And besides, Westram will not allow Marguerite and Petra to have anything to do with it any longer and so, without any more hats to sell, it must close.'

'Quite honestly, I am not surprised that Westram would put a stop to it. But that is no reason for us not to marry.'

She frowned. 'How would we manage?' Her frown deepened. 'On your gambling?'

He shrugged. 'What else?'

She nodded slowly, frowning at the toast. Finally, she pushed the plate away, her grey eyes lifting to focus on his face, thoughts, like shadows, swirling beneath the calm surface. 'We were both very clear at the start of this adventure that neither of us wanted to marry. Nothing has changed.'

He wanted to howl with frustration. Bang his fist on the table. He took a deep breath. 'Nothing? A great deal has changed. Do you think Westram will not insist on this marriage? If I renege, do you think he won't ask for satisfaction?'

She looked shocked.

Hah. Got her. A feeling of triumph filled him. She was right, he had not wanted to get married when they first met. But that was then and now things were different. Warmth spread through his veins at the idea of Carrie as his wife. He was definitely fond of her. And she seemed fond of him. Perhaps it was love, of a sort. Perhaps love did exist?

She gave a little jerk of her chin. 'Do you think your father will be happy at you marrying a cit, as you nobles call us?'

Blast it, he really wasn't sure if the old man was behind this turn of events or if he would be opposed to it. 'It is none of the Duke's business what I do and I neither know nor care what he thinks.'

She narrowed her gaze and took a deep breath. 'All right, let me stop beating around the bush and get down to brass tacks. I am not going to be forced into marrying anyone, not by Westram or anyone else.'

Forced? He felt as if he had been stabbed through the heart. The pain left him speechless.

Her chin came up and she looked him straight in the eye. There was a glassiness about her gaze that looked suspiciously like tears. 'I will not marry you, Avery, and

I wanted you to know this, because that is what I intend to tell Lord Westram before you call on him at eleven o'clock and I will ensure that he listens.' She rose to her feet and headed for the door.

'Carrie,' he said, giving her a smile that ought to soften her anger. 'Be reasonable.'

'I am being reasonable. Reasonable and sensible. Please, get this through your head. Our little fling was wonderful, but it is now at an end and we are not getting married.' She strode out.

He started after her, but he could hardly chase after her through St James's in his dressing gown. He rubbed at the growth of beard on his chin. And he could hardly turn up on the Earl's doorstep in disarray if he wanted to make a good impression.

His gut dipped. Nor could he force Carrie to wed him if she didn't want to.

He actually had the strange feeling she was trying to give him a way out of the whole mess. Instead of feeling pleased, or grateful or relieved, for the second time in his life he felt desperately hurt.

Only this time, he wasn't going to run away the way he had after what happened with Alexandra. This time he was going to fight for the woman he loved.

Loved?

Dammit all. He did love her.

And he did not believe she cared nothing for him, not after last night. Apparently, he was going to have to find a way to convince her of his love and to woo her into loving him back.

Oh, no, Carrie Greystoke, this was definitely not the end of their affair. Not if he could help it.

Chapter Fourteen

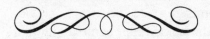

Only an idiot would be tempted to marry a man like Lord Avery.

And Carrie counted herself an idiot. She stopped a few yards from Westram's hotel and dried her tears with her handkerchief, then blew her nose.

She took a deep breath. She was not going to allow Westram to force Avery into marriage. He had forced her first husband up to the mark, she certainly would not allow him to do the same thing to Avery. If she had known more about Jonathan, she would never have agreed to his proposal.

Although with the pressure from her father to accept after Jonathan had offered for her—well, it was no use going over old ground…it was the present she had to deal with. She had her sisters-in-law to think of now, too. They had agreed to stick together. To renounce the married state and help each other. The idea had been to take a lover should the opportunity present itself, not end up in church marrying the man.

So what if Avery had stolen her heart? It was the sort of thing men like him did. He made a living by making foolish women fall for his charm. And foolish men, too.

At the gambling tables. Unlike the situation with Jonathan, whom she knew little about before they married, she *did* know all about Avery. Even if Westram wasn't pressing him to marry her, she could not be with a man who loved the thrill of a wager.

What if he promised to give up his gambling? The strength of that hope took her aback. Oh, she really did need her head examined if she thought he would keep such a promise.

When the next wager came along that offered the chance of easy coin, he'd be off risking his life by swimming across the Thames or climbing a steeple. That was the sort of thing her first husband had done she had learned after his death. People had spoken of his exploits with awe and fondness. It had made her so very angry.

She certainly wasn't going to sit at home waiting for the news of Avery's death in some misadventure. She simply could not do it.

Her mind kept running in circles. Tossing up what ifs and maybes until she could not think at all. This was so unlike her. But oh, she did so wish things could be different. They couldn't. And even if Avery gave up gambling and wagering on ridiculous outcomes, she would not marry a man who had to be forced to the altar for the sake of his honour.

What had that gypsy fortune teller said, something about the head ruling over the heart if she wanted true happiness? Then that was her answer. Logic and reason, not sentiment.

She strode into the hotel without hesitation. She knew exactly how to go on. She had visited merchants who had come to Nottingham on business with her father. In those days, her father had been a force to be reckoned with among the merchants and no one had taken any notice of him bringing his daughter along.

Here, the porter looked at her askance.

Well, he would. Young women did not usually call on gentlemen unescorted. Blast, she should have thought of that and brought Tansy with her, but she needed her to mind the shop. 'I am here to visit my brother-in-law,' she said firmly. 'Lord Westram.'

The man's eyes widened. 'What name shall I give, ma'am?' His expression was polite enough, but his eyes held doubt.

'Mrs Greystoke.'

He wrote a note and gave it to a lad in livery standing at attention near his desk. 'If you would take a seat for a moment or two…' he suggested.

She nodded and perched on one of the chairs scattered around the lobby. She chose one with a good view of the stairs.

A few moments later, Westram ran down them, looking harassed and flustered. He had a brief word with the porter before coming to her side. 'There is a private parlour we can use.' He took her arm and escorted her up to the second floor. The windows of the small room looked out over the Strand where not long ago she had gone to visit an elephant.

'What are you doing here, Carrie?' he asked once they were seated.

'I have no intention of marrying Lord Avery, so it is absolutely pointless you meeting with him this morning.'

He reared back. 'So the blackguard got you to do his dirty work for him, did he? Well, it won't wash. I will not allow such an insult to my family name to stand—'

'Enough.' She inhaled a deep breath and calmed herself. 'Please, Westram. Believe me when I say the blame is mine. I approached him. I am sorry if you are disappointed in my behaviour. I certainly did not intend to cause you any anxiety. I can assure you nothing like this will ever happen again, but I am not marrying Lord Avery.'

She could hardly be any plainer.

'*You* approached *him*?'

Dash it, why was he focusing on that part of her apology? 'I am a widow, Westram. I assume that has not escaped your attention? He came to my shop with another lady and I found myself charmed.' She launched into the other thing she had hoped she would not have to say, but now felt obliged to offer. 'If you are concerned about *my* lack of decorum somehow tainting the reputation of your sisters, I will leave Kent immediately and break off all contact with them.'

Westram stared at her. 'I must say I am surprised at you,' he said his voice gruff. 'I thought you were the most sensible of the three of you.'

At the sight of the pain in his expression, she felt bitterly ashamed that she had let him down.

He reached out and patted her hand. 'I wish you had talked to me first. That sort of fellow, well, charm, it's his stock in trade,' he said heavily. 'But then I should have realised you weren't as up to snuff as you seem.'

She wasn't sure if he was insulting her or being kind, he spoke so gently. Why would he be kind? 'No doubt you think because I am of common stock, I do not know how to go on.' She ungritted her teeth and forced a smile. 'As I understand it, as a widow I am permitted some licence to pursue my own interests.'

He stiffened. 'I believe I made myself clear that you

were all to look for husbands,' he snapped. 'Lord Avery is a well-known philanderer. You cannot believe how many people couldn't wait to tell me my widowed sister-in-law had taken up with the *ton*'s most idle rake. And if you think I am happy about the idea of having to hand over blunt in settlements to that fellow who will likely just gamble it all away in a single sitting just as my—' He ran a hand through his hair and closed his eyes briefly.

'As your brother did,' she finished his sentence. 'Which is why I will not marry him, despite his kind offer.'

Westram sagged back in his chair. 'This is all my fault. I should have insisted you all came with me to live at Castings.'

Worry and sorrow filled his normally austere expression.

'You have had the care of your family for a very long time, Westram. You did your best to protect your sisters and now me. I honestly regret causing you this worry. To be honest, I made a mistake in marrying your brother. I had no idea he was wedding me in order to pay off his gambling debts, leaving nothing for my future should he die. I should have been told beforehand.'

He opened his mouth to speak.

She put up a hand. 'The past is the past. It need never be spoken of again, but I hope you will not insist I marry another ne'er-do-well.' Inwardly she winced, for she did not really think Avery anywhere near as bad as Greystoke, but it seemed strategic to use Westram's overdeveloped sense of responsibility against him in this particular instance.

'Devil take it, Carrie,' he said on a sigh. 'All right. If you are really opposed to the match, then I will get rid of the fellow. I'll pay him off.'

'No need,' she said, feeling very sad inside, hollow and achy. 'I have been to see him. He will not call.'

'You went to see him?'

She nodded.

'Alone at his lodgings? Are you mad?'

'No one saw me.'

'Someone will have seen you,' he said heavily. He straightened his shoulders. 'Well, I'll just have to do my best to scotch any rumours that arise.'

'Why not return to Gloucestershire as if nothing had happened. I shall not be seeing Lord Avery again and everything will die down soon enough.' The same way the drama over the deaths of Westram's brother and brothers-in-law had died down. 'By next Season it will all have been forgotten.'

Westram gave her a sharp look. 'You are a very intelligent woman, Carrie. It is a pity you were not as perceptive when it came to being charmed by a blackguard like Lord Avery.' He waved a hand. 'Never mind. I agree with your suggestion. But this shop thing must stop.'

She pressed her lips together, trying to marshal her arguments. 'I do not—'

'If you want me to forget about this affair with Lord Avery, then this is my price.'

Damn him, he was not at all a stupid man. She and his sisters would have to find another way to earn an income. That was if the other two would even welcome her back into their fold. She inclined her head. 'As you wish.'

He nodded sharply. 'It is what I wish. I will send round a note to Thrumby, asking him to send me his outstanding bills.'

She drew herself up straight. 'You need not do so. Mr Thrumby's bill is paid in full.'

His jaw dropped. 'You mean you actually made enough to pay your rent?'

'We made a healthy profit. Which is why you should let us continue with the endeavour.'

He shook his head. 'I cannot have it said that my sisters have gone into trade.'

Heat scalded her face.

He had the grace to look chagrined. 'I apologise. There is nothing wrong with being in trade, per se. It is simply that if my sisters are to marry again, they will need to see that their reputations are spotless. It is the way of the world, Carrie. There is nothing I can do about it.'

He was a good brother and he cared about his sisters. She could not fault him for that, much as she resented his high-handed interference. But then that was really her fault, wasn't it? If she had stuck to selling bonnets, instead of getting involved with Lord Avery, they would not be having this conversation.

But without Lord Avery, their little enterprise would not have been nearly so successful.

Oh, dear. What a pickle it all was to be sure. But there was clearly no gainsaying Westram on the matter. He was determined to have his way and she had given him all the ammunition he needed to shoot down their plans. 'I will need one day to close up the shop and dispose of the stock.'

His sisters were going to be so disappointed. The thought made her heart sink even further.

Westram nodded. 'I'll send my carriage around first thing in the morning.'

'Westram has no right to interfere in our business,' Petra said, pacing to the drawing-room window and back. 'We should simply ignore him and continue on as planned.'

Carrie, who had arrived the previous evening to deliver her news, could not remember seeing her sister-in-law so agitated. 'We cannot. Mr Thrumby will not allow us to keep the shop without Westram's approval. I do not think your brother will change his mind, do you?'

'He tends to be one of the more stubborn sort,' Marguerite said. 'My concern is all the women we employed to help us. We will have to find a way to pay them.'

At least she had a bit of good news on that front. 'This past week was surprisingly successful. We had almost no hats left and the nightgowns were exceedingly profitable as the ladies paid top prices for the few that were left. There is definitely enough to pay for their work. There will be little left over for us, though.'

Not enough for them to show Westram they could manage for themselves and did not need his support.

'And what are we to do with all the bonnets and nightgowns they made in the meantime? There has to be something we can do.'

'I suppose we can give them to charity,' Marguerite said. 'I must say I did not expect Westram to take a pet over an affair with a gentleman.' She turned her gaze on Carrie. 'Surely you were not terribly indiscreet?'

Carrie shrank inside. 'We were not exactly circumspect. The idea was to bring customers to the shop.'

'While I can quite understand why the son of a duke would be interested in you, Carrie, I don't understand why he would involve himself in helping our business.'

Startled, Carrie stared at her. 'I believe you have it the wrong way around. His interest was primarily in our commerce. It is how he earns his living.' That and gambling. 'He is cast out by his father.'

'Then he must have done something dreadful,' Marguerite said. 'And you are better off not associating with him.'

So Carrie had told herself repeatedly. Telling herself and believing it were two very different things, though.

Petra's face grew thoughtful. 'He is need of funds, then?'

'He is. He has arrangements with several shops in town. If the ladies he brings to them buy their wares, he receives a commission.'

'Ladies?' Marguerite said sharply.

Carrie ignored the stab of pain in her heart and the realisation dawning on her sister-in-law's face. The look of pity.

Petra came back to the sofa and perched beside Carrie, looking at her intently. 'I have an idea.'

'Someone needs to have an idea,' Marguerite said on a sigh.

'You said he offered for you,' Petra went on. 'Marry him. Then Westram can have nothing to say about the shop.'

Carrie gasped. Her heart stilled. Her stomach fell away. Longing filled her. She shoved it away. 'Marry him? Certainly not.' She hoped she sounded convincing, because the fluttering in her stomach was internally giving her the lie.

Petra made a dismissive gesture. 'You must like the fellow. And it will simply be a business arrangement. We will have to include him in the partnership, of course. But we cannot let our business go, when it is just beginning to be successful.'

'No!' Carrie exclaimed. 'We agreed we all wanted our independence from husbands. That we would stick together in this matter.'

Marguerite nodded, giving her sister a frown.

'Besides,' Carrie continued, 'while Lord Avery is everything that is charming, he has an unsteadiness of character that I cannot like. And,' she added for good measure, 'I would never marry again out of convenience.'

'Oh, pooh!' Petra said indelicately. 'You cannot mean to say you expect to find true love a second time? If indeed you found it the first time.'

The hurt in her voice was hard to hear. But it was more than that, a sort of disillusionment.

'Enough, Petra,' Marguerite said, clearly noticing nothing amiss, which made Carrie think perhaps she was imagining something that wasn't there.

'We agreed when we set up house that *none* of us wished to marry again,' Marguerite said. 'Marriage is nothing but a disappointment. This independence of ours was supposed to relieve us of the necessity of relying on men.'

While Marguerite never spoke of her husband, she was certainly the one who had been the most vocal of the three of them about never wanting to marry again. Setting up house here in the country had been her idea. Carrie had really let her down. 'I am so sorry.'

'It is not your fault,' Marguerite said.

'No,' Petra said, her blue eyes flashing. 'It is Westram's and we are left still relying on his support.'

'That is different,' Marguerite snapped.

'I don't see how?' Petra said. 'And if Carrie was married, then she could act as our chaperon and we would never have to be answerable to Westram for anything again.'

Unfortunately, Petra was right. But she was not the one being asked to marry a man who had been forced up to the mark.

'I am sorry,' Carrie said. 'Truly I am. But I cannot marry Lord Avery. Not after—' Her voice broke.

Petra drew in a breath, her eyes wide, and full of sympathy. 'Oh, I am sorry, too, Carrie. I did not mean to hurt you. I know you loved Jonathan, but I thought if you had taken a lover, you were ready to move on. I did not mean to be unfeeling. And besides, you are right, we did agree we would stick together no matter what. Please, forget I so much as mentioned it.'

Argh. Now she felt like a complete fraud. She should have scotched their romantic notions at the very beginning, but she had felt like such a fool when they had both appeared so happy in their marriages.

'It was a fling, nothing more.' The words hurt dreadfully. 'Neither of us wishes to marry and I won't have him forced into it.'

Petra sagged back against the chair cushions. 'Since Westram won't entertain our names being associated with at shop, mayhap we can find someone to run the shop while we are silent partners. Westram never said anything about not making hats, did he? His objection is purely about trade, I believe. What about the young woman you hired to help you, Carrie? Do you think she could manage it alone?'

Carrie winced. Tansy had been devastated to learn she had lost her position. Carrie had convinced Mrs Thrumby to take her on as a chambermaid.

Marguerite put up a hand and shook her head. 'No.

We are not going behind Westram's back again. We have to find something less objectionable.'

Carrie felt her shoulders stiffen.

Marguerite looked conscience-stricken. She put her arm around Carrie's shoulder. 'Oh, my dear, I did not mean that the way it sounded. It is not me who finds trade objectionable. It is Westram and he is being an ass. But he is doing his best according to his lights, that is all. And sneaking around behind his back again will be just the ammunition he needs to insist we return to living under his roof.'

'Oh, Lord,' Petra said. 'I never thought of that. It is the last thing we want.'

Carrie hugged Marguerite back. 'I just wish I had more to offer. My portion is so small it hardly helps at all.'

'Having you here with us is enough,' the older girl said. 'Never fear, we will think of some way out of this conundrum.'

An idea occurred to Carrie. 'Perhaps Lord Avery would buy the business. We could put him in touch with the ladies who have been making the hats and the nightgowns. They would be glad to work for him, I am sure. And we would be solvent for a time.'

'Oh, bravo,' Marguerite said. 'If that were possible, it would give us some breathing room to find another way to support ourselves.'

Chapter Fifteen

Carrie tossed the third sheet of paper into the fire in the drawing room. Her sisters had gone about their own chores and left her to it. The note to Thrumby had been easy. She hadn't given him any details—she couldn't until she had Avery's answer—but simply requested that he not rent out the shop to anyone else until she'd had a chance to sell the business to someone who would need the premises.

After almost a week, he had replied in the affirmative.

The letter she now had to write to Avery was proving much harder. She'd been pretty scathing in their last meeting. And while she didn't mind humbling her pride for the sake of her sisters-in-law, she was worried that she'd be tempted to throw herself at his feet and beg him to make his proposal again—if he would still have her. And that would never do, despite that her stupid heart kept telling her she was making a terrible mistake by letting him go. Her head was very sure she was doing the right thing.

Trusting your head will ensure your safety, I confess.
Trusting your heart is taking a chance when.
Only one path leads to true happiness.

Doing the right thing should not make one feel so miserable. Should it?

Besides, though she had agreed to write this letter, Avery had made it quite clear he intended to continue with his travels and his gambling at some time in the future. He had never intended anything more than a short-lived affair and nor had she. The more she had thought about it, the more she kept thinking she had got her sisters-in-law's hopes up for nothing.

She swallowed the lump in her throat.

The door opened and the maidservant gave her a beaming smile. 'Lord Avery to see you, mum,' she announced and gestured him in.

The breath caught in Carrie's throat. It couldn't be. But it was.

Somehow, she had forgotten how handsome he was. All she could do was stare at him as if he was a vision.

He bowed. 'Mrs Greystoke. How glad I am to have found you in.'

Where else would she be? And what on earth was he doing here? She glanced down at her letter. Writing to him was one thing. Greeting him in person was another altogether. Her tongue felt awkward. Her mouth dry. She gestured to a chair. 'Won't you sit down?' The words were little more than a breathless whisper.

'Thank you.' He took a straight back chair near the hearth. She sat on the sofa a little distance away.

Marguerite bustled in, followed by Petra. 'Lord Avery, how delightful of you to call.'

A shadow passed across his face, but he rose to *his* feet and gave the two ladies an easy smile.

Carrie made the introductions. Petra joined Carrie on the sofa, while Marguerite sat close to Avery. Too close.

'I believe Lord Avery came to have private words with me,' Carrie said pointedly.

Marguerite cocked an eyebrow. 'Indeed. That is hardly proper.'

What sort of game was she playing? Had her sister-in-law changed her mind about asking him to take over the shop for them? Carrie felt all at sea. Indeed, she felt rather unwell. Thinking about Avery was bad enough, but seeing him here in the flesh was almost more than she could bear.

'Did you have a good drive down from town?' Petra asked.

He inclined his head. 'I rode. It was very pleasant.'

'You are lucky it did not rain,' Marguerite said. 'The weather has been exceedingly inclement recently.'

'I was indeed fortunate,' he said, smiling. 'It seems my luck is holding.'

Luck. What was he saying? Fortune smiled on the brave? Hardly. Who could have been braver than her husband and his two companions if reports of the battle were to be believed? And look what had happened to them. Believing in luck was no way to live. So why had he come?

'I hope the stables were able to accommodate your horse?' Marguerite went on. 'We rarely have visitors.'

'They were most accommodating. Thank you.' His smile was so charming both of her sisters beamed back at him. Of course they would. All the ladies fell at his feet. She wanted to bash them both over the head. She wanted to flee.

'Excellent. You will stay for dinner, of course,' Marguerite said calmly. 'I have asked the housekeeper to prepare a room for you, where you may refresh yourself.'

Carrie stared at her, mouth agape.

Avery also looked bemused, but he recovered in an instant. 'That is most kind of you, my lady.' He glanced at Carrie as if seeking her agreement. 'I would not wish to impose, however?'

What could she say? It was getting late. He would never make it back to London before dark and there wasn't an inn for miles. Not a decent one, anyway.

'It is no trouble at all,' she said, but her tone was a little terse and he grimaced.

She had not meant to sound unwelcoming. Indeed, her heart was thumping so loudly at the very sight of him, she was sure he must hear it. But having made up her mind to never see him again, having him here, under the same roof, was just too unsettling. The longings she was sure she had under control were now struggling to the fore, doing battle with all the good reasons she had lined up to defend her decision to refuse his offer of marriage.

'Naturally, it is no trouble,' Marguerite said. 'If you would care to follow me, I will take you to our house-keeper who will show you up. We keep country hours here and dinner will be ready in an hour.'

Again, Avery glanced her way, as if seeking guidance, but she gave a little hitch of her shoulders. Clearly Marguerite had something in mind and, until Carrie knew what it was, there was nothing she could say.

Perhaps she intended to tackle him herself about their idea. Indeed, it might be the best way to get him to agree. A man who was well fed and content was more likely to be accommodating.

She just wished she knew what his intentions were in coming here. Surely he did not intend to pursue his suit? She didn't think she could bear it.

* * *

Despite Carrie's obvious discomfort in his presence and monosyllabic answers to his questions, Avery found himself glad he had come. Her sisters-in-law were lovely women and thoroughly charming. How could their husbands had gone off to war and left them to fend for themselves? Idiots.

Likely that was why Carrie seemed so averse to marriage. Well, she needn't worry. He would never abandon her, if that was her fear. He would make her understand this. Somehow.

If only he could get a few minutes alone with her.

He had talked to Laura and John before leaving to come here. John's clientele had picked up remarkably over the past couple of weeks and he had been very clear he and Laura no longer needed anyone's financial help. John had also given Avery a bit of a bear-garden jaw about finding sensible employment and settling down.

You would think the man was a saint instead of the cheeky blighter who had run off with a duke's daughter. Still, Avery was pleased to see his sister so happy and his brother-in-law finally finding his feet, leaving Avery free of the financial burden of his sister.

'Would you like another helping of compote, Lord Avery?' Petra asked.

He leaned back in his chair. 'No, thank you. I could not eat another bite. Your chef has excelled himself.'

'Oh, we don't have a chef,' Marguerite replied.

'Then you have an excellent cook.'

The woman seemed to swell with pride. Good. He needed these women on his side. 'And may I say that the hats you ladies produced for your shop were amongst the most well made and creative any of the ladies of the *ton* have seen for a long time.'

Marguerite beamed.

'Lady Marguerite designed them,' Carrie said. 'She has a great deal of talent in that regard.'

'It is a great deal too bad her talent is to be wasted,' Petra added.

'Westram is determined the shop is to be closed, then?' Avery asked.

'He is determined that none of his sisters shall become shopkeepers.' Carrie was looking at him oddly. She glanced around the table. 'I suppose now is as good as any time to put our proposition to you.'

The other two ladies nodded their agreement.

Avery straightened. Another proposition? His body heated, remembering her earlier proposition. The one he'd initially turned down. But this could not possibly be that sort of proposition, this was something else entirely. He forced his mind to focus.

Carrie blushed and hung her head as if she'd guessed his thoughts and was ashamed.

Dash it, that was not what he wanted at all.

'Tell me,' he urged.

She straightened her shoulders as if bracing for a rejection. 'We wanted to offer you the chance to buy the shop and the millinery business.'

She wanted him to become a shopkeeper.

Why was he surprised? She would likely see shopkeeping as infinitely preferable to his current modes of making a living. And it would provide the ladies with some additonal finances.

It would certainly infuriate both the Duke and Westram. Just for that reason alone he was tempted.

Carrie was watching him closely, as were her sisters-in-law.

Was there something here he was missing? He'd learned to study his hand closely before he made a wager. 'I need to think about it.'

Carrie looked disappointed, but Marguerite smiled sweetly. 'You can let us know your decision in the morning.'

He frowned. 'Why the rush?'

'We employed women in the village to make more hats and nightgowns because we were not able to keep up with the demand by ourselves,' Lady Petra said. 'We have paid them for their work, but they are relying on the future income. We have to inform them one way or the other.'

'I see.' If he did this, he would have to come down to Kent all the time and would likely see Carrie, too. See her and be kept at arm's length, the way she was keeping her distance now. No, he would not be able to live with that.

He needed her answer to his proposal, if he could ever get her alone. Unfortunately, he had a feeling he already knew what her answer would be. She had not been pleased to see him. Not one little bit. He would simply have to change her mind.

'If you do not wish to buy the business,' Carrie said, tightly, 'perhaps you might know of someone who will.'

That did not bode well. Something in Avery's chest gave an unpleasant squeeze.

'Carrie,' Marguerite interjected. 'It is perfectly reasonable for Lord Avery to request a little time to think about our offer.'

She nodded, but her jaw hardened. 'Very well.'

Had he been wrong about her having deeper feelings for him?

Damn it all. Why was he surprised at her indifference? Or hurt? She had been quite clear that she wanted to use him right from the very beginning and the only reason she was entertaining his presence now was because he could be of further use.

The pain of that knowledge went far deeper than he would have expected. Could he really feel that strongly about a woman who wanted nothing to do with him? It seemed so. And yet he couldn't really blame her. He was a man who lived by his wits. Did she think he could not provide for her adequately? It was ironic, after he had been providing for Laura these many months.

'I will also try to think of who else might be interested,' he said, smiling despite the pain in his chest.

Lady Petra and Lady Marguerite exchanged glances.

'I think it is time for us to retire to the drawing room and leave you to your port,' Lady Marguerite said, rising.

'I think I would prefer to take tea with you in the drawing room, if you ladies would not object,' Avery said, standing. 'I plan on leaving early in the morning.'

And before then, he needed a private word with Carrie. No matter how much it hurt, he wanted to hear her answer when he laid all of his cards on the table.

Avery followed the ladies to the drawing room. At the door, Carrie hung back. 'If you don't mind, I will not join you. I seem to have a headache.'

She walked briskly away.

Oh, this was not going well at all.

Carrie paced up and down her bedroom. Why on earth had Marguerite put Avery in the chamber next to hers when there were two other guest rooms to choose from.

Once the maid had left, Carrie had been indulging in

a good cry as a way of saying goodbye to Avery—again. A painful never-ending endeavour, when the sound of men's voices had penetrated her wall. First Jeb, then Avery.

The words were indistinct, but since no doubt Jeb was there to ready him for bed, Avery must be undressing.

Her mind's eye imagined his coats coming off. Jeb hanging them over a chair, ready for him to take away and brush while Avery disposed himself on the sofa in that masculine sprawl she so adored. Now attired in his shirtsleeves, he looked deliciously informal.

Jeb knelt, removing Avery's boots and rolling off his stockings.

The manservant's voice rumbled again. 'Been a fine summer so far, my lord,' Carrie imagined him saying.

'It has indeed.' Avery's charming smile would be in full effect as he held out his wrists for Jeb to remove his cuff links. Avery lifted his chin and Jeb removed the ruby pin that had winked and glittered in the candle-light at dinner.

A light metallic tinkle made her think of the tray on the dressing table. No doubt Jeb placing the valuable items there.

Avery, meanwhile, unwound his cravat from around his throat and tossed it on top of the coats, white on black.

Avery's tenor now, quite distinct from Jeb's baritone. 'Have you always lived on the Westram property?' She imagined him saying in that polite charming way he had.

'I have, my lord,' Jeb replied. 'Born in a cottage not far from here.'

'It is a lovely corner of England.'

Jeb grinned, looking pleased. 'Ah, that it is.'

He reached out to help with the shirt buttons, but Avery waved him off with a genial smile. 'Unpack my valise, would you, there's a good chap. I've a couple of clean shirts in there.'

While Jeb emptied the valise, Avery pulled the shirt off over his head, revealing that mouthwateringly broad torso.

Carrie collapsed on the sofa, breathing fast at the image her mind was so vividly recalling. A pair of wide shoulders, a smattering of crisp dark hair and the heavily muscled arms of a horseman—or a swordsman.

His strong large hands went to the buttons of his falls. He paused, looking at her from beneath lowered lashes, tempting and teasing with his eyes.

Her breasts became full and heavy, the place between her thighs tingled and pulsed. Unable to help herself, she cupped one breast and her other hand drifted between her legs, gently circling, imitating the way he had touched her on their last night together. Heat rippled along her veins.

Her eyelids drooped, her body warmed, breaths became shallower, faster. She wanted…

The voices next door silenced. A door closed. Footsteps whispered along the corridor in the direction of the servants' stairs. Now alone, Avery lounged on the sofa in the glorious dressing gown he'd worn the day she went to his chambers looking relaxed, at ease yet as lithe as a cat.

She moaned softly, imagining kneeling beside him, untying the belt. Letting the robe fall open to reveal the strong column of his neck and the dark hollow at the base. The bones a sharp contrast to the smooth male skin displayed so openly.

She leaned forward to kiss that tender spot, feeling the warmth of his skin against her lips, his cheek resting lightly on the top of her head while he stroked her back.

Her lips cruised from his throat to his neck to the shell of his ear. He sighed with pleasure at her kisses. She stroked her hands over his chest, revelling in the heat of his skin against her palms, the rough texture of the hair, the tight little nipples beading beneath her touch, the way hers tightened now beneath her fingers.

She pulled the dressing gown down over his arms and he helped her take it off, leaving him naked to her view. His wide chest and narrow waist and jutting erection.

She collapsed back on to the sofa, her fingers delving into her core, stroking and circling and... A wave of gentle pleasure and heat rippled outwards, leaving her limp and panting and...disappointed.

She dragged herself out of her trance. Emptiness filled the space behind her ribs. How foolish to have thought that, in discovering what every wife should know, she would find some contentment with her lot as a widow. Instead, she had found only greater longing and deeper despair than ever she had felt at the loss of her husband.

His death had only left her feeling cheated and angry. This new loss made her feel sad. And alone.

She sat up, clenching her hands in her lap. This must never happen again. She had to stop her foolish imaginings about Avery. She had her sisters-in-law to think about now. They had made a pact to support each other in their bid for independence. They had agreed none of them wanted marriage. She would not go back on her word.

Certainly, Avery, no matter how much desire she felt

for him, was not the sort of man she would ever wish to marry. He spent his life taking risks at the card tables or on the throw of a dice or—she shuddered—on the ability of a man to swallow yet another sword.

With a man like him, a wife would spend her life expecting the bailiff at the door or, worse yet, discovering he'd died risking his life for some nonsensical wager.

She had to do what she'd promised herself she would do and put him out of her mind.

For ever.

She climbed up into bed and pulled the covers up under her chin. She would not think about Avery sleeping in the bedroom next door.

She definitely would not.

Chapter Sixteen

Finally, Avery was alone. He'd thought the lad assigned to assist him would never cease his chatter and go. At least Lady Marguerite had pointed out Carrie's chamber, so Avery didn't need to go prowling around trying to discover her whereabouts. He could have kissed the woman when she let that bit of information fall from her lips, though why she had done so, he was not exactly sure. If it was to trap him into making an offer to Carrie, she needn't have bothered. It was the first thing on his agenda.

And if she would not see him alone, then he was damn well going to do it with a house full of sisters and servants looking on. Because he wasn't leaving here until she agreed to their marriage. Or until she gave him a good reason as to why she would not. He poured a glass of the brandy someone had thoughtfully left on the dressing table and swallowed it down. He shrugged into his dressing gown, pulled the belt tight and squared his shoulders.

Now to accost the lioness in her den. Hopefully, she didn't have her door locked.

Having checked there was no one lurking in the corridor, he strode the few steps to Carrie's door. The handle turned easily and the door swung back at a push. He breathed a sigh. One hurdled crossed.

Once inside, he closed the door behind him. The air in here seemed warm and somehow sultry. Sensual enough to stir his blood. A slight whisper of air caught his attention. There. In the bed, half-hidden in shadows, propped up on her elbows. Carrie. Watching him. Yes, a lioness in her den. He could not help but recall her magnificent anger the last time they'd met when her voice came to him in a fierce whisper. 'What are you doing in here?'

Not the welcome he'd hoped for, certainly, but at least she wasn't screaming or running to the bell pull to summon a servant. He held up his hands in a gesture of surrender. 'I came to talk.'

She muttered something under her breath.

'I beg your pardon?' he asked, stepping further into the room.

'I said, how like you to take such a risk.'

He frowned. 'Don't tell me you have a pistol in your hand and were about to shoot me for a burglar.'

'All right, I won't.'

'Won't what?'

'Tell you—'

'Never mind that. Will you give me leave to talk to you?'

She heaved a sigh. 'I don't suppose you would leave were I to say no?'

He winced. Apparently, her mood was no better than it had been at dinner. He lit a candle from the banked fire in the hearth and moved nearer the foot of the bed. She blinked at the light.

She looked warm, deliciously flushed, almost as if… Could she have been…? A surge of hot blood made him lose focus. He reined in his lust. If she preferred to seek solace alone, that was her right.

But dammit all…

He stepped back. 'I beg your pardon. I assumed this might be a good way to catch you alone, since your sisters-in-law made it impossible downstairs. Perhaps you will grant me an audience tomorrow?'

She grimaced. 'Not like you to be so formal, my lord. Now you are here, I suppose it is as good a time as any other.'

She swept a glance over him. 'I hope Jeb made a satisfactory valet?'

Off balance at the change in topic, he glanced around for somewhere to sit. There was a chair beside the window, but it was a little far away. He opted for perching on the end of the bed. 'Jeb was most attentive.'

She glared. 'Give me that candle, before you drip wax all over the counterpane or set the bed curtains afire.'

He handed it over and she put it in the candlestick on the bedside table.

Now he could see her properly. Her hair neatly plaited and laying over one shoulder. Her plain cotton nightgown buttoned up to her chin. Her eyes wide and unfathomable.

Clearly aware of his assessing gaze, she folded her arms across her chest and shot him a glower of what looked like resentment, but not before he noticed that her nipples had tightened and pressed against her nightgown in a most interesting way.

'What did you want to talk about?' she asked.

'Us.'

Her gaze slid away. 'There is no us. Our personal arrangement is at an end.'

Was he really going cast his pride aside to profess his love like some callow youth or would he be better off appealing to her practical side and work on gaining her trust?

The latter might be more successful, since there was nothing to suggest she held him in any great esteem and certainly there was nothing to suggest her heart was involved.

That was something he would work on. If she would allow it.

'Why not extend our arrangement? It was profitable for us both.' He grinned. 'On more than one front.'

She clearly caught his meaning because her frown deepened. 'Westram wouldn't like it. He has made that very clear.'

'He made it clear, he expected a wedding. Perhaps a betrothal would satisfy him for the nonce.'

She looked unimpressed. 'I had no intention of marrying and nor did you until Westram arrived on the scene.'

'I have missed you.' Hell, where had that come from? She'd been gone barely a week, but the subtle change in her expression told him this might a better tangent. He recalled his first impressions when he stepped into the room and—'I think you have been missing me, too.'

She dropped her gaze to the counterpane and picked at a non-existent thread. 'Nonsense. Why would you think so?'

He leant forward and tilted her chin with one finger. 'Haven't you?'

Slowly she raised her gaze to meet his. No coward, this woman. It was what had impressed him from the very first, the way she squared up to him.

'I've missed some things about our liaison,' she admitted bravely.

He couldn't stop himself. He kissed those luscious lips and, after a small resistance, a slight stiffening of her body, she made a low groan in her throat and kissed him back, pulling his head down with feverish gasps and moans that had him hard in an instant.

He flung the covers back and shrugged off his dressing gown, aware of her greedy gaze on his already responding erection. A feral triumph filled him at the heat in her gaze and the evidence of her arousal, the flush of her cheeks, the hardened peaks of her breasts lifting the soft cotton of her gown.

A growl rumbled up from his throat and in seconds he had the nightdress over her head and flung aside so he could feast his gaze on his sensual Amazon lover.

She opened her arms to him with a smile so seductive and welcoming a breath caught in his throat. Unable to resist the invitation, he fell upon her like a ravening beast.

Apparently, he had not merely missed her, he had been starving for her, for this. She wrapped her legs around his thighs and he slid into her slick heat in a dizzying rush. Ready. She was so damned ready.

His mind darkened. His lips found her full ripe breasts and he latched on, suckling as her bucking hips urged him to drive home deeper and harder.

Her cries of pleasure were sweet music to his ears and her urgent desire for his body sent a hammer beat of blood through his veins.

For a brief moment, he tried to pull back, to slow things down, but her sheath was so tight around his shaft, and the feel of her hands wandering his skin so very urgent, that he followed her lead, drove into her in time with the upward thrust of her hips and, when he felt her come apart, only a long-honed instinct for self-preservation had him withdrawing at the last moment before he followed her into bliss.

He wasn't exactly sure how he managed it. Likely because he'd been more ready for the onslaught that had completely ambushed him last time.

Thrills rocked him, drained him and lasted for ever, yet was over far too soon. He rolled clear and cleaned off her belly with a corner of the sheet. Replete and overwhelmed by the power of the orgasm that had ripped through his body, he basked in the warm haze of satisfaction. Never had he been so shattered.

Or felt so good.

He pulled her close, nuzzling her ear, stroking whatever part of her he could reach. 'Lovely,' he murmured. 'You are lovely.' Warm darkness enveloped him as he heard her sigh.

'Oh, Avery.'

With her firmly entwined in his arms, positive she could not leave him before he had a chance to have his say, he let himself drift.

A slight shift of Carrie's arm drew a sleepy sound of protest from Avery. He tightened his grip. She abandoned the thought of getting up and tried to process what had just happened.

Whatever it was, it was her fault. She had no doubt if she had told him to leave he would have done so. Instead, when he had slipped through her door, all she could think of was that she had not worn her pretty nightgown.

What on earth was the matter with her? Did she have no sense when it came to men? First, she married a totally unsuitable man because her father had wanted it so badly. Only to discover Jonathan had only married her to pay off his debts and to have him reject her as a person. Now she was considering marriage to one who had the power break her heart. One, for that matter, who seemed in no hurry to leave her bed. Good lord, what would the maid say if she found them? Or, worse yet, what would her sisters-in-law think.

Well, they wouldn't mind the bed part, that had been agreed to, but the fact that she was so very tempted to let him convince her to marry him, that was a whole other story. She could not be married after she had sworn to stand by them through thick and thin. She certainly could not marry a man who—

Dash it. Why did he have to be a gambler?

Her heart sank. If she was honest with herself, that was the real reason she had rejected his offer. The only reason. Because her sisters-in-law would understand. And even him being forced up to the mark wasn't an impediment. Because even if he didn't love her the way she loved him, they liked each other and it was possible that it could grow into something stronger.

No, it was the gambling, the recklessness of it that held her back.

Yet the thought of not accepting his offer and imagining him going off and finding another lady on whom to lavish his affections had her heart in a permanent spasm.

'What is going on in that head of yours?' Avery yawned. 'I can hear the wheels turning.'

For a moment, she considered blurting out her fears. How he would laugh. After all, everyone gambled. It was *de rigueur*. Only the merchant class frowned upon wagering.

She turned on her side to face him. 'You said you came to talk.'

'I did, *chérie*. Somehow I got sidetracked.'

He flashed her a wicked grin and her insides tightened. Oh, he really was a naughty man. Not at all the sort of man her far more serious nature needed. 'I hope you are not here to try to convince me to marry you.'

'I am here to explain why it would be a good idea.' He kissed the tip of her nose and brushed a strand of hair back from her face.

At least he wasn't spouting poetry and other such nonsense. But oh, she could understand why women fell for his charm.

'If you must say your piece, I will listen, but do not expect me to change my mind.'

He gave her a look of admonishment. 'Please do me the courtesy of hearing me out *before* you decide.'

She pressed her lips together, determined not to let him charm her into doing something she would most certainly live to regret.

'Think about it, Carrie. If you were married to me, you could continue operating your shop and your sisters-in-law could continue selling their wonderful hats and Westram could say nothing about it.'

She thanked heaven she and the others had already had this conversation. 'They will not go against Westram's edict. The millinery business is not an option. So we are right back where we started.'

'Surely Westram wouldn't object to a hands-off approach? Provided your names are not known, what could possibly be his objection?'

The dear man, he really wanted to help. She placed a hand flat on his cheek. 'He is adamant.'

'So how does he expect his sisters to maintain themselves?'

'He doesn't. He wants them to marry again.'

'Understandable.'

'Is it?' A little flash of disappointment took her by surprise. Why would she have thought he was different to any other male of the species, thinking that all women needed a man to rely on.

He gave her enquiring look.

'The reason we came here was that none of us wanted to marry again. We wanted our independence.'

He frowned. 'Then why did you ask me to be your lover?'

'You know why. I was curious about something that had been denied me. Besides, the three of us had agreed that being widows meant that we were free to enjoy lovers if we so wished.'

'Lovers.' His tone was heavy.

'Surely you are not judging me when you flit from one lady to another on a whim.'

He had the grace to look chagrined.

'Besides,' she continued, 'I have no intention of taking any other lovers.' She could not even think about it, not when there would only ever be one man she loved.

He rose up on one elbow, looking down into her face, his gaze searching her face intently. 'Am I to understand from that admission that you do care for me? At least a little.'

'Of course I care for you,' she almost snapped at him.

'You don't think I would do this...' she waved a hand to encompass them, the bed, the room at large '...if I did not care for you.'

He lay back down. 'Good. Very good.'

She frowned, but he seemed to be thinking and it was a long pause before he spoke again.

'So now you can no longer gain income through the shop, apart from selling it to me, how do you plan to support yourselves on an ongoing basis?'

'We haven't come up with a solution yet.' She sighed. 'And if we do not solve the problem, Westram will solve it for us.'

'By marrying you off.'

'Yes. And that is not an option.'

He did not seem disturbed by her vehemence. Indeed, he seemed almost pleased.

'Then why not pre-empt the fellow and marry me? We get along well. We like each other. And to be brutally honest, I have never enjoyed a lover the way I enjoy you.'

A marriage of convenience in other words. 'You plan to support a wife on your earnings from gambling when you do not make enough to afford decent lodgings?' She didn't mean to sound scornful, but she could not keep her feelings out of her voice. 'I have nothing to bring to such a marriage. I am honour bound to continue to pay my portion into this household. Without my contribution, they would have no choice but to return to Westram. We worked it all out very carefully. I cannot do that to them.'

He stiffened. 'If I can support my sister, I cannot see why I cannot support a wife and her sisters-in-law.'

'You support your sister?'

'I did until recently. Very handsomely, too, I might add. Thankfully, her husband can take up the reins now that his clientele has picked up.'

'You supported her with your winnings at the tables?'

'That and… Well I have given up my other source of income.'

'Your special ladies.'

'Yes. It wasn't all that profitable and I only started it to help out an old friend. It added a bit to the coffers, but I won't miss it.'

The man was nothing if he was not resourceful, but… 'I cannot see myself relying for room and board on the results of a game of *vingt-et-un*.'

'Pooh. That is a game for novices. I don't play games of luck. I play whist. It is a game of skill and I rarely lose.'

'But it also has an element of chance. You must lose sometimes.'

'Of course.' He sat up, forearms resting on his bent knees. She ran a hand over his lovely naked back. How would it be to have this lovely man in her bed all the time? As her husband. Oh, she wanted to say yes so badly it hurt.

A hot hard lump rose in her throat. 'I can't do it.' She hated how weak she sounded. She swallowed, hating the burn behind her eyes. 'I cannot marry a man who risks everything on the turn of a card. My first husband spent all my money paying off gambling debts and then he died because of some stupid wager and I cannot live day to day wondering if you might do the same.' She sniffed.

He was looking at her over his shoulder, his eyes grave, his lips unsmiling. He said nothing.

'There. Now you have it. The truth. I am a coward. Please do not ask me. I am sorry.' She buried her face in her hands. 'You must think me such a plebeian to concern myself with such things.'

'I did not know that about your husband.' His voice sounded cold. Remote. 'I knew he went off to war and got himself killed, but I did not know it was because of a wager.'

'Hardly anyone knows and Westram asked us not to speak of it. No one actually seems to know the full details, but what is undeniable is that all the money from my settlements was used to pay Jonathan's gaming debts. They were huge. Westram was nearly ruined keeping us out of debtors' prison. The day after our marriage Jonathan made some sort of stupid wager, I presume to recoup his losses, and went off to war and got himself killed, along with his two best friends. No doubt he lost the bet into the bargain. How can I place my future in the hands of another man who lives by taking those sort of risks?'

He stared at her. 'You think he got himself killed because he didn't want to be married to you or because he lost the bet?'

She flinched. Pain twisted in her heart. 'Probably both. What am I to think when...when he did not even come to my bed before he left?'

His mouth became a thin straight line. 'I beg your pardon for asking you to take such an unwarranted chance on marriage to me.' He got up and threw on his dressing gown in silence. 'I fully understand your reticence and can quite see why you think we might not suit.'

'I am sorry,' she whispered.

'You cannot be sorrier than I.' He bowed.

Only Avery could bow while wearing a dressing gown and make it look like the most elegant movement in the world.

She was still warmed by the thought when he left the room and closed the door behind him.

Then, cold, alone and lonely, she let her tears run free until she was too exhausted to remain awake.

In the morning, she learned he had left at first light.

It had taken Avery two days to get an appointment to see his father. Finally he knew exactly what he had to do to ensure Carrie's happiness. Heavens, her first husband had been an absolute bastard. Now he understood some of the things that had puzzled him about Carrie. Her withdrawals. Her frowns. They'd all occurred when the subject of gambling had come up.

And no wonder.

He'd sent Westram a note rescheduling their meeting. Westram's reply had been stiff, bordering on insulting, but Avery had swallowed his pride.

Westram was simply doing his duty, protecting the women of his family, no matter how much the idea stuck in Avery's throat that the other man had the right to protect Carrie while he did not.

Pride swallowing was the order of the day, apparently, for he was now in the company of a man he'd sworn he would never again have anything to do with.

Shadows lurked in the corners of the room, because the curtains were drawn against evening drawing in. The chamber smelled like old dust and old man. With his brother standing at his shoulder in a show of support, Avery tried not to stare at the father he'd not seen for five years. To his dismay, the Duke had shrunk in on himself in the intervening years, grown older, his dark hair completely white now. He hunched into a shawl someone had placed around his shoulders as if he felt cold, despite the heat from a blazing fire. Yet the old man still had the same piecing glare that had always made a youthful Avery feel like an insect under a microscope.

'So, finally, you decided to do your filial duty,' the old man grumbled, sipping at his glass of port. He groaned and shifted the bandaged foot propped on a padded stool.

Avery gritted his teeth, both in sympathy at the old man's obvious pain and annoyance at the truculent tone. Ah well. He'd sworn to Bart he would not let the old fellow get under his skin. 'I came to tell you to stop interfering in my business.' Damn, he'd meant to approach this a little more tactfully.

'Hah,' the old man said, rolling the stem between gnarled fingers and watching the way the light played on the ruby liquid. 'Why would I bother?'

'You bothered before, remember.'

The old man shot him a glare from beneath white bushy eyebrows. 'I was right, wasn't I?'

Avery hesitated. If his fathered hadn't interfered, he would have been married these past five years. To a woman only interested in his money whom he'd barely given a thought to in a very long time. And he would never have met Carrie. But that was beside the point.

'I know it was you who went to Westram. Telling tales.'

The Duke glanced at Bart and back to him. 'You should know better than to lift the skirts of one of the nobility. Even if she is widow.' He glowered at his port.

'I hear she's a cit, to boot.' There was a slyness in his gaze when he lifted it to meet Avery's glance.

Damn him. 'You will speak of the woman I intend to marry with respect.'

His brother moved to his father's side. Took the glass of port from his shaky hand and set it on the table.

'Why would you marry the girl?' the Duke asked. 'Seems you are getting what you want without it?'

'I am marrying her because that is what she deserves. And I do not care what you have to say about it, quite honestly.'

'And how do you plan to support a wife? She happy about your philandering with every married woman in town? Likes the idea of being married to a man who spends his nights in London's hells, does she?'

'I will support her by way of my birthright.' Hell, this was coming out all wrong.

'Will you now?'

He reined in his anger. He was angry because he'd had to come here cap in hand, but this was for Carrie, not for him. She deserved the best he could give her and this was it.

'I acknowledge you were right about Alexandra.'

The old man leaned back in his chair. His eyes widening. 'Well-a-day! I never thought I'd hear such an admission fall from your lips. A right stubborn one, you always were.'

Avery relaxed somewhat. This was the father he remembered. Irascible. Outspoken. But not completely unreasonable. Except when it came to the marriage of his offspring.

'I came to ask you to sign over the estate of Fenward to me, as Mother requested and you agreed.'

'It wasn't part of the settlements.'

'But it was her intention.'

The old man shook his head. 'Only if I thought you were ready to take on the responsibility. Even she knew you for a harum-scarum. What do you know about managing an estate? You've spent your life in ladies' boudoirs or at the tables and have nothing to show for it.'

'I haven't forgotten anything I learned as a boy under your tutelage.' Indeed, the very idea of having his own estate was one of the things that had kept him going all these years. If he hadn't needed to help Laura, he would have bought one by now.

The Duke glanced up at his eldest son, who gave him a grin. 'I told you he'd come around.'

'You did. Took him long enough. I tell you this, my boy, I was beginning to despair of you. You always had a good head on your shoulders. I couldn't believe it when you wanted to marry that dizzy-headed puss. I hope this widow of yours has a bit more sense.'

'She does.' He hesitated. 'Are you saying you accede to my request?'

'Of course. Been keeping Fenward for you, boy, if you ever decided to come to your senses. Runs along beside Wrendean. You'll also manage that one. For your brother if you'd rather do it for him than for me. I'm not long for this world. Your brother will need all the help he can get.'

Avery didn't like all this talk of death. But he wouldn't put it past the Duke to play on feelings of guilt. He was a cunning old so-and-so. He narrowed his eyes. 'I'll expect a wage, if you want me to take on Wrendean as well.'

The old man waved a hand. 'I will leave all that to your brother.'

Bart nodded. 'There is nothing I would like better.'

'And Laura?'

He knew he shouldn't be asking. He'd got far more out of this interview than he ever expected or even hoped. But he hated that his father had cast out his sister.

'Another stubborn one,' his father said, reaching for his port.

Bart put the glass in his hand.

The Duke took a sip. 'Well, I ain't dead yet. Had that jackanapes of a husband of hers not come here demanding I agree to their wedding and laying out all kinds of conditions about what I would and would not do, I might not have lost my temper. Damn his eyes. Sent him to the right about, as he deserved.'

Avery closed his eyes. Of course, that would have set the Duke's back up no end.

The old man fixed him with a stare. 'Don't think I don't know you and Bart have been helping the pair of them behind my back.'

'Mostly Avery,' Bart said. 'Since you've made it too difficult for me to do much.'

'Then you shouldn't go behind my back.'

Avery rolled his eyes. 'What else were we to do?'

'Nothing,' the Duke snapped. 'You are her brothers. I am glad to see you have at least that much sense of duty. I've been keeping an eye on that husband of hers, too.'

Argh. Now they would be in for a lecture.

'He'll make a fine barrister,' the Duke said.

Avery gaped at his father, who seemed oblivious to his surprise.

'Going to do well for himself,' the Duke mused as if surprised. 'I've already had some old friends send business his way.'

So that was why things had recently turned around

for John. Avery sank on to the edge of the seat in front of his father, the fondness he'd tried to bury for so damn long welling up. 'You really are an old curmudgeon.'

The Duke ruffled Avery's hair, the way he had when Avery was a boy. 'And you will be just like me if you aren't careful.' He leaned back in his chair with a sigh. 'Send for Sprake. I'll take that damned medicine now, my boy,' he said to Bart. 'Makes me so damn sleepy. Needed my wits about me, dealing with the likes of you two.'

'Yes, Father,' Bart said.

'You can't be thinking of cocking up your toes,' Avery said, feeling a sudden sense of panic at the weakness his father was showing. 'You have yet to get either of your sons to the altar.'

'Not thinking any such thing,' his father said wearily. 'See him out, Bart, and make whatever arrangements are needed. You have carte blanche.'

Clearly surprised by this magnanimity, Bart rang the bell and Sprake rushed into the room with a bottle of tonic and a spoon. 'You see, your Grace,' the elderly valet said. 'I told you, you needed this, but, no, you weren't going to take it. Too proud.' He shoved a cushion at the Duke's back and loosened his collar.

Avery hated seeing his father so fragile.

'What are you still doing here?' the old man asked. He curled his lip. 'Thought you had a lady to see.'

Avery narrowed his eyes for a moment. There was a glint of amusement in his father's eye and, yes, triumph. Damn the old man, he had finally got what he wanted. An acknowledgement that he was right. And a wedding in the offing.

And Avery discovered it was like a weight off his

shoulders. If not for meeting Carrie, he might never have swallowed his pride and made peace with his father before it was too late. Something he now knew he would have regretted for the rest of his life.

Carrie. A pain pierced his heart, for his own pride might yet have caused him to lose her.

He must now convince her to change her mind and set his whole world to rights.

He hoped she would listen. He had never felt this nervous when betting on a mediocre hand of cards with a hundred guineas on the outcome. But then cards were games of skill and he knew what he was doing.

In the game of love, he risked losing everything.

Tomorrow he would learn his fate.

Carrie's umbrella did nothing to keep her skirts dry, the wind drove the rain so hard. The weather had been fair when she'd caught the stagecoach from Sevenoaks. Jeb had been far from happy dropping her off at the inn, but she had insisted. She didn't want anyone witnessing her embarrassment should Avery turn her from his door.

What she would do if he did so, she wasn't sure. Throw herself on Westram's mercy, she supposed, assuming he was still in town.

Evening was already drawing in when she turned the corner on to Avery's street. She hesitated. Stopped. The street was empty except for a lad huddled in a doorway with his broom and one or two gentlemen holding on to their hats as they hurried on their way.

Turn back, her mind whispered.

This might be your only chance, her heart argued.

Squaring her shoulders, she marched the last few

yards to the house where Avery lodged. More doubts assailed her.

She swallowed them down and banged on the door.

The same porter who had opened it to her the first time opened the door with a glare.

'I am here to see Lord Avery.' She had certainly learned how to be imperious from her sisters-in-law. The thought bolstered her courage.

The porter bowed her in. 'You know where to find him.'

Heart thumping hard in her chest, she walked up the stairs to the first floor. Obviously, her heart wasn't quite as brave as it had pretended to be out on the street.

Only one path leads to true happiness.

This had to be right. She'd chosen with her mind once. She had to give her heart an opportunity.

She knocked. Scratched, really. Was she hoping he would not open the door? That he would be out and she could scurry away telling herself she had tried?

She raised her hand to knock again, more loudly.

The door opened.

Avery stood there, looking sartorially splendid as he always did, clearly dressed to go out.

A pain cramped her chest. Was he off to meet one of his special ladies?

His face lit up and her fears disappeared.

'Carrie?' He scanned her up and down. 'Good Lord, you are soaking wet. Come in. Take off your wet cloak.' He whipped it from around her shoulders. Took her by the hand and led her to a chair. 'Sit here, by the fire. Warm yourself.'

He was on his knees building up the fire, no sooner had the words left his lips.

A long sigh escaped her. She had been so worried about his reception. This was all she had hoped for and more.

'What the devil are you doing out on a night like this? And how did you get here? Not in that open gig, I hope.'

'I came on the stage.'

'What? Is Westram so nip cheese he will not afford you a post chaise?'

'Westram knows nothing of this journey.'

He frowned, sitting back on his heels as the flames of the fire took hold. 'Your sisters-in-law? Do they know?'

'Of course.'

Indeed, they had encouraged her when she had explained her dilemma and asked if they would be terribly upset if she pursued her suitor.

'You should have at least brought a maid if you are going to visit a single gentleman in his lodgings. Though really you should not be doing that at all.'

How else was she to speak to him? Send him a note and hope he might reply? 'La, sir, it is not the first time.'

He rearranged the coals in the fire. 'No,' he agreed, watching the flames take hold. 'It is not. What message of importance do you bear for me this time?'

Her heart stumbled. This was it. Taking the risky path and hoping for happiness.

'I changed my mind.'

He looked startled.

Dash it, where were all the elegant words she had rehearsed in the long hours on the stage? Left behind in that cramped little box, it seemed.

'I mean, I will accept your proposal of marriage if it is still on offer.'

Not exactly elegant, but to the point.

His brow cleared. 'I see.'

'I quite understand if you have changed your mind,' she hastened to add. 'You are under no obligation, of course. But...' she looked at him shyly '...you were right—there are some great advantages to be had in our union.'

At that he looked a trifle disappointed. 'Yes, indeed. As I said.'

'Of course the disadvantages may outweigh them now you have come to think about it a bit. I am a little long in the tooth. I am a widow who comes with baggage. I will always do my best to help my sisters-in-law, howsoever you earn your living. My settlement is small and you cannot expect anything from Westram, he was quite done up paying for his brother's debts as I told you.'

'Are you trying to talk me out of my offer?' He sounded amused.

Oh, dear, she really was making a mull of this. 'I simply don't want there to be any misunderstandings and I shall quite understand if you have changed your mind.'

Understand and be devastated.

He glowered. 'If that rapscallion husband of yours hadn't got himself killed, I would be ready to murder him about now.'

'If Jonathan was still alive, none of this would be happening.'

He chuckled. 'Ever the practical one.'

She swallowed. Was that good or bad? 'Someone has to be practical. I am hoping we can make enough from the shop—'

He frowned. 'So you changed your mind about that. Why?'

Cold fingers travelled down her spine. This was the question she dreaded. 'Remember the fortune teller?'

He looked surprised. 'I do. But surely you are not basing your decision on her words.'

'Not really. Well, perhaps in part. These were her words to me. *Trusting your head will ensure your safety, I confess, trusting your heart is taking a chance when only one path leads to true happiness.*'

For a moment he looked hopeful, then the frown returned. 'So is it your head you are trusting?'

She knelt down beside him and, leaning against him, put her arm around his waist.

His own arm crept around hers.

'I trusted to safety when I married Jonathan. Father was right about Westram being a good provider for his family, though he had no idea Jonathan's debts were so outrageous. I am safe, even as a widow, with Westram in charge, but it is not true happiness. My heart tells me you are the man meant for me.' She hesitated. 'Something in my heart also tells me you feel the same way about me.' She gave a little laugh and it broke in the middle. 'Of course if you do not—'

He turned towards her, gazing into her eyes. 'How could you doubt it, my dearest darling Carrie? I love you. I think I have since the moment I saw you.'

'You were too bosky to know anything,' she said, her heart filling with a bubble of joy she did not know how to contain.

'I most certainly was not.' He gave her a look. 'And you? How do you feel?'

She sighed. 'Oh, Avery, I thought my heart was broken when you left Kent. I realised a while ago that I loved you, but I thought I was doing the right thing, knowing I could never be happy marrying a gambler. But without you, being safe and secure seemed like so much dross after you left. I fell in love with you, the man who is kind and generous and caring. I do not want to change you.'

He picked her up in his arms and settled himself on the sofa where he commenced kissing her silly. When they finally broke for breath, he twirled one of the strands of hair that had escaped her pins around one finger and gave it a little tug.

'I was coming back down to Kent tomorrow to give it one last shot,' he said.

Shocked, she gasped. 'You were?'

'You made me see things I refused to look at before.' He gave a small laugh. 'You see, I am not really a gambler at heart. I never bet on anything unless I know I can win. Even so, I fully accept that no woman wants to live her life worrying about whether her husband will lose everything they own. So, I went to see my father.'

'The Duke?'

'We came to an agreement.' He sounded grim.

'Was it so very dreadful? You know you do not have to do this for my sake.'

'Turns out I am doing it for my own sake, too. Without a reason on which to hang up my pride, I would never have gone to see him and I would have regretted that deeply.' He swallowed. 'He's aged terribly in the years I have been absent.' His voice softened. 'Though he's still as autocratic as ever. It seems we both regret our row, though of course he is positive he was in the right.' He smiled fondly. 'He was, actually. But he could have found a less unpleasant course of action.'

He let the strand of hair spring free and kissed her

cheek and then her lips, before continuing. 'I went to him to tell him to stay out of my business, since I thought he must have learned you were related to Westram and set him on us. He denies the latter, but I am still not so sure. I also insisted he hand over the estate my mother left me.'

She could scarcely believe it. 'You have your own estate?'

'Yes. He also offered me the position of land agent for one of the nearby ducal properties, one I know well and that will bring a good income.'

Her head was spinning. She could not quite believe all he was saying. 'Are you saying you intend to give up gambling? For me?'

'For us, love. Though I believe the odd gentlemanly wager is not a crime.'

'No. No, of course not. Avery, I love you. And I trust you to do what is right.' She did. How could she not have realised that before?

He smiled and his face took on a boyish cast. 'The estate is in a lovely part of England.' He glanced at her intently. 'That is if you do not mind burying yourself in the country.'

'I love the countryside. Living in Kent for more than a year, I have come to realise how much I prefer it to the city, though the city is where I grew up.'

He breathed a sigh of relief, lifted her off his knee and settled her on the sofa. He went down on one knee before her and her heart did a little dance of happiness.

'Dearest Carrie, will you do me the very great honour of becoming my wife?'

She reached for his hand, took it in hers, kissed it and rubbed it against her cheek. 'Yes, Avery, I will.'

He kissed each of her hands in turn. 'Then you make me the happiest man in all of England.'

He rose to his feet and pulled her to hers. 'Now we must get you to the Westram town house. I'm not having the gossips saying this marriage was forced on you. Everything is going to be absolutely above board.'

Avery looked so happy, it was only now Carrie realised that there had always been shadows behind his mischievous flirtatious gaze. Those shadows were gone, replaced with a light she could only describe as love. The fact that the light was for her was the most amazingly wonderful thing in the world.

The fortune teller had been wrong. Following her heart had also led to the safety and security of her one true love's arms.

'I do love you so,' she said, unable to contain her happiness.

He whirled her about with a laugh, then gazed down into her face. 'I wasn't sure you would take the risk. I have not been the most stable of fellows, these past many years.'

'It is no risk at all when love is involved. We will face whatever comes along together.'

Gravity filling his face, he cupped her cheeks in his hands. 'That, my darling, we will.'

We. It was such a wonderful word when compared to you and I and them. 'I do have one favour to ask.'

'Anything, my sweet. I'll never gamble again. I'll buy you the moon. Ask, it is yours.'

'If we are going to observe all the proprieties now that we are engaged, can we get married tomorrow? I really don't think I can wait any longer to, er…have you as my husband.'

He looked startled. Then laughed. 'If that is your true wish, then it shall be done. I am certainly happy not to wait. I will go to Doctors' Commons for a special licence right after I speak to Westram.'

'Thank you.'

She flung her arms around his neck and kissed him.

Epilogue

Sunbeams filtered through the window in the bedchamber where Petra and Marguerite were helping Carrie dress for her wedding. She'd chosen a simple gown of pale primrose and wore flowers made by her sisters-in-law in her hair.

Petra retied the bow at the back of the dress. 'That is better. Now you are perfect.'

Strangely enough Carrie felt perfect. It was the way Avery looked at her that had made her feel that way. Avery. Today they would be wed. She could scarcely believe it.

'You are sure you wish to go through with this?' Marguerite said, her expression one of concern. 'Do not let Westram force you into something you do not want.'

Her palms grew damp inside her cotton gloves. This was the only part of marrying Avery she had been dreading. Saying goodbye to her sisters-in-law.

After the ceremony she and Avery were travelling north to one of the Duke's properties and from there, in two weeks' time, they would move on to their new life together.

'I am going to miss you both terribly,' she said and swallowed the lump forming in her throat. 'But I do love Avery and he loves me.' It sounded so wonderful to say those words and to mean them and feel sure.

'I should say so,' Petra said with a teasing smile on her lips. 'I have never seen a man so besotted as he has been these past three weeks.'

Carrie puzzled over the words. Surely Petra's husband—

'I know,' Marguerite said almost too briskly. 'Yesterday Westram grumbled that he could no longer walk around the house without tripping over him.'

Carrie chuckled. It was true. And she loved it.

Her eyes went a little misty at the thought of Avery's impatience to get their wedding over and done. Not that she had felt differently, but Westram had insisted there be nothing havey-cavey about the marriage and had vetoed their intention of getting a special licence.

While their wedding was to be a small affair in the Westram town-house drawing room, everyone who ought to be invited had been, including the Duke. They had all accepted, too. Waiting three weeks for the banns to be called had been the longest weeks of Carrie's life and yet they had also flown by, she had been so busy. Petra and Marguerite had come to town to help with the preparations and to help her shop for her trousseau. A new one. Avery wanted nothing of her first marriage to haunt the beginning of theirs. For once, she had agreed with the extravagance.

Petra briskly twitched at Carrie's skirts. 'I must say, though, this bridegroom of yours is not one to let grass grow beneath his feet. The ladies in Westram village were delighted to hear they are to continue supplying the shop now that the Thrumbys have taken it over.'

'I was so pleased that Thrumby agreed,' Carrie said. 'Tansy was thrilled, too, now she's going to help them in the shop again. She hated being Mrs Thrumby's chambermaid, despite being grateful for the job.' She gave her sisters a regretful smile. 'Now the only people my departure inconveniences are you. I feel so badly for letting you down.'

In a flash, both girls put their arms around her and they clung together for a moment. 'Nonsense,' Marguerite said, her voice a little hoarse. 'Your happiness is more important than anything. Petra and I will find a way to keep ourselves busy and earn some money to boot.'

They drew apart. Carrie took a deep breath. 'About that.'

Marguerite raised a brow. 'You know we agreed you were not to worry about such things.'

'I haven't. I promise. Avery has. He went to see Mr Thrumby and finally convinced him that since he will continue to use Marguerite's designs, he must give you a share in the profits from them every quarter.' She did not think it worth mentioning that Avery upon his third visit had told Thrumby what a mistake it would be to annoy the son of a duke. Avery hadn't wanted to play the ducal card, as he had put it, but needs must. 'Oh, and should you happen to show something you have designed to the village ladies and they make it then you are to receive a commission for that too.'

Petra and Marguerite gasped. 'But what about Westram?' Marguerite said.

'These are royalties, Marguerite,' Carrie said. 'Your name will never be attached to the shop in any way. Avery spoke to Westram and has agreed it is not the same as being in trade.' She shook her head. 'Though to be honest I really feel you ought to be credited with your work. And you, too, Petra, for you taught the ladies how to turn the drawings into beautiful hats.'

Both sisters looked pleased. 'It's fine,' Petra said. 'We don't need recognition, but we could certainly use the funds.'

Carrie let go a breath. She hadn't been sure the women would accept the arrangement with or without Westram's approval.

'I don't know how to thank you, Carrie,' Marguerite said, giving her another hug. Petra put her arms around both of them.

'It is what sisters do,' Carrie said and received a very tight squeeze from both of hers.

A knock sounded at the door. They broke apart, smoothing their gowns and dabbing their handkerchiefs beneath watery eyes.

'The guests are all assembled, ladies,' the butler said, smiling broadly.

As they started down the stairs, Carrie's heart started to pound. What if Avery wasn't there? What if she was fooling herself and he left her right after the ceremony?

No. Not Avery. He would never do that to her. They loved each other.

They walked in procession across the hall and into the drawing room. At the fireplace the minister was waiting with Avery before him in a beautifully fitting dark blue coat with silver buttons and buff pantaloons. His brother standing beside him was similarly attired.

Carrie knew the room was full of people, knew the Duke was there, and Avery's sister, and Westram and other relatives, but she only saw Avery. It was if her vision had narrowed to encompass only him. She hesitated.

He turned and gave her such a heartfelt welcoming look, she felt utterly beautiful. Then he was walking towards her with his hand outstretched. She reached out and took it. Together they walked to the front of the room.

'Dearly beloved,' the minister began...

Beloved. Yes. Those words described her feelings to the full and the love and pride and joy in Avery's face told her he felt the same way, too.

* * * * *

AN EARL FOR THE
SHY WIDOW

This book is dedicated to you, my good friend and teacher, Sandra Atri.

Thank you for your patience and understanding, and for making me want to go to the gym instead of dragging my feet.

It has been a great year and I am looking forward to the next one.

Chapter One

September 1813

Autumn sunlight flooded into the tiny drawing room at Westram Cottage. Lady Petra strode to the window. Beneath a blue sky, a slight breeze stirred the leaves of a nearby oak tree and nodded the heads of the red roses along the path to the front door. A perfect afternoon for a ride, *if* one had a horse.

She sighed and wandered back to her chair. She picked up the embroidery she'd been working on a few moments before. A handkerchief for her brother Red, the Earl of Westram. So boring. She cast it aside and got up to straighten the portrait of her mother on the opposite wall.

'Petra,' her older sister, Lady Marguerite Saxby, said, 'please stop pacing. You are making me dizzy.'

Remorseful, Petra spun around. 'I am sorry. I did not mean to disturb you.'

Auburn haired and green eyed, Marguerite was seated at the table going through her correspondence. As usual, her luxuriant tresses were pinned back severely beneath her widow's cap. Although she returned Petra's smile, there was sadness in her eyes. Marguerite hadn't looked anything but sad since she was widowed.

Did Petra have that same look? She strode to the glass over the mantel and peered at her reflection. Unlike her older siblings, she took after her mother with blonde hair and blue eyes. Did she also look sad?

She closed her eyes against her reflection, unwilling to admit to sadness. Yet perhaps she could acknowledge regret. After all, it was partly her fault that she and Harry had had such a blazing row.

She had been so happy for the first few months of her marriage. It had come as a painful shock to realise that Harry, already bored with his brand-new wife, was seeking his entertainments elsewhere. If she'd been a proper *ton*nish wife and simply ignored his infidelities, brushed it off as something every fashionable husband did, things would have turned out very differently. But it had hurt so much, she could not remain silent. And the more she complained, the worse he behaved until, during their last argument, she'd accused him of not loving her any more. He'd shouted back that he had *never* loved her and had only married her because his father insisted on it.

He'd said she was a stupid little girl who had ruined his life.

The pain had left her speechless.

The next thing she knew he had stormed off to fight the French. Worse yet was him taking her brother and her brother-in-law with him. Not only had Harry broken her heart, but her stupid naivety had cost her sisters their husbands.

She turned away from the glass.

'Do you not have mending to do?' Marguerite asked.
'All done.'

'What about the garden? Doesn't it need attention?'

Petra shook her head. 'Every time I pick up a shovel or pull a weed, Jeb leaps in to take over. Red seems to have given him very definite ideas about what a lady should or should not do. Honestly, I miss making hats.'

'Make one for yourself,' Marguerite suggested.

'It is not the same. Besides, I have more hats than I need. I feel so useless.' Earning an income from their fledgling millinery business had been thrilling, until their brother Red had put a stop to it. He had been horrified to discover his sisters were engaging in trade.

They still received some income from the hats Marguerite designed, but the manufacturing had been handed over to the new owner when they sold the business. Ladies of quality did not enter into the world of commerce.

Marguerite scanned the next letter in her pile. 'Carrie sends her love and says the dog Avery bought her will have a litter of puppies at the end of November, and would we like one?'

'How adorable. Tell her yes.'

Marguerite nodded. 'It would be good for you to have company on your walks. A dog would be just the thing.'

Petra joined her at the table to read over her shoulder. 'She does not say what sort of breed they are? Hopefully, not too large.'

'I will ask her when I reply. You are right. We do not want anything too big.' She set the letter aside and picked up the next one.

Petra wandered over to the sofa and glanced down

at her fingers, rubbing the calluses she'd earned from their millinery efforts. They were already disappearing.

A great many things had changed in the past few months. Their widowed sister-in-law, Carrie, was married, and happily so, while Petra and Marguerite continued to go against their brother's wishes and maintain their independence. Neither of them wanted to marry again. Once was enough for Petra, certainly. In her experience, men promised you the moon to get what they wanted, then did exactly as they pleased. She had been little more than a child with stars in her eyes when she married Harry. How hurt she had been to discover he'd only married her because his father had wanted the connection to nobility. She certainly wasn't going to make that sort of mistake again.

Marguerite gasped, 'The Thrumbys have sold the business.'

'What?' Petra hurried to look over Marguerite's shoulder.

'Avery included a note with Carrie's letter. Here, read it for yourself.'

Petra scanned the note written in a firm male hand. The Thrumbys had received an offer for the business from a Bond Street competitor and had agreed to sell. The new owner created her own hat designs, therefore Marguerite's were no longer needed.

'At least they will continue to employ the ladies in the village to make up the hats,' Marguerite said, her voice full of resignation. 'The quality of their work is exceptional.' She gave Petra a wan smile. 'All due to you, dearest. You taught them well.'

'Dash it all. That is so unfair. We needed that income.' She bit her lip at the pained look on Marguerite's face. 'Now what will we do? Ask Red for help, I suppose.'

Marguerite shook her head. 'No. We will think of something. In the meantime, we will be frugal.'

They were already careful with every penny. 'I wish I could help more.'

Marguerite pursed her lips. 'We will have to cut back on meat... It is so expensive.'

'Well, Red better not hear about that, or it will be all the excuse he needs to put us back on the marriage mart.'

Marguerite paled. 'He is sure to find out eventually. I have to think of some other way to augment our income. Sometimes publishers need illustrators for their books. I will write to them and send some examples of my drawings. Perhaps I can use a nom de plume.'

Petra nodded. 'Good idea.' A recollection of something she'd seen on her way to the village popped into her mind. 'Why don't I see if I can pick some blackberries for jam? We have lots of sugar in the pantry.'

Marguerite gave her a grateful smile. 'Excellent idea. A good supply of preserves will help us through the winter.'

It wouldn't be enough, though. But Petra had an idea about that, too. The countryside was full of free food if one knew where to look. Blackberries were just the start.

Not too many minutes later, Petra had equipped herself with an old straw hat, a large wicker basket and covered her oldest spring muslin with an apron that had seen better days.

Outside, a light breeze cooled the warmth of the sun and she strolled along swinging her basket until she arrived at a blackberry bush hanging over the lane. The last time she noticed it, the brambles had been covered in little white flowers. Now the prickly canes were weighed down with gleaming clusters of black fruit.

Unfortunately, they were on the other side of a ditch and hanging over the top of a dense hedge far too high for her to reach.

Bother. They hadn't looked so high when she was travelling in the trap.

The other side of the bush grew in a field belonging to the Longhurst estate. On that side, the berries were temptingly easy to reach even for a short person such as she. A wooden stile a few feet from where she was standing offered perfect access to the field and the blackberries.

Besides, who would care? No one had lived at Longhurst since she and her sisters had arrived at Westram more than a year ago. According to the locals, the new Earl was away fighting on the Peninsula and cared not a bean for the estate. In consequence, there was no one to care if she trespassed. Besides, it wasn't as if he had planted the brambles. They were part of nature's bounty.

After a quick glance up and down the road, she hiked up the skirts of her old blue gown and climbed over.

Wary of fierce thorns bent on ripping her clothes to shreds, she pushed into the bush using her basket as a shield. Soon it was full of shiny blackberries and becoming quite heavy. A trickle of sweat ran into her eye and she wiped it away on the corner of her apron.

She picked a berry and popped it into her mouth.

Mmm...delicious. And exactly right for jam. She tasted another just to be sure.

The jingle of a bridle and the sound of a horse's heavy breathing had her whipping around.

A tall fair-haired man with an amused expression on his handsome face gazed down at her from the back of a huge brown horse. He leaned forward and let his glance travel down her length. It lingered at her feet.

She glanced down. Heat rushed to her face at the sight of her stockings bared to her garter at the knee because her skirts had tangled with the thorns when she turned. She pulled them free.

When she looked up again, his light blue eyes were twinkling and he wore a charmingly boyish smile. The sort of smile a man knew would cause the nearest female to forgive him.

Her stomach fluttered wildly. She tried to ignore it. Harry had worn the same sort of smile when he sought her forgiveness each time that he had strayed. As an unmarried girl, she had adored that smile. As a wife, she had come to dread it. She'd learned it meant he'd made yet another conquest and was trying to jolly her along as if it meant nothing.

No, a gentleman's smiles and promises, no matter how charming or sincere they seemed, were definitely not to be trusted. She schooled her expression into cool politeness and dipped a curtsy. 'Good afternoon, sir.'

'Good day to you, wench.' His voice was deep and rich and smooth. 'May I ask what you are about?'

Wench? Pinpricks shot across her shoulders. 'What does it look like I am doing? I am picking blackberries.' Dash it. She should not have responded so sharply.

'*My* blackberries,' he said with another smile.

Oh. She winced. 'Then you must be Lord Long-hurst.'

'Indeed.' He inclined his head slightly.

It seemed the wanderer had at last returned. 'Well, sir, this fruit may grow on your property, but since they grew without the aid of any man or woman, it might be argued that they have no particular owner.'

He frowned. 'Are you one of my tenants?'

He thought she was a farm labourer's wife. Dash it all—was she supposed to wear her best gown to go blackberry picking? For a moment she was tempted to play along, but she did not know this man or his character. At first glance, he looked handsome and charming, but she knew better than to judge anyone by appearances. Or at least, she did now. Besides, it would be embarrassing when he later caught her out in her lie. 'No, sir, I am not a tenant of yours. I am Lady Petra Davenport. I reside at Westram Cottage. I am pleased to make your acquaintance, Lord Longhurst.' She bobbed a small curtsy. As a formal introduction, it would have to do.

He removed his hat and gave her another winsome smile. 'So, we are neighbours. Please purloin as many blackberries as you desire.'

Had she not already explained they were not exactly his to offer? She smiled back sweetly. 'As you can see, I have already helped myself to as many as I need.' She frowned. 'Besides, rather than galloping around the countryside and fussing about a few dozen black-berries, I should think you would rather spend your time setting your estate in order.' She gestured to the acres of hay spread out before her.

The amusement in his face faded. Oh, dear. Why

had she let her tongue run away with her when she knew she was in the wrong? If she had known he had finally taken up residence, she really would never have climbed his fence. She opened her mouth to apologise, but he forestalled her with a pleasant smile and a bow.

'As you say, ma'am. I do indeed have a great deal of work requiring my attention. I wish you good day.'

He signalled to his horse to move on and the animal obediently took a short run at the stile. Rider and beast cleared the obstruction in magnificent form. The sound of hoof beats faded into the distance.

A bruising rider herself, she could not help but admire his skill. And he looked so good on a horse. Dashing. Oh, no. She was not going to think of him that way. She shook herself free of such musings. He was simply a new neighbour with whom she had made an acquaintance.

She stomped out of the bushes and heard the sound of tearing. Blast, she'd caught her apron and now she would have to mend it. Well, it would be something to do when she had finished making the jam.

Hopefully she would be busy enough that it would take her mind off his face and that lovely smile. Smiles like that caused nothing but trouble and heartache, yet it seemed that she had still not learned her lesson.

Good Lord, he might even be married. A man didn't stop being charming to ladies, just because he was wed. If anyone knew that, she should.

He'd called her a wench! Mortified heat scalded the back of Ethan's neck. How was he supposed to recognise her as a lady? Not a ribbon or a ruffle to be seen. Tangled up in a blackberry bush, her legs displayed for all to see and with deep red juice staining her full lips, she'd looked like a roundheeled lass ready for a spree.

He was lucky he hadn't given in to the urge to kiss those luscious, ripe lips. Not something he was in the habit of doing or even thinking as a general rule, but in her case, for some reason he could not quite understand, he had been very tempted indeed. Fortunately, the lady's tart remarks had reminded him that no matter how attractively dishevelled a woman might be, he was an officer, a gentleman and an earl with duties and responsibilities to King, country and his family name.

But there really had been something deliciously pretty and alluring about her... He winced. He had thoroughly deserved the sharp edge of her tongue when she caught him ogling the slender legs bared to his gaze. Right now, he did not need the added complication of any sort of lass, common or noble, in his life.

Honestly, though, what sort of lady went about the countryside without even a maid?

Dash it, kissing her wouldn't have crossed his mind under normal circumstances. His army duties had kept him too busy to worry about the ladies, except for the occasional foray when he was on leave, until Sarah had begun to pay him particular attention. Her own husband had been killed, but she had remained on the Peninsula as companion to her sister, the wife of one of his fellow officers. Sarah had stirred up feelings he thought he'd long buried in response to a childhood fraught with drama. A sense that perhaps he did warrant affection from someone. His parents hadn't thought so. They had been far too involved in themselves to pay attention to their only child.

When Sarah had entered his life almost a year ago,

she'd been attentive and, well…loving, if he even understood the meaning of the word. There was no denying he'd been smitten. He should have known better than to believe a woman could actually care for him in the way he had thought Sarah did.

Fortunately for him, a brother officer had heard her talking to her sister about how life as the wife of an earl would suit her very well. How she liked the sound of being called Lady Longhurst and would enjoy the privileges a title brought, even if it did require marriage to him. His friend had teased him about how popular he was among the ladies now he was an earl.

Ethan had come to his senses with a jolt and only just in time, because if their relationship had gone much further, he would have been honour-bound to take Sarah to the altar. A lucky escape indeed.

Bitterness rose in his throat like gall. How had he not seen through Sarah's smiles to the truth beneath? It was the first time any woman had trapped him with her wiles and it would also be the last. But apparently, those few weeks of so-called affection had left him feeling that something serious was lacking in his life and made him vulnerable to the first pretty lady he came across now he was back in England.

Damn it! Didn't he have enough to keep him occupied, adjusting to his new position in life without the sort of distraction a pair of blackberry-stained lips brought? He hadn't even known he was the heir to the Earldom until he received a letter from a lawyer hired by some busybody third cousin twice removed who had searched down every line of the family tree, going back as far as his great-great-grandfather to search him out.

Apparently, it had taken some digging to discover

that his great-grandfather, the fifth son of the Earl, had been bribed to take his wife's name in order to inherit the wealth of an old Cornish mining family. With only daughters to their name, the Trethewys had thought they were getting a nobleman, but instead Great-Grandfather Trethewy had been a ne'er-do-well gambler who had lost most of the family fortune the moment he got his hands on it. As a result, both families had cut the connection. Certainly, if Ethan's father had known he was related to an earl, he would have used it to his advantage in some way.

Even after Ethan learned of the title, he had put off returning to England for as long as possible. The army was his life. All he had known since he was a youth. He hadn't mentioned the inheritance to anyone, but somehow the news must have reached Sarah's ears and she had decided to set her cap at him, and make him think she genuinely cared for him. Not once had she mentioned knowing about the title.

He'd been cut to the quick when he realised that was all she'd really cared about.

Not long after he uncovered her deceit, the same busybody third cousin, Lady Frances, had written to Wellington, asking why the General was keeping the last Longhurst Earl captive on the battlefield when he ought to be taking up his duties at home.

Wellington, damn his eyes, had insisted Ethan return to England and take up the reins of his estate. The moment Ethan had put things in order here, he intended to get back to what really mattered. War with the French.

As he galloped up the drive of Longhurst Park, a grand old house with a winding drive lined with trees, his mood darkened further. The previous Earl had left the estate in a wretched mess, as evidenced by a pile of unpaid bills his man of business had presented to Ethan with the expression of a man who saw disaster looming.

Paperwork. Ethan hated it, but he'd been battling his way through it every day since, determined to bring things into some sort of order.

At the stables, he handed Jack over to O'Cleary. The handsome black-haired Irishman narrowed his gaze on Ethan's face. 'What has you so hot under the collar?'

Ethan didn't get hot under the collar. He never unleashed his temper on anyone. He was a big man and, out of control, could do a lot of damage. It was why he had decided to become a soldier in the first place. He gave O'Cleary a look that ought to make him shrivel in his boots, but only made the fellow glare back.

Ethan didn't know when it had happened, but at some point O'Cleary had become more friend than servant. They were of a similar age and Ethan respected the man's skill with horses, but O'Cleary's perceptiveness and frank speaking had also earned his admiration and, yes, a sort of friendship.

Ethan sighed. 'I met a lady on the way back. I thought she was a dairymaid or some such stealing my blackberries.'

'Your blackberries, is it? Since when do you care about brambles?'

Since a lovely young lady with lips stained red had come to his attention. 'She was trespassing on my land.'

'Ah.' He gave Jack a pat.

'Ah, what?'

'Who is she, then?'

'Lady Petra Davenport. She lives in Westram.'

O'Cleary narrowed his eyes. 'Fancy her, do you?'

Ethan glared at him. Much as he might *fancy* Lady Petra in passing—what man would not when she was so excessively pretty?—he certainly had no more interest in her than that. 'You will not speak of a lady in that manner.'

O'Cleary's black brows climbed into his hairline. 'It is protective of this lady, you are?'

As if. The lady needed no protection from him. 'A gentleman protects all ladies.'

'Ah.'

Could O'Cleary be any more irritating? Possibly. If given the chance. 'Are you going to let my horse stand there all day? Or are you going to see to his needs?'

O'Cleary grinned, his blue eyes full of laughter, saluted and walked Jack off.

Ethan stomped into the house. The memory of a pair of shapely legs had him smiling, too, until he tripped over the end of one of several rolled-up rugs. Like the rest of the house, the study was full of pieces of furniture, chairs upended on chairs, tables and consoles stacked willy-nilly. There were even stacks of ancient newspapers and journals on the floor, leaving little room to walk. The last Earl had been a jackdaw, collecting anything and everything. It was ridiculous.

He groaned. He really hated the business of being an earl. He took off his coat, rolled up his sleeves and hefted the rug that had tripped him on to his shoulder and headed for the barn.

To the devil with the paperwork, this was a task he could get his teeth into. In a few hours he might actually be able to see the floor.

Sitting in the front pew in St Bartholomew's Church, Ethan was aware of the many curious gazes landing on him as the service wore on. As an officer, he was used to being watched by his men, but this was a different kind of observation. The gazes were not only assessing, they were hopeful. No doubt they were all hoping to meet him in the melee outside the church at the end of the service. He braced himself and polished up his most charming smile, despite that he'd prefer to go straight home.

It would not be neighbourly. And while he had no intention of staying any longer than necessary, in the army one learned to adapt to local customs.

Naturally, he'd received a call from the Vicar the day after he had arrived at Longhurst. The worthy fellow had made it very clear it was an earl's duty to set a good example for the villagers by attending church every Sunday. Naturally, Ethan agreed. It had been no different in the army. Officers were required to set a good example in all things.

The Vicar had beamed at his assent and further pronounced that, as Earl, he would, of course, want to subscribe to the front pew that had been a tradition in his family for many years. A not-unreasonable request. Unfortunately, Ethan discovered he not only had to pay this year's subscription but also that of the previous fifteen years, since his dear departed predecessor had refused to have anything to do with St Bartholomew's.

He really did despise the former Earl.

Of course, he'd paid up with as much good grace as he could muster. It was what one did, despite the fact that the payment ate a large chunk of his army pay, making another visit to his man of business in Sevenoaks mandatory. While he had absolutely no hope of discovering a nice little nest egg hidden among the Earl's

papers, there were still a few tenants left on the estate
and he needed to know what rents had been paid and
what required collecting.

The congregation filed out and he followed. Right
away, he noticed that women outnumbered the men.
He frowned. Why would that be? Naturally, he also
spotted one woman immediately, Lady Petra, in a particularly fetching bonnet and a fashionable gown and
spencer clearly designed to bring out the blue in her
eyes. Strangely, her tiny stature stood out as much as
his large one. Or perhaps it was that his gaze had sought
her out as one of the few people he recognised, even if
theirs had been a rather unconventional meeting. He
recalled the neat turn of her ankle and her dainty feet
as much as he remembered her face. Would she acknowledge their acquaintance? Likely not, given her
unfriendliness at their first meeting.

He waited his turn to speak to the Vicar, who
greeted each person with a few brief words as they
filed out into the sunshine. The man had the aesthetic
look of a monk rather than a Church of England cleric.
His sermon had been all fire and brimstone about the
evils of drunkenness.

'Good sermon, Vicar,' Ethan said when it was his
turn to receive a nod and a handshake.

'It is unfortunate that those who really need to hear
the words of the Lord do not open their ears.' Reverend
Beckridge smiled thinly. 'But never mind. I am glad
to see you here today, my lord. Let me introduce you
around.'

'I would particularly like to meet other landowners
in these parts,' Ethan said.

Beckridge frowned. 'Unfortunately, the owner of the

largest property, Lord Compton, attends the church in Ightham. While his estate is in this parish, the church there is closer to his abode.' He sighed. 'I do not blame him, I suppose, but St Bartholomew's could use the support.'

'I am looking to hire some farm labourers. Perhaps there is a farmer or two among the congregation?'

'There are indeed. But you will find them also short of men. What with the war and the lure of the better-paying factories in the North... But first let me introduce you to the two widowed ladies, who recently came to Westram. Lady Petra and Lady Marguerite, Lord Westram's sisters. In the past year, they have made quite a stir with their industry.'

Lady Petra was a widow? At such a young age?

Ethan found himself inexorably guided to the small knot of women chattering on the path leading out to the road.

At the centre of the group, Lady Petra's bright smile lit her pretty face as if the sun had deigned to send down a ray of light especially for her, yet it became somewhat brittle as he approached, as if she was steeling herself for their inevitable meeting.

The Vicar introduced everyone, including his wife, a sharp-eyed, round-faced lady who eyed him with speculation in her gaze.

'Lord Longhurst and I are already acquainted,' Lady Petra said with a challenging glance. 'We met over a basket of blackberries.'

Instead of his usual easy conversational gambits—the weather, the news—he found his mind going completely blank while he stared at her luscious mouth. He forced himself to speak. 'We did indeed.' It sounded unfriendly.

Her smile dimmed a little.

Lady Marguerite, a much taller lady, with auburn hair and green eyes and a plain mode of dress, looked puzzled. 'You met over... Why, Petra, you didn't say you had met Lord Longhurst when you went blackberry picking.'

Lady Petra smiled sweetly, too sweetly, perhaps fearing he might reveal the awkwardness of their meeting. 'I must have forgotten.'

He winced. If she had wanted to forget, why had she mentioned it now? Women. There was no understanding them.

'You are welcome to pick my blackberries whenever you wish, Lady Petra.'

Lady Petra raised her eyebrows, reminding him that she did not in fact believe they were his to offer. 'How very kind of you, my lord.' She dipped a curtsy. 'If you will excuse us, Lord Longhurst, Vicar, we don't wish to be late for lunch.'

While her sister looked surprised, she trailed after Lady Petra and both ladies climbed into a waiting pony and trap. He watched them drive away, one blonde, petite and pretty and dressed in flounces and ribbons, the other an elegant redhead and plainly gowned. Both attractive in very different ways.

'Such a shame,' the Vicar's wife said. 'To be widowed at such a young age.'

'This war has taken a great many young men,' the Vicar said.

'I am sorry to hear it.' What else could one say?

'Such pretty ladies will not be single long,' Mrs Beckridge added, somewhat pointedly staring at Ethan.

He smiled pleasantly, ignoring the hint. Sarah had

been another widow left in penury by the death of her husband and looking for a replacement. She hadn't tangled herself up in a blackberry bush in order to meet him; she'd twisted her ankle when leaving the dance floor and stumbled into him.

He wasn't fool enough to be taken in twice by way of a pretty ankle. He would do his own choosing of a bride and Lady Petra seemed far too sharp-tongued to make a man a comfortable wife. Besides, when he married, as he would have to do, he'd choose someone solid and dependable who didn't need him to devote his whole attention to her needs and whims. Someone he could leave in charge of things here in England while he returned to his army career. His real life.

'You *really* think I should take Long Longhurst some of this jam?' Petra looked at the prettily covered pots she and Marguerite had filled a few days before.

'I most certainly do.' Marguerite frowned. 'They were his blackberries after all. It is only polite. Besides, it is not wise to risk upsetting our neighbour needlessly.'

Marguerite had not been happy upon learning the details of her meeting with Lord Longhurst.

Petra did not want to meet him again. While his smile seemed friendly enough, she had the peculiar sensation that it hid his true feelings. It seemed to set her at a distance rather than be truly welcoming. Not to mention that he was just too handsome for any lady's peace of mind. 'You really are making a mountain out of a molehill, Marguerite. They grow wild. He could not have said a word about it if I had picked them from the lane.'

Her sister's eyes widened, probably because Petra had spoken with heat. 'But you did not pick them in the lane. You trespassed on his land in order to gather them.'

Petra huffed out a breath. 'Very well, I'll take him a pot.'

'Two, I think.'

'Two? After we did all the work?'

Marguerite sighed. 'Do as you wish. You will anyway.'

Petra stilled, pained by the accusation. Her siblings often teased her about being the baby of the family and overindulged, but she did not think they truly meant it. 'What is that supposed to mean?'

Marguerite shook her head. 'It means nothing. I am sorry. I am feeling a little out of sorts.'

Petra gave her sister a closer look. Marguerite looked pale and tired. Instantly she regretted their argument. 'Is your head aching, dearest?'

Marguerite rubbed a fingertip against her temple and gave her a wan smile. 'I think there may be a storm brewing.'

Petra glanced out of the kitchen window to where Jeb was doggedly hoeing between the rows of cabbages. The sky was clear, all but a few wispy clouds, but Marguerite had always been prone to headaches before the arrival of a storm, so perhaps the weather was about to change. 'Go and lie down. I will bring you a cold compress.' She grinned. 'And after that I will take Lord Longhurst two pots of our lovely jam. I promise to charm him out of the boughs.'

'Ask him to come for afternoon tea.'

Not likely, when the man was so standoffish, though

it was probably her fault. She had been rather sharp with him. And a bit dismissive at church. So what if he was an attractive man? It meant nothing to her. She could at least be civil to him. Dash it all, she really ought to mend some fences if only to declare a truce. They did not have to like each other, but they ought to be able to manage a polite friendliness.

'Go on upstairs,' she said, shooing her sister out of the kitchen. 'I'll bring you a tisane before I go.'

Marguerite gave her a grateful smile. 'You are a dear.'

Relief filled her. She hated being at odds with Marguerite, particularly when she carried some of the blame for her sister's sorrow. If only she hadn't said those things to Harry and driven him away… Perhaps her family was right in saying she was too used to getting her own way. Well, she had got her own way as far as marrying the man she wanted, and look what a terrible mistake she had made. She would be very careful about what she wished for in future. She delivered Marguerite's tea and set off to walk to Longhurst Park, making sure to take her umbrella.

The crested wrought-iron gates to Longhurst Park were open, not in invitation so much as in careless abandonment, the weeds and vines having grown so high it would take a full day of chopping and pulling to free the gates from captivity and have them working again.

The curving drive, lined by lime trees, fared no better. The gravel sprouted tufts of grass and the lawn looked more like a hayfield. As she rounded the bend, though, she was enchanted by the sight of the house. Lovely old red brick gave the place a warm homely look. As she got closer, however, she was saddened to see that a few of the windows had been boarded up and that some of the tiles on the roof were missing.

What had Longhurst been thinking in letting the house go to rack and ruin these past two years? Perhaps he didn't care because he had estates elsewhere like her brother, who owned more than one property.

She glanced skyward and grimaced. It seemed Marguerite had been right. The clouds that had been fluffy and white when she left home were thicker and showing signs of grey.

When no one opened the front door at her approach, she pounded the knocker against the heavily carved wood and stepped back. This portico could certainly use a coat of paint.

The door swung back.

Petra blinked in surprise at the sight of a dark-haired, sullen-faced young man in his shirtsleeves and riding boots. He looked more like a groom than a footman.

'Good day,' she said briskly. 'Lady Petra Davenport to see Lord Longhurst.'

His eyebrows shot up. He opened the door wider. 'This way, ma'am.' The brogue of Ireland coloured his voice.

He ushered her into a gloomy hall with marble pillars and a grand staircase leading up to the first floor. Footmen's chairs lined the walls as if there ought to be a dozen men waiting to open the door. Tables and chests and cupboards were piled on top of each other in one of the corners. Very odd. The Earl must be moving things around.

Instead of asking her to wait while he enquired if his

master was home, the servant led her down a corridor and to a room she guessed would be an antechamber where visitors would wait.

Only—

'A Lady Petra Davenport to see you, my lord.'

Petra's jaw dropped. There at the desk sat Lord Longhurst, also in his shirtsleeves, his blonde hair tousled as if he had run his fingers through it more than once.

The servant left and closed the door behind him. His footsteps echoed on the floor outside and she could hear him whistling as he walked away. How very peculiar.

After a second's pause, Lord Longhurst shot to his feet, reaching for a jacket slung over the back of his chair. He shrugged into it. 'Lady Petra Davenport? Lady Petra?'

He quickly buttoned the coat. There was nothing he could do about the shirt open at the throat. She tried to keep her gaze focused on his face and not drift down to the strong column of his neck or the intriguing sight of crisply curled golden hair peeking seductively above the stark white linen.

'How may I be of service?' he asked.

Service? An image of a broad naked chest flickered across her mind. Good Lord, had her mind really jumped to those ways in which a man could service a woman? Was that why she missed Harry, not for himself, but for the delights of the marriage bed? Could she really be so wanton? Besides, she wasn't very good at bed sport, as Harry had called it, or he wouldn't have gone seeking his pleasures elsewhere. *Boring*, was what he'd called her. Too innocent, whatever that meant.

Sadness filled her. She should never have confronted him. Should never have expected fidelity from him. She knew better now.

She lifted her chin. 'I brought you some jam.'

He blinked as if her words made no sense. He looked gorgeous, almost vulnerable standing there with a puzzled look on his face and his long, strong fingers covered in ink. Then he smiled and a dimple appeared in a jaw already showing signs of fair stubble. Her heart clenched.

And no wonder. He had looked magnificent up on his horse the first time they met, and like a handsome soldier at church on Sunday, but here, now, he looked like every woman's dream of a man in need of a woman's care.

She could even imagine running her fingers through those wavy locks to bring them to some semblance of order. How would they feel? Silky or coarse? And would he let her help him tie the cravat he had discarded on the corner of the desk? Or better yet, let her help him remove his shirt to reveal the full glory of that wide expanse of chest so tantalisingly covered with billowing linen?

Mind blank, she inhaled a deep breath.

His gaze dropped to her bosom. The room warmed. The air crackled with something that made her skin tingle. For a second, her head seemed too light for her shoulders, as if she might float away.

Would he also find her boring? The thought brought her back to earth with a bump.

Longhurst's forehead furrowed as if he had finally figured out her words, but not their meaning. 'Jam?'

'From the blackberries I picked.' Goodness, her voice sounded so small and weak she scarcely recognised it. She straightened her shoulders. 'We made jam out of the fruit.'

She walked deeper into the room, aware of his gaze tracking her every movement as she skirted a couple of armchairs.

'My word, you have a lot of furniture,' she said in awed tones.

He grimaced. 'You would not believe the half of it. I've moved out most of what was in here. At least now you can actually see some of the floor. The house is stuffed full of furniture and knick-knacks. It seems my predecessor liked to collect things.'

No wonder the entrance hall had been so cluttered. She reached into her basket and, like a magician pulling rabbits from a hat, drew out three jam pots one by one and placed them on the desk. 'Blackberry and apple. The apples picked from *our* tree,' she said pointedly.

He stared at the pots as if he had never seen jam before. He swallowed. 'I see.'

Her heart beat a little faster. Too fast.

'As an apology for purloining your blackberries,' she added, completely unnecessarily, but it filled the silence.

His gaze rose to her face. 'There is no need…' He gestured at the jam.

Why could the man not just say thank you and leave it at that? 'If you do not eat jam, then please feel free to give it to your servant.'

His blue eyes widened and then he smiled. Her stomach did a somersault. 'I do beg your pardon, Lady Petra. Thank you for the gift.'

That smile would be the death of her when she ought

to know better than to be taken in. She dipped a curtsy. 'Then I will bid you good day.'

'No. Wait. I mean— Would you like—'

They gazed at one another in silence for a long second or two. She seemed to have trouble drawing in a breath. 'Would I like…?'

'May I offer you a cup of tea before you leave?' Longhurst finally said. 'I am sure O'Cleary is taking good care of your horses and groom for the nonce.'

'Oh, there are no horses or groom. I walked.'

Astonishment filled his expression. 'You walked from Westram. It must be more than two miles distant.'

'About that, I should think.'

He frowned.

Did he not approve of a lady going for a walk? 'I grew up in the country, my lord. I am quite used to using my legs to get about.'

His gaze shot down her length and back up to her face and she recalled how much he had seen of her legs the last time they met. Heat scalded her cheeks and his eyes filled with awareness. Bother, they were never going to get past their first meeting. Mortified, she prepared to turn away.

'But you will take some refreshment before you set out for home.'

It wasn't expressed as a request, but rather as an order and she felt her hackles rise, but then again, she *was* thirsty after her long walk. And she had promised Marguerite to charm him out of the boughs. 'A cup of tea would be most welcome, my lord. Thank you.'

Strangely, he looked relieved. 'Excellent.' He strode for the door and turned when he reached it. He gestured to a chair beside the desk. 'Please, Lady Petra, be seated. I shall not be more than a moment or two.'

And then he was gone.

More orders. The pile of papers on the desk looked highly intimidating and important. She took a turn about the room. It was indeed full of strange items, from ill-thrown pots to finely blown glass ornaments.

Having established that she was not going to instantly obey any man's order, she dusted off an armchair near the window with her handkerchief and perched on the edge of it.

Perhaps he was so dictatorial because he was a soldier used to commanding men on the battlefield. She sighed. She did not like to think about war and battlefields. She hated the whole thing. Poor Harry. Had she really driven him to take the King's shilling? She still couldn't believe she would never hear his laughter again and never be irritated by his devil-may-care ways. While she hadn't made the wisest choice in a husband, it didn't mean she didn't miss him. After all, she had known him most of her life. Her mistake had been not making sure he loved her as much as she loved him before they wed. To discover he saw it purely as a marriage of convenience had been devastating to say the least. He'd called her a silly romantic, as if it was some sort of flaw.

Well, she was a romantic and not ashamed of it either. She couldn't be happier for Carrie and Avery, who had clearly fallen head over heels in love.

Chapter Two

When Ethan found no sign of O'Cleary in the kitchen, he put the kettle on the hob. Damnation. He'd left his cravat in the study. He dashed upstairs and, well used to dressing in haste, soon had a new cravat tied neatly at his throat.

Returning to the kitchen, he found O'Cleary setting a tray with cups and saucers. 'Where the devil were you?'

'Putting the carriage to. I assumed you wouldn't send her back on Shanks's pony. Er...my lord.'

Mollified by O'Cleary's anticipation of his wishes, he grinned. 'Well done.'

'Hmm. Had you not better get back to your guest?' He ran a discerning eye over Ethan and pulled a comb from his pocket. 'Here. This might help.'

Ethan dragged the comb through his hair. 'Thanks.' He strode back to his study.

Lady Petra was gazing out of the window when he arrived. Despite the dust on her hems and the tendrils of hair escaping from their pins around her face, she looked good enough to eat.

Blast it. He had forgotten to ask O'Cleary to add biscuits to the tray. If indeed they had any. She would think him as even more of an ill-mannered brute than she must do already. Why on earth had he made such a stupid invitation?

'Tea will be along shortly,' he announced.

She jumped as if she had been so far away in her thoughts that she had not heard him enter despite the fact he had not been in the least bit quiet about it. Her blue eyes were filled with sadness.

He stiffened. Was it something he had said? Was she one of those females who needed treating with kid gloves? She seemed so self-sufficient, but perhaps it was all an act intended to keep a man on his toes.

Women did that. Pretended. His mother had always fussed over him, as if she loved him, but only when his father was about, to make him jealous of her attentions. Sarah had pretended she cared about him just to gain his title.

Lady Petra's eyes widened as her gaze took him in, clearly realising he had tidied himself up. What? Did she think he had no manners? If he had been a bit rough around the edges when he first joined the army at the age of fifteen, his fellow officers had soon put him straight.

She smiled and he felt like preening at her obvious approval, when he really didn't care if she approved of him or not. He smiled back, it was the obvious thing to do. When in doubt, smile. He'd learned that from his mother's interactions. She'd always stalked off if he'd shown the least sign of being unhappy. Any upset had always brought heaps of coals down upon his head. His mother had told him quite plainly that she had enough trouble with his father without him adding to it.

However, Lady Petra's smile faltered at the sight of his own. 'I really did not intend to put you to so much trouble.' Her voice was light, nicely modulated, music to the ears of a man mostly used to the coarse words of soldiers. Perhaps that was why he had found Sarah so alluring after twenty years of all-male company.

Twenty years. A long time. And yet he was still in his prime at thirty-five. And lucky to be alive, given how long he'd been fighting for his country. Something he'd sooner do than sit here entertaining a lady in his drawing room.

A lady far too attractive to be a soldier's wife. A man would surely worry about leaving such a lovely woman behind when he went off to war. He forced the wayward thought aside.

'No trouble at all, my lady. You'll find O'Cleary is a dab hand at brewing a pot of tea.'

'O'Cleary?'

'My batman. Well, no longer a batman, more a valet-cum-butler-cum-groom. He let you in.'

Her eyebrows rose. 'A man of all work, then.'

'A good description indeed.' He couldn't hire any proper staff until he knew exactly how the estate stood financially. The account books had been left to keep themselves during the last few years of his cousin's illness, as far as he could tell.

Her brow furrowed. 'I understand you inherited the estate more than two years ago?'

His mouth tightened. 'I did, but other, far more important matters engaged my attention.'

She looked shocked.

Could no one truly understand that he did not want this title? He was an army man through and through and here he was struggling with information about yields and labourers and bushels and baskets and... Bah! It was his duty and he would do it, but that didn't mean he had to like it. Well, he would get it licked into shape, provide it with a countess and an heir and get back to what really mattered in short order.

'The French. The war.'

She coloured. 'Yes, of course.' She did not, however, sound convinced. But then she might not, considering how she had lost her husband.

O'Cleary entered with the tea tray, picked his way around the clutter and set it down on the table in front of Lady Petra with a smile and a wink. 'The shortbreads are a bit singed. But I cut off the worst of it.'

Ethan cringed at the sight of jagged edges and burnt crumbs. 'You will have to excuse us, Lady Petra. We are bachelors used to army tack. Take them away, O'Cleary.' O'Cleary was still not used to the new-fangled oven in the kitchen. He was more used to cooking over a campfire.

O'Cleary reached for the plate, but Lady Petra Davenport put out a hand to forestall him. 'Thank you, Mr O'Cleary, I am sure they are fine.'

The smile she gave O'Cleary and the grin he gave her back made Ethan want to grab his batman by the collar and heave him out of the door. He blinked at the odd urge. He didn't have a jealous bone in his body. Deliberately so. He'd learned early that it was a pointless emotion.

'That will be all, O'Cleary,' he said gruffly. 'I think Lady Petra can manage from here.'

O'Cleary walked out whistling. The idiot.

The lady poured out cups of tea and added milk. 'The village will be delighted that you have finally moved in.'

'I am glad *they* are pleased.' He picked up his cup and took a sip. Somehow, she'd got it exactly the right strength.

'You do not like the idea?'

'No.' He squeezed his eyes shut briefly. Why on earth was he telling her this? But now he had said it, he could hardly call a halt to the conversation. Even he knew that was the height of rudeness. 'I know nothing about farming or managing an estate. The army is my life.' He sighed. 'I am not cut out for this.' He made a gesture to encompass the house, the land and the whole of Kent.

He'd also been a fish out of water in his father's house, never knowing how to please the man who had sired him, never knowing whether his mother would react to her husband's rants by blaming Ethan for whatever it was Father had decided was wrong that time. Joining the army at fifteen had been a welcome relief from the mayhem in his home. Since then he'd seen himself as a confirmed bachelor. A free spirit.

Lady Petra offered him the plate of biscuits.

He munched on one absentmindedly until he hit a burnt bit. He grimaced, glad to see she had not taken one.

'A good bailiff should be able to help you,' she said. Was that a note of encouragement in her voice? Surely not. She was simply making conversation.

'Indeed. But how does one tell good from bad? Looking through my cousin's estate diary, I have the feeling the man he employed was a charlatan.' What was it about her that had him revealing his concerns? She would think him a terrible bore. It just wasn't done. Unless she was deliberately trying to lure him in with kindness as Sarah had done. He inspected her expression, but could detect no ulterior motive. But then he wouldn't, would he? Ladies were experts at hiding their real thoughts and feelings.

'Perhaps you could ask around among your fellow peers,' she said.

Fellow peers? Did he know any? There was the chap the Vicar had mentioned, Compton, who also served as the local magistrate living near the next village over. Perhaps he should ride over and introduce himself. Though what they would have in common, he could not imagine. 'Good thought.'

She looked surprised and pleased.

He frowned. Had she not expected him to acknowledge her idea as helpful?

She sipped at her tea. 'If I might offer another suggestion...'

He tensed. No doubt this was where he learned the real purpose for her visit. He did not relish making his lack of interest plain. 'Please do.'

'Well... If I were you, I would mow the field where we met as soon as possible. It is perfect for harvesting and if you cut it right away you may get another crop before the winter.'

Why hadn't he thought of that? Because while his horses ate hay, and he made sure they had enough, he'd never questioned how it arrived in the stable. It was not his concern when he had a war to fight. The commissary looked after those sorts of details. 'I will certainly look into it, thank you.'

She gave him an odd look and finished her tea. 'And now if you will excuse me, I really should be getting home before my sister wonders what has become of me.'

Ethan glanced out of the window. 'My carriage awaits you.' To his surprise, the old coach looked in a lot better shape than it had looked the last time he had inspected it and with Jack between the poles it looked almost lordly.

'Truly, my lord, I am quite happy walking.'

'Nevertheless, Mr O'Cleary will be pleased to drive you since Jack is in need of the exercise. I have not had time to hack him out today.'

'Very well. Since you make it impossible to refuse without seeming disobliging, I will avail myself of your kind offer, my lord.'

He blinked at the forthright speech. No beating around the bush or simpering for this lady. He liked it. He knew where he stood. Unless she was using it as a ploy? Well she would not find him easy to gull, so he would just take her words at face value until he discovered the truth.

And thank heaven she had accepted his offer of the carriage. If she had not, he would have had to walk her all the way home, using up a great deal of time which he really did not have. And yet... He glanced out of the window. A walk with a pretty widowed lady on his arm would be very pleasant indeed.

And just the sort of entanglement in which he would not allow himself to indulge.

He escorted her outside and helped her aboard.

Once he had shut the door he went forward to speak to O'Cleary seated on the box. 'No racing, not on the way there or on the way back.' He glanced up at the sky. The clouds didn't look particularly threatening, but one never knew for certain in England. 'Not even if it rains.'

O'Cleary grinned, touched his hat in acknowledgement of the jibe and set Jack in motion.

Lady Petra lifted her hand in farewell as the coach swept away.

Mow the hay. It was the first helpful suggestion anyone had given him and that it had come from such a pretty lady who looked as if she would be more at home in a London drawing room than in the wilds of Kent was quite a surprise.

Although she had not looked quite so ladylike when she'd been picking his blackberries. He squashed the image that popped into his mind.

Likely someone had encouraged her to make herself useful to a bachelor earl. After all, why would the sister of an earl march about the countryside delivering jars of jam if it wasn't to get his attention?

Two mornings after her visit to the Earl, Petra set out to collect mushrooms for the stewpot before the dew was off the grass. She had noticed a fairy ring of them, as they had called them as children, in the same hedgerow where she'd picked the blackberries. She certainly was not going with the expectation of meeting His Lordship, but if she did, she had her excuse ready. After all, while he hadn't specifically mentioned mushrooms, he had told her to purloin all the blackberries she wanted, so why would he object to her picking mushrooms, as long as she offered him some of her bounty?

A tiny tickle of something pleasant stirred low in her body at the thought of meeting Longhurst again. The same sensation she had felt when he was staring at her bare legs. Never before had the memory of a simple glance caused such feelings.

Nor even Harry had had that sort of visceral effect on her, which was what made it so very strange.

When they first came to Westram, she had suggested to her sisters that as widows they ought to be free to take lovers. It had been her anger at Harry's abandonment, both before and after he died, that had made her suggest such a wicked idea. An anger that had faded into regret over time. And she certainly hadn't actually expected to have an opportunity to put such an idea into practice out here in the depths of Kent. No, the last thing she wanted or needed was more hurt in her life.

Besides, this outing was not about her seeing Lord Longhurst again, it was about providing food for their table.

She climbed the stile into the field. At this time of year, the birds were quieter, though there was still the odd cheep as they darted about, feasting on blackberries and grass seeds. The crisp morning air seemed to predict autumn just around the corner. The dew caught the sun's rays and glinted as if there were diamonds scattered across the top of the grass. It would not remain long; a breeze was already ruffling the long stalks like wind upon water.

She found the mushroom ring she had spotted a few days before, and after carefully bruising one of the caps to ensure it turned pink and not yellow, she cut them off and gently placed them in her basket. The next mushroom she found was a giant puffball hiding in the stinging nettles at the foot of an elm tree. It was large enough to provide both her and Marguerite with an excellent breakfast. Careful to make sure the nettles did not touch her skin, she cut the stalk and soon it was also sitting in the bottom of her basket.

She continued up the rolling stretch of land, making her way to the brow of the low hill which ran through the centre of the field.

Because the grass was so long, most of her harvest grew against the hedge, where the vegetation thinned out. Mushroom picking was easier in woods or a pasture with short grass, but since she had promised Marguerite she would not go into the woods alone, she continued up the hill.

By the time she crested the rise, her basket was brimming with assorted mushrooms and it was time to turn back. She stretched her back and looked about. Two men with their shirts off were hacking at the grass at the far end of the field.

Apparently, Lord Longhurst had taken her advice.

She squinted against the sun's brightness. Oh, goodness. If she was not mistaken, one of those men was His Lordship himself and the other shorter, leaner figure, Mr O'Cleary.

She frowned. With only two of them working, and at the rate they were progressing, it would take ages to mow this field. After that, they would have to pile it into hayricks to dry. It would take days to finish. Why on earth had he not hired any help?

Unable to contain her curiosity, she continued

working her way along the hedgerow, picking one or two mushrooms and then glancing up to see if they had noticed her presence while pretending she had not noticed them. As she drew closer, she could see both men in all their glorious detail, though she really only had eyes for the taller blonde giant of a man.

Lord Longhurst's chest was broad and well muscled, like a statue of a Roman god, and his arms as he swung the scythe were the most enticing sight she had ever seen. Oh, heavens, the way the muscles in his back rippled with his movement made her insides tighten in a most shocking way. She fought the strong desire to run her hands over that back and down his spine and… She could not remember ever seeing a flesh-and-blood man who could serve as a model for a Greek god. Such a gorgeous specimen of the male of the human species.

She fanned her face. What on earth was the matter with her? She could not recall ever having such wayward thoughts before. Not even when Harry was alive and still treating her as if he loved her. With Harry, she realised, she'd been all girlish giggles and eager to do anything to get his attention. With this man, her reactions were far subtler in some ways and earthier in others she simply did not understand.

Good Lord. What would Longhurst think if he knew the direction of her mind? He'd likely be as shocked as she was.

The next glance revealed His Lordship pulling his shirt over his head. A sense of disappointment gave her another shock. No, no, she wasn't disappointed. She was pleased because he must have seen her. Yes, indeed he had because the moment he was decently covered he strode to meet her.

As he drew close she became aware of trickles of moisture working their way down from his hairline to his neck. Oh, and the way his shirt clung to his skin was positively delicious. No, no, she meant indecent.

She mentally shook her finger at this new wanton version of herself and composed her face into an expression of polite surprise. 'Good day, Lord Longhurst. A perfect day for working in the fields, is it not?'

He smiled and her heart gave an odd little clench. Oh, she was a fool for those boyish open smiles. She always had been. But she'd also learned those smiles also hid a good deal of boyish vice. Definitely not to be trusted.

'Yes,' he said. 'Although I have to admit, while the sun is a boon, I am grateful for the breeze.'

As was she, as a gentle waft of air carried his scent towards her, earthy sweat mingled with the fresh scent of soap. She inhaled deeply and caught him looking at her with an odd expression.

Surprised by her inability to control such reactions in herself, she swallowed and was startled to discover her mouth was quite dry. 'I have been mushroom picking,' she said, holding out her basket and sounding more frog-like than she would have preferred. She swallowed again. 'Half of these are yours.'

He looked startled and peered down at the fungus. 'Are you sure they are edible? I have heard there are many poisonous kinds.'

Did he think her an idiot? 'I have been picking mushrooms for almost as long as I could walk. You may trust I know what I am doing.'

She and Marguerite had gone on foraging expeditions with their cook, who had taken pity on their motherless state. She'd been a dear old stick and taught them lots about the bounty to be found in the country. She'd also taught them the rudiments of cooking, never expecting it would come in useful later in their lives.

Petra liked being outdoors. Even in those days Marguerite had preferred standing at her easel creating art to tramping around the countryside in all kinds of weather. Now Petra wished she had spent more time in the kitchen, but fortunately their maid, Becky, wasn't a bad cook and between them all they managed to put decent if simple food on the table.

His Lordship made a wry face. 'I appreciate the offer, but I am not sure O'Cleary knows how to cook much besides boiled beef, turnips and potatoes. He'd likely ruin them.'

The way he'd burned the biscuits. A man in Lord Longhurst's position should be able to hire a proper cook, should he not?

'I apologise if I seem ungrateful,' he added, likely to fill the uncomfortable silence.

She pulled her thoughts together and shook her head. 'Not at all. I was thinking what a shame it is that you do not have a cook, that was all. You might find one at a hiring fair, there are several local ones over the next few weeks.'

'Yes,' he said vaguely. 'Perhaps after we are done here, I will look into it.' He glanced over at where O'Cleary was quenching his thirst using a long-handled dipper in a bucket they must have filled from a stream. He dipped it again and poured the water over his head.

'It is hot, thirsty work,' she said.

'And we have barely made a dint in it.'

'What about hiring some men from the village to help you?'

He shook his head. 'The other landlords are keeping them busy. We will do as much as we can and that will have to do.'

The determination in his voice gave her pause. It seemed he did care something about his property.

The last time Harry had joined her brothers during a harvest, he had tossed the hay about and chased her around the stooks and generally caused much hilarity and disturbance. His carefree ways were what she had loved about him as a girl and what had been so annoying about him when they were wed.

She hesitated. 'Would you mind if I made a suggestion?'

Another suggestion? It had been Lady Petra's idea that he mow this field. Was she now spying on him to see if he had followed her instructions? Or was her motive something different? An excuse for her to meet and flirt with him? Before he'd left the Peninsula, his fellow officers had teased him about all the ladies who would be lying in wait for him in hopes of catching an earl. And Sarah had proved just how right they were. He would do his own choosing, thank you very much. A simple bargain between sensible people was all he needed. No pretence of stronger emotions. The very idea of the sort of destructive passions his parents had engaged in made him feel ill. He was not about to be trapped into such a hideous life by a scheming woman.

Lady Petra's presence out in this particular field so early in the day certainly seemed highly suspect. A lady of her stature would have no need to grovel around in the fields to put food on the table. No, there must surely be some ulterior motive for her appearance today.

He needed to be careful. 'Suggest away.' He braced for what might next come out of her mouth.

'You are chopping at the hay, rather than mowing it. You need to take wider, slower swings. It will go much faster and will be a lot less tiring.'

His mouth dropped open. She was now instructing him on how to use a farm implement? Given her petite form, he doubted she could even lift a scythe, let alone swing it. The damn thing was as heavy as it was awkward.

No doubt she was one of those females who liked to pretend she knew something about everything and hand out orders to large and apparently slow-witted men like himself. 'I see.'

She coloured delightfully and for a moment he forgot his annoyance. Which irritated him even more. 'Perhaps you would like to demonstrate, Lady Petra?' he challenged.

'Yes, that might be of more use than trying to explain.'

He stared at her in astonishment and followed her when she pushed through the long grass to where O'Cleary was back to plying his scythe.

She stood watching him for a moment.

'Have you never seen anyone mow grass?' she asked.

'Of course I have,' Ethan said. He certainly couldn't wait to see what sort of hash she was going to make of this with her tiny arms and hands and in her long skirts and fancy bonnet.

She put her basket aside, lifted her skirts and tucked the hems up at the sides into the waistband of her apron, once more revealing those charming calves and finely turned ankles.

His mouth dried.

O'Cleary turned around and dropped his scythe with a low whistle.

'Don't be ridiculous,' she snapped. 'You've seen lasses working with their skirts hiked up before now.'

O'Cleary turned bright red and Ethan knew exactly what sort of work he was thinking of.

Lady Petra frowned reprovingly. 'Dairymaids and such.'

O'Cleary lowered his gaze. 'Yes, my lady.'

'Give me your scythe.'

O'Cleary handed it over. It was nearly as tall as she was. 'I usually use a smaller one,' she said. 'They make them in various sizes.' She grasped the handles. 'Stand back, please.'

She took a long slow swing at the stems at ankle height and a swathe of hay keeled over. She took a step forward and swung again and another swathe went down in defeat. In two swings she'd cut as much as he had with ten.

Clearly growing up in the city with a customs clerk for a father had not prepared him for the life of an earl with a country estate. Neither had life in the army.

'I see what you mean,' he said, relieving her of the scythe and handing it back to O'Cleary. 'May I try?' He didn't want her exhausting herself.

'Certainly. Before you start always make sure there is no one close by. Swung with force, the blade can do considerable damage to a human limb.'

To his nonsensical male disappointment, she stepped back, untucked her skirts and brushed them down, looking perfectly demure.

'O'Cleary,' Ethan growled, 'stay well back.'

He picked up the scythe he'd been using and swung as she had done. The damn thing nearly flew out of his hands.

'It is more about the swing than the force,' she said.

He tried again, this time achieving a smooth half circle that was not nearly as tiring as what he had been doing before. He tried a few more swings and was surprised by how much progress he made.

'Excellent,' she said. 'Mr O'Cleary, it is your turn to try. Move a little to the right so you are parallel to His Lordship but well clear of his blade.'

O'Cleary touched his forelock and did as instructed. Soon he, too, was swinging in great form and moving forward steadily.

So much for his cynicism. Lady Petra really did know what she was talking about. He leaned on his implement. 'Thank you, Lady Petra. We will have this field done in no time.'

She beamed at him and he grinned at her. Her smile faded. 'With only the two of you it is going to take a few days, even so.'

'It will,' he said, unsure what he had done to wipe the smile from her face. Women, they were all the same. He just did not understand them. Indeed, he had no wish to understand them, even if they were as pretty as a picture. 'I ought to get back to work. Thank you again.'

He hefted the scythe and joined O'Cleary, swinging his scythe in easy arcs. The next time he looked up, she was gone from view.

* * *

Over the next few hours, he and O'Cleary made amazing progress, but every now and then the vision of a tiny lady with her skirts caught up, expertly swinging a scythe, popped into his mind.

He felt like he'd been ambushed and had not yet got his troops back into proper order.

Chapter Three

Perched on an upturned bucket, Petra watch Jeb groom Patch with a critical eye. When she had lived at home, she'd had her own riding horse, Daisy, and had learned how to care for her. She enjoyed working with horses, but this was another thing Jeb had decided was too lowly to be undertaken by a lady. So, having helped Becky make the bread first thing this morning, she'd come out to watch Jeb work, mostly so she would not disturb Marguerite at her drawing.

'How old are you, Jeb?' she asked.

He straightened and turned to face her. 'Sixteen, my lady.'

So young! Yet hadn't she known exactly how her life should be at sixteen? Wife to Harry, whom she'd assumed would become a gentleman farmer.

Why had she not seen that, while Harry had enjoyed his visits to her brothers, he was not the least bit interested in the land? He'd liked the hunting and the rollicking around the neighbouring villages getting up to all sorts of tricks, which she had known nothing about. After their marriage, he had made it perfectly clear that residing in the country would be a sort of living death for him. He declared he belonged in town, where he could continue to enjoy the company of his friends and, as she discovered later, any female who happened to come into his orbit.

A pang seized her. She quelled it. She never allowed herself to think about his unfaithfulness. It was simply too demeaning.

She sighed. Red had been right in cautioning her against setting her sights on Harry, but in those days, she had been so sure of everything. Now she felt as if she knew absolutely nothing, although her stupid body seemed to be attracted to the first handsome man to cross her path since Harry died.

Which was nonsense. She hadn't given a thought to that sort of thing before she married, so why would she need to think it about it now she was a widow? She was a lady after all, not some lowly maiden.

Jeb was staring at her. Oh, yes, he'd told her his age. She frowned. 'That means you started working here when you were fourteen. Isn't that rather young?'

Surprise filled his expression. 'Why, no, my lady. Me da started work up at Longhurst Park when he was nobbut ten. Under-groom he were then. He said we were spoiled going to school and not working till we were fourteen as our ma insisted upon.' He grinned. 'To hear tell, it was a fine life up at the Park till the old lord up and died. The fellow that came after him was sickly and spent most of his time in London, so he had no need of the horses or the staff. I was supposed to train there when I was old enough, but it were not to be.' He went back to currying Patch's flank.

'Where does your father work now?'

Jeb shrugged. 'Died of the lung disease three years ago. Leaving Ma to raise five young 'uns on her own. God's blessing it were when this here job came up or we might have ended up on the parish.'

Guilt assailed. Why had she not known this? But it was Red who had hired Jeb before she and her sisters had arrived in Westram. 'I suppose your mother is helping the other ladies with the millinery now?' She winced, as even that work wasn't certain.

'Nah, my lady. She cooks for a family out beyond Ightham.' His gaze held sadness. 'She gets home one day a month. The little 'uns miss her, but me and my older sister do the best we can with them. Suzy does a bit of lacemaking, but it be hard for her to do much with the baby an' all.'

'Baby?'

'Ah, he be four now. Right little handful.' He grinned fondly. 'The other three help out.'

This vision of Jeb as head of a family was shocking. And for a mother to be separated from her young children! A vision of singed biscuits popped into her head. 'Your mother is a good cook, then?'

'Yes. Trained she did, up at the Park when she were a lass. Had to give it up when she married me da, of course, but he had a good job by then.'

A good cook. Now, that was something. 'When will she be home next?'

Jeb rubbed the back of his neck. 'Next week, I reckon, my lady. Sunday.'

'Do you think she might be willing to cook for us here on that day?'

Jeb turned to look at her. 'What, my lady?'

'I would like to invite a guest for dinner, but we

will need someone to cook for us. Your mother can take home any leftovers, and, of course, we would pay her for her time.'

His eyes lit up. 'I'll have my sister write and ask her, but I am sure as how she would be pleased to help out. A bit of extra never goes amiss.'

Hopefully Marguerite would not object to spending a little bit extra next week. Now if she could convince the Earl to accept her invitation, she might kill two birds with one stone by finding His Lordship a cook as well as help Jeb's family out by having their mother live at home. The thought pleased her inordinately, even if it did mean having to entertain the Earl for dinner.

Ethan tied Jack to the fence in front of Westram Cottage. At first, he'd thought to refuse the ladies' invitation to dine with them, but the thought of a half-decent meal, instead of O'Cleary's stew, was far too tempting for any man, especially one who liked his food as much as Ethan did.

Besides, strangely enough, he was looking forward to seeing Lady Petra again. Which wasn't moving the next project on his list in the right direction.

According to his man of business, who had his office in Sevenoaks, he was not entirely destitute. He'd offered the heartening news that if Ethan was careful in the management of the estate, and if he perhaps found himself a suitably wealthy bride, he should come around very nicely.

The noose tying him to this estate was growing ever tighter, but he still had hopes of returning to his army career. After much discussion, Ethan had reluctantly agreed to the man of business making discreet enquiries regarding the availability of such a bride. He had indicated his preference for a sensible woman who would understand the concept of a marriage of convenience. Preferably one who had some experience of country living and all that it entailed, so he could leave matters in her hands. There were to be no commitments or promises until Ethan had met the lady.

He marched up to the ladies' front door and rapped the knocker. After some discussion with O'Cleary, he'd decided not to wear his uniform. Since a military man had little use for civilian clothes, his wardrobe was limited, but he did have a coat he'd bought from Weston on a whim during one of his visits to London. It wasn't exactly evening wear, but O'Cleary had agreed it would do for dinner in the country. Though why on earth the batman thought himself an expert in the matter Ethan didn't know.

A maid guided him to a small parlour at the front of the cottage.

The two ladies rose to their feet when he entered. He gave them his warmest smile and bowed. 'Good day, ladies.'

They dipped their heads in unison.

'Please be seated, Lord Longhurst,' Lady Marguerite said. She glanced at the servant. 'That will be all, thank you, Becky. May I offer you some sherry, Lord Longhurst?'

'Thank you.'

He took his glass when she poured one for each of them. Both ladies perched on the sofa. He sat opposite in the armchair and raised his glass. 'To your very good health.'

'Your health,' they replied.

He took an appreciative sip of his drink. The sherry was of excellent quality.

A silence descended. Ethan dragged out his party manners. 'What a snug house you ladies have.'

'Thank you,' Lady Petra said. 'We like it very much.'

'There is one thing I do not quite understand,' he said, recalling some earlier musings. 'The village has your family name and yet your family does not own any property in these parts, apart from this cottage.'

'It is quite a long story,' Lady Marguerite said. 'But it is not an unusual one. It dates back to Oliver Cromwell's rule.'

'Do not tell me your family once owned Longhurst Park?' Blast, he had not anticipated that when he asked the question, though he should have. He really ought to find out more about this branch of his family's history. He just hadn't thought it important before now.

'Oh, no,' Lady Petra said. She chuckled. 'Actually, it is Lord Compton who is the usurper.' Her amusement lit her blue eyes like sunlight dancing on water. He found himself enchanted. He suppressed the sensation. He had seen that sort of conspiratorial amusement on his mother's face. It had been a lie then and was likely one now, too. Ladies' smiles were not to be trusted, even if they were pretty and enticing.

'Petra, you really should not say such things,' Lady Marguerite said. 'It is all water under the bridge. While Compton Manor, then known as Bedwell Hall, did belong to our family, our ancestors supported the idea of a republic. After the Restoration, we lost the title and the land. Charles the Second bequeathed Bedwell to the Comptons, all except this cottage, which was occupied by an elderly lady who had maintained her loyalty to the King.'

'A very stubborn old lady apparently.' Once more Lady Petra's eyes twinkled. 'My family says I take after her.'

Lady Marguerite shook her head fondly at her sister. 'You are not stubborn, my dear, unless you do not get your own way.'

Both ladies laughed. Once again Ethan was struck by the younger sister's angelic beauty. Her laughter was a sweet light sound and her eyes gleamed with mischief. She was the sort of woman who stood out in a crowd and drew every man's eye when she smiled. The sort of woman who would lead a less sensible man a merry dance.

His suspicions about her having an ulterior motive returned in full force. He really should have declined this invitation. He certainly did not want to create any false impressions or hopes.

Lady Marguerite continued the story. 'It wasn't until the Stewarts were gone that our family wormed their way back into the good graces of the royals and were granted the property in Gloucestershire. Danesbury is where Westram has his seat now.'

'Yet you choose to live here in Kent?'

'Yes,' Lady Marguerite said, lifting her chin as if she expected him to take issue with her words. 'We like our independence.'

Lady Petra nodded her agreement.

Perhaps he was misjudging her motives after all.

The maid peeped in. 'Lady Marguerite, I am to tell you dinner is served.'

'Thank you, Becky,' she said, standing.

'May I?' Ethan offered both ladies an arm. He escorted them into a small dining room overlooking the garden at the back of the house. The French doors were wide open, admitting a light breeze along with the scent of roses.

He seated the ladies and then took a chair. 'Your garden is beautiful,' he said.

'That is Petra's doing,' Lady Marguerite said. 'She has a talent for making things grow.'

Lady Petra smiled. 'I have always had an interest in plants. How about you, Lord Longhurst?'

He grimaced. 'I enjoy eating what the land produces, my lady, but my knowledge beyond that is severely limited. But not for long, I hope.'

The little maid carried in an assortment of dishes, including a magnificent roast of beef, assorted vegetables and puddings.

Having carved the roast and made sure each lady's plate was full, Ethan got down to eating his own meal with a will. Food like this had not been coming his way recently.

The conversation, led by Lady Marguerite, revolved around the weather, the need for a church roof and some information about other families in the neighbourhood.

Finally, Ethan, put down his knife and fork. 'That was the best meal I have had in months, if not years.'

Lady Marguerite looked pleased. 'Surely you exaggerate, my lord.'

'Not at all. Everything was cooked to perfection. Your chef is to be complimented.'

'Actually, she is not *our* cook,' Lady Petra said. 'We hired her for the day.'

He frowned. 'Do cooks hire themselves out by the day?'

'Not as a general rule, but she is looking for a permanent post near to Westram. We do not need a full-time cook, unfortunately.'

Everyone needed a full-time cook if they could afford one. Again, his irritation at Westram's niggardliness with his sisters raised its head. But it was none of his business. Indeed, he had no idea why he would care.

'Perhaps you would like to hire her,' Lady Petra suggested idly. Too idly. He narrowed his eyes on her face. Why was she so interested in his household arrangements? The sort of arrangements that would normally be within a wife's purview. Was she seeing herself in that role? No doubt she thought an earl would be a very good catch.

Even so, the thought of having meals like this on a regular basis was so tempting as to make Ethan's mouth water.

'Are you sure I would not be depriving you of her services, if I hired her?'

'Oh, no,' Lady Petra said airily. 'Becky manages our everyday needs and, since we rarely entertain, we do not have need of a cook. Mrs Stone comes highly recommended. Indeed, she used to work at Longhurst Park years ago, so she should fit right in. And it would mean she could live at home with her family.'

The lady did protest too much. He frowned. 'Did you invite me to dinner so I might be convinced to hire this woman?'

Lady Marguerite looked embarrassed.

'Is it so terrible?' Lady Petra asked. 'Is it not our duty to help our neighbours and friends? Besides, what better way to know if she will suit than to sample her skills?'

She looked a little disgruntled. What? Had she not expected him to see through her ploy? Was she like so many others, including his father, who thought him lacking in intelligence because of his size?

Indeed, he also felt a little disgruntled. He had thought—well, perhaps vaguely hoped—she had invited him because she valued his company, but it seemed that it had been an attempt to manipulate him into hiring a cook. A very fine cook, to be sure, but he did not intend to be manipulated by any woman ever again, especially after his lucky escape from Sarah.

The maid entered with a tray containing desserts. A fruit compote, an apple pie and a lemon mousse. Everyone served themselves. Ethan partook of the pie and a little of the mousse.

Any idea of resistance immediately disappeared. Mentally he shook his head at what he knew would next be coming out of his mouth. Complete and utter surrender. 'Ask the cook to report for duty as soon as she is able.'

Both ladies seemed happy with his pronouncement, Lady Petra exceedingly so, blast the woman. O'Cleary would be delighted in the extreme. Ethan, however, could not quite shake his earlier sense of being ambushed once again.

From now on it would be best if he avoided Lady Petra completely.

Chapter Four

As was their usual wont on a Thursday, Petra and Marguerite walked to the village of Westram. Their first stop was the post office.

'Quite a few letters for you today, Lady Marguerite,' Mr Barker, the postmaster, said. 'And one for you, Lady Petra. Franked, they are.' He beamed, his red wrinkled cheeks looking like apples left too long in the sun.

All the letters had been franked by Westram or by Lord Avery's father—a duke, no less. Their connections to the nobility seemed to thrill Mr Barker, as if somehow the more noble the frank, the higher it lifted those who lived in the village.

'Thank you, Barker,' Marguerite said, stuffing the letters into her reticule after a glance at the sender's name and address.

'One is from Lord Westram,' Mr Barker said. 'Will he be visiting you any time soon?'

'Not to my knowledge,' Marguerite said, handing over her outgoing letters and opening her purse.

Perhaps Lord Longhurst will be good enough to

frank them for you?' he said, gesturing to the window with his chin.

Across the road, Lord Longhurst was talking to the Vicar's wife, Mrs Beckridge. 'That will not be necessary,' Marguerite said.

Marguerite hated asking anyone for anything. She was determined they would be completely independent. While she had not said anything at the time, she had been quite disturbed when their sister-in-law, Carrie, married so soon after they moved to Westram. Disappointed, Petra had thought, though Marguerite had hidden it well. It had certainly made their task of living independently a little more difficult, despite the fact that Carrie's new husband did all in his power to assist.

Their mail dealt with, they went back out into the street. Mrs Beckridge waved them over. Petra would have preferred to ignore her, since she tended to pry. Also, the thought of meeting the Earl made her feel hot and cold by turns. There was something about the man that fascinated her, she had discovered at dinner the other evening, and the strength of those feelings made her uncomfortable. However, since Marguerite was already crossing the street, she could hardly put her head down and walk the other way.

'Lady Marguerite, Lady Petra,' Mrs Beckridge gushed. 'How lovely to see you.'

Longhurst bowed. 'A pleasure, Lady Marguerite, Lady Petra.'

Petra curtsied. 'Lord Longhurst.'

'I was right at this moment telling His Lordship about the gypsies who have taken up residence in

Crabb's Wood at the edge of his land. I am sure you ladies will agree with me when I say something really should be done about them.' She made the pronouncement in a voice of doom as if predicting the end of the world.

'What sort of something?' Petra asked.

'Why, chase them off, of course. We don't need the likes of them around here, stealing babies and washing off the line.'

Marguerite frowned. 'Whose baby did they steal?'

'No one's as yet,' the Vicar's wife admitted. 'But as I mentioned to my dear husband this very morning, it would be preferable not to give them the chance.'

'Utter rubbish,' Marguerite said with a shake of her head.

'The Vicar thinks *I* should chase them off, does he?' Longhurst asked.

'Well, it is *your* land they are sitting on. Disgraceful people. Next, they will be knocking on doors selling charms for warts or lucky heather. Most un-Christian behaviour.'

'A gypsy band used to camp near Danesbury when we were children,' Marguerite said.

'Our papa always hired them to help with the harvest,' Petra added. 'It was why they came back year after year. We certainly never had any trouble with them. Why not offer them the job of cutting your hay, Lord Longhurst? I wouldn't be surprised if a previous earl used their services and that's why they set up camp on your land.'

Mrs Beckridge made a sound of disapproval. 'Not with my husband's approval, I assure you, Lord Longhurst.'

'What an excellent solution, Lady Petra,' Lord Longhurst said. 'When I enquired at the Green Man, I was told there was not a man hereabouts in need of gainful employment. I will ride over there tomorrow and see if I can hire them on.'

Petra looked up at the sky. Mare's tails were riding high above them. 'I would go today if I were you. The weather is about to change. You may have only a day or so before it rains.'

He looked startled. 'You can tell that?'

'Really, my lord,' Mrs Beckridge said. 'Do not encourage them to remain in the district. Please, send them to the right about, as my husband would say. We do not need their sort around here.'

'Your husband does not have several fields of hay in need of mowing and no men to help,' the Earl said with a pleasant smile.

Petra could not help herself. She beamed at him.

He recoiled slightly, as if he did not welcome her approval of what was a very sensible response to the Vicar's wife.

Mrs Beckridge shook her head. 'Far be it from me to dictate your actions, my lord, but were my husband here he would say the same thing.'

'I am sure he would,' Longhurst said. He bowed. 'If you will excuse me, ladies.'

All three ladies watched him stroll away. Petra had never seen anyone stand up so well to Mrs Beckridge's forceful personality. Perhaps he did not yet understand the lady's position and reputation in the village. No doubt he would when the Vicar heaped coals of fire on his head at the church service on Sunday. It would be interesting to see how he reacted to that.

'Why are you so set against these gypsies?' Marguerite asked Mrs Beckridge. 'I certainly have not heard of any abductions or theft associated with them.'

'Not yet, you haven't,' Mrs Beckridge said sullenly. She pressed her lips together. 'Likely, I should not make mention of this, but I fear I must warn you.'

'Of?'

Mrs Beckridge glanced about her and then drew closer, lowering her voice to a whisper. 'One of them tells fortunes.'

Marguerite shook her head at the lady. 'It is only a bit of entertainment, Mrs Beckridge. No one truly believes in it.'

Mrs Beckridge sniffed. 'People around here believe all sorts of blasphemous nonsense. All I can say is do not let yourselves be taken in.' She nodded her head and stalked off.

Marguerite sighed. 'More fire and brimstone to look forward to on Sunday. I should have kept my opinions to myself.'

'Perhaps she ought to have been a little less forceful in hers,' Petra said.

Marguerite chuckled. 'Every time I see the woman she rubs me the wrong way. If she said "Up", I would likely say "Down". I think your suggestion was the best. Give them some gainful work and leave them in peace. It is all anybody wants. Come along, I need to buy some bread.'

It would be interesting to see if the Earl actually went against the Vicar's wife and offered the gypsies work. They were people who really understood the land and who worked hard. And if they occasionally poached a rabbit, well, why not? The rabbits didn't belong to anyone any more than the blackberries did, even if the law said otherwise.

When Petra came in from the garden after a satisfactory hour of pulling weeds without any interference from Jeb, she found Marguerite in the hallway tying on her bonnet. 'Where are you off to?'

'Oxted. We are almost out of candles and the stall at the market there is cheaper than our shop in the village.'

'Not to mention that it would not do for our neighbours to know we are burning tallow in the private rooms.' Beeswax ones were kept for visitors and used only sparingly.

Marguerite pursed her lips for a second, then chuckled. 'Precisely.'

Marguerite always looked far too serious for her twenty-seven years. She was not the same person Petra remembered growing up in the Westram household in Gloucester. She had seemed to change after her marriage. She rarely laughed any more. It lifted Petra's heart to see her sister smile for once. 'I'll come with you. I have nothing else to do today.' It would be like old times, going shopping with her sister, even if it was a small village market and not London's Bond Street. Indeed, it would likely be more enjoyable.

Jeb had already brought around the pony and trap when they got outside and seemed ready to argue when he realised there would not be room for both him and Petra and he would therefore be left behind.

At a raised eyebrow from Marguerite he touched his cap and returned to the barn.

They set off at a spanking trot and as they passed the scene of the great blackberry robbery, Marguerite waved her whip. 'It seems Lord Longhurst took your advice.'

The field was more than halfway to being mowed by five men with their shirts off and expertly swinging scythes. Stooks of hay dotted the pasture. Petra could not help searching for one particular man, but she was disappointed. Lord Longhurst was not among the workers. 'It would seem so,' she said non-committally.

'It is good to see Lord Longhurst is taking his estate seriously at long last,' Marguerite said.

'It is indeed. Though I do not know how long he intends to stay. He prefers life in the army to life as a country gentleman, I believe.' As Harry had. Though Harry preferred life in town, he'd seen the army as a means of escape from an unwanted wife. She swallowed down her feeling of mortification. She had married the wrong man and she wasn't going to make that sort of mistake again.

The conversation turned to other topics, but Petra could not help wondering about the whereabouts of Lord Longhurst.

'I wonder if there will be any servants looking for employment at the fair,' she said.

'We cannot afford to hire more help,' Marguerite said sternly. 'I am not going to ask Red for more money when he is so hard-pressed.'

Their brother, the Earl of Westram, had inherited the Earldom only to discover its financial affairs in a state of disarray. When Marguerite and Petra had insisted on their independence after their husbands died, they had promised not to be an additional burden on their brother. Marguerite was determined to stick to their agreement.

'I wasn't thinking of us,' Petra said. 'I was thinking of Lord Longhurst. He needs a housekeeper and a butler.'

Marguerite frowned. 'I am sure it is not our place to be telling Lord Longhurst how to run his affairs.'

'I was not going to do any such thing. I simply thought if I saw any likely candidates I could mention Longhurst Park. Mr O'Cleary is not only looking after the horses and opening the front door, but he is serving tea—in his riding boots.'

Marguerite looked suitably scandalised. 'Very well. If you feel you must. But please do not let your kindness result in any sort of gossip or scandal. I do not want Red using it as an excuse to force us back beneath the family roof.'

It was not that they did not like Red; they did—indeed, they loved him dearly—but Red's idea of being a good head of the household was to find them each another husband. Neither of them wanted that. 'I promise you, I will be careful. Besides, there may not be any suitable people to be had so late in the Season. The Earl also needs a bailiff,' she mused, but one would not expect to find one of those at a fair.'

'Why don't you offer to take on the job?'

Petra's jaw dropped. Her heart gave an odd little thump. 'Me? Westram would never approve.'

Marguerite gave her an odd look. 'I was joking, Petra.'

Yes. She had to be. But the idea was just so appealing Petra could almost see it in her mind's eye. She'd followed Red about when their father was teaching him about the land before he went off to university. She loved the rhythm of the seasons, watching things grow and bear fruit. Unfortunately, Harry's father had been a mill owner and his only interest in land was how many sheep it had and how much wool it produced. And Harry had turned a pale shade of green when she'd suggested they live in the country.

She had been too blinded by his easy-going manner and handsome face to see the true man beneath. What a little fool she had been.

Their arrival at the Red Lion brought her uncomfortable thoughts to an end. Marguerite handed over the pony and trap to an ostler, and arm in arm they walked to the market held at the foot of Oxted's market cross.

Petra left Marguerite haggling over candles and wandered off to see what else was on offer. An enquiry led her to where servants were hiring out their skills, but there she found only a couple of dairymaids seeking employment. Lord Longhurst didn't have any cows as yet.

Oh, well, she hadn't really expected a housekeeper or a butler to fall into her arms. Which also meant she had no excuse to visit Lord Longhurst. Just as well, since she seemed drawn to the handsome man whose obvious ignorance about running an estate made him seem vulnerable. Seeing him at a loss made her want to offer her aid, when she should be keeping her distance if she didn't want the villagers to start gossiping.

Vulnerable? Longhurst? Surely not. Now she was making up stories in her head.

She wandered aimlessly among the stalls until she discovered a small crowd gathered around a shabby wagon sporting a pole from which fluttered an array of brightly coloured ribbons.

'What is going on?' she asked a portly farmer in a linen smock.

'Gypsies.' The disgust in the word was palpable.

'If you dislike them so much, why do you remain?'

His mottled red cheeks darkened to crimson. 'I heard as how they had a couple of horses for sale. The bidding will start shortly.'

'I see.' About to move away, she stopped at the sight of a young woman obviously far along in her pregnancy emerging from the wagon, grinning cheerfully. 'Madame Rose says it will be a boy,' she announced.

The farmer cursed beneath his breath. 'Fortune telling. Against nature that is.'

How odd. Mrs Beckridge had mentioned the gypsy camping in Crabb's Wood who told fortunes. Could this be the same one? Petra edged closer.

A man appeared at her elbow. 'Want your fortune told, miss?' He cleared his throat. 'I mean madam.'

How did he know? Was her widowed state written on her face or could he see the outline of her wedding band beneath her glove. She curled her fingers into her palm. 'I...er... Why not?' It would be the only way she would know if this was the woman the Vicar's wife had spoken of.

The man helped her up the steps. 'Cross her palm with a bit of silver and Madame Rose will tell you all you need to know.'

It would be interesting to see what sort of nonsense the woman came up with. Petra knew exactly what her future held. A quiet life in the country with her sister. She climbed the three steps and pushed aside the canvas blocking the way.

The interior of the wagon was a great deal larger than she had expected and lit by lanterns hanging from hooks. Bright red fabrics edged with glittering gold adorned a narrow cot and the table behind which sat a young woman, rather than the old crone Petra had expected. Clothed in brightly coloured scarves decorated with intricate gold stitching, with large gold rings hanging from her ears and a multitude of gold bangles jingling at her wrist, she looked exotic. The woman thrust out a hand, palm up.

Petra dropped the thruppence into her palm and the coin seemed to disappear. 'How did you do that?' she asked.

'Curiosity kills the cat,' Madame Rose said, her voice heavily accented. She grinned cheerfully. She was actually quite beautiful, with dark hair and eyes and skin the colour of polished oak.

'What do you want to know?'

Petra swallowed. 'Your man out there said you would tell me my fortune.'

The dark eyes stared at her unblinking. 'Is it the name of your second husband you are seeking?'

Petra froze. 'How did you know I am a widow?'

The girl shrugged. 'How do I know anything?' She shuffled a deck of cards with rather horrifying-looking pictures on their fronts.

A cold shiver trickled through Petra's veins. 'I have changed my mind.' She turned to leave.

Something grabbed her. She glanced down at the long fingers gripping her wrist. Strong, elegant fingers.

She raised her gaze to meet that of Madame Rose. The woman smiled. 'It is not the future that interests you. Most of all you wonder about the past.'

Petra squared her shoulders and turned back to meet the woman's scrutiny head on, for she had realised that, despite her youthful appearance, Madame Rose was a woman with a very old soul. 'I cannot deny there are things about the past that I question. But don't we all?'

The girl nodded. 'The person who could answer your questions has passed over.'

She shivered. 'Yes.'

'Sometimes the spirits are cruel with their answers.' She laughed and it was not unpleasant or mocking, rather it held sympathy. 'Your future is more easily discovered.'

It was too late to change the past, and besides, the woman was talking in riddles. 'Then I will settle for that.'

She removed her glove and held out her hand.

Madame Rose traced the lines across her palm. 'You are fortunate indeed. I see a long life, with two paths. One leads to discontent, the other to happiness. Yours is the choice.' She sat back. 'Good day, my lady.'

What? Petra stared at her, mouth open. 'That is it?'

'It is what I see.'

Behind her, the curtain at the door drew back, flooding the interior with harsh daylight, making the furnishings look tawdry and cheap and the young woman behind the table look weary and older than her years.

'This way, madam,' the man outside said.

Petra stumbled out and down the steps.

'What did she tell you, sweetheart?' one of the men

gathered outside called out. 'I'll marry you, if it's a husband you want.'

Petra smiled brightly. The man meant no harm. 'She said to avoid men like you at all costs.'

A chorus of laughter greeted this sally.

A hand grasped her elbow. She spun around, ready to defend her person. 'Lord Longhurst,' she gasped.

'Lady Petra. Allow me to escort you.' A fierce frown on his normally smiling face made her feel breathless. Her heart beat a little faster than normal. No, no, it was the stares of the crowd that had her feeling on edge.

'I would not put you to any trouble, Lord Longhurst,' she said, trying to maintain the easy brightness of her smile.

'It is no trouble at all,' he said in his lovely, deep, calm voice. 'Since I am going your way.' He held out his arm.

She cast him a look askance. 'How do you know where I am going?'

The twinkle returned to his eyes and his brow cleared. 'Naturally, I go in whichever direction you are headed.'

Was he flirting with her? 'Very droll, sir.'

He chuckled. A rich warm sound that started up a flutter in her stomach.

She felt oddly light-hearted. She repressed the urge to giggle like a schoolgirl. That was the Petra of old. She was a sensible woman now and a widow.

'You are not here alone, I presume,' he said rather more seriously. 'Your maid is nearby?'

'I am here with my sister. She is shopping in the market.'

'Your sister approves of your visit to the likes of

Madame Rose? Surely you do not believe in such nonsense?'

She felt herself bridle. Men always thought they knew best. Even lackadaisical Harry after they'd wed.

'You don't believe she can tell fortunes?'

'Certainly not.' He looked down at her from his great height and there was a troubled look in his gaze. 'Nor do I believe a sensible woman like yourself would believe it either.'

He thought she was sensible? Most men looked at her face and diminutive figure and decided she was nothing but dizzy headed. A warm feeling in her chest spread outwards.

'While I do not consider myself foolish, sir, it seems to me that there are mysteries in this world that cannot be accounted for by logic or the church would be doing a very poor trade indeed.'

His beautiful blue eyes widened. 'Such heresy! Mrs Beckridge would be aghast.'

She laughed. 'I trust you not to betray me, sir.'

'Upon my honour, I will not,' he said. 'I am a gentleman. Besides, I have to admit there is something of the truth in your words. It is my belief mankind does not know all the answers as yet.'

'I see.' She smiled. 'I presume you were not about to seek Madame Rose's wisdom yourself?'

He grinned. 'Lord, no. I came to bid on some horses.'

'Then I must not keep you from your transaction.'

'All done. Two plough horses and a carriage horse, much to Jack's relief.'

'Jack?'

'My mount. I brought him home with me from

Spain. He was not best pleased at the idea of doing all the work on the estate since all the horses were sold off by my cousin before he died.'

They strolled along the line of stalls. Merchants called out, encouraging them to inspect their wares.

'Better to sell them off than keep them eating their heads off to no good purpose. The land has not been worked for several years, I think.'

He sighed. 'If I had realised how badly my cousin had left matters I would have come sooner and found someone to oversee matters. With the war going badly and Wellington needing every experienced officer... Well, it is of no matter now. Hopefully I can come to grips with it and find the right man for the job.'

Her heart sank at the implication in his words. 'You maintain your intention to return to the army?'

'My place is with my regiment. While I do not wish to appear a braggart, I believe I am needed.'

Could he not see he was also needed here? What difference did one man risking his life on the Peninsula make to the war effort when so many people depended on him here at home? 'Your cousin had been ill for some considerable time, I gather. The locals say he rarely came to Longhurst. Had he come here more often, things might have gone better. I am surprised he did not discuss these matters with you as the heir apparent.' She winced. 'I beg your pardon. It is not my business to speak of your cousin in such a way.'

'He was a very distant cousin. I had never even heard of the man until the lawyers contacted me.'

Startled, she gazed up at him. His expression was grim. 'You did not know you were the heir?'

'No. I was unaware of the connection until I received a letter from a lawyer two years ago. They traced back three generations to find me apparently. The task was made more difficult by one of my great-great-grandfather's younger sons taking his wife's name and breaking all connection with his family.'

'But you did not return the moment you knew you had inherited.'

He shrugged. 'I saw no need to leave my duties until another person of whom I was not aware, a third cousin or some such, wrote to the General demanding my immediate release.' The disappointment in his voice was palpable.

'It is hard to imagine that someone would prefer the battlefield to the peace and quiet of the English countryside.' The very idea made her shudder inwardly.

'Is it?'

'Many families have lost sons and husbands in this dreadful war. Why do men have to fight and seemingly take pleasure in it?' The bitter edge to her tone came as a shock to her. 'I have to beg your pardon once again, my lord. I do not have the right to criticise. I am sure there is good reason for it, but—'

'You lost a husband to the war. Who better to criticise? I must also admit to having the occasional doubt. A man who does not is not using his brain. But I believe the freedom of our country is quite possibly at stake.'

Unfortunately, it was true. Still, she had the feeling that some men went off to war for the sake of glory and honour, without a thought for those left behind, rather than because they felt it was the right thing to do for King and country.

They walked in silence while he carefully guided her around knots of people chatting between the stalls.'

'I believe I see Lady Marguerite,' he announced.

Petra envied him his height. She could see nothing past the shoulders of people around her. Yet despite his height, he had managed to adapt his long stride to her exceedingly short one, when most men had her trotting to keep up. Indeed, it had been a most pleasant stroll and he hadn't once treated her like an ornament to be seen and not heard. Instead he had listened to her opinions as well as giving his own.

Harry had been charming and fun when he was in the mood, but often acted upon a whim and only asked her opinion when it was too late. Unfortunately, as a schoolgirl, his charming smile, teasing ways and seemingly undivided attention had completely blinded her to his true character. She had learned the hard way that one could not judge a book by its cover.

'Is something wrong,' Lord Longhurst asked, leaning closer. 'You look distressed.'

Oh, dear. Her thoughts were showing yet again. 'Not at all.' She forced her thoughts to take a more pleasant direction. 'I see you have made a good start with the haying.'

'I took your advice and visited the gypsy encampment. They were pleased to be offered work and got started right away. I also visited Lord Compton and he said I should come here today to look for horses. Thank you for the suggestions.'

Surprised by his open admission that she had been helpful, she gazed at him open-mouthed. The men in her family had always dismissed her ideas out of hand. They always thought of her as little more than a baby. Sometimes they had even used her ideas as if they were their own. 'You are most welcome,' she said, beaming at him.

He frowned slightly.

'There you are,' Marguerite said at their approach. She looked relieved. 'I could not think where you had got to.'

Petra waited for Lord Longhurst to inform on her, but he said nothing, although he was regarding her with a rather cynical light in his eye, as if he expected her to lie.

'I went to see if there were any possible housekeepers at the hiring fair. Lord Longhurst needs one, but there was no one suitable.' She took a deep breath. 'And then I stopped at Madame Rose's caravan.'

'Madame Rose?' Marguerite echoed, looking puzzled.

'A housekeeper?' Lord Longhurst said, sounding surprised.

'You had your fortune told?' Marguerite asked.

'Yes, Marguerite. Yes, Lord Longhurst, a housekeeper. I will continue to ask around.'

'Thank you. I do not believe I deserve such kindness.' He looked a little bemused. Oh, dear, did he think she was interfering? Before she could ask him, he bowed. 'Ladies, may I leave you to your errands? I have some horses to collect.'

She and Marguerite dipped curtsies. 'Good day, Your Lordship,' they chorused.

'Madame Rose!' Marguerite said again, turning back to Petra. 'What, pray, were you thinking?'

Blast it. Now Marguerite would not let the matter rest. Yet what else could she have done with His Lordship standing there looking at her as if he expected her to prevaricate.

Yet she felt better about it than she would have if she had kept the truth from her sister. 'I'll tell you all about it on the way home. Not that there is much to tell.' She certainly wasn't going to mention what Madame Rose had said about her finding a second husband. Because nothing like that was ever going to happen.

Chapter Five

'Where are you going, dearest?' Marguerite asked in an absent voice as Petra glided along the hall to the front door.

Blast. Petra should have known the slightest sound would alert Marguerite to her presence, although Petra had hoped to slip away unnoticed. 'Gathering chestnuts.' She held up her basket. 'There should be plenty on the ground by now.' Chestnuts were a treat eaten hot from the fire and would keep until Christmas in the pantry.

Marguerite closed her sketchbook and turned to face her. She frowned. 'Not from the tree on the village green, I hope. Mrs Beckridge would dine out on that for weeks.'

'Certainly not.'

'Then where?'

'There is a huge tree in Crabb's Wood.'

'Isn't that part of Lord Longhurst's property? If so, that would be stealing.'

'It is not stealing if one has permission.' She crossed her fingers behind her back. She did have permission of a sorts. He might not have included chestnuts specifically but he had said she was welcome to purloin his blackberries. She hardly thought he would have a different reaction in the matter of chestnuts.

Marguerite nodded. 'Don't be late for tea.'

Petra let go a sigh of relief. She'd half expected her sister to ask her not to go.

'Ask Jeb to go with you,' Marguerite added. 'He can pull down the lower branches for you.'

Dash it. Exactly what she needed. A nursemaid. 'Very well.'

She made good her escape and went in search of Jeb. He was mucking out. 'Want to go for a walk?' she asked.

He frowned. 'I have to finish this, Lady Petra. After that, I have windows to clean. Perhaps afterwards…'

She had done what Marguerite required, in fact at least, if not in spirit. 'Never mind. I will ask you another time.'

Duty done, she set off for Crabb's Wood with her basket over her arm. It had been a few days since she had been able to provide anything for their dinner table. Chestnuts weren't exactly a staple food, but they could help stretch a meal or make an evening fun.

A glance at the sky had her wincing. The weather had been fair for the past few days, but today's clouds had dark hearts and a less-than-friendly look about them. Hopefully she could gather enough nuts to make the outing worthwhile before it rained.

Instead of taking the winding lane, she took a shortcut across the corner of Lord Longhurst's land to where the river took a sweeping curve into Crabb's Wood, a copse mostly made up of ash and hazel and the odd oak. The ancient sweet chestnut trees were foreigners and had arrived in England with the Romans.

She followed the track along the river's edge for a while and then moved deeper into the woods. The woods had been ill tended for several years and she had to pick her way over fallen tree trunks and push through undergrowth. As she walked, she kept an eye out for distinctive spear-shaped leaves among the detritus.

She had a rough idea of the location of the tree she had spotted on one of her many walks, but it took a while to find it. After stopping to get her bearings a couple of times, she finally found herself standing in a golden carpet of leaves. She scuffed around with her feet to expose the spiny-skinned fruit. A few of them had turned yellowish brown and had burst open, making it easy to pick out the shiny brown nuts cupped inside. Most of the shells were still green and she carefully rolled them beneath her foot to break open the prickly casing. The thorns were so wickedly sharp they would easily pierce her gloves and did so when she extracted the exposed nuts if she wasn't careful.

After a half hour of shelling and picking up the glossy brown nuts, she had gathered what had fallen and looked up into the tree. There were still plenty of chestnuts on the branches. One of the branches was barely out of reach and her basket was nowhere near full yet. If only she could reach…

A thick branch the wind had brought down caught her eye. It might give her the two or three inches she needed. She dragged it over and stepped up. The branch rolled, she teetered and fell backwards, managing to land on her feet. 'Bother.'

This time she took more care, got her balance just right and reached upwards. She could touch one of the leaves with her fingertips but could not quite... get hold of it.

'Lady Petra! What are you doing?'

She fell backwards and was caught in strong arms and held against a hard, warm chest. The owner of the chest helped her get her balance and immediately stepped back.

She spun around. 'Lord Longhurst!'

'What are you doing?' His voice held curiosity, not anger.

'Gathering chestnuts. I was trying to reach that branch.' She pointed upwards.

He glanced up at the tree. 'Ah, I see.'

'I have gathered all I can from the ground, but not as many as I hoped.'

'Let me help you.' He easily reached up and brought the branch down to eye level. She could not help watching the ease with which he forced the branches to bend to his will. How she envied him his height and his strength, but when he grabbed for a cluster of nuts, he hissed in a breath and shook his hand. 'Why does anything tasty have to have thorns?'

She laughed, knowing he was also thinking of the blackberries. 'I suppose it is the tree's way of protecting its babies.'

He grinned. 'I suppose it is.'

'Pick them at the stem and drop them. I will peel them.'

He threw down several bunches before letting the branch go with a swish. He pulled down another branch and another, until he could reach no more, while Petra expertly stepped on the green prickly shells and rolled the nuts free.

'So that is how it is done, is it?' he said, standing back and watching her. 'There were sweet chestnuts in Spain and Portugal, but I only ever saw the nuts themselves. The camp women gathered them. They gathered beechnuts as well, when they could, and turned them into flour and a concoction that tasted a bit like coffee.'

'I haven't seen any beech trees in these woods, have you?'

'There is one on the far side, closer to the house.'

Was he offering her the fruits of that tree, too? If so, he was a kind and generous man.

His big riding boots made short work of the rest of the chestnuts and now her basket looked invitingly full and was becoming heavy.

'I think that will do for now,' she said. 'It is time to head for home.'

'Let me escort you. Which way do you go?' He took the basket from her hand, not giving her an option to say no.

Mentally she shrugged. If he wanted to assist her, why not? 'Back to the riverbank, where the walking is easier, then to where the lane crosses the bridge.'

'Ah, so that is where the river goes.' He held back a branch so she could pass.

'What were *you* doing in this part of the woods?'

'I was following the river along to see where it went after it left my lake. I heard noises in the undergrowth and was wondering what sort of wild animal I would find.'

'Instead you found me.'

'And glad to do so. I was wondering if you might be a bear or a wolf.'

She laughed. 'In England?'

He grinned. 'Not really. I thought of a deer, actually.'

'Yes, there is the occasional deer. Are there wolves and bears in Europe?'

'There are.'

'And you slept in tents there?'

'Sometimes. But they don't come near the campfires and we would keep them going all night.'

'Oh, I see.'

At last they were back to the river and they could walk side by side in relative comfort. 'People must walk along here frequently,' Longhurst observed.

'I expect some of the villagers fish here.'

'Oh, so the villagers also poach on my land, do they?'

'I would not be surprised, since you do not have a gamekeeper. Despite their claims otherwise, they are no different from the gypsies when there is a chance of some free fresh food.'

'Not unlike you.'

She laughed and he joined in. 'Touché, my lord.'

They rounded the curve. A figure lay face down on the track ahead of them, face almost touching the water, one arm dangling in the river up to the elbow.

Longhurst dashed forward with a cry of alarm before Petra could stop him.

The lad leaped to his feet. One of the gypsy children. He looked terrified. He snatched up his jacket, dived past Longhurst, flew past Petra with his bare feet stirring up leaves and disappeared into the trees.

Longhurst stood, arms folded, watching him go. He shook his head ruefully. 'I thought he was injured.'

'Just another poacher, I am afraid,' she said with a smile.

'Poaching what? Frogs? If so, he's welcome to them.'

She winced. 'No, not frogs. If I am not mistaken he was guddling for fish.'

'Why would he cuddle a fish?'

She chuckled. 'Not *cuddle*. *Guddle*. Catching fish with his hands.'

'Not possible,' he declared.

'It most certainly is. I have done it myself. Did you learn nothing as a boy?'

'I didn't learn that. And how did a lady like yourself learn the way of it anyway?'

She rolled her eyes. 'I had two older brothers and a gamekeeper who didn't mind showing things to a mere girl, as it happens.'

'I had neither siblings, nor gamekeepers. I grew up in Bristol. All the fish I ever ate appeared on our table by way of the fishmonger.'

Clearly, his education had been sadly lacking. She glanced in the direction the boy had fled. 'Well, if you wanted evidence of the gypsies poaching, you have it now.'

'Never mind that. I want to learn how to guddle a fish. Can you teach me?'

A drop of rain hit her cheek.

She glanced up. 'Another day, perhaps. Apparently, it is about to rain.'

He glanced up, too. 'Dash it, you will get wet.'

'Rain is good for the complexion, so they say.' She picked up her basket. 'Good day, my lord.'

To Ethan, rain pattering on leaves had its own special sound. He'd grown up in a bustling city where the noise of wheels grinding on cobbles and the strident shouts of costermongers were constant. When he'd joined his regiment on its first march in Portugal, he'd been amazed by the different sounds and smells he'd encountered while sleeping rough.

The loamy smell of the earth beneath his feet intensified. Soon the trees would not protect them from the falling raindrops. He also knew all about the unpleasant sensation of being soaked to the skin. He really ought to find them some shelter. If she would accept it.

Never had Ethan met a woman quite like this one. She irritated and amazed him at one and the same time. Every word out of her mouth was designed to establish her independence. Since leaving home, he'd become quite accustomed to meeting strong-minded women, having met a good few of them during his time in the army. Even so, most of them were more likely to seek his help than rebuff an offer of aid.

Not to mention their attempts to attract his attention in other ways. Those sorts of entanglements he'd avoided like the plague. Other men's wives, no thank you. For some reason that seemed to make them chase him all the more. It seemed now this youthful and exceedingly attractive widow was turning the tables on him. She wanted nothing to do with him, which seemed to pique his interest all the more. It really was annoying to say the least.

Unfortunately, he could not allow her to walk home in a downpour unescorted and call himself a gentleman. He lengthened his stride, caught up to her and held out his arm. 'Allow me, Lady Petra.'

'Don't be ridiculous,' she said. 'I told you before I am quite used to walking by myself. Indeed, I enjoy it.'

Could she be any more brutally honest about her

lack of interest in his company? Likely so, given the opportunity. He simply continued to hold out his arm as he walked beside her. One did not argue with a lady.

Her foot must have caught in a tree root because she stumbled and grabbed for his forearm. Hmm, he hadn't noticed anything projecting from the dirt. Indeed, the path looked remarkably smooth and well worn. Perhaps she had manufactured a stumble, to take advantage of his arm without seeming to give in? Interesting.

'I must say I am impressed with your knowledge of agricultural matters,' he said. 'I have a great deal to learn.'

She brushed back a stray lock of hair from her cheek. 'I was a complete pest as a child and spent all my time following my father and my older brother around the estate. They called me their little limpet.' She chuckled. 'I don't think it was an endearment as much as an expression of exasperation. Nevertheless, whatever my brother learned from my father, I learned, too, along with my father's love of the land.'

'Does Westram feel the same way about his estate?'

'I think he sees it as his duty to pass the estate along in the shape my father passed it to him, if not better. There were several bad harvests that set us back somewhat. However, I am not sure that he loves it exactly.'

'I can sympathise.'

'Because you prefer the army.'

'I do.' He sighed. 'There is a great deal more to this farming business than I thought. The signs of neglect are readily apparent even to a layman such as me. I see it taking a great deal more time that I expected.'

'And a great deal of effort,' she added.

And a great deal of money that he did not have.

A flash of lightning turned her face a ghostly shade. 'Oh, dear,' she said, quickening her pace. 'It seems we are in for a thunderstorm. We should hurry.'

He could not agree more. Sheltering beneath trees was the worst place to be with lightning about. The wind tossed the branches above them hither and yon, the heavens seemed to open and what had been a gentle rain a moment before turned into a waterfall rattling on the leaves and their heads and shoulders. He whipped off his coat and put it over her head. 'This way,' he shouted, pointing down a fork in the path.

'The lane to the village is that way,' she protested.

'But we can find shelter this way.'

She nodded and he took her hand and hurried her along. The silly little sandals on her feet and the tight fit of her skirts were not conducive to speed. If she were not such an independent little thing, he would pick her up and run. Just the thought of her in his arms heated his blood despite the chilly water soaking through his shirt.

Another flash of lightning.

To hell with it. They were both getting soaked to the skin. He scooped her up and ran. No doubt he would pay for this indignity to her person, but better that than she catch a chill from spending too long out in what was now a downpour.

After a second or two, she relaxed and clung on around his neck, making his job easier. They reached the edge of the trees and the lake spread out before them. He ran for the odd little structure he had found the previous day while out walking. A series of man-made caves formed into a grotto like the ancients might have visited. In no time at all they were safely beneath the vaulted ceiling. He set Lady Petra down on her feet.

As a shelter against a storm it wasn't that wonderful. Water rushed down the walls and across the floor into the stream running down the centre. He took her hand. 'Come on.' He led her deeper into the cavern, until they reached the whole purpose of the ridiculous structure. A pool—and, glistening in the half-light provided by an opening in the roof, the statue of Venus in its centre—fed by the stream, its glassy surface of yesterday now broken by ripples as the raindrops splattered down.

Around the pool, stone benches at strategic angles provided visitors with a view of the statue.

Lady Petra shivered.

'I know. It's chilly,' he said, 'but at least it is dry.'

'And not as dark as I was expecting.'

'Stay here. I'll be back in a moment.'

'I'm not sure where else I would go.' The bravery in her voice gave him an odd sensation in his chest. He dispelled it with a chuckle that echoed around the chamber.

She also chuckled, her voice mingling with his in the dark reaches of the cave.

Yes, laughter was often the best way to be rid of discomfort.

Ethan ran back to the entrance, took a deep breath, bracing himself for the next dash of cold rain, and ran back into the trees. He managed to find some reasonably dry twigs and a thick branch and was soon back in the cave with his hoard.

He really wished he had thought to bring several large branches into the tunnel upon his last visit, but then he had not been expecting to be forced to shelter here. He carried his armful back to the reflecting pool and Lady Petra.

She had removed her sodden bonnet and set it on one of the benches while she perched on one of the others, clutching his coat around her as protection against the chill. The sight of her snuggled into his coat gave him a strange feeling of warmth inside.

'What do you have there?' she asked.

'The makings of a fire. We can try to dry out a bit while we wait for the storm to pass.'

'Oh. I see.'

He laid out the wood in front of her bench and reached into his pocket. In the army, he never went anywhere without his tinderbox and old habits died hard. He unwrapped it from its oilskin.

'Goodness me,' she said. 'You are well prepared.'

He wanted to grin like a schoolboy at her tone of admiration. Nonsense. The happiness inside him was simply gladness he would soon be warm and dry. He got the fire going without difficulty, and while it was only a small blaze, it offered a measure of comfort and a warm glow to the cold rocks.

'I had no idea this was here,' she said, glancing around.

'I found mention of it on one of the maps in the library and came to take a look at it a day or so ago.'

'Why on earth would anyone want to build such a thing?'

'In the last century they thought it romantic.'

'Oh.' She shivered.

'I must say, it is better when the sun is shining. Quite pretty, in fact.'

'I'll take your word for it,' she said, her tone dry. She shivered again and hunched inwards.

Of course, she was cold. She wasn't used to such hardships.

'Allow me,' he said and briskly rubbed her shoulders and arms. Damnation, her skirts were soaking wet and clinging to her very shapely legs. 'Get closer to the fire.'

She inched to the edge of the bench nearer the flames. 'The last thing I expected today was a thunderstorm.' She groaned. 'Marguerite is going to be so worried when I am late for supper.'

They stared into the flames in silence. How many nights had he sat thus on campaign, sitting around a campfire, wet and tired to the bone? Too many to count. There had been companionship with his fellow officers, but it was nothing like the feeling of contentment he had now, sitting next to this tiny woman in the depths of the English countryside.

The feeling of peace threatened his equanimity. As a boy, the brief periods of peace in his household usually presaged an enormous storm of passion between his parents far worse than the thunder and lightning of the storm outside their cave.

She shivered and leaned towards the flames. Shadows flickered on the walls and glimmers of firelight danced across Venus's pool. Silence descended.

'Do you think the storm will last long?' She glanced up at the fissure above the water, where the raindrops trickled down its edges and dripped into the pool.

They seemed to be falling a little less heavily than they had been. 'Let us hope not.'

She nodded and rubbed her upper arms beneath his coat.

Usually she sounded so sure of herself. Right now, she sounded uncomfortable. Some people were afraid of storms. 'Move up closer to me,' he said. 'We will be warmer if we share our body heat.'

At first, he thought she would refuse his offer of comfort. He wasn't sure why he felt this need to offer her protection against the elements, but when she shifted closer, he put an arm around her shoulders, holding her loosely so she would realise she could break his hold any time she wished. After a second or two he felt her relax and her trust made him feel warmer than any fire. He hoped some of that warmth would transfer through his skin to her.

To Petra there was something especially pleasing about the feel of such a sturdy forearm around one's back. She leaned closer, resting her head against his shoulder, and became aware of the strong, steady heartbeat against her cheek and the scent of his cologne. Something manly and spicy.

His calm solid presence kept the dark in the corners of the cave at bay. She'd hated the dark, ever since Jonathan had locked her in a wardrobe when she was a child and then went off with his friends. Jonathan had always been a bit of a beast.

She'd never told her brothers how much the dark terrified her, but Harry had winkled it out of her one night. And then he had teased her unmercifully as was his wont. Worse was when he came home drunk and blew out the candle on her nightstand, leaving the room horribly dark until she pleaded with him to light it.

Once it was lit, she would pretend she didn't care, but he'd laugh and tell her he would make love to her so she would forget all about her foolish fears. It never quite worked, but she never admitted that he some-times left her less than satisfied, especially after he'd been carousing.

Sitting with Longhurst's arm lightly curled around her shoulders, she had the sense that he was not the sort to play cruel jokes on her or anyone else. How could that be? She barely knew anything about him. She wanted to know more. But she did not want him to think she was prying so she remained silent.

Warmth from his large body trickled through her skin and, what with him at her side and the fire at her front, she began to feel quite toasty.

Her eyes drifted shut and her breathing slowed. It was a lovely sensation: half-awake, half-asleep and knowing she was safe. A slight movement of his chest. A light touch to her hair. Tingles danced down her spine. Had he kissed the top of her head? Her breath caught. Dare she turn her face up to his and seek an-other, better kiss?

No. No. There had been no hint of interest of that sort from him. She must have imagined it. She held still, trying to recapture the peace and calm of mo-ments before, but her heart was racing far too fast to do more than pretend to be at ease.

The sound of rain hitting the pool diminished to a steady drip.

'Lady Petra, I think the storm is over,' he said qui-etly, as if trying to awaken her gently from slumber. He removed his arm from about her shoulders and shifted away from her, leaving her feeling chilled.

She sat up slowly as if she had indeed drifted off. 'Oh, my goodness.' She patted her hair, smoothed it back from her face. The fire had died to a mere glow.

He rose and kicked the ashes about until the fire was no more, giving her time to recover her wits and retrieve her bonnet. When she went to remove his coat, he placed his hands on her shoulders. 'Keep it for now. Until we see how it is outside.'

She did as he requested, unwilling to lose the warmth of it. Or the scent of him that clung to it. He took her hand and led her outside into daylight.

She blinked in the brightness. What she had not noticed on their mad dash was a lake in front of the cave, set in a shallow depression and surrounded by trees. Long grass and rushes grew along its banks. At the other end, where the lake began to narrow, a grass-covered three-arched bridge crossed from one side to the other. Its reflection in the still water was one of the loveliest things she had ever seen. 'What a pretty view.'

'I thought so when I found it yesterday. It is too bad it is so overgrown. Another project to be undertaken once the land provides an income.'

She heard weariness in his voice. 'Hopefully it won't take too long,' she said encouragingly. Although, once he had his income, he would likely leave and return to his beloved army. Disgruntlement filled her. Why did people who did not care about the land get to inherit, while those who did care looked on in sadness? It was the way of the world, according to Marguerite.

He took her arm and they walked back through the trees to the lane. Petra found the silence oppressive, as if the real world had closed in on them and come between them.

Unable to bear it, she tried to think of something to say that would lighten the moment. 'Since you grew up in Bristol, I am surprised you did not choose the navy over the army.'

He made a scoffing sound. 'I'm a dreadful sailor. My father took me sailing once. I turned pea green and spent the whole time leaning over the side, hanging on for grim death. Father was not best pleased.' He grimaced. 'It was the same when I travelled to Portugal and back. The navy was definitely not an option for me. It is the only bad thing about going back to my regiment.'

In other words, he would not miss Longhurst Park. Sadness filled her. 'I see.'

'I was lucky that Mother's brother offered to buy me a commission as soon as I was old enough.'

'How generous of him.' What sort of uncle sent a boy off to get killed in the war?

'Yes, he was a generous man. He didn't have children of his own and I used to visit him from time to time as a lad. We became good friends over the years. I missed him greatly when he died.'

'And your parents, do they still live?' She winced. What a foolish question. He would not be the Earl if his father was alive.

'My father died of an apoplexy about ten years after I left home. My mother went into a decline and died shortly afterwards.'

'I am sorry.'

'Thank you, but there is no need. We were not close.'

How very cold that sounded. Her family had been so very loving, even Jonathan when they were younger. Longhurst's tone suggested he would not welcome further questioning. And really, it was none of her business.

A large puddle lay across the path at the edge of the woods.

Without a word of warning, Lord Longhurst whisked her up in his arms.

She cried out in surprise. 'My lord, I—'

A second later he was putting her down on the other side. He glared at her. 'Don't tell me you would rather have splashed through it in your sandals and soaked the hem of your skirts,' he said gruffly.

Not at all. Being swept up in such a way for the second time in one day, was rather…lovely. It made her feel particularly feminine. She took a deep breath.

He held up his hand. 'Come, let us not argue about such a trivial matter.'

His words gave her brain time to work. She could certainly not encourage him in such outrageous behaviour by telling him she had thoroughly enjoyed it. 'Very well. But, my lord, you must leave me here to continue my journey alone. The villagers are used to seeing me walking by myself. To see you escorting me through the village would give rise to all sorts of unwanted speculation.'

'My dear Lady Petra—'

Was she his dear? Her heart gave a heavy, painful thump. No, that she could never be. He was a soldier and a man who would leave here at the drop of a hat and without a backward glance. 'Please do not argue, my lord, unless it is your intention to ruin my reputation.'

'Certainly not.' He sounded offended. No matter. It was better to offend him than have the whole countryside gossiping about them and Westram getting to hear of it.

His expression became grim. 'While I cannot like the idea of your walking alone, I do take your point, my lady. I must therefore acquiesce to your request.' He frowned. 'However, before we part there is something I would like to ask you.'

For a second her heart seized. Ask her? Could he be thinking of a...proposal? No, no, what was she thinking? They were scarcely even friends. 'Ask away.'

'About the field you recommended we mow first. I've been reading about crop rotation and such and I was wondering if you would advise ploughing and planting this year, or leaving it fallow.'

Stunned by his willingness to ask her advice regarding such a complex matter, she stared at him.

His frown deepened. 'Is this not a sensible question?'

'Yes. Yes, indeed. Perfectly sensible.' But gentlemen did not ask ladies for such advice as a general rule. She swallowed.

'Perhaps you do not know?' He sighed. 'So far you are the only person to offer me anything helpful regarding the estate. All Mrs Beckridge suggests is that I chase off a band of gypsies, who as far as I can judge are doing no one any harm at all and are the only ones available to work in my fields.'

'Except they are poaching your fish and quite possibly your rabbits, you know.'

'As you so rightly pointed out the other day, things that exists in the wild belong to no one person. They are welcome to them. There are far too many of them anyway.'

He sounded so fierce, she wanted to laugh. She kept her face straight. 'To really give you a good answer to your question about the field it would help to know how it has been used in the past. I have not lived here long enough to know that myself, I'm afraid.'

He shrugged. 'I have been through the estate journals. But to be honest, they might as well have been written in hieroglyphs for all that I understand.'

She winced. 'It is quite possible. I understand that each bailiff has his own form of shorthand as a way of preserving their positions. I might be able to make sense of it, if I were to see the notes.'

'Would you be willing to look at them?'

She hesitated. What would people say? What would Red say?

His expression froze. 'I beg your pardon. I should not have asked.'

Why not? 'I would be happy to help.' Delighted, in fact. It was so long since she had anything truly useful to do.

'I'll bring them over tomorrow. We can go through them together. I am determined to understand this stuff.'

His eagerness was enchanting. As was his willingness to seek her advice. She stilled. Shook her head.

'No?' he asked.

'Perhaps it would be better if I come to Longhurst. No one will see me if I cut across country, or, if they do, they will think I am out on one of my rambles, but everyone will see you arrive at my door. And everyone will make assumptions. Before you know it, my brother will be knocking on your door asking about your intentions. Red is very dear, but completely misguided in matters regarding his sisters.'

His expression became serious. 'I would not like to go behind your brother's back.'

'Nonsense. We are simply making sure we do not incite gossip about something perfectly innocent.'

'Visiting a gentleman alone in his home is just as likely ruin your reputation.'

'Only if it becomes known. My lord, I am a widow. I am free to come and go as I please, provided I remain discreet.'

He frowned. 'Then it shall be as you wish.'

She shrugged out of his coat and handed it to him. 'I will come to Longhurst at around eleven on Friday.'

'I shall look forward to it.'

As she walked away, she was aware of his gaze following her down the lane until she turned the corner.

A few moments later the Vicar and his wife came driving along the other way. See, she was right. If he had escorted her home, there would have been all kinds of questions and innuendo.

The Vicar pulled up when he came alongside her. 'Good day, Lady Petra.' His gaze scanned her person. 'It seems you got caught in the storm.'

'I did. Fortunately, I found some shelter under a tree. I am only slightly damp.'

He eyed her up and down. 'You were fortunate indeed. It was quite a shower.'

Mrs Beckridge leaned forward with a sugary smile. 'My dear Lady Petra, you must hurry home before you catch a chill. I am surprised your sister permits you to wander around the countryside alone.'

Petra gritted her teeth but managed a smile. 'Thank you for your concern, but as you say, I really must be getting home. I bid you good day.'

She set off at a brisk pace, praying they would not turn around and offer to drive her to her door. There really was something about the Vicar's wife she did not like. The sound of the vehicle continuing on its way was a great relief. All she had to do now was think of an excuse Marguerite would believe to be out of the house for an extended period on Friday.

Or perhaps she should just tell her sister the truth.

And if Marguerite thought it a bad idea to visit Lord Longhurst in his home? Alone? Petra really did not want to fight with her sister.

She would think of something.

Chapter Six

Ethan paced his study. Lady Petra should have been here by now. He should not have listened to her worries and should have sent his carriage. After all, she could easily have brought her maid, or even her sister. It was not as if they were doing anything untoward. No matter how much he might like to.

He quelled that thought the instant it formed, but it did not quell the heat in his blood quite so easily, damn it.

A few moments with his arms around the woman, one brush of his lips against her hair, and he could not stop thinking about her. Which was simply not on. And if by seeking her aid, he was putting her reputation in danger, then he should cease and desist immediately. Particularly since his man of business had written to inform him the he believed he'd discovered the perfect heiress. The daughter of a foundry owner somewhere in the North.

If he wanted to take a look at her, he could meet her in town during the course of the Season, when Parliament resumed. He did suggest that Ethan should not delay in making his interest known, if she proved suitable, since more than one destitute lord was in the market for a wealthy bride.

Damn it all.

He strode for the window, looking out and squaring his shoulders. There was no help for it. Unless Lady Petra could see a miracle within the pages of the journals, he would simply have to buckle down and do his duty as his title demanded.

No matter how irksome. Still, once done, with the aid of a good bailiff and a wife to oversee things, he could head back to his regiment.

He swung around at a sound behind him. Lady Petra in the doorway with a smile on her face. Thank God. How long had she been there? He frowned, hoping she would not recognise the pure joy he felt at the sight of her. Joy? Nonsense, it was relief, that was all.

Like a beleaguered battalion upon the arrival of re-inforcements.

'I am sorry I am late,' Lady Petra said, pulling off her gloves, revealing her dainty hands. 'My sister needed some last-minute help with the household chores.'

Why was a lady of her distinction required to do menial tasks? Why did her brother not take better care of his widowed sisters?

'Are you late? I had not noticed.' He certainly wasn't going to let her see how anxious he had been for her arrival. He knew only too well that women used such displays of weakness against a man. His own mother had been a master at the art.

Her face fell. 'I asked Mrs Stone to send up a tea tray. I hope you don't mind.'

The hesitant speech made him feel like a brute. 'Not

at all.' He gestured to the desk. 'I have set the relevant journals on the desk, if you would care to take a look at them.'

After his boorishness, he wouldn't be surprised if she refused.

She removed her bonnet, tucked her gloves inside it and looked around. 'I see you have managed to get rid of the furniture in the hall.'

'O'Cleary and I carted it into the barn. We thought we would put it in the attic, but it is already completely full of yet more furniture.'

'What will you do with it all? Sell it?'

'If anyone wants it. Or burn it, perhaps. I cannot keep it in the stables for ever.'

She winced. 'It seems like a terrible waste, I must say.' She made her way to the desk and looked at the stack of journals he'd set there. 'I suppose I should get on.'

In no time at all she was seated at his desk, poring through the entries, cross-checking between the various years and flipping back and forth.

With her head bent over her work and the sunlight from the window catching her hair and making it glint like gold, she looked lovely. Such a pretty woman. The recollection of her cuddled up against him in the grotto made him wish for an excuse to hold her again. He pushed the thought aside and paced the room, waiting for her judgement.

O'Cleary brought the tea tray and collected it again, and still she studied the ledgers.

Finally, he could bear it no longer. 'What do you make of it?'

She glanced up as if startled by the sound of his

voice, as if she had forgotten he was present. A humbling thought.

Then she smiled and he forgot all about books and estates and titles and could think only of how much he would like to kiss those pretty lips. He froze.

She tipped her head as if she saw something in his reaction, then stared back at the pages before her. 'Bring a chair and I will share what I have understood so far. But I need your help.'

He sat beside her, aware of her arm so close to his, drinking in the sight of her delicate nape as she pointed to an entry in the ledger before her. He forced himself to focus on the page.

'I can understand what it says with regard to what was planted and when, but I cannot for the life of me understand where.' She pointed to a series of letters and numbers.

He stared at them. 'Those look like map references to me.'

'Really.'

He searched through the pile of papers and pulled out a dog-eared map which had neatly printed letters and numbers and arrows pointing in all directions scattered all over it. 'Yes, I saw this earlier and couldn't make head nor tail of it, except that it's obviously a map of the estate.' He pointed to the number she had indicated in the journal and then to a corresponding section on the map. 'Those coordinates refer to this location, I believe. It is not done exactly correctly, but it is plain this location is what is meant.'

'Oh, my goodness. Very well, what about this one?'

Slowly but surely, they worked through it together and a pattern emerged, linking the ledgers to the maps.

'Well done, Lady Petra. Finally, there is clarity.'

She beamed. 'Well, without your knowledge of maps, I would never have figured it out. This is very dissimilar to the way my father's bailiff recorded his journals. Now we have figured out the key, next we have to understand exactly which field was used for which purpose.'

'Can I help?'

'Of course.' She handed him a sheet of paper and the ink stand. 'I think we need to focus on the hundred-acre field that you mowed and see if we can trace exactly how it has been used these past four years. Seven would be better, if you have the information.'

He shook his head. 'There are no records older than four years as far as I can determine.'

'Then we must work with what we have.'

The determination in her voice was heartening. And he was equally determined. Though it had surprised him, he was glad his map-reading skills were as useful here as they had been in the army. He had a knack for it. It had been part of the reason he had risen to the rank of Major. That and his attention to duty.

They worked through the details in the journal, matching them to the map, until they had recorded each of the previous years.

'Judging from this, I would say you should plough now and plant root crops,' she said, leaning back in her chair with a smile that held not a little satisfaction.

The urge to kiss her mouth was almost overwhelming.

He straightened, putting distance between them. 'I agree. That accords with what I have been reading in the agricultural journals.' He grimaced. 'Now I need to buy a plough and hire a ploughman. Not to mention find a bailiff.' This business of caring for the land was indeed an expensive proposition. All the outlay came ahead of any income.

He turned the pages of the most recent journal until he reached the last few pages. These were written in a different hand. A more flowing script, albeit one that looked a bit shaky in places. There were names, dates and amounts beside each one, along with letters and numbers that must be some sort of code. 'Do you have any idea to what this might refer?'

Lady Petra shook her head. 'I have no idea what it is. It is like nothing else in the ledger.'

As he had thought. He grimaced. 'Unfortunately, these I believe I understand all too well. It is a record of enormous expenses. The only thing I can think of to account for these large amounts are gambling debts. This must be why there is no money left in the coffers.'

She looked as shocked as he had felt the first time he saw them. 'Oh, dear.'

'Exactly.' He closed the journals. 'Is it not time for you to be heading home?'

She glanced at the clock. Her eyes widened. 'Four o'clock? Already? I told Marguerite I would not be gone above two hours.' She chuckled. 'I'll be in trouble again. Poor Marguerite. I really am a sad trial.'

'Next time I see her, I will thank her for allowing me to take up so much of your time. I wish I had some way to thank you, as well.'

She gazed at him with a soft glow in her eyes. 'Nonsense, my lord. It has been my very great pleasure.' She grimaced. 'However, I think it would be better if you did not say anything to Marguerite. I simply told her I was going for a walk.'

He glanced at the pile of ledgers. 'And there are still a great many more puzzles to solve. We have only tackled one field.'

'I know. Would you like me to help you with the rest of them?'

He could not believe what he was hearing? 'You would do that?'

'As and when I can. If you think it would be helpful.'

He could do it by himself, but it would take a great deal longer than it had taken them together. Relief filled him. 'Helpful does not describe the value of your contribution.'

A smile lit her lovely face. 'Then I shall come as often as I can.'

'In the meantime, I'll see if I can borrow a plough from Lord Compton, because it seems my cousin cared nothing for farm implements and sold them off with the horses. Ploughing cannot be that hard.'

Her eyes widened. 'You mean to plough it yourself?'

'Why not? Drive up and down in straight rows. How difficult can it be?'

'I do not know. I have never tried, but I do recall my father saying a good ploughman was worth his weight in gold.' She glanced down at the journals. 'Like a good bailiff. Yet it is possible to learn.'

'Then I shall learn.'

She laughed, stood up and stretched, revealing the delights of her petite figure in a very intimate way. No doubt she had no idea what the sight of her breasts pressing against the fine fabric of her gown did to a man. For although she was a widow, she seemed almost too young and innocent to have ever been a wife.

He frowned at the wayward thought.

'I will come again when Marguerite goes to market next Friday, unless something untoward occurs,' she declared as she tied her bonnet and pulled on her gloves. 'There are a great many more acres for us to worry about. One by one we shall solve the mysteries of the estate.'

Her confidence was heartening. Perhaps his sojourn in England would be shorter than he had at first thought. For some reason, that thought did not make him feel as glad as he would have expected.

'No mail today,' Petra sang out as she entered the drawing room.

Marguerite threw down her pen. 'Dash it. Are you sure?' She looked worried.

'Of course. Why what were you expecting?'

'Final approval of the drawings I sent off to a publisher last week.'

'Your drawings are being published?'

She blushed. 'I was asked to colour some drawings of parts of plants for a book, and they requested some samples of drawings of specific flowers. I am hoping they might use them.'

'That is wonderful. Amazing.' She rushed to her sister and gave her a hug.

Marguerite sighed. 'It would be wonderful if they accept the drawings. Colouring pays very little.' She had the household ledger open in front of her.

Petra's heart sank. 'Is there a problem?'

'We don't have enough money to last us through the winter, if they reject the work.'

'They must pay for work they requested, surely?'

'They made no commitment. They rejected the last one I sent.'

Petra recalled how upset Marguerite had been. 'But your work is wonderful and now you know what they are looking for, I am sure it will be fine. The letter will likely come tomorrow.'

'I hope so.' Marguerite did not sound convinced.

'I could set some traps for rabbits to tide us over.'

'You won't find any rabbits in our garden. Jeb has made sure of that.'

'No, I'll set traps the in the field Longhurst had mowed a few days ago. I've seen rabbits there.'

'Did His Lordship give you permission?'

He had said he didn't mind if the gypsies poached his rabbits or his fish. He had also given her permission to purloin what she wanted in the way of blackberries. 'He did.'

'He gave you permission to hunt rabbits?'

'Not rabbits exactly.'

'Oh, no, Petra. I am not having my sister arrested for poaching. I want to see permission in writing.'

'Very well, I will send him a note.'

Marguerite nodded and went back to her ledger. 'Perhaps we can do with less coal if we don't heat the bedrooms.'

Petra sat down and scribbled off a note, then went in search of Jeb to deliver it. He was nowhere around. Then she remembered that he had said he was going to take Patch to the farrier, since she had a loose shoe. She would just have to take the blasted note herself, even though she knew Marguerite would not approve. On the other hand, perhaps it was better this way, because if Ethan was home and gave permission right away, she could set her traps on the way back.

She put on her hat and coat and marched across the fields to Longhurst, picking hazelnuts from the hedgerows as she went. If Longhurst wasn't home, then her trip would not have been completely wasted.

As it happened, she met Lord Longhurst riding up his drive as she crossed his lawn from the other direction. He really was a fine figure of a man on a horse. Her unruly feminine side gave a little sigh of appreciation. It had apparently lost all sense of decorum.

He dismounted as soon as he came up to her. 'Lady Petra, to what do I owe this pleasure? I wasn't expecting you today, was I?'

'No. I came to ask permission to trap a few rabbits on your land.'

He looked surprised, but then smiled. 'You are an endless source of surprise. Help yourself. You know you may.'

He looked so handsome when he smiled she almost forgot her manners. 'Thank you. Would you like one?'

He grinned. 'I didn't like to ask but, yes, O'Cleary and I would appreciate some fresh meat.'

'Very well. Either tomorrow or the day after. In the meantime—' she held out her note '—would you write your assent to my trapping on your land? That way Marguerite will not live in fear of my imminent arrest for poaching.'

He chuckled heartily. 'I will do better than that.' He tore a leaf out of a small notebook with a pencil attached and scribbled his permission. 'There you go. You did promise to teach me to guddle, don't forget.'

'So I did. Would you like to go tomorrow afternoon? I can check my traps at the same time.'

'I would be delighted. Fresh fish for dinner will be a welcome change.'

'Good. I'll meet you at the stream where we saw the boy.'

'You *are* still coming on Friday, as promised?'

Her heart picked up speed. At this rate she would be seeing him every day this week. She really ought not to do that. 'I will.'

'Excellent. May I offer you some tea before you leave?'

She was sorely tempted, but if she did not leave now, then she would not have time to set her traps before dark and it would be two more days before they would have fresh meat on the table.

'I will take tea when I come on Friday, if that is all right. I really must be getting along.'

He bowed. 'Until tomorrow, then.'

'Yes. Tomorrow.' She headed back across the lawn, before she changed her mind and went for tea instead.

Ethan arrived ahead of the appointed time. A good officer always checked the lie of the land before he engaged in a sortie. He'd also organised things the way he wanted them and had ascertained there were no gypsy boys lurking about. Now he would meet Lady Petra before she entered the woods. He strolled along the path to the spot where the river emerged into sunlight. From here he could see the bridge, the lane and anyone walking along from the village.

The next person to come along was a farmer on a

wagon. He pulled up at the bridge and Petra jumped down, giving him a wave as he started his horse moving again. She waited until he was out of sight, then hopped over the stile.

Ethan waited until she was close enough to hear him. 'Lady Petra.'

She smiled.

And it was if the sun had come out from behind a cloud. He glanced upwards. There wasn't a cloud in the sky. But the day definitely felt brighter and warmer. He shook his head at such nonsensical flights of fancy. They walked into the cool of the woods and when they were out of sight of the road, he tucked her hand in the crook of his arm and matched his steps to hers. He was pleased that she made no demur about his escort.

When they reached the chosen spot, she released him with a sound of surprise. 'You brought a blanket?'

He had spread it out where the boy had been lying. 'I didn't think you would want to get your gown dirty.'

She chuckled. 'Well, I did wear something old for the task, but it was thoughtful of you. Thank you.' She raised her eyebrows. 'I see you also brought fishing rods. Is that in case my method of catching fish does not work?'

'Insurance,' he said. Perhaps he should have had a bit more confidence in this guddling of hers, but, when O'Cleary had explained fully what the term meant and since the gypsy boy clearly had not caught anything by this method, Ethan had decided that reinforcements might be required.

'Well, let us see, shall we?'

She removed her gloves, her spencer and her bonnet. She was wearing a dark blue gown with the tiniest little sleeves. She stretched out on her stomach on the rug, so that most of her shoulders hung out over the water. 'Come on, then,' she said to him, 'you cannot learn the way of it standing there.'

He stretched out beside her.

'Lie very still,' she whispered, 'and look down into the water until you see the trout.'

At first, he could see nothing but ripples and waving weed and pebbles. Slowly, his eyes became accustomed to the watery scene and the shapes became more defined. A brown fish was right beneath him, all but his head hidden by the bank's overhang. One really had to look hard since the fish seem to blend in with its surroundings. 'I see it.'

'First you gently ease your hand into the water, about a foot away from him.' She suited her actions to the words. 'You stay like this until he stops noticing you.' The fish shifted position as if to take a look at her hand. Fascinated, Ethan watched her dangling hand. It did not move for a very long time. Eventually, the fish returned to its original position.

She slowly moved her hand a little closer. She repeated this until the fish no longer took any notice of her at all as she gently and rhythmically stroked along its side.

The fish seemed to go into a trance.

'Now,' she whispered, 'I will catch him beneath the belly and toss him up on the bank.'

With a twist of her wrist, she flipped the fish up on to the bank. It stared up at him in puzzlement. 'Poor thing,' he said. 'I can't believe that a fish would let you tickle it, then simply pull it out of the water.'

'There is something they like about having their skins stroked. It seems to send them to sleep.'

'It feels like a mean trick.'

'But a good way to get dinner on the table if you do not have a rod.'

The fish began to jump around. Petra dispatched it and pulled out a knife to gut it.

'I'll do that,' he said firmly, taking the knife from her hand.

'Do you know how?'

'I have seen it done many times.'

'Seeing and doing are not the same necessarily.' She sat back on her heels and watched. She nodded when he was finished. 'In your case, it seems it is.' She turned back to the river. 'Now it is your turn to try.'

They lay side by side, staring into the water.

'I see one,' she said. 'There.' She pointed.

He saw it, too. He took off his jacket, rolled up his sleeve and lowered his arm into the chilly water. He did exactly what she had done and the fish flicked its tail and disappeared.

'Slower,' she said.

They found another one and he lowered his hand at a snail's pace.

It worked. Soon he was also stroking down the fish's side with a fingertip. The scales were slippery. The fish's gills slowed. It let him close his hand around its belly.

He tossed it up on the bank. Petra fell upon it.

'What a beauty,' she said.

They continued fishing and soon had a good haul.

'What are we going to do with all this fish?' he asked. 'I certainly can't eat that amount in one sitting.'

'Take what you want for dinner and I will take the rest. I will smoke what we cannot eat right away. It will help us get through the winter.'

He sat up and dried his arm on his shirt tails. He was looking forward to fresh fish for dinner. Smoked fish he could do without. He had eaten far too much of it during his army days. Smoked fish. Dried meat. Hard biscuits. He certainly did not miss the food.

They had caught ten good-sized trout and they worked together to get them cleaned, tossing the offal back into the water, where it would feed other fish.

She grinned at him. 'You brought your rods for no purpose.'

'I am assuming that guddling is not always an option?'

'No. The conditions have to be right. We would have been glad of the rods had it been cooler or cloudy.'

'Well, I must thank you for my lesson.'

'You are a good pupil. My brothers were hopeless at it. They could not sit still long enough. Sometimes you have to get into the water with the fish. We are lucky here, the overhanging bank makes it a perfect spot.'

He touched the bare arm that had been in the water. 'You are freezing. You need to put on your coat.'

'I am not in the least bit cold,' she objected.

He gave her a look. 'You will not be pleased if you catch a cold.'

'Believe me, I don't catch cold so easily. I must go now. I need to prepare this fish so it does not spoil, and I want to check my traps.'

He shrugged. 'As you wish.'

She frowned as if surprised he did not insist more.

Why would he? She would only take him to task for fussing.

He could not, however, stop himself from saying one thing. 'I will see you on Friday as you promised.'

'If I can get away. If I am not there on Friday, I will come at the first opportunity.'

And with that, he had to be satisfied. He rolled down his sleeve and put on his coat. Once they had split their haul, they went their separate ways.

Or at least, she headed back the way she had come. Ethan followed her from a distance, moving quietly through the undergrowth until he was sure she was safely back in the lane. Why had he not simply insisted on escorting her?

Because she would refuse and he really did not want to have to insist. If he did that, she was sure to turn cold on him.

Chapter Seven

Petra hurried along the path in the woods. She had not been able to get away to help Lord Longhurst with his books for five days now. She had been so busy with smoking the fish they had caught and dealing with the rabbits, then a storm had blown in, leaving Marguerite with a bad headache. Today was the first day she was able to slip away.

The ring of metal against wood rang out through the forest. A woodcutter clearing up the deadfall, no doubt. It seemed Lord Longhurst had taken her advice on that matter also. She smiled. Not only was he a handsome, charming man, he was also the most sensible male she had ever met.

Deciding to avoid being seen, she circled the clearing, but could not resist a peek. She started as she realised it wasn't a woodcutter at all. It was His Lordship stripped to the waist once again and swinging an axe. The muscles in his arms rippled with each powerful strike. Sweat gleamed on his sculpted torso. The man was so beautifully proportioned with his wide strong shoulders and tapered waist he might have been used to model Atlas himself.

Unable to resist, she crept closer to get a better look. And stepped on a twig. At the snap, he turned. Their gazes met across the clearing. Heat shimmered in the air. She could scarcely breathe for the pounding of her heart as she remained fixed in his bright blue gaze for what felt like a very long time, but must only have been seconds.

He lowered the axe head to the ground. 'Lady Petra.'

'Lord Longhurst.' My goodness, how breathless she sounded. She forced herself to take a deep breath and draw closer, as if he was not half-naked and radiating heat from his exertions. Indeed, he was the most tempting sight she had ever seen. 'I was on my way to see you.'

'I thought you had given up on me, to be honest, so I have been plodding along on my own and making a bit of headway.'

Was he saying he no longer needed her assistance? Disappointment filled her. Sadly, she stared at him, drinking in the sight of him as if she was about to lose something precious and dear to her heart. Shocked by her reaction, she cast him a bright smile that felt brittle and false. 'I am sorry I was unable to send you a note on Friday to let you know I would not be coming as promised.'

'Never mind. You are here now and I have some questions.'

Relief flooded through her. Impulsively, she touched his arm. His heat permeated through her cotton gloves and his muscles shifted slightly as if surprised by her touch. The strength beneath her fingers inspired awe. 'I am so very happy you still need my help.'

She gasped even as the ill-thought-out words left her lips. Yet they were honest, were they not? The truth.

His eyes widened a fraction, as if he, too, sensed more to the words than their actual meaning.

She swallowed. 'I mean—'

'I missed you,' he said gruffly. 'Your help. Your smile. I—'

And then, without knowing who had made the first move, she was in his arms and kissing him as if her life depended on it.

His mouth moved over hers, his lips soft yet hungry, his tongue tracing the seal of her lips, requesting rather than demanding entry. She parted her lips and welcomed the blissful strokes of his tongue and tasted the nectar of his kiss.

She pressed against that beautiful broad expanse of chest, loving the hard feel of him against her soft flesh. Her insides tightened unbearably and she arched her back, aligning her body as close to his as possible. The blood rushing through her veins made her dizzy with excitement.

A large warm hand lay flat on her back, holding her steady so he could explore her mouth fully. His other hand stroked over her derrière and gently pulled her close as he rocked in counterpoint to the movement of her hips.

Pleasure became an exquisite ache in her core. Wild with desire, she ran her hands over his back and up to his lovely shaped head, where she speared her fingers through the damp curls at his nape.

Finally, when she thought she would never draw breath again, he broke their kiss and rested his forehead against hers, breathing hard.

'Ethan,' she whispered.

'What is it, my...dear?'

His little hesitation gave her pause. What had he been about to say before he changed it. *My love?* Surely not. Perhaps he had been going to say my lady and had realised it did not really fit the circumstances. That was far more likely.

'Should I apologise?' Ethan asked, his voice gentle. 'Because you know, I am not at all sorry.'

She laughed, the awkward moment forgotten, and stroked his beard-roughened cheek with the tips of her fingers. 'It is I who should apologise. I believe I caught you unawares. But I am not at all sorry either.'

He chuckled softly. 'You have no idea how glad that makes me.' He let out a sigh. 'I cannot deny that I find you attractive in the extreme and knowing that you reciprocate makes me happy.'

Her heart lifted, then plunged as he stepped back.

Sorrow filled his expression. 'What has happened here, between us, makes it clear that we must not meet alone again.'

'I don't understand.' Heat rushed to her face. Why was she arguing? Why was she not simply shrugging and accepting his rejection as any sensible woman would? But after the joy of that kiss she needed to know what held him back. 'What harm do we do?'

He grimaced. 'None. We clearly enjoy each other's company. And your knowledge has been invaluable. Indeed, if I had a choice, Lady Petra, I would request your hand in marriage, we are so well suited.'

Her jaw dropped. He wanted to marry her?

'But needs must. I have to marry for money. There is no help for it if I want to rescue this estate.'

She laughed awkwardly. 'I certainly cannot help you there, my lord. I do not have a penny to my name.' She fixed her gaze on his face, willing him to listen. 'Nor am I on the marriage mart. I do not seek to marry again. And since, at least for the moment, we are both free to seek our...' How did one put this? Heat rose in her face, but she soldiered on, for was this not one of the only advantages to being a widow? 'To seek our entertainments where we please. Does it not seem opportune that we have found each other at this moment in time? As if the fates have brought us together? There can be no doubt that there is more than mere friendship between us.'

His eyes widened.

She tried not to flinch. 'Oh, dear, now I have shocked you with my boldness. I apologise.'

He caught her hand in his, brought it to his lips, and kissed it gently. 'Not so much shocked, my dear, as pleasantly surprised. You are a desirable, beautiful woman. The attraction between us strikes me anew, each time we meet. But for your sake, I would not dishonour you by proposing anything untoward. Or anything that you do not want.'

Her heart soared at his reluctant admission that he also desired her. She wanted this. She wanted him. And she was free to indulge herself, provided she did not make a scandal. Why should she not enjoy the attentions of a man she had come to like very much?

She moved closer, ran her free hand down the bare expanse of his chest and was delighted by the way his nipples hardened in response. She looked up into his face, unable to hide her feelings of hope. 'Then it seems we are perfectly in accord in our desire for a brief affair.' She glanced around at their surroundings. 'And who knows how many opportunities the future will offer us to be alone? Should we not make the most of it right now?'

His voice deepened and became husky. 'I am honoured that you trust me enough to make such an offer.'

'But?'

He groaned. 'But nothing. I have no willpower where you are concerned.' He pulled her close and kissed her deeply. After a few heady moments he drew back and gave her a small peck on the cheek. He left her side and she felt a sudden chill until she saw what he was about. He collected a bundle on the ground she had not noticed before. His coats and shirt and, of all things, a blanket.

'I planned to eat luncheon out here, so I could get as much work done as possible today,' he explained at her quizzical look. He spread the blanket on a patch of soft green moss beneath the limbs of a large oak. 'A soldier learns to take along what comforts he can,' he said, grinning up at her from his knees on the grey wool blanket. He held out his arms to her with the expression of a naughty boy who has just found something wonderful, like a grasshopper or a frog, and had plans for it.

'How exceedingly fortuitous for me,' she said, shaking her head at him and going to him with laughter bubbling in her chest.

She hadn't felt quite this giddy since she was a girl. She sank down on her knees beside him and he undid the strings of her bonnet. He carefully removed it and set it aside. 'Now I can see your pretty face properly,' he said with satisfaction. 'And kiss you properly, without fear of crushing your hat.'

He did just that and as she gave herself up to kisses that were almost magical, he gently eased her back on to the blanket so that he was leaning over her, kissing her lips, nuzzling at her throat and exploring her ear, until she felt like she would explode with the heat and pressure building inside her. Her core ached for his touch, for the pressure of his body against hers. Out of pure self-preservation of her sanity, she took his hand and placed it where she needed it. He lifted his head and smiled down at her.

'Anxious, are we?'

She was panting and scarcely breathing for the excitement bubbling in her veins. Why had she never felt such overwhelming sensations before? It was almost unnerving. She'd enjoyed making love with Harry, mostly. It was really the only time that it seemed as though she'd had his full attention, once they were married. But the storm going on in her body right now was making her dizzy. She did not understand it all. 'It would seem so,' she gasped.

Realisation dawned on his face, along with a hint of regret. His dropped a small kiss on her nose. 'Yes. Of course. You have missed your husband.'

That wasn't it all. But how could she explain the wildness inside her that had been building since the moment she met him?

He smiled as if he understood her silence, though he could not possibly understand anything at all. 'Let us do this properly, shall we?' he said.

'Is there any other way?' she said more boldly than she actually felt at that moment. A doubt niggled at the edges of what remained of her brain. Would she meet his expectations? Harry had accused her of being boring and after a few short weeks had gone elsewhere for his pleasure.

Ethan gave her a sweet smile. 'Let us hope not.'

Lying on her back, her face eager, bright and flushed, Petra looked strangely innocent for all that she was so bold. He liked her daring. Certainly, he would not have let things go so far had she not made it perfectly plain what she wanted.

He'd been wanting this for days when he usually didn't allow himself to want anything at all. One day at a time had been his philosophy for years. It avoided disappointment. That was until he met Sarah. He'd allowed himself to dream of a different future then. And hadn't that been a stark reminder of why his usual philosophy worked so well?

The here and now was what counted and he was going to make sure she enjoyed their encounter as much as he did. More. Because not only was that what a gentleman did, it was what he wanted for her. It was what she deserved.

Luckily, he had been blessed with the tutoring of one of the most accomplished courtesans in London while he kicked his heels waiting for his orders to come through. She'd had other moneyed clients whom she charged a fortune, but for some reason she had picked him to be her lover on the side for those few short months. Perhaps she'd felt sorry for him. Or enjoyed showing off her prowess to a younger man. He'd never asked. One did not look a gift horse in the mouth. And it was certainly a gift that was being offered to him now. A liaison with a widow, with no strings attached.

But Petra was a different proposition to a courtesan.

Or even Sarah. Beneath her prickly outer shell, he sensed she had a delicate centre that would be easy to crush. A soft heart that had likely been crushed in the past.

The thought gave him pause.

'You truly are sure you want this?' he asked, gazing into her deep blue eyes already hazy with desire from their kissing.

'Positive,' she said, smiling at him. A shadow passed over her expression. An expectation of hurt? 'Unless… you've changed your mind?'

He didn't want to hurt her for the world. 'Not a chance,' he said, kissing first her chin and then her collarbone where it peeked at him above the neckline of her muslin gown. He swirled his tongue around the little hollow of her throat and she shuddered. 'I simply want you to be sure.'

And he did not want her to feel as if she did not have a choice.

'I am sure.' Her eagerness sent the blood from his brain straight to his shaft.

'I am happy to hear it.' He smiled down at her and she smiled back. It was if they shared a secret, though he had no idea what it was. But whatever it was, it deserved a kiss.

As they kissed, he undid the bow at the neck of her gown and eased it down over her shoulders. Such delicate pale skin compared to his, which was bronzed by the sun of many summers abroad. Reverently he traced the rise of her breasts where they swelled above her stays and chemise. Small breasts, but beautifully formed. He kissed them one at a time and she gave a soft moan and arched towards him.

It would be easy to hike her skirts and lie between

her thighs, but he wanted to reveal all her loveliness, to pleasure her as she deserved. 'Let me help you out of your gown,' he murmured close to her ear.

He helped her to stand and turned her around, kissing her lovely nape as he undid the tapes of her gown and her stays. They fell to her feet and, stepping out of them, she turned to face him with a shy and mischievous smile.

He really liked those smiles. He never wanted to see her sad or unhappy. He drank in her beautiful shape, tiny yet with curves in all the right places, and marvelled at his good fortune.

She raised her eyebrows and pointedly glanced down at his breeches, where his erection must be evident through the tight fabric. 'Do you need help?'

Good lord, he must have been standing here staring at her like some besotted fool. Quickly, he disposed of his boots and stockings and, turning his back, peeled off his breeches.

When he turned to face her, she was once more sitting on the blanket, watching him with an avid expression. He felt like preening.

Inwardly, he laughed at his schoolboy inclinations around her. He'd always told himself that one lover was like any other. That women in general were to be treated with kid gloves and not to be trusted, but with this one he seemed to be constantly battling to retain his guard.

When she opened her arms to him, her high, pert breasts pressing against the filmy fabric of her chemise, he forgot all about such thoughts and fell to his knees beside her, losing himself in her kisses, savouring the hot dark warmth of her mouth with his tongue.

While his lips paid homage to her mouth, his hand found one small breast, its tip furling tight as he circled it with his thumb. With a last lingering kiss to her mouth, he lowered his head and kissed the hard little nub. He suckled, the muslin a sensual counterpoint to the silkiness of her flesh against his tongue.

She sighed her pleasure and her hips arched towards him. He pushed the chemise up to her waist and gazed down her length. The pale gold curls at the apex to her thighs were damp with her desire. He petted the pretty curls and she parted her thighs, giving his fingers access to her hot wet core. He stroked his fingers along her slit until he found the source of her pleasure. She made soft keening noises that drove him nearly insane with desire.

And when her fingers curled around his shaft, squeezing and stroking with a knowing hand, his mind went dark. The urge to plunge into her rode him hard. But he was so bloody big and she was just so tiny.

He rolled over on his back, bringing her with him. She squeaked in surprise, but when she found herself straddling him with his erection pressing against her belly, she smiled and rose up and took him in.

How he survived the first shock of sliding into those tight warm depths without losing control he didn't quite know, but he gritted his teeth and hung on. At first, she seemed uncomfortable with the position, but with his hands clasped around her waist he helped her find a rhythm and depth that suited her and soon she rode him with the skill of a woman who knew what she liked.

The pleasure on her face was nearly his undoing. He shifted within her until he found the spot that sent shudders rippling through her and made her cry out. A few swift strokes and she came apart.

As she collapsed on his chest, he withdrew from her body, and his own petite mort racked him from head to toe.

He lay panting and boneless for what seemed like for ever. At long last, his breathing returned to normal and a great lassitude came over him. He forced himself to lift her off his chest and cleaned them both up with his shirt tails.

With a sigh of satisfaction, she curled up against him. He enfolded her in the crook of his arm and covered her with his shirt. Hopefully, she would not regret the gift she had bestowed on him when she awoke. He fell into warm darkness.

A heavy weight pressing on her hip brought Petra to her senses. What…? Oh, yes. Ethan. Warm and alive and one exceedingly heavy thigh across hers. Recollection flooded in. The way he had given her control. The unbelievable pleasure. The complete loss of herself in those last few moments, like falling apart and reforming as someone new.

Had he felt the same thing? Was it something that happened only occasionally during lovemaking? Nothing in her marriage had prepared her for such a shattering experience.

Yes, there had been pleasurable sensations when Harry made love to her…but that explosive ecstasy she'd just felt? No. Compared to the way Ethan made love, Harry seemed clumsy and rushed. As if he'd always been in a hurry to be done with her. The withdrawal thing she did understand. Harry also had not wanted children. He'd wanted to wait. He'd been having far too good a time as a newly minted member of the *ton*.

The warm heavy weight shifted as Ethan rolled away. She quelled a shiver at the loss of his heat. 'Oh, my goodness,' she said, opening her eyes, surprised to see the sun still shining and glinting through the leaves above their heads. She felt as if she'd slept away a whole night when in truth it must have been only a few moments.

He rose on one elbow to look down at her. 'Are you all right?'

She stretched. All right? She felt wonderful. Full of energy and lax all at the same time. She smiled into his concerned expression. 'I am more than all right. Thank you. That was lovely.'

A warm smile lit his face and his eyes danced. 'My pleasure, I assure you.'

They both laughed.

'I think perhaps we should dress in case anyone comes along,' she said, running her hand over his heavily muscled flank and down over the hard, round buttocks. They were positively delicious. So masculine and firm. Sensual. It was going to be a shame to cover them up.

'Yes, I suppose we should,' he murmured, leaning forward to lick at her breast.

Her nipples hardened instantly. Tension began building deep in her core.

She glanced down at his now-flaccid member resting against his magnificent thigh. Even at rest it was impressive. And already hardening.

As quick as that, she wanted him again. Wanted to

live through that amazing exquisite delight. If it was possible to feel such things a second time?

He rolled away and rose to his feet. 'You are right, my dear. We do not want to be discovered. Think of your reputation.' He pulled on his shirt and helped her to rise.

Disappointed, she sighed, but nodded agreement. They had already risked a great deal out here in the woods where anyone might trip over them. Discovery would without a doubt put paid to her and Marguerite's independence. She really could not do that to Marguerite. She must be more careful next time.

Oh, heavens, was she already planning a next time? Was she really so wanton?

He helped her into her stays and gown, fastening them with all the expertise of a ladies' maid. Clearly, he had done this before. A pang of jealousy took her by surprise.

To hide her chagrin, she sat down to put on her sandals. 'If I am to help you today, we should hurry.'

He hunkered down beside her and took over tying the strings. His hands were large, but he accomplished the task with meticulous dexterity. He shook his head. 'I think you should not come to Longhurst today.'

She froze. He didn't want her at his house? Did he think less of her because of what they had done? Had he found her lacking in some way as Harry had done? Cold trickled into her chest.

'I told Mrs Stone I would be gone all day,' he said. 'It might look strange if we were to arrive there together.'

Cold was replaced by a flood of warmth. He was thinking of her, not himself. Oh, how she loved—appreciated—his generous nature. Harry had only ever thought of himself. 'You are right. I shall come tomorrow.'

'If it is convenient.'

'I will make it convenient.'

'I will give Mrs Stone an errand in Sevenoaks.'

She giggled. 'Perfect.'

'Do you want to know what is even more perfect?' he said, smiling and picking a leaf out of her hair.

'What?'

'There are beds at Longhurst, with nice, soft mattresses.' He grinned in triumph as if he had produced a rabbit out of a hat.

She could not help laughing. 'It sounds heavenly.'

Chapter Eight

Over the next week or so, Petra had found every excuse to be out of the house. Hazelnuts ready for gathering, elderberries ripening in the hedgerows and even a visit to a sick neighbour on the other side of the Parish when Marguerite was otherwise engaged.

While they were not ladies of the manor, since Longhurst had no wife, someone had to take on the role, particularly since Mrs Beckridge found the idea of visiting ill people distasteful.

Petra never went home to Westram Cottage without completing her stated task, but always managed an hour or two in Ethan's company, either in his arms or poring over the journals. Or both. Little by little, together they uncovered all the secrets in the journals. And little by little, she grew closer to Ethan until on the days she could not go to Longhurst for one reason or another, she felt lost.

Today was one of those days. She put aside her needlework and went to the window to see if the rain had abated. She had not seen Ethan for two days and she missed him terribly. She felt as if she could not breathe. No, it wasn't only him she missed, it was the enjoyment of working with him, of imparting all her knowledge to someone who sincerely appreciated the help.

And, if she was honest, she adored their interludes in bed where she'd experienced that indescribable pleasure each and every time.

Sadly, there was no sign of a break in the weather.

'What on earth is the matter, Petra?' Marguerite asked, putting down her pen. 'That is the third time you have looked out of the window.'

Petra winced. There really was no excuse she could think of for going out on such a miserable day. She flopped down into a chair. 'I am bored.'

A pained look crossed Marguerite's face. 'Are you, dearest?'

Petra hated giving Marguerite pain. 'It is this weather, getting me down, that is all.'

'Perhaps life in the country does not suit you after all?' Marguerite sounded as if she had an idea on her mind.

Petra straightened. 'What are you saying?'

Marguerite glanced down at the letter she had been writing. 'I was thinking a visit to London might do us both good.'

A chill entered Petra's chest. 'Are we running out of money? Do we have to return home to live with Red?'

'No. At least, not yet. But things are getting a little difficult, as you know.' She glanced at the empty hearth. They had agreed to hold off lighting the fire, despite the growing chill of autumn, and were both wrapped in warm shawls.

'So how will going to London help?' Petra tilted her head. 'You can't be thinking about marriage.'

'Certainly not,' Marguerite said swiftly, sharply. 'I need to meet with the publisher, personally. I am owed some money.'

'But Red—'

'It will never come to Red's ears. Unless you tell him.'

Petra gasped, 'I would never say a word. But someone is sure to tell him we are in town.'

Marguerite smiled grimly. 'I will tell him we are in town. He will understand perfectly, when I say we need to shop.'

Oh, indeed. Petra grinned. Red assumed that all women wanted to do was spend money in the shops. His series of mistresses had trained him well, poor dear. But to leave Westram and go to London meant leaving Ethan. She wasn't sure she wanted to do that.

'You go. I will stay here and look after things.'

Marguerite folded the letter and added it to a bundle of folded papers, which she proceeded to wrap in brown paper. 'Nonsense. I could not possibly leave you here alone. And anyway, I'm not yet sure whether I will be going at all. It will depend on the answer to this letter.'

Petra went to her side as Marguerite daubed sealing wax on the strings around the parcel. 'What is that?'

'Some drawings that I am hoping to sell. I saw an advertisement in the newspaper for a sketch artist.'

'Is there anything I can do to help?'

Marguerite pressed her lips together. 'I don't know if my sketches will be accepted, but if they are you will need to take on more of the housekeeping. I hate to burden you with it.'

Petra gasped, 'Do you think I am so spoiled I would not willingly do whatever is needed?'

Her sister closed her eyes briefly. 'It is not that. Of course it is not. You have always done your share and more. It is my fear that it may all be for nothing.' She sounded...mortified. 'I am not sure they are any good.'

Marguerite was sensitive about her art. She rarely let anyone look at it.

'They are sketches of what?'

'Samples of my work. Diagrams. Watercolours. So they can see what I can do.' She shrugged. 'It is for a book.'

'There is more to it than that.' Petra just knew it.

'I am trying to make sure of our independence,' Marguerite said. 'And that is all that needs to be said.'

Petra eyed the package. There was no address on the outside. 'Do you want me to take it to the post office?' It might give her an excuse to run across the fields and visit Ethan, if only for a few minutes.

Marguerite snatched it up. 'I prefer to take it myself. I won't be long. When I come back, we will see if we can turn some of the elderberries you collected into cordial before they go bad. I am sure we have enough sugar on hand. Perhaps you wouldn't mind taking them off the stems in the meantime.'

She whisked out of the front door and was off down the lane with her umbrella over her head before Petra could argue.

Dash it all. Why was Marguerite being so secretive? But then they all had secrets, didn't they? Petra wandered into the kitchen and eyed the basket of elderberries she had picked two days before. She sighed. If she was going to bring fruit home, then she really ought to be prepared to deal with it. She pulled the scissors out of the drawer and began snipping off the stems.

What would Ethan be doing on such a wet day? Would he be staring out of his window, hoping she might come? Likely he would not expect her in such weather. Perhaps he was out riding his estate, verifying the information in the journal, as he so often did on the days she could not go to him. Or paying a visit to Lord Compton. The two men were becoming fast friends. Or at least that was how it appeared.

More to the point, would he be disappointed if she and Marguerite went off to London before she had finished helping him with the journals?

She sighed more deeply. Really. Be honest. Ethan now knew exactly what needed to be done before the start of winter. He simply did not have the money to do it. All they had done recently was try to prioritise which things must be done and in what order, until he came up with a way to finance it.

Two days later, Ethan glanced at the library clock. If Petra was coming today, she would have set out by now. The rain of the previous few days had cleared out and it was a bright crisp autumn day. Ethan shrugged into his coat. He really did not like her wandering the countryside alone. If he left now, he would likely meet her before she had got too far across the fields.

She always scolded him for going to meet her, but he could tell she was also pleased. And seeing her pleased made him happy. Made him forget the dire future looming over him, though the future was rapidly becoming the here and now.

It would soon be time to present himself in London. He had received several letters from other peers of the realm asking for his support on one issue or another in the next session of Parliament. Those letters had reminded him that if it turned out he could not continue to be a soldier, there were things he could do in government to help with the war effort. Things that might improve the lot of the men fighting for their country.

And then there was the matter of the potential bride his man of business had discovered. The man had more or less indicated that if Ethan didn't stir his stumps in regard to the marriage mart, she'd be snapped up by some other poverty-stricken nobleman.

He opened the library door and discovered Petra walking down the hallway with a couple of rabbits dangling from a string. He grinned. 'Poaching again, I see.'

She laughed. 'Marguerite makes a wonderful stew. Send them over with O'Cleary and come for dinner tonight, so you can find out for yourself. It is Mrs Stone's day off today, I believe?' Her eyes twinkled saucily.

'What a clever girl you are,' he said and kissed the tip of her nose, pulling her into the library and closing the door so he could kiss her more thoroughly. How he was going to miss this closeness once he brought home a bride.

Although… No, he would not disrespect any woman who became his wife, despite the fact that many married men kept a mistress. And he certainly would not disrespect Petra by persuading her to continue their relationship after his marriage, no matter how much the idea appealed.

'Wonderful. I shall have Jeb deliver a note of invitation when I get home.'

He took the rabbits and, finding O'Cleary in the stables, gave him the necessary instructions. By the time he returned to the library, Petra had removed her bonnet and her spencer and was seated in his chair at the desk.

'I have had another thought,' she said, peering at the map they had carefully drawn together. 'If we—'

He went around behind her and kissed the delicate nape of her neck.

She shivered, then laughed. 'Don't you want to hear my idea?'

He removed the pins from her hair, watching in delight as the fine golden tresses tumbled around her shoulders. 'I always want to hear your ideas,' he murmured into her ear, delighted to see the fine hairs on her arms stand to attention.

She turned her face up to his, offering her lips for a kiss. He took full advantage and words were forgotten as he brought her to her feet without breaking the kiss, taking her place in the chair and seating her so she straddled his lap.

She moved slowly and sensually against his groin.

He groaned and undid his falls and she sank down on to his erect cock. 'I missed you,' he groaned. He missed her the way he would miss an arm or a hand. He felt incomplete when she wasn't there. He kept waiting for the feeling to die a natural death, but each time they were together it only grew stronger.

Not that he would ever admit such feelings out loud.

He would never give a woman that sort of power over him. Those wild sorts of passions led to a great deal of unhappiness and jealousy as he'd seen first-hand with his parents. No, he did not like feeling this way about Petra. Which was why he was willing to consider the northern heiress as a bride. A sensible convenient marriage was all he would ever need. One that would allow him to return to the war, if at all possible.

He sank lower in the chair and gave her free rein to take her pleasure as she pleased. He loved watching her face as she moved on him. Loved the sensation of hot wet tightness around his shaft. The slide of her inner muscles stroking him brought him close to the edge and it was almost beyond his control to wait for her to find her release. While she pleasured him, he undid the bow at her neck and unfastened the hooks and eyes of the front-closing stays she had taken to wearing just for him. It was always a delight to expose her beautiful breasts to his gaze and his hands and his tongue. He loved their firm softness and the way her nipples hardened to the touch of his tongue.

He suckled. A few moments later she fell apart. Desire beat a demand in his blood. He lifted her clear and she grasped his member and brought him to completion, expertly catching his seed in the tails of his shirt before collapsing against his shoulder.

He curled his arms around her. If only he could protect her from the future. He could not. He lifted her so she sat comfortably in his arms. Entwined in his chair, satiated and content, the minutes passed. If he was honest, he had never been this contented in his life. A very foolish admission. 'I missed you, too,' she said sleepily.

His heart ached in a painfully sweet way at her words. Foolish sentiment. He was a soldier. An earl. Sentiment had no place in his life. 'Tell me your idea.'

She sat up and he helped her straighten her clothing and she lifted up so he could button his falls.

'It is about using the fields for grazing animals.'

'I have no cattle to graze.'

'Exactly. Why don't we lease out the fields to those who do?'

'Are there people who need grass for their animals?'

'Yes. There is an article about it in this journal. The demand for wool from sheep is going unfulfilled at the moment, because France is blocking ships from reaching us. There is not nearly enough grazing land for the growing number of flocks and people are leasing out patches of land all over the place.'

She shuffled through the papers on his desk and found a journal he had not yet had a chance to read. She flipped through the pages until she found what she sought. 'Here. This is it.' She handed it to him.

He scanned the article. 'How do we locate such a person?'

She gave him a smile of triumph and took the journal back. She opened it to a page at the back and pointed to a paragraph set in bold type. 'We advertise.'

We. It was if this situation between them could go on for ever, even though she knew full well it could not. On numerous occasions she had indicated that it must end soon. Pain sliced through his chest. He swallowed.

She stared at him, concerned. 'You don't like the idea?'

He shook his head to clear it. 'I like it very well. Indeed, it is brilliant.'

'Would you like me to draft up something for you to send in to the journal? Merino sheep would do very well on your fields and they fetch a good price at market. Their grazing would bring a good income, I should think. We will have to look into what sort of prices others are asking. Lord Compton might know. I believe he pays for grazing for some of his cattle.'

She pulled a sheet of paper and a quill towards her.

A sound made him look up. The sound of a door opening. He frowned. Was O'Cleary back from Westram already? If so, he must have ridden—

The library door swung back. Mrs Beckridge stared at them, slack jawed.

'My lord,' she gasped. 'Lady Petra. Oh! Oh!'

Petra leaped from the chair, but it was far too late. With her hair in disarray around her shoulders, her gown obviously askew and sitting on his lap, there was nothing she could have said that would have done any good.

Instinctively, Ethan rose to his feet and put Lady Petra behind him. He gave the Vicar's wife his best parade-ground stare. 'Madam, what right have you to intrude on my privacy in this way?'

Attack was always best when faced with an enemy.

'Well, I never. Wait until the parish hears about this revolting spectacle.'

Anger rose in a red haze before his eyes. 'If I hear one word about your visit here today, your husband will be looking for a new living."

She turned white, then a mottled shade of red before she turned and fled.

'That's torn it,' Petra said flatly, coming out from behind him.

'Marry me,' Ethan replied, knowing it was the only thing he could say.

She looked aghast. 'Certainly not. She won't say anything. Not with her husband's livelihood at risk.'

He didn't trust the woman an inch. 'It is the only way.' Though God knew how he would support her.

She stared at him for a long moment and he was sure he saw longing in her gaze. She brushed her hair back from her face and gave him a bright smile. 'I am a widow. I can do as I wish. In our circles it is quite normal. No one would say a word. That woman had no right barging in on you like that.'

If he'd been able to afford a butler, she wouldn't have been able to barge in on him. 'Think of your reputation here in Westram.'

'Oh, pooh. Even if she does say something, who is going to take any notice of that old bat? The villagers despise her.'

'People love scandal.'

'Well, I don't care a fig for it.'

'Petra—'

'No, Ethan. I won't be forced into a marriage neither of us wants and that is final.'

Her rejection stung, whereas he should have felt relieved. He ought to argue with her. Make her see things his way, but if she truly did not want him... Well, he certainly wasn't going to force her, was he? The last thing he wanted was an unwilling wife.

She went to the mirror, pinned her hair up neatly and donned her outer clothing. On her way to the door, she paused. 'I don't think dinner tonight will be a good idea, do you?'

He closed his eyes briefly. 'No. I do not.'

She smiled sadly and left.

At first everything seemed normal when Petra and Marguerite entered the church the following Sunday. She'd certainly heard not a word of gossip that would lead her to believe that Mrs Beckridge had spoken a word of what she had seen at Longhurst Park.

Petra could only be thankful that the busybody woman had not entered a half hour before.

She and Marguerite took their usual seats in the second row. Ahead of them in the closed pew, Ethan was already seated, his broad shoulders in his tight-fitting coat a most enjoyable sight for any woman. And especially enjoyable for her, because she knew intimately what lay beneath the snug blue fabric.

As usual the service began right on time, but Petra felt the back of her neck prickle as if someone was watching her closely. Using the excuse of adjusting her hassock, Petra glanced back and met Mrs Beckridge's piercing and challenging glare. *How dare you show your face in the house of the Lord*, the look said.

Petra pretended not to notice and, staring to the front, lifted her chin.

No other member of the congregation sat beside them, but that wasn't unusual. The villagers usually occupied the seats further back and while Mrs Beckridge occasionally sat with them, it was her wont to visit herself upon various families over the course of the weeks, as if it was an honour to be bestowed.

It wasn't until the sermon began that she realised

the reason for the challenge in that unfriendly look. The Vicar read from Corinthians chapter six regarding sexual immorality and preceded to call down hell and damnation upon anyone who ignored the warning contained in the scripture. Petra's face became hot. She prayed no one could see her blushes. Ethan's shoulders squared and he kept his gaze fixed firmly on the Vicar's face, but even from this distance she sensed his anger. Oh, heavens, what if Ethan said something to him? Might people conjecture and put two and two together? They had met other parishioners from time to time when out on their rambles around the estate.

Petra forced herself not to look around at the congregation to see if anyone was looking at her, but a glance at Marguerite's grim face made her heart sink. Had Mrs Beckridge said something to her sister?

At the end of the service, Marguerite nodded stiffly to Mr Beckridge and hurried to climb into the pony and trap before anyone else left the church yard. They set off at a spanking pace. Heat and cold flushed through Petra by turns. Had the Vicar spoken to Marguerite? Or had Marguerite guessed the reason for her many absences from home this past month?

'Insufferable man,' Marguerite snapped. 'He was looking right at me.'

Petra gaped at her. 'I thought he was looking at me.'

'What reason would he have to look at you? No, it was me he was looking at. Once or twice he has cautioned me about the temptations of two women living alone. Horrid man. How could he think such things? I should have known better than to…'

'Than to?' Petra asked.

Marguerite gritted her teeth. 'I gave him a piece of my mind. Blast it, I told him it was none of his business what I did or who I did it with… I should simply have agreed and assured him nothing of that nature would cross our minds.'

Petra's jaw dropped. 'He thinks we are Sapphists?'

'He is an idiot. He didn't precisely say we are living in sin, he just hinted that we might be tempted to do so.'

'Where would he get such a peculiar idea?'

'From his wife, no doubt. Oh, heavens, if he says one word of that sort to Red I am going to strangle him. You know, I really think it would be better if we went to London tomorrow, instead of waiting until next week. Out of sight is out of mind. We will start packing as soon as we get home.'

'Marguerite, you were not the object of that sermon. He would not dare make such an unfounded accusation.' Inwardly she winced. 'However, there is something I must tell you.'

Marguerite slowed the horse to a walk and turned in her seat. 'What?'

'Yesterday, Mrs Beckridge caught me sitting on Lord Longhurst's lap in his library.' How angry he must have been at the Vicar's sermon.

Marguerite let the reins go slack and the pony stopped. 'She what?'

Petra swallowed. 'She barged in on us. He and I have been having an affair.'

Marguerite closed her eyes and tipped her head back. 'So that is all it was.'

'All?'

She pursed her lips. 'Well, of course, it is a serious matter, but nowhere near as odd as his other accusation. And besides, I assume Longhurst made you an offer? Or if he did not, he certainly will now.'

She took a deep breath. 'He did make me an offer and I refused.'

'What? Why?'

'Because I don't wish to marry again. I certainly don't wish to marry a man forced to the altar by Mrs Beckridge. Besides, we all agreed we could take lovers if we wished when we came here.'

'As long as we were discreet about it!'

'I was discreet. The woman walked in on us unannounced.'

'Typical.'

'Of me?'

'Of Mrs Beckridge! Blast it. This is sure to get to Red's ears and he'll be racing down here—'

'Ethan—' she winced at the slip '—Lord Longhurst said that if she uttered one word to anyone, Beckridge would lose his living. I don't think either of them would dare say anything outright.'

'I see.' She picked up the reins and set the pony in motion. 'Well, we are still going to London tomorrow. And, Petra, it would be better if you did not visit Lord Longhurst again, in case someone else stumbles in on you. Someone who can't be forced to remain silent.'

It was what she had already decided. Particularly since his offer of marriage. Somehow, him making the offer and her turning it down had felt like the world had shifted, leaving them on opposite sides of a crevasse too wide to cross. It was too wide to cross. Over and over, Ethan had talked about returning to the army. She would never marry a man who cared only for war. She'd lost one husband to it, she certainly didn't want to lose another. And losing Ethan would hurt far more than losing Harry had.

She stilled. Was that true? Was she really so smitten with Ethan? If she was, it was exceedingly stupid of her. She should know better.

'I'm sorry, Petra,' Marguerite said softly.

'Do not be.' Petra smiled brightly. 'I had already come to the same conclusion.' After shedding a few tears.

Marguerite patted her hand. 'You know, if my errand in London is successful, in time we can buy a cottage of our own and not be dependent upon Red.'

And everyone would be happy.

Then why did she still feel so terribly sad?

Chapter Nine

Ethan watched the Westram ladies depart from the church in haste. He had his temper in check. Barely. 'Interesting sermon, Vicar,' he said through gritted teeth.

'Thank you, my lord.' Beckridge rubbed his hands together. 'There are a few members of our little congregation who were squirming in their seats.'

He actually had the gall to look smug.

'And your reason for selecting that particular message today?' Ethan could not keep the dangerous note from his voice, no matter how hard he tried.

'Actually, it was my dear wife who suggested that it had been a while since we had last addressed the topic. The ladies employed at the Green Man are no better than they should be and have been getting bolder by the week. A little reminder never goes amiss.' The Vicar beamed.

A sly and clever woman, the Vicar's wife. Ethan could hardly object to a sermon directed at the village's round-heeled wenches. Not without raising suspicions in the Vicar's mind. But it was a fine line his wife was walking. A very fine line indeed and Ethan would not hesitate to make good on his threat if one shred of gossip impinged upon Petra's reputation.

Unfortunately, since she had not accepted his offer of marriage, he was honour-bound to end their idyll. And since that was the case, he no longer had an excuse to put off going to town to take his place in the House of Lords. It was also time to meet his prospective bride before making a commitment.

'There is another matter I wish to raise with you, my lord,' the Vicar said.

Ethan eyed him warily. 'And that is?'

Beckridge glanced at the departing congregation. 'If you would care to honour me by taking a cup of tea in my study, my lord, we could discuss the matter in private.'

The hairs on the back of Ethan's neck rose. He narrowed his eyes on the Vicar's face, but he saw no guile, nothing untoward. Damn it all. It looked as if this was a discussion he could not avoid.

It would be as well to discover what the man had on his mind and, since the Vicar's abode was beside the church, it should not take long to dispense with the matter.

Once they were seated in the small study each with a cup of tea and the maid had closed the door behind her, the Vicar leaned forward in his chair. 'It is about these gypsies.'

Gypsies. Ethan felt the stiffness leave his body. The result of a protective urge that seemed to overtake him in regard to Petra, when he knew that lady could take care of herself. 'What about them?'

'The last time my wife raised this matter, you indicated you knew of no wrongdoing on their part which would make you require them to move on.'

This was likely the reason for the woman coming to his house in the first place. And no doubt now she thought she had the means of getting what she wanted by making Petra's life uncomfortable. Yes, Mrs Beckridge was indeed a clever woman, but he was not one to be held to ransom. He'd learned a great deal about strategies for dealing with enemies in the army. He was known for it. 'And you have some knowledge of their wrongdoing you would like to impart?'

'No direct evidence, my lord.' He shook his head. 'But two reports of stolen laundry in the past week lead me to think they are up to their usual tricks.'

'Have these thefts been reported to the constable or the magistrate?'

'I am not aware that they have.'

'Then they ought to be.'

The Vicar waved a hand in dismissal. 'The villagers do not like to bother such people with trivial matters, my lord. Indeed, it is unlikely that either of those persons would lower themselves to investigate the theft of a couple of handkerchiefs and a chemise, not when the matter can be easily resolved by moving the gypsies along.'

'And if it is not the gypsies, laundry will continue to disappear and I shall have lost useful labour.'

The Vicar goggled. 'You continue to employ them, my lord?'

'I do. They are currently harvesting the deadfall in Crabb's Wood.' He'd arranged it when he realised he wouldn't have time to finish the work before he removed to London for the opening of Parliament.

'How do you know they will not steal the wood from you?'

'If I am not concerned, I do not see why you should be, sir.'

Looking very unhappy, the Vicar drew out a kerchief and blew his nose loudly. 'I see.' He was no doubt wondering how to break the news of his lack of success to his wife.

Ethan took pity on him. 'When that task is done, they intend to move on to their winter quarters in the south country.'

The Vicar beamed. 'Soon?'

Ethan nodded. 'Very soon.'

The Vicar reached down and opened his desk drawer and pulled out a small bottle. 'A drop of brandy to liven up your tea, my lord?'

The man was a tippler. No wonder with a wife like his. Ethan accepted a splash of brandy in his tea and sipped appreciatively. 'Are there any other matters we need to discuss, Beckridge?'

'Nothing at all, my lord.'

Ethan was very glad to hear it.

When Red had learned of his sisters' intention to visit London, he'd sent his carriage for them. To their surprise, he was waiting for them on the doorstep of the family town house in Grosvenor Square, looking as pleased to see them as they were to see him.

Red rarely left Gloucestershire. Their visit to town seemed hardly likely to draw him forth, but they accepted that it had with gladness.

He kissed them both on the cheek and escorted them indoors. By the time they had gone up and removed their outer raiments and directed the staff with regard to their belongings, the tea tray was awaiting them in the drawing room.

At first, Petra had been so pleased to see her brother, she had noticed nothing amiss. However, now she had a chance to observe him more closely sitting beside Marguerite on the opposite sofa, the lines around his mouth and eyes seemed deeper than they had been a year ago.

Yet, despite his drawn looks, he was beaming at them as if he was genuinely pleased to see them, so she refrained from commenting on his appearance.

'I knew you would tire of the country eventually,' he said to Marguerite.

'Nonsense,' Marguerite said. 'We simply need to refresh our wardrobes, that is all.'

Red nudged her with an elbow. 'Who needs a fashionable wardrobe stuck out in the middle of nowhere? Unless some country squire has sparked your interest.' He waggled his brows.

Petra's cheeks heated. Not that she'd ever felt any need to alter her dress for Ethan. He had never seemed to notice what she was wearing. Indeed, he seemed to prefer her wearing nothing at all. Her whole body went hot.

Marguerite also coloured.

Petra frowned. Had her sister met someone and not seen fit to mention it? More likely she was embarrassed because she did not intend to tell Red her real reason for coming to town. No doubt she was worried that he might see her being paid as an artist as something less than desirable.

'We still go to church every week, Westram,' Marguerite said reprovingly. 'You would not have us attend with worn hems and flounces turned more than once, I assume?'

His face fell. 'Certainly not.' He drew in a breath. 'I should tell you, however, that the moment I heard you were coming, I accepted several invitations on your behalf. Thought you might like to get about a bit.'

Marguerite glared at him. 'Now, why would you do that without asking us?'

'Because people would think the worst of me if you visited London and were not seen in polite company. That is why.'

'Think the worst of you? What nonsense. What on earth would give you such a notion?' Marguerite said. 'Besides, no one would be any the wiser about our presence here, unless you told them. Really, Red, could you not have consulted me first?'

He stiffened. 'Actually, it was Miss Featherstone who said it would look most odd if it appeared you had gone into hiding from the public eye.'

'Miss Featherstone,' Petra echoed. 'What business is it of—'

His face darkened.

'Red!' Marguerite's voice rose in volume. 'You have finally offered for her.'

He gave a shamefaced grin. 'I did.'

A flicker of emotion crossed Marguerite's face. Worry? Then she smiled. 'Congratulations, my dear. I wish you both very happy.'

'Oh, Red, if it is indeed what you want, I am so pleased for you, too,' Petra said.

Petra and Marguerite had never understood his devotion to the lady in question. She was so high in the instep as to be insufferably rude to everyone she met. But the match had been arranged between their parents years ago, before they were born, and he had never looked at another woman. Not a respectable woman anyway.

'Have your finances finally come about?' Marguerite asked.

He grimaced. 'With my prospective father-in-law's help. In addition to advancing funds for improvements to the estate, he has made a great many…er… helpful suggestions with regards to its management over the past year. Within a month or so I will be solvent and there is no longer any reason to put off the wedding.'

No reason, except that Petra could not imagine a worse sister-in-law than Miss Featherstone. While the world generally described her as handsome, Petra always thought of her as horse faced. Not that there was anything wrong with horses. Nor would she dislike anyone simply because of their looks. She was not so petty.

Unfortunately, Miss Featherstone had never liked Red's sisters and had called them spoiled and frivolous. Naturally, the scathing words had got back to Petra by way of her friends. She had never told Marguerite.

'What else does Miss Featherstone think?' she asked Red sweetly. 'Perhaps she thinks it is time we married again?'

Red looked distinctly relieved. 'As do I, my dear Petronella.' Red only called her by her full name when he thought he could lord it over her. When she was a child, she'd always stuck her tongue out at him when he had done so. Right now, she felt like hitting him over the head.

'Well, it doesn't matter what she thinks,' she said briskly. 'Or what you think for that matter. I am not marrying anyone.' She couldn't bear to think of it after the way she felt about Ethan. She froze. She didn't mean it quite that way. Ethan was a friend. A close friend whose company she enjoyed to the fullest. As a widow it was permitted. It was a delightful affair that was now over. 'And you cannot force me to do so.'

'Or me,' Marguerite said quietly and with a great deal less heat.

Red rubbed the back of his neck, something he did when faced with a conundrum. 'Unfortunately, it is… I mean my whole future happiness depends on… You have to understand—'

'Spit it out, for heaven's sake,' Marguerite said. 'I am assuming you have made us part of your agreement with her father.'

'I agreed that I would ensure that I was not carrying any more expenses than the estate can afford. As he pointed out, the income Westram Cottage would bring would be a boon if I could rent it out.'

'We will pay the rent,' Marguerite said immediately.

Petra gasped, 'Marguerite, how can we?'

Marguerite squared her shoulders. 'You will let me worry about that.'

Red looked unconvinced. 'I am sorry, my dears. I wish I could simply let you have your way in this, but you must either find husbands or come and live with me and Miss Featherstone once we are wed.'

A shudder rippled through Petra. Living as a poor

relation under that woman's roof would be utterly intolerable.

'Perhaps Carrie—' she started to say.

'What are you suggesting?' Red snapped. 'Would you have it said I refused to care for my widowed sisters? Lady Avery is not even a relative.'

'She is our sister.'

'She *was* your sister-in-law and has now married into another family altogether.'

'Anything would be preferable to—'

'Petra,' Marguerite said calmly. 'Let us not get into a brangle with our brother. Red, if I can prove to you I can support Petra and myself, will you accept that you are no longer responsible for either of us?'

Red eyed her warily as if anticipating some sort of trap. 'If you could prove it to my complete satisfaction, I suppose so. Provided you are not planning to go into trade again. Miss Featherstone was appalled when I told her of your foray into the world of commerce.'

She would be appalled if they as much as breathed fast. Heaven knew what she would do if she learned about Petra and Ethan. Probably die of apoplexy. In which case, she maybe ought to tell her. She squashed the uncharitable thought.

If the woman made Red happy, who was she to criticise? But if he was happy, why did he look so careworn? He looked years older than his twenty-five years.

'At the end of one week and I will pay you three months' rent in advance and show you that I have enough keep Petra and me in style. If I cannot do this, we will agree to abide by your wishes.'

Investments? Agree? 'You might be willing to agree—' Petra said hotly.

'Trust me,' Marguerite said, the look of appeal in her gaze so intense Petra felt compelled to acquiesce.

'Very well, sister,' she said, forcing a smile. 'I will trust you.' But she hoped like anything she wasn't making a huge mistake.

Red nodded his satisfaction. 'In the meantime, I shall be happy to foot the bill for one ballgown each. You will need them for my wedding, therefore I will make you a gift of them. And, my dears, it really would please me greatly to see you out and about in society while you are here.' He gave them a pleading smile.

Who could resist when he asked so nicely? And Petra had to admit it would be pleasant to catch up with old friends and all the latest on dits. She glanced at Marguerite, who nodded grimly.

Petra put down her cup. 'Very well. We shall attend these events.'

Red rubbed his hands together. 'Excellent.'

Marguerite rose. 'I think I need a rest after our journey.'

'I'll join you,' Petra said. 'I hope you know what you are doing,' Petra added when they were on their way up the stairs.

'So do I,' Marguerite said quietly. But she did not sound at all certain.

Petra felt as if she had jumped from the frying pan into the fire.

For one mad moment, she felt like running back to Ethan and telling him she had changed her mind about his offer of marriage. She forced herself to remember he had offered for her only because he had been honour-bound to do so. She reminded herself that Harry had been similarly forced to offer for her and had clearly resented it. Not to mention that, as delightful as a man could seem before a wedding, once married, they held all the power and had no qualms about doing exactly what they wanted.

So far Ethan had shown nothing but good qualities. But then she had thought the same about Harry. One never knew for certain what lay beneath a person's surface until they had no reason to hide.

She'd been disappointed once. She would not take the risk a second time.

Ethan was in London but had yet to contact the lawyer who was supposed to introduce him to his prospective bride. Instead, he'd been investigating other alternatives to return his estate to its former glory. While he knew he had to marry, eventually, he wanted to do it when *he* was ready, not because of financial exigencies. Unfortunately, none of his enquiries to his fellow peers had borne fruit. While marrying an heiress was his very last choice, no other solution had come to the fore. The day when he would have to knuckle down and admit there was no other way was drawing ever closer.

The image of pretty little Lady Petra floated across his mind. Too bad she was not a wealthy widow. He pushed the wish aside. It was pointless thinking about how much he enjoyed her company. Or how well they suited. His emotions when it came to Petra were far too strong. He did not want that sort of marriage. He wanted peace in his house.

Her suggestion of leasing out his fields had been a good one, but upon deeper investigation he had concluded it would not bring enough income. His barns needed repair as did the cottages for the people he needed to employ on the estate. To put it bluntly, he needed a huge infusion of funds. If only there was some way other than marriage...

A diminutive lady with bright yellow hair swirling around on the dance floor caught his eyes.

Petra? His heart leaped with joy.

For a moment he thought his eyes were deceiving him. She always looked lovely, but tonight in a ball-gown of a celestial blue that matched her eyes and her hair elaborately dressed, with jewels at her throat and wrists, she looked ethereal. Otherworldly. Not in the least like herself. Yet stunning. Was this the real Petra rather than the woman who tramped across his estate in all weathers to lie in his arms?

Clearly, she was enjoying herself thoroughly. He glared at her partner, a handsome man with rich auburn hair. Apparently, it hadn't taken her long to attract an admirer, for there was no denying the warmth in her gaze as she gazed at this man.

Lord Pelham wandered over to stand beside him. 'I hear you are going to make your debut in the House of Lords next week, Longhurst?' He'd briefly met Pelham at an event earlier in the week.

He bowed. 'I am.'

'Where do you stand on the Corn Laws?'

Ethan frowned at the older man. He'd been reading about the matter, about the artificially high price for bread. 'It is hard to justify keeping the cost of such a basic food item so high.'

'And yet without the necessary protection of our income, men like you and I will be ruined and the men who buy bread will have no work and no money at all. Trust me, it is for the good of the country that we landowners must stand together.' The older man gave him a hard look.

'Thank you for your advice.' Ethan wasn't convinced. He needed to read more from both sides of the question before he made any decision.

Clearly assuming he had a convert, the other man beamed. 'You are most welcome. If there is anything else I can do to help you, let me know.' He bowed and moved to join a group of men on the far side of the room.

Petra had concluded her dance with the tall redhaired nobleman and was now standing beside her sister, whose severe manner of dress and air made her appear more unapproachable than usual. One could not imagine Lady Marguerite dancing. She also looked very much like... Of course. The man Petra had been dancing with must be her brother, the Earl of Westram.

A feeling of relief rushed through Ethan. He made his way to Petra's side and bowed. 'Lady Marguerite. Lady Petra. What a pleasure to find you here.'

Petra beamed. 'Lord Longhurst, I had no notion you were coming to town.'

She had. He'd mentioned it. Was that why she was here? Hardly likely, she'd already turned his proposal down. Unless she had changed her mind? If so, would he be glad or sorry? Good Lord, he had never felt so conflicted in his life. Or at least not recently. 'Would you care to dance?'

The request left his lips before he had time to think about the possible implications.

Petra's eyes widened a fraction and then she smiled.

She glanced at her sister, who made a shooing motion with her fan. 'Just don't leave the ballroom.'

Good lord, had Petra told her sister of their affair? The back of his neck became hot, much as it had in the church when that idiot Beckridge had lectured the congregation about sexual morals.

He led Petra on to the dance floor.

Their opportunities for conversation were limited and their words easily overheard, so he restricted himself to pleasantries until the end of the dance.

'May I bring you some refreshment?' he asked politely.

'That would be lovely,' she replied in kind.

He led her to a chair beside a small table at the edge of the ballroom and then sent a footman off to fetch a cooling glass of punch.

She laughed when he sat down beside her. 'Handled with the efficiency of a major.'

He raised an eyebrow. 'I didn't spend twenty years in the army and not learn something.'

'How lovely to see you here.'

'And you. You look as at home here in town as you do in the countryside.'

She sighed. 'I had forgotten how much I enjoyed dancing. Perhaps we can convince the landlord of the Green Man to hold the occasional assembly. We would need subscriptions from enough people to make it worth his while.'

She was going to be returning to Westram.

For a moment, he felt incandescently happy. Until he remembered his purpose for coming to London. When he returned to Longhurst, he would likely be returning as a prospective bridegroom, if not married already. His mood darkened immediately.

'You don't like the idea?'

He forced himself to smile. 'I think it an excellent plan.'

'Mrs Beckridge will not like it,' she mused.

'Then together we will rout her.'

She smiled. 'As you did the other day.' She blushed. 'Oh, I should not have mentioned that.'

'It is hard to forget. The woman was gobbling like a turkey when she left.'

She laughed out loud. 'It is a sight I shall never forget as long as I live.'

The sight he would never forget was Petra as she came undone.

They gazed at each other and he knew he was going to miss her for the rest of his life.

'Would you really make Beckridge leave if she starts to gossip?' Petra asked curiously.

He sighed. 'I would not turn him out, but I must say I find his sermons highly unpleasant and his wife even more so. I am thinking I might try to offer him some sort of lure to make him leave of his own accord.'

Petra nodded her approval of his idea.

Her sister walked purposefully over to where they sat, clearly intent on breaking up their tête-à-tête.

Regretfully, Ethan gave up his seat. 'May I fetch you some refreshment, Lady Marguerite?'

'Please,' she said with a stiff nod.

He did as he was bade and sent a footman over with the glass of ratafia since he had already used up the requisite amount of time with the ladies and had no wish to give the gossips fuel for their conjectures. On moving away from the table, a guest touched his arm. When he turned he saw it was Pelham. 'May I introduce my niece? Ermintrude, this is Lord Longhurst. Longhurst, my sister's daughter, Miss Lambton.'

Nonplussed, he stared at the girl. Why... He kept his face expressionless, but inwardly he cringed. This was the way the marriage mart worked. Pelham would not be so anxious to make the introductions if he knew the state of Ethan's finances. So far, he and his man of business had managed to keep that to themselves. He bowed. 'I am pleased to meet you, Miss Lambton.'

Finally, the girl raised her gaze to his face. She did not look at all happy to meet him. 'My lord,' she said, her voice dull.

Her uncle whispered something in her ear and she forced a smile.

Pelham rolled his eyes and leaned close. 'She's nervous,' he whispered.

Ethan set out to make the lady feel more comfortable. While he could not say that she warmed to him, she did deign to walk the circumference of the room on his arm. She responded to his remarks in monosyllables for the most part, but when a new set formed she agreed to dance with him. She danced with precision, but not with Petra's grace and verve.

When he allowed himself to glance over to the table where he had left Petra, she was gone. He had wanted to tell her what the future held. Clearly a ball was not the place to reveal his intentions.

Perhaps she would consent to drive out with him. He'd discovered a natty curricle among the myriad articles in the back of the stables at his town house. It would be easy to rent a pair of horses to pull it. Unfortunately, the town house was included in the entail or he would have sold it in a heartbeat. The place was also in need of care and attention and a good clearing out. It, too, was stuffed to the gills with furniture and assorted knick-knacks. In fact, it was even worse than Longhurst Park had been.

Chapter Ten

Petra should have been surprised to receive Ethan's note three days after the ball, asking if she would drive out with him at the fashionable hour. She was not. She was, however, surprised at how thrilled she felt at the notion.

Marguerite absently agreed that it would be perfectly all right for her to accept the invitation. Her older sister clearly had other matters on her mind. She had been disappearing on errands of her own. On one occasion, two days after their arrival, she'd seemed particularly dispirited. When Petra had asked her point-blank what was wrong, Marguerite had smiled vaguely and said she would reveal all when the time was right. Then she'd locked herself away in her chamber for two days.

Did Marguerite have a secret lover? Had she been rejected? Or was she still pining for Saxby and this visit to London had brought all her memories of her late husband back? Petra's heart ached for her sister, but what could she do if Marguerite would not talk about her troubles?

Ethan arrived a few minutes early, but Petra was

ready and waiting in the drawing room when his curricle pulled up outside.

With Marguerite nowhere to be seen, or to remind her of the proprieties, she dashed down the stairs before the doorbell rang. When the butler opened the door, she beamed at Ethan, who looked splendid in a coat of blue superfine with silver buttons. He whipped off his hat and bowed. 'Lady Petra, how good to see that you are ready.'

One of her brother's footmen had taken charge of the horses and he held them steady while Ethan helped her up and once more took control of the reins. In just a few moments, they were moving out into the traffic and heading for Hyde Park.

Ethan pulled around a parked brewer's dray and neatly avoided a hackney carriage coming in the other direction.

'The traffic is busy today,' Petra remarked.

The offside horse started at a piece of paper blowing across the road, but Ethan held him in check. 'It is always busy in London, I think.'

'And noisy,' she added when three hawkers competed for attention for their wares at the corner of the street.

He grinned at her and nodded. It was only a little less noisy when they turned into Hyde Park given the many carriages making their way sedately up the row, in order that their occupants would have plenty of time to see and been seen. And, of course, there were the pauses while acquaintances greeted each other and looked each other over.

Fortunately, the weather, while cool, did not threaten rain.

'That is a very fetching bonnet, Lady Petra,' Ethan

said, looping the reins expertly around one hand and half turning to face her.

'Thank you. I made it myself.'

He looked surprised. 'You are very accomplished, I must say.'

She smiled at the compliment and addressed the thought uppermost on her mind. 'Did you have a purpose for inviting me to drive today, or was it merely for the pleasure of my company?'

His lips twitched. 'You are also very forthright. Which I like very much,' he hastened to add.

'Do you, indeed? Then I shall never hesitate to speak my mind when I am with you.'

A short pause ensued. 'I did advertise my fields for grazing and, as luck would have it, Compton needed somewhere to put his dairy herd, since one of his fields flooded and it will be weeks before it is fully drained. He also loaned me an old plough share. It needs repairs, but O'Cleary thinks he can mend it.'

'That is good news.'

He shook his head. 'It is a step forward, but it is nowhere near enough.'

'Perhaps you can lease out more fields.'

'I will lease as many as I can, but even if I had animals on every field, it will not be enough to cover the expenses, unfortunately.'

Dash it. She had hoped— 'Perhaps you need to marry an heiress,' she said, thinking of her brother and Miss Featherstone. She had decided that was the only reason Red could possibly want to marry the woman, hence the reason for his haggard appearance.

'You are not the first person to make that suggestion.' His voice was dry.

A pang seized her heart at the thought of him marrying someone else. Or perhaps it was because he, too, seemed content with something so cold-blooded as a marriage of convenience. She tried not to show her disappointment. After all, she had known he would have to marry sooner or later, but for some reason she had hoped it might be later. The back of her throat ached with…unshed tears? Surely not. She must have a cold coming on.

'Do you have someone in mind?' she asked calmly, hoping he would notice nothing amiss with her voice. 'Or would you like me to make discreet enquiries among the ladies of my acquaintance? They often know about these things.' She winced, fearing she sounded a little bitter.

'You would do that for me?' He frowned.

'If you wish it?' Was she mad? She hated the idea.

'I see.' He urged his horses a few steps forward and lifted his hat to a group of ladies walking along the path. 'There is actually someone waiting in the wings, but I have not yet met the young lady in question.'

He didn't sound happy; he sounded stoic.

'You would rather not.' She felt a little more cheerful.

'It is not my first choice to be sure.'

Naturally he would not say more because he was a gentleman.

'When you meet her, you might be pleasantly surprised.'

'Why, Lady Petra, you sound as if you are trying to marry me off.' His laugh had a hollow ring, though his blue eyes were twinkling. He was trying to make them both feel better about what was to come. And for that she was grateful.

'What about selling your town house?' she asked.

'Entailed. It seems that the Longhursts have been

a feckless lot and decided to make sure the property remained in the family.'

'There is nothing else of value?'

'Only my horse, but I would only have to buy another, so selling Jack would be a false economy. Even if I lease out the town house *and* the estate, it won't bring in enough income to put the estate into anything like order.'

Together they had worked out just how much would be needed. It had been an enormous sum.

Back to the heiress, then... 'Yes. It seems your hands are tied. I can think of nothing else you could do that would result in vast sums of money.'

'Nor me.'

People did marry for money and often they were happy. Sometimes they were not and if she were going to wish something for Ethan, it would be his happiness. 'Would a bank give you a loan?'

'It would, if I had any collateral.'

They reached the end of the row and turned out of the park. Their hour was up.

He sounded like a man preparing to lead a forlorn hope. 'Perhaps you should think about it for a day or so. Something might turn up.'

'I have done nothing but think about it.' He heaved a sigh. 'I can certainly wait a day or two more, since the duns are not yet at the door.'

'I am very glad to hear it. Do you go to the Frobish-ers' ball next week?'

'I have not replied to the invitation, but I can do so. Do you go?'

'Yes. Perhaps by then one or other of us will have come up with a solution.' Other than marrying an heiress. She really hoped so.

* * *

Ethan sighed and threw the agricultural journal aside. He'd spent all afternoon going through every last article to no avail. There really were no shortcuts for a landowner. It took five years at least for every damned thing to get to a point of profitability.

He'd received word from O'Cleary that the plough had been repaired and asking which field was to be turned over first, and could he please see about hiring a man to do the work. But if Ethan didn't have money for seed, what was the point in laying out money on hiring a ploughman? He'd have to go home and see to it himself.

Someone thumped on the front door with a fist. Ethan started. He'd not hired on any servants for the London town house, because he had decided that even though he slept here each night, he would neither pay calls nor receive any here. The house was a mess and it had to be cleared out before he could think of entertaining anyone. Another expense he'd have to face soon.

In the meantime, if someone wanted to meet with him, then he met them at his club, where he took all of his meals, thus keeping his expenses to the minimum.

Not having O'Cleary's help here in town had been an inconvenience, but he was perfectly capable of dressing himself and shaving.

The knock came again. He got up and looked down into the street and saw a very familiar face looking back up at him from beneath her umbrella. Lady Petra. Standing in the pouring rain.

He wasn't exactly dressed for afternoon callers, but nor was he going to leave her standing on his doorstep for any old passer-by to see. He tightened the belt on his dressing gown, wended his way round the multitude of furniture that took up every inch of floor space and opened the door. He quickly pulled her inside.

She took in his state of undress and beamed. 'I am sorry if this is an inconvenient time to call, but Marguerite went out and I had an idea.'

'An idea?' Hope lifted his heart. 'Let me help you out of that wet coat.' She undid the buttons and he eased her out of the nonsensical thing. The thin fabric offered almost no protection against the elements and barely skimmed the high waist of her gown. Her skirts were soaked at the hem.

'Yes.' She looked about her. 'Sell everything. All the furniture. The lamps. The rugs. They can't possibly be included in the entail. Surely that would help?'

He gave her coat a shake and draped it over a chair. She took off her bonnet, stripped off her gloves and handed them to him. He draped them over another chair. He shook his head. 'They won't fetch anything approaching what is needed. Like the stuff at Longhurst, most of it is only fit for the rag-and-bone man or the fire.'

'You already thought of it.' She sounded disappointed.

'I had a man come round yesterday. He offered to take it all away as a job lot.'

'You must pay him to take it?'

'Yes. Only then can I lease out the house.'

Her face fell. 'And here I thought I had the answer.'

'Thank you for the attempt, but you know you really shouldn't be visiting me here. Wasn't I supposed to see you at Frobisher's ball tomorrow night?'

'We are not going after all. Marguerite came home

after lunch and announced that we are going home first thing in the morning.'

'Why the haste? What has happened?'

'I have no idea. Red is furious with her, but apparently she was able to pay him three months' rent in advance for Westram Cottage so we can go home.'

'And you came here because you thought you ought to let me know I would not see you at the ball.'

She nodded. She gazed up at the picture in the hall. Like all the paintings in the house it had acquired a thick coating of dust and grime. 'This picture looks familiar.' She touched the surface and her fingertip came away with a black smear. She frowned and looked at the picture again. 'It looks like a painting Marguerite tried to copy from a book when she was going through her Italian phase,' she said slowly. 'She enthused about it for an hour at least. His name is Canal something. I remember that because that was mostly what he painted. Venice canals.'

Ethan knew nothing about art and artists. he simply knew when he liked something. The dealer who had come to value the furniture had only looked at one painting and had declared it a copy of a Reynolds, and a poor one at that.

'There was a diary at Longhurst recording the grand tour of one Joshua Trethewy,' he said. 'The previous Earl's father. I didn't take much notice of it when I realised it didn't have anything to do with the estate, but one of the pages I opened recorded several purchases in Venice of what he called "scribbles" that his mother had asked him to buy.' Along with recording a great deal of other nonsense, like masquerades and the licentious behaviour engaged in by young men out on the town. If the tone of the journal was anything to go by, Joshua would indeed have bought second-rate copies of artwork and spent the bulk of his money on the ladies of Venice, about whose beauty and sensuality he waxed on and on.

Petra turned away from the picture and stared at the clutter of furniture littering the hallway. Footmen's chairs, carved chests, sculptures of assorted sizes and materials all higgledy-piggledy. 'My goodness, it is the same as it was at Longhurst. Your cousin had some sort of problem, I think.'

'All the rooms are the same. Let me show you around. If you can see anything worth salvaging, I would be glad to know it.'

They moved from room to room. Each chamber was full to overflowing with items. 'It is awful,' she exclaimed. 'Who needs five beds in a bedroom?' she asked, peering into one of the guest chambers where the beds were in pieces and the mattresses piled in a corner. 'All these things must have originally cost a fortune.'

'I should think so. And I doubt any of it is worth more than a farthing or two it is so out of style and ugly.'

'What a terrible waste,' she said with a sigh.

'If he would have only spent half of it on the upkeep of the estate...' He let his words trail off. He did not want to mention his need to marry money yet again. If he was honest with himself, instead of trying to pretend otherwise, he really wouldn't mind marrying Petra, if she would have him. He felt comfortable with her. She had become a good friend. Not to mention he thoroughly enjoyed their lovemaking. The fact that she also made his heart beat a fraction too fast was something he could control. Unfortunately, since she had no fortune, it was not to be.

Finally, they reached the only room in the house that was anything like normal, the state bedroom where he slept. Even it had three armoires.

She walked into the room and stroked the beautifully embroidered counterpane. 'I suppose, since you will soon be offering for your heiress, this is the last time I shall see you alone.' She gave him a shy little smile that held a world of meaning.

His heart sank at the thought of them parting, even as his body tightened at the blatant invitation in her words and glance. 'I suppose it will.'

'It would be a shame to waste the opportunity,' she said, holding her arms out to him.

He pulled her close and kissed her.

Ethan's kisses were simply lovely. When he held her in his arms she felt precious and feminine. It was easy to believe that they could be together for ever, when they really could not. As the daughter of an earl, she understood that the nobility married to advance their influence or fill their coffers. Her father had been indulgent in allowing her to choose her husband for love.

It hadn't worked out terribly well.

Ethan would be a lot happier marrying his heiress, knowing that his family line was safe and his estate could be brought back from the brink of disaster, than marrying a poverty-stricken widow but, oh, how she wished she had money. But then he would be marrying her for her money, just as Harry had been convinced by his family to marry her for her connections.

No, she really would not want that. She sighed.

He pulled back and gazed into her face. 'Sweetheart, what is wrong? If you do not want this, please say so. I would not have you regret this for the world.'

She managed a smile. 'Of course I want this.' She gave his shoulder a push. 'It was my idea.'

'Then why the sigh?'

'I was thinking how I would miss this, being with you.'

'Me, too. Let us not think about the future, but enjoy the now. It will be a good memory for us both.' The concern in his face touched her heart.

'Yes, I would like that. It has been a lovely friendship, but in future we will meet as mere acquaintances, in the village and at church, but we will each have our memories.' It would be hard to meet him under those circumstances, knowing there would be no more memories to make.

'First I need to get you out of that wet gown. I don't want you catching a chill.'

'That is your excuse anyway,' she said, laughing and undoing the ribbon holding the bodice closed. He lifted the gown over her head and stepped back as if to admire the view. A moment later he was tugging at the laces on her front-closing stays. 'These will just be in the way, don't you think?'

'Most definitely.'

He pulled her close and his kiss was hard and seemingly as full of longing as her own and she gave herself up to the wooing of his lips and the soft strokes of his tongue and the shivery sensations caused by his caressing hands. She wanted this to be wonderful for him, too. A fond memory of the bliss they created together.

She certainly could not imagine herself ever doing this with any other man.

She pulled the pins from her hair and let it fall around her shoulders. He speared his fingers in her tresses. 'Mmm...' he murmured against her lips. 'I love the feel of your hair. It is so soft and silky.'

'It feels good to me, too,' she said, hot prickles running down her spine.

He picked her up and lay her on the bed. He gazed down at her. 'It looks like spun gold spread out on the pillows.'

She wrinkled her nose. 'Sadly, it is only hair or I would give it to you to sell.'

He shook his head and gave her the smile that always made her heart tumble over. 'I couldn't bear for you to part with it.'

She held her arms out to him. 'Come to bed, dear Ethan. Let us not waste time talking.'

He divested himself of his dressing gown beneath which he was wearing nothing at all. What a beautiful man he was in his bare skin and fully erect. Gorgeous. And clearly interested in her as a woman.

He toed off his slippers and climbed up to lie beside her. Leaning on one elbow, looking down at her, he took a lock of hair and raised it to his nose. 'I will never smell lavender without thinking of this moment, or taste blackberries without remembering how we met, or eat a trout without seeing you in my mind's eye stretched out on your stomach on a riverbank.'

A pain pierced her heart, so agonising she could scarcely breathe. 'Ethan,' she murmured, hoping her laugh did not sound forced to his ears, for she wanted him to believe she was happy, 'you say the loveliest things.'

He shrugged and gave her a sweetly shy smile. 'It is the truth.'

She thought for a moment. 'I will never pass a field of hay without recalling you swinging a scythe with your muscles glistening in the sunlight and shifting beneath your skin. I will never eat fish without re-membering your expression when you guddled the first time. It was adorable.'

He gave a gentle tug on her hair. 'Now you are teas-ing me.'

'It is the truth. And I will never ever pick chestnuts without wishing you were there to lend your help.' She reached up, pulled his head down and plundered his mouth for if she did not kiss him right then and there she might very well cry.

As if sensing her anguish, he kissed her back and gently palmed first one breast, then the other, making them feel full and heavy, with her nipples tightened to hard little peaks. She rolled towards him, align-ing their bodies, seeking blindly for the closeness she needed.

He groaned and kissed her with urgency and aban-donment, until she could no longer think about any-thing but the demands of her body, her longing for him to be inside her and her need to feel his weight.

She parted her thighs and he came over her, set-tling his body into the cradle of her hips. The muscles in his chest became hard ridges, as he supported him-self on his hands, as did those on his belly. He really was too beautiful.

'Ah, sweetheart,' he said. 'When you look at me just so, I believe I could move mountains.'

Slowly he entered her body and began to move in long delicious strokes.

She moved against him, lifting her hips in counterpoint to his thrusts. The pleasure built and she brought her legs up and around him. Bringing him even deeper inside her body.

He suckled on one nipple, then the other, while she hugged him close, holding on for dear life as she reached for the delicious undoing of body and soul.

The sweet pain of it tore her asunder. She had never experienced such undoing before Ethan and likely never would again. He withdrew from her body and reached his own climax. Sated and lax, she lay panting beneath him. He pulled the counterpane over them both and she fell asleep in his arms, knowing it really must be for the very last time and trying with a monumental effort not to cry.

Chapter Eleven

With winter approaching, Petra found herself more and more housebound. But then she had no real reason to go anywhere, did she? Longhurst Park remained unoccupied while His Lordship stayed in London, no doubt wooing his heiress and preparing to take his seat at the opening of Parliament the following week.

She would have liked to have been there for that. She would have felt so proud of him.

A letter arrived from Red while she and Marguerite were at breakfast one morning. Miss Featherstone had agreed that their wedding would take place in the spring.

'Finally,' Petra said. 'Though I don't understand why they would wait yet another six months.'

'She is a fortunate woman,' Marguerite remarked. 'I hope she appreciates him the way she ought.'

Petra laughed. 'No doubt she expects him to appreciate her.'

Marguerite sighed. 'Poor Red.' She rose to her feet. 'Time to get back to work.'

'How is it coming along?'

She winced. 'It's hard to come up with new ideas.'

'You haven't shown me any of your drawings for weeks.'

Marguerite looked out of the window. 'That's because there hasn't been much to show. I am working mostly on the drawings from nature the publishing house contracted.'

'They certainly take up a great deal of your time.'

She gave an uncomfortable laugh. 'They do indeed. It is dull stuff, I assure you. It is mostly the insides of flowers, their reproductive organs. Very technical and tedious. I'll show you the one I am working on before I send it off.'

'I'd like that.'

'I was wondering if you wouldn't mind going to market with Jeb today, so I can finish it. I need to get it in the post tomorrow.'

Mind? She'd be thrilled to get out of the house. Anything to take her mind off missing Ethan.

She dressed warmly and went out to tell Jeb the good news that he would only have her company for the drive to Oxted.

He grinned good-naturedly and helped her up into the trap. 'When be His Lordship returning from London?' Jeb asked.

Petra stiffened. 'I have no idea, Jeb. Why do you wish to know?'

'Me ma says it ain't the same cooking for no one but Mr O'Cleary and him taking all his meals in the kitchen, like.'

'I am sure he will be back as soon as his business in London allows.' And then Mrs Stone would have two more mouths to feed.

Her throat filled with unwanted tears. She swallowed them down. 'Are there things you need for the stables?' she asked.

'Yes, my lady. I need corn for Patch here and some nails. We got a board or two coming loose on the potting shed.'

Petra added the items to her list.

Shopping at the market in Oxted was uneventful, though she found the haggling to get the best price tiring and rather distasteful. It ought to have been enough to keep her mind busy, but she still had to stop herself from thinking of Ethan every time she noticed a tall fair-haired man. He wasn't living at Longhurst and therefore he would not be at the Oxted market.

While Jeb went to buy feed, she purchased the items on her list. No more tallow candles either. The advance from Marguerite's contract had allowed for a few little luxuries.

She counted the money left in her purse once she'd bought all the required items. She had enough remaining to buy some good-quality tea. She wandered along the stalls. A hand clutched at her shoulder.

She swung around, half expecting to find a cutpurse at her elbow. To her surprise it was Madame Rose. She was not wearing her gaudy outfit today, apart from her large hoop earrings and her bangles that tinkled softly as she moved.

'My goodness,' Petra exclaimed. 'You gave me a start.'

'I beg your pardon, my lady,' the woman said in her heavy accent.

Petra smiled politely. 'Was there something you wanted?'

The woman narrowed her eyes on her. 'You are sad.'

Petra frowned. 'Nonsense.'

'You miss the one who makes you unhappy. You will see him soon.'

'If you are talking about my husband, you are barking up the wrong tree,' she said with an airy laugh. 'I won't be seeing him any time soon.'

'I speak of the big man. The fair lord.'

Why did everyone suppose she knew Ethan's movements? She glared. 'If you mean Lord Longhurst, of course I will see him. We are neighbours and he will be returning to Longhurst with his wife before very long.'

Madame Rose shook her head, her earrings swinging back and forth, until Petra could not help but wonder if they might hurt her. 'You can see the future, my lady?'

'Of course I cannot see the future. I simply know of his plans.'

The woman smiled knowingly. 'There is many a slip between cup and lip, and many a child born of love.'

Petra's mouth dropped open. Unthinking, she pressed her hand against her belly, before she recalled it wasn't possible. Things had all gone as they should this month with her courses.

Madame Rose raised her eyebrows and her eyes danced wickedly. 'Give a message to the lord when you see him. The woods are finally all cleared and we are wondering if he has other work for us to do since it is too late now for us to seek other quarters for the winter.'

'You plan to stay at Longhurst all winter?'

'If His Lordship will allow it.'

'You should speak to Mr O'Cleary. He is sure to be in touch with His Lordship.'

'You will see His Lordship first.'

She didn't want to see Ethan. It would only remind her of how lonely she had been since she left him in London and how lonely she would continue to be. Sometimes she wished she had never set eyes on him at all. At other times she knew that she would not have missed their few weeks together for the world.

Madame Rose patted her arm. 'It is all right, little one. You will find the man of your heart.'

Dash it all, these platitudes of hers were annoying. 'Please speak to Mr O'Cleary.' She turned and hurried back to find Jeb.

Since Jeb wasn't much of a conversationalist, on the way home Petra found herself reliving her conversation with Madame Rose. Mrs Beckridge was right. The woman was a charlatan, playing on the emotions of unhappy women. Petra was sorry the gypsy band had chosen to linger in this corner of Kent.

As they passed through the village, she told Jeb to pull up so she could collect the mail from the post office.

She jumped down from the trap and went inside.

Mrs Beckridge was at the counter. When she turned to leave and saw who was waiting behind her, she recoiled, a look of disgust on her face.

Petra flinched inwardly, but pretended not to notice the look or Mrs Beckridge. But the woman wasn't satisfied with being ignored. She leaned close and hissed, 'You think yourself so high and mighty, but you are no better than the wenches at the Green Man. Tell Lord Longhurst those gypsies have to move on. No one dare hang out their laundry while they are still about.' With a stiff nod, she hurried out.

The postmaster eyed Petra askance.

'How are you today, Mr Barker?'

'Fair to middling, Lady Petra.' He frowned. 'It really is a shame His Lordship lets those gypsies stay on his land, you know.' He gave her such an odd look; her stomach fell away. Had Mrs Beckridge reported what she had seen to others despite Ethan's threat?

'Then you take the matter up with His Lordship,' she said matter-of-factly. 'Do you have any mail for Westram Cottage?'

'Ah, I would, were I to see him. My wife lost her best petticoat this week. Right cross she is about it, too. Perhaps if you hadn't agreed with His Lordship that it was all right for them to stay...' He checked his pile of letters. 'Nothing for you ladies today.'

'Thank you.' She made her way outside.

So that was what the artful Mrs Beckridge was about. Letting people blame her for Longhurst's decision. How ironic that she was just as unhappy with their presence in the area as everyone else. Perhaps there was something she could do. Madame Rose had said they had finished clearing the woods, so perhaps Petra could convince her and her family to move on.

Or better yet she should write to Ethan and tell him that the problem with the laundry continued and his presence was required.

That was a much better idea.

She didn't feel comfortable talking to Madame Rose after what the woman had said to her.

Ethan could not wait to see Petra and to tell her his news. Her letter about the gypsies had come at a most opportune moment. He pulled up outside her cottage and jumped down. Petra was on her hands and knees working on her garden.

She got up at the sound of his footsteps and her gaze filled with pleasure. 'Ethan.' She started forward, then stopped, her cheeks turning red. 'How good to see you, Lord Longhurst.' She glanced towards the cottage. 'I didn't know you were back from London. May I offer you tea?'

He'd arrived late last night. Too late to visit Westram Cottage.

'Thank you, that would be delightful.'

Inside, she offered him a seat and rang for the tea tray. 'How was your journey down from town?'

'Excellent. I left the moment I got your note, though I cannot stay long. I have to take my seat in Parliament on the fourth.' It was a task he would be glad to have out of the way. He had planned to speak with Petra after that, but receiving her note had changed his mind and he'd come straight away.

She nodded. 'I wish I could be there to see you make your first speech.'

'It is not a speech as much as a question. Pelham advised me to keep it short, unless I have plans to become a great orator, which, I assure you, I do not.'

He frowned. She looked paler than usual. Unhappy. 'What is this issue you are having with the gypsies?'

'Apparently, they are stealing laundry left and right.' She gave a short unhappy laugh. 'As predicted by Mrs Beckridge.'

'You know for certain they are involved?'

She got up and went to the window, looking out as if she did not want to see his reaction. Or maybe to hide hers. There was more to this than met the eye.

'Who else could it be?' she said evasively. 'I know I did not agree with Mrs Beckridge at first, but it seems we both might have been wrong. Now they have finished clearing the deadfall, could you not ask them to leave?'

'I told them they could stay for the winter if they wished. I do not generally go back on my word.'

Damn it all. This was not what he wanted to talk to her about. And yet he was loath to discuss a more delicate matter while this topic put them on opposite sides of the fence.

She turned to face him. 'What if they were caught in the act? Would you ask them then?'

He closed his eyes briefly. 'It would certainly be in their interests to go if one of their number was caught in a criminal act.' He narrowed his eyes on her face. 'It is not the only reason you have for wanting them to leave, is it?'

She sighed. 'No. The villagers seem to be blaming Marguerite and me for their continued presence here. Because we took their part against the Vicar's advice. They don't say anything, but they are not as friendly towards us as they once were.'

'The Beckridge woman again, I suppose.' Damn her. If she couldn't make trouble one way, she found another to accomplish her ends.

'Most likely.' Petra smiled unhappily. 'Though I think she didn't need to say much on the subject to have them up in arms after the loss of valuable items. Next, they fear their homes may be pillaged, I am sure.'

As a landowner, it was his responsibility to protect his neighbours. Both the villagers and the likes of the two lady widows. And he wasn't having her made unhappy because of a point of honour. 'You say they have not yet been caught in the act?'

'Unfortunately, no. I was thinking of setting a trap.'

He started. 'You would need to be very careful. Any creature who is cornered can be dangerous, but it is a good idea.'

'That was why I wanted your help. I was thinking of spreading one of our tablecloths on the laurel bush in the front garden. It wouldn't be the first time we have used it to dry larger items.'

'You are going to use yourself as bait?' He did not like that idea at all.

'Who else can I ask? Besides, the villagers might be grateful to us if it was Marguerite and I who were the ones to finally capture the thieves.'

'You really care what these people think of you, don't you?'

'Naturally. We live here. To be ostracised by our neighbours would be horrible.'

Well, he had a different answer for that problem, but now was not the time. 'When do these thefts occur?'

'Usually in the evening. Honestly, I had no idea how often people forget to bring their laundry in at night, though I believe they are being a lot more careful now. We have not had any incidents for two days.'

'Then this is what we shall do. I will return here after dusk and set up a perimeter with O'Cleary around the laundry and we will nab our thieves.' He stood up. 'Wait to put out your linens until after I have gone.'

'Thank you, Ethan. I knew I could count on you.' His heart warmed at the words he'd never heard from a woman before.

She came forward, hands outstretched, and he took

them in his. So tiny. So easily broken. He raised one to his lips and brushed his lips against her knuckles. 'You know you can call on me for anything at any time.'

Her eyes went moist for a moment, as if tears were close to the surface, but her bright smile made him think he was likely wrong. 'I know it,' she said huskily. 'Though I will try not to take advantage of your kindness.'

He wanted her to take advantage of him as often as she wanted. The idea pleased him and he smiled back. Only just in time did he stop himself from taking her in his arms. That would come later, after he put paid to the petty thieves who were causing her concern.

Instead of folding her into his arms, he picked up his hat and gloves. 'Once you have put out your laundry, stay inside the house with the door locked.'

Petra could hardly sit still. Every little sound made her jump. Putting aside her book, she glanced out of the window and shook her head at herself. It wasn't fully dark yet. Soon, though. She could scarcely see to read. Was Ethan out there already? What if he came too late?

He wouldn't. He was a man one could rely on. It was one of the things she liked about him. She got up, lit the candles and pulled the curtains closed as they usually did at this time of the evening.

Marguerite raised her head from the stocking she was mending. 'Is something wrong, dearest?'

'No. Why do you ask?'

'You sighed.'

Oh, dear. She really did not hide her emotions very well. 'I am not finding this book as entertaining as I thought I might.'

'What is it?'

Petra looked at the cover, having chosen it from random off the shelf and not read a word. '*The Vicar of Wakefield* by Oliver Goldsmith.'

'You do not like it? I found it vastly entertaining. Indeed—'

Petra tossed the book aside. 'I am simply not in the mood.'

'Then I suppose you are not in the mood to read it to me,' Marguerite said, laughing. 'Take out your mending, my dear. I know you have some.'

Petra winced. How could she bear to sit reading or sewing when Ethan might be outside apprehending a criminal? What if the man was dangerous? 'I will read it to you when I return from the privy.'

'You are surely not going outside now?'

'It is not yet full dark. I won't be but a moment.'

Marguerite grimaced. 'Surely it would be better to—'

Petra whisked out of the room before her sister could finish. It was all very well using the chamber pot, but it then had to be emptied—besides, the privy was simply an excuse. She snatched up her cloak and quietly unlocked the back door, intending to sneak around to the front garden to see if her tablecloth remained where she had left it. Of course, she could have gone upstairs to look out, but it would be difficult to see exactly what was going on.

She hadn't gone but a few steps when someone grabbed her from behind and covered her mouth with a large warm hand. The scent of cologne gave her attacker away. Ethan. She relaxed. He turned her around and lifted her hood over her head. 'That bright hair of yours,' he whispered.

Oh, she had forgotten about that.

'I might have known you would not wait indoors,' Ethan muttered in her ear. He pulled her down the path and into the shelter of the hedge.

'No one came?' she whispered.

'Not yet.'

'Is Mr O'Cleary here also?'

'Yes. Hush.'

She subsided into silence, pleasantly tucked against his large warm body. Petra prayed Marguerite would not come looking for her as the minutes ticked by. A squeak of hinges. A burly shape freezing at the sound, then tiptoeing along the path and across the grass. In a second, the tablecloth was torn from the bush and bundled beneath the interloper's cloak.

Ethan and Mr O'Cleary stepped forward. 'Hold,' Ethan ordered sternly.

The thief squawked, made a dash for the gate and was caught around the waist by O'Cleary, who raised his fist, then stepped back, startled.

'I have a pistol,' Ethan warned.

The thief made a choking sound. Mr O'Cleary uncovered the light of a lantern he must have brought for the purpose.

A scared face scrunched up at the sudden glare.

'Good Lord!' Ethan exclaimed.

'Oh, goodness!' Petra gasped. 'Mrs Beckridge?'

The woman drew herself up straight. 'Someone had to do something to get His Lordship to listen to reason.' Despite her bravado, her voice shook.

'Nonsense,' Petra said curtly. 'How dare you try to

put the blame for the thefts on the gypsies? And what is more, you will return everyone's belongings first thing in the morning and apologise for giving them such a scare. Lord Longhurst I assume you will deliver this woman to her husband?'

'That I will. And I will be having a few words with that worthy gentleman.'

Mrs Beckridge moaned.

'Lady Petra,' Ethan said, 'I will call tomorrow to let you know the conclusion of tonight's events.' He bowed and grabbed Mrs Beckridge's arm. 'This way, madam.'

The front door opened. Marguerite stood framed in the doorway with the light behind her and a coal shovel raised above her head. 'Who is out there? Show yourselves,' she quavered.

'It's all right, dearest,' Petra called back. 'It is only I.'

'What on earth is going on?'

'A slight case of mistaken identity,' Petra said, going to her side. She hooked her arm through her sister's and drew her back indoors, trusting Ethan to handle the matter satisfactorily.

She trusted him more than ever she had trusted Harry. She liked him, too. A great deal more than she should for someone who had sworn never to marry again.

Chapter Twelve

Ethan was disappointed when it was Lady Marguerite who met him at the door, but her greeting was warm. 'Quite the adventure last night,' she said, smiling at him.

'Indeed, it was.'

'I assume the Beckridges will not be remaining in Westram?' She sounded pleased. Everyone had sounded pleased.

'They are packing up and preparing to move as we speak.'

She nodded. 'Petra is dying to hear all about it. And she will tell *me* all about it later. You will find her in the kitchen garden. She is expecting you.'

Finally. 'Thank you.'

'Go around the side of the house. I would offer to take your hat and coat, but the wind is rather chilly this morning.'

He did as she suggested and found Petra on her hands and knees weeding an herb garden. She sat back on her heels at his approach. 'Lord Longhurst.' She laughed. 'You always catch me at the worst possible moments.' She gestured to her muddy hems and gardening apron.

As far as he was concerned, any moment he caught her was a good one.

He took her hand and helped her to her feet, inhaling the scent of lavender and thyme and rosemary. 'I am probably earlier than you expected. I apologise, but I thought you might be anxious to hear about the rest of last night's adventure.' That was his story and he was sticking to it. At least for now.

'I am all agog.' She gestured to a wooden seat overlooking the rest of the small garden and the view of the fields beyond. 'Come, let us sit and be comfortable and you may apprise me of all that occurred after you left here.'

He seated her and sat beside her. He crowded her a little more than he ought to, but that was how he felt at the moment. The need for closeness.

'I could not have been more shocked to discover our thief was the Vicar's wife,' she said.

'Nor could Beckridge. At first, I thought they may have schemed up the idea together, but his shock was real enough. He had assumed his wife was tucked up in bed with a headache. His jaw almost hit the floor when she appeared with us on his doorstep.'

'What on earth did he say?'

'Well, it seems Mrs Beckridge rules the roost in that household, so he tried to support her in her exaggerated claims about the gypsies, but when I threatened to call the magistrate and the constable, he collapsed and admitted she was in the wrong.' Though she had threatened to reveal all that she had seen in his study the day she had barged in on him and Petra. A few pithy words had convinced her husband to ensure her silence. He'd also made sure she understood that in his noble circles, widows did as they wished, as did gentle-men, and that neither he nor Petra gave a damn what people like Mrs Beckridge and her social ilk thought.

That the woman believed that about Petra simply proved her stupidity.

'She really is an awful woman,' Petra said.

'Beckridge is a fool to let a woman lead him around by the nose.'

She stiffened slightly.

He frowned. 'I mean in regard to his vocation, his dealings with his flock. He should have known better.' He wasn't sure he had made things any better. The ground beneath his feet felt a little slippery.

'Did you call the constable?'

'Not when Beckridge agreed to leave immediately.'

She nodded. 'That sounds fair.'

He breathed a sigh of relief. 'He said he had been thinking about going to America anyway. He had a let-ter from someone he knows out there indicating they were in need of a pastor. He asked for references.'

'Did you give them?'

He was back on dangerous ground. 'I said I would think about it.' He took a deep breath. 'I did tell him that I would only do so if he promised not to let his wife run amok again.'

'It would be better if you extracted that promise from Mrs Beckridge.'

He gazed at her, at the tightness around her mouth. Of course. This was where he was going wrong. And he definitely did not want to be going wrong at this moment. It would not do at all given his real purpose in coming here today.

'You are right,' he said. 'And so I shall insist.'

Her posture relaxed. Hallelujah.

'There is another matter I wish to discuss with you,' he said.

She perked up. 'About the estate?'

'In a manner of speaking. You will recall the painting you noticed in the hall in my town house. The view of Venice.'

'I do.'

'Well, upon your departure, I got to thinking about the agent who initially offered to take all the items in the house off my hands. He was also quite eager to look at what we had put out in the barn here at Longhurst, with a view to disposing of them. There was something familiar about his name.' He could not keep the note of excitement out of his voice.

'Ethan?'

'I recalled a bill of sale among the papers my cousin left. When I located it again, it was a receipt for a French table and the price was exorbitant, except that someone had scribbled on it the word *Versailles*. I asked around and eventually was given the direction of an agent who purchases French items for the Prince of Wales. He came and looked at the piece and confirmed it indeed could well have been purchased for the Palace of Versailles along with several other items that he looked at. For the paintings he recommended another expert. It turns out the picture you spotted is the genuine article by Canaletto.'

She was staring at him, wide-eyed. 'It must be worth a fortune.'

'My cousin's collection is almost priceless apparently.'

'Oh, my word. What are you going to do?'

'Sell it.' He shrugged. 'Or most of it. My predecessor should never have spent the money he did on all that stuff when the estate needed funds so badly. I am assured that there are several collectors, including the Prince himself, who will be more than happy to pay a fair price for the artwork and the furniture as soon as the provenance is fully documented. And he saw no problem at all with that.'

She beamed at him. 'That is amazing. Wonderful. I am so pleased for you.'

He grinned back at her. 'Now I can finally put the estate to rights. Which leads me to the last reason I came here today.'

He sought the item he had tucked in the watch pocket in his waistcoat and went down on one knee. He smiled at her. 'I think you know how fond I am of you, Petra. I believe you do not hold me in aversion either. I would like to beg for the honour of your hand in marriage.'

At first, she looked surprised—nay, shocked. And perhaps a little pleased. Slowly, though, her expression turned to one of dismay. 'Oh, please. Do not.' She averted her face.

Pain seized his chest. What the hell was the matter with him? He should have known better than to have expected her to behave in a rational manner. His mother never had. One day hot. One day cold. He got to his feet staring down at her. 'I beg your pardon. I must be under some misapprehension about your feelings towards me.'

'No. No. I like you very well, Ethan. Truly I do. I do not wish you to feel that you must marry me, because of what Mrs Beckridge might say to others. I will not do it.'

He shook his head. 'My offer has nothing to do with that woman, I assure you.'

'Are you saying you…love me?'

Love? Did she really expect such a thing? His mother and father had thrown the word around as if it meant everything and nothing. He had certainly not felt more than mild affection for them, as one must for one's parents.

'I am fond of you. I have affection for you. We deal well together. I can now offer you an estate with good prospects which we can build together. Is that not a more solid foundation for a marriage that some passion that is likely to be over within a few months of marriage?'

Her face drained of colour. What had he said to make her react so?

She inhaled a deep breath and rose to face him, or rather look up at him, she was such a tiny thing. He stepped back a little so as not to overwhelm her. She gave a faint smile at that.

'Ethan, I am truly honoured by your proposal. Deeply touched.'

She didn't sound touched, she sounded hurt. As hurt as he felt. He gritted his teeth.

'As you know, I am determined not to marry again.' She winced. 'I do hope we can remain friends, but I think it would be better if we did not see each other again for a while.'

Friends. As clinically as a surgeon with a knife, the word sliced something in his chest to ribbons. It was the oddest and most painful sensation he had ever known.

Even more painful than his mother's frequent rejections of him. As he had when he was a boy, he bore the pain in silence. He bowed. 'As you wish, Lady Petra.'

He walked away.

Was that a sniffle he heard?

Hardly likely. Perhaps she was laughing at him.

Heart aching so painfully she could scarcely breathe for the pain if it, Petra watched Ethan walk away. Had she really suggested they remain friends? It would not be possible. Meeting each other, even casually, would cause the utmost embarrassment for them both. She should have tried harder to express how honoured she was by his proposal, but truly, receiving such a cold offer was worse than knowing he had intended to marry an heiress for her money.

She sank on to the wooden bench.

What was wrong with her that the men she fell for could only manage a lukewarm affection for her rather than love? What was it Harry had said?

I'm very fond of you, old thing, but this marriage was all your idea. I wanted a commission in the army. Once Pa realised he could be related to an earl, there was no talking him round. It was marry you or be kicked out on my ear. No one ever said anything about love. Besides, in our set no husband hangs off his wife's sleeve. I'd be ridiculed.

She'd loved him so desperately from the age of about fourteen she hadn't realised it had been all one-sided. She'd been so angry at his words she'd told him he would make a terrible soldier. A few days later, he'd entered into that silly bet with her brother Jonathan and Neville Saxby and all three of them had gone off to prove their worth.

All they'd managed to do was get themselves killed.

Well, she knew better than to enter into that sort of marriage again. But, oh, she was going to miss Ethan. Somehow, turning down his offer of marriage this time seemed a whole lot worse than saying their lovely goodbye when they knew there was no choice for him but to marry an heiress. Likely because for a moment she had actually thought he was requesting her hand because he loved her.

But he didn't.

And since she loved him, she'd be right back where she was with Harry. Watching her husband sneak off to make love to whichever woman caught his fancy and knowing that her love was not returned. Not to mention that now he had all the money he needed to set the estate to rights, he'd soon be dashing back to the war and his beloved career. No, turning him down was the right thing to do. For them both.

She closed her eyes to ease their burning. When on earth had she fallen in love with Ethan anyway? It really should not have happened. It was meant to be a fling, nothing more. She really was the worst sort of fool.

She brushed the back of her hand across her eyes and it came away wet. Dash it all. What did it matter that he didn't love her? She had been perfectly all right before he came along, and she was perfectly all right now.

She went back to her weeding. Unfortunately, she had no idea what sort of plant she was yanking from the ground. She could not see them through her tears.

She didn't care.

* * *

Petra walked alone to the village a few days later to discover her neighbours still abuzz with the news of the Vicar's departure and the mysterious reappearance of their missing articles.

'His Lordship said it was all a mistake,' Mr Barker said, scratching behind his ear when he held out a small stack of mail. He tapped one of the notes. 'Franked by Lord Westram, that one there is.'

Petra smiled, though her cheeks felt stiff. 'Thank you.' She didn't feel much like smiling these days, but Barker didn't seem to notice the falseness. Nor did he release the letters.

'Odd that. The Vicar going and the laundry reappearing, don't you think, Lady Petra?'

Gossip. The villagers loved gossip and conjecture. She had delayed going to the village as long as possible in order to avoid this kind of discussion, but Marguerite had been worried about the mail piling up and had been too busy to come herself. 'I really have no idea.' She tugged at the letters and finally he released them.

'He said it weren't the gypsies after all.' He sounded doubtful.

'I am sure he knows what he is talking about.'

Barker shook his head. 'Odd, I call it. Very odd.'

Petra turned to leave.

'Don't forget your package, Lady Petra.'

Why could he not have mentioned a package right away? She frowned. 'I do not believe I am expecting a package?'

'It is quite large. Shall I have my lad deliver it?'

'How large?'

He went behind his counter and pulled out a huge square parcel and set it on the counter. 'Heavy it is, too.'

'Who is it from?' Marguerite often sent parcels out, but nothing so large and she had never had one in return.

'From London. Sherman's Antiquities and Fine Art.'

It must be one of Marguerite's pictures, then. 'Thank you.' She eyed the package. 'I think I can manage it.'

When she stepped out into the street, it was still raining hard and she tucked the package awkwardly under one arm while she opened her umbrella. Intent on getting out of the rain as fast as possible, she put her head down and started walking. She collided with someone coming the other way. The package slipped sideways. She grabbed for it and dropped her umbrella. Blast.

'Why can't you look where you are going?' she said as she snagged the handle.

'I beg your pardon, Lady Petra.' A deep, rich and terribly familiar voice.

Heat rushed to her face. The pain around her heart intensified. 'Longhurst,' she snapped and whipped the umbrella back over her head. 'Good day. I am in a bit of a hurry.'

'Allow me.'

He neatly extracted the parcel from under her arm.

'There is no need,' she protested, reaching for it.

'There is every need.' He tucked the parcel under his left arm and it fit there easily. He then held his other arm towards her.

Short of giving him the cut direct there was little she could do. She rested her hand lightly on his sleeve.

She raised her umbrella over her head and they walked in silence. Like an old married couple. And yet like strangers. She had burned her bridges with Ethan and this sort of reminder was just too much to bear.

Finally, she could stand it no longer. 'I can manage the rest of the way by myself.' She sounded stiff and unfriendly.

He did not break his stride. 'I will see you to your door, Lady Petra.'

Blast. If she had acceded to the offer of the postmaster to send his lad, she would not have had to suffer this.

'Do you think it will clear up later?' he asked in the most normal of tones.

She glanced up at the sky. 'I think it is set for the day. Marguerite said she was feeling a headache coming on.'

'Ah. I wondered why you were walking alone.'

She gritted her teeth in case she told him to mind his own business. She wasn't angry at him exactly, merely the circumstances. But there *was* something she needed to say to him. 'The villagers are putting two and two together with respect to the Beckridges's departure and the reappearance of the missing laundry.'

'I expected it, to be honest. I went to see Compton the morning after we caught her in the act. I decided that, as magistrate, he should be made aware of the whole. It is bound to come to his ears and better he heard about it from me. He suggested we let them work it out for themselves, so they do not continue to blame our gypsies.'

'Our gypsies?' she said, surprised.

'My gypsies, I suppose, since they are on my land. I have spoken to their leader and told him what happened. I explained that as long as nothing else untoward happened during the course of their stay in Crabb's Wood, then the villagers would understand that they were not to blame. He understood completely and then informed me that their plans had changed. They had received word of work from another band and had decided to move on after all.'

'How ironic. Mrs Beckridge would have been so pleased to know that her efforts were successful.'

'Though not in the manner she intended.' He sounded amused.

She glanced at his face and saw he was smiling. Unable to resist, she smiled back. 'All's well that…'

'Ends well,' they finished together and laughed.

It was strange that they could be so in accord on some things and so on the outs with regards to others. Her heart gave a little pang. Regret. It was going to be a long time until she did not feel regret.

He opened the front gate for her to pass through and followed her to the front door. Under the porch she closed her umbrella and stood it in the corner to dry. Fortunately, it was their maid's day to work and she opened the door before Petra needed to search for her key. Longhurst handed her the parcel. Petra turned to face her escort and forced a bright smile. 'Thank you for your help, Lord Longhurst.'

'You are very welcome, Lady Petra. It was nice to be able to assist you for a change.' His smile turned a little wry. He bowed and walked back out into the downpour. He didn't so much as flinch when the rain beat down on his shoulders.

Oh, mercy. What was she thinking? She should have offered him her umbrella. 'Lord Longhurst,' she called out.

When he turned she held it out. He waved it off and continued on his way.

She ought to have felt proud of how she had handled their chance meeting, instead she felt more miserable than when she had set out for the village.

'I put the package on the dining room table, my lady,' the maid said, helping her out of her coat and bonnet.

Petra glanced in the mirror to straighten her hair. 'Can you let Lady Marguerite know it has arrived?' Whatever it was.

'But it is addressed to you, my lady.'

'Oh.' She hadn't as much as glanced at the name of the addressee. 'What can it be? I haven't ordered anything.' Something from Red? Or perhaps from Carrie? She was a frequent correspondent, but Petra could not think what she could be sending that was so large.

'You will have to open it and see, my lady.' Becky bustled off.

Petra wandered into the drawing room and inspected the parcel. It was indeed addressed to her. She untied the string and peeled back the paper. A painting.

'Oh, my word!' She sank down on to the nearest chair.

The maid hurried in. 'Is something wrong?'

'I— No, nothing is wrong exactly.'

'That is a nice picture, my lady. What place is that?'

'Venice,' Petra said faintly. He had given her the picture of Venice. She gazed at the signature, now easily visible since the picture had been cleaned. Canaletto. Out of curiosity, she had asked Marguerite about him on her return from visiting Ethan that day. She had gone on and on about the fellow, but at the time Petra had assumed Ethan's picture to be a copy. This painting was worth a fortune.

The maid gathered the brown paper up. 'There is a note enclosed, my lady.' She handed it over. It was from Ethan.

I want you to have this.

Without your help this picture and many like it would have been given away to an unscrupulous dealer.

Keep it or sell it. It is yours to do with as you wish.
Longhurst

Oh, the wretched man. How could he? And he had carried it for her all the way home and not said a word. He must have known exactly what it was.

The tears that she thought had been all used up burned the back of her throat and forced their way from beneath her eyelids.

'You don't like it, my lady?' Becky asked worriedly.

Petra wiped her cheeks. 'It is not that. It was just the surprise.'

And the generosity.

And the foolhardiness.

Chapter Thirteen

'A package for you, my lord,' O'Cleary said. 'And your new bailiff, a Mr David Carter, is waiting in the hall.' O'Cleary set the large square parcel on a chair.

Ethan frowned at it. It couldn't possibly be what he thought it was. 'Show Carter in.'

He got up and tore a corner of the paper. Yes. Unfortunately, it was. Damn it.

'Good day, Lord Longhurst.'

The young man standing on the threshold had been recommended to him by Lord Compton when he had visited him to discuss the Beckridge affair.

Ethan shook hands with the young man and gestured for him to take a seat. He rang the bell for O'Cleary and gave him instructions as to what to do with the painting Lady Petra had returned.

She wasn't going to like his solution.

'There is a great deal to do here, Mr Carter,' he said, resuming his seat.

'Yes, my lord. I took a bit of a look around before I came here. I can see that things have been let go for a while, but with a bit of work it will soon recover.'

Petra would like this young man's attitude.

'Excellent. When can you start?'

Carter looked surprised. 'Don't you want to see my references, my lord?'

'Compton's recommendation was enough of a reference for me,' Ethan said. He himself was also a good judge of character. Most of the time.

He hadn't been too smart in regards to the art-dealer chap. But then he knew nothing about that sort of person. Fortunately for him, Lady Petra had an eagle eye.

She would no doubt like the look of this young fellow.

Damn it. Every time he thought about something, he tried to imagine what she would say, what she would think. Sometimes he even heard her voice in his head, laughing or teasing. He really would have to stop thinking about her. She had rejected his offer and that was that.

'You should still take a look, though, my lord.' Carter handed over a sheaf of folded references.

Ethan went through them. They were all glowing. And all from men who were known to be honest.

He put down the last one and raised his eyebrows. 'So when can you start?'

The other man blushed and smiled. 'In a month's time, my lord. My current employer has sold the property and the purchaser has his own bailiff.'

'How very fortunate for me,' Ethan remarked and entered into negotiations about terms and conditions and salary, based on yet more suggestions offered by Lord Compton.

* * *

'This has to stop,' Marguerite declared. 'This is the third time this painting has come back to us.'

'I can't accept it,' Petra replied exasperatedly. 'You know I cannot. What on earth would Red say to a gentleman offering a lady who is not related to him such a priceless object?'

'I shall go and speak with him,' Marguerite said.

'No. I will go and speak with him.' This time he would listen to reason.

'What did his note say this time?' Marguerite asked curiously.

'If you don't like it, sell it.'

'That was it?'

'A lot of nonsense about paying back a debt to me and his sincere gratitude. It isn't seemly.'

'It might have been more seemly if you had not bedded the man.'

Petra stiffened. 'That is not nice.'

'It is the truth.'

And it was the real reason the painting had to go back. They had been lovers. If Mrs Beckridge had not walked in on them, if there was no possibility of anyone ever learning of their affair, then she might have gladly accepted the gift in recognition of her help with his estate. But since the truth might one day come out, accepting the picture might well look like the spoils of a paid-off mistress. It was that she could not abide.

She had loved Ethan, still did love Ethan, and despite that he did not love her in return, she did not want their relationship tainted by what could be perceived as some sort of commercial transaction.

'It is too bad we cannot sell it, though,' Marguerite mused. 'It would solve all our financial problems.'

'I thought we were out of the woods.'

Marguerite pursed her lips. 'They accepted three of the four botany pictures. I have not yet received another commission.'

'What happened to the fourth one?'

'They decided not to use it.'

'Still, they will have paid you for the work, surely?'

'I have already told you before, that is not how it is done.'

Petra turned back to the package leaning against her chair. She hadn't even bothered unwrapping it. She could not keep it, no matter what. It would hurt too much every time she looked at it. And she certainly could not sell it. 'I will return it myself this time. Do you need the trap today?'

'No. I am going to be working indoors all day.'

She didn't sound happy. Marguerite used to love her painting and drawing. 'Don't do it if it bothers you,' Petra suggested. 'We can find some other way to get income.'

She'd had a million ideas when it came to Ethan's property, but then there were a great many more opportunities to be had on a large estate like Longhurst Park. Their cottage had none.

Marguerite smiled. 'I'm sorry. I am being defeatist. I can do this. I know I can. Take Jeb with you to Longhurst, dearest. Please.'

She didn't need to be reminded to play the part of a proper lady, but she let it pass. There would be no more sneaking into Ethan's home for her and if it made Marguerite feel better to play her part as the responsible elder sister, so be it.

Walking across the lawn, the sight of the little trap travelling up his drive both gladdened and saddened Ethan's heart. An oddly disturbing mix of emotions he did not like to recognise. He certainly knew the purpose for the visit, however. He put down the chair he was carrying and waited for the trap to pull up.

'Good day, my lady,' he said when Petra halted beside him. He nodded at Jeb. 'Your mother is baking biscuits today. You'll find O'Cleary hanging about in the kitchen getting in her way.'

O'Cleary had been helping move the furniture out of the barn, but at the sight of the trap he had developed a sudden need for biscuits and tea.

Jeb grinned. 'I'll take this inside, shall I, my lady?' He hauled the painting out from behind the seat.

'Please do,' she said, her expression cool.

Ethan waited until Jeb was out of earshot. 'All right. You win. I will not send it back again.' There really was no point. She not only did not want him...she clearly did not want anything *from* him.

'Thank you,' she said quietly.

Now she thanked him. Damn it all.

She flicked her whip in the direction of the chair. 'What are you doing?'

He gestured to the growing pile of furniture on the lawn. 'Making a bonfire.'

She gasped, 'You are going to burn it?'

'No choice. It is full of woodworm. That pile is from the attic, but the rest of it is just as bad. I am advised that if I do not want woodworm getting into the structural beams and bringing down the house, it must be burned. It certainly cannot be sold.'

'The pictures, too?'

'Not the pictures themselves. Only the frames.' He shook his head. 'My cousin must have bought something that was infected and they have been having a feast. I really hope I am in time to save the house. I had a chap come down from London to look at it and we have to cut out a couple of diseased sections from the joists, but he says that fortunately the furniture was keeping them too busy to do much damage elsewhere, though it was only a matter of time. I hope he's right.'

Shock and then sympathy filled her expression. Sympathy was better than nothing. He'd take what he could get.

She stared at the pile. 'What a terrible waste.'

He'd been shocked himself. 'Fortunately, none of the items in the town house are similarly affected and the stuff here was less valuable to begin with. The items in London were collected by my cousin's great-uncle.'

'And these?'

'My cousin collected what was here at Longhurst Park. He did not have as good an eye as his predecessor. Most of these are reproductions or badly made to begin with. They wouldn't have fetched much even without the woodworm.'

'I see.'

'Honestly, the previous Earl clearly had no clue what he was doing. He simply could not help himself. Whatever he saw he had to buy. That list we found in my study was not a record of his gambling expenses, but a record of everything he bought for outrageous sums.

I wish he'd had the same compulsion with regard to farm implements. Those we could have made use of.'

'Do you think he suffered from some sort of mental imbalance?'

He narrowed his gaze. Was she wondering the same about him? 'I have no idea.' He looked over at the pile. 'There are one or two items I wish I could have saved, though.'

'Is there no other alternative?'

'There are treatments, I'm told, but nothing is guaranteed. I won't take the risk of losing the house over sentimental rubbish.'

She looked puzzled.

'I had to get rid of the desk in the study. And the chair.'

She gave him an oddly wry smile. 'Sentimental rubbish indeed.'

Damn. He'd obviously said that wrong. 'The memories are all I need.'

Her eyes widened.

A hit. He forced himself not to smile.

'Well, I am truly sorry things turned out so badly for the items here.'

'Me, too. Right now, I'm sleeping on the floor and we still have a great many more rooms to clear.'

'We?'

'Me and O'Cleary. Until the paintings and furniture in London are all evaluated and sold, I still don't have any ready cash to hire the extra help I need and I refuse to go into debt over something I can easily do myself. The dealer thinks we should start seeing income from the auctions at the town house in about two to three weeks.'

'I can lend you Jeb to assist, if you could use his help. He has little enough to do at Westram Cottage at the moment.'

His first instinct was to refuse her offer the way she had refused his painting. But that would be cutting off his nose to spite his face. 'I will accept, provided you allow me to pay his wages for the time he spends here.'

She smiled so sweetly something in his chest clenched and the pain was suddenly so intense his knees buckled. He locked them tight.

'Yes,' she said. 'That would be fair. You can pay him when you have sufficient funds.'

He grinned at her. For a woman she really was quite sensible. 'Good. Send him over in the morning, if that suits you.'

'I'll do better than that. I'll have him set to work now.'

'Even better. By the way, I should tell you I hired a bailiff. He is to start in a month's time.'

'Excellent.' Her tone was just a little too hearty. Could it be that she did not like the idea of him replacing her help? He held that thought close to his heart. It eased the pain somewhat.

'I am sure he would be delighted if you could pass on any of the information you learned over the last few weeks,' he said, hoping for another hit with her. Which was just plain daft at this point. 'I will, of course, try to do so, if you feel it would not be appropriate to speak with him yourself, but you understand it all so much better than I.'

Ah. Yes, there it was. That brightening of her expression that he liked so much.

'I would be delighted to assist him, if needed. But

you should not be so modest. You learn quickly and I am sure you have a good grasp on what is required.'

And so, like the picture, she neatly returned the compliment.

Clearly his case was hopeless.

They waited in silence for Jeb to return so Petra could give him his instructions. It wasn't many minutes before he and O'Cleary arrived on the drive.

'Jeb, His Lordship needs your help for the next few days. Mr O'Cleary will find you a place to sleep.'

Jeb frowned. 'I should ask Lady Marguerite first.'

'No, you should not,' Petra said firmly. 'If she was here now, she would say the same thing. We can manage very well without you at Westram Cottage for a few days.'

O'Cleary grinned. 'A right welcome sight he will be, me lady. Big strapping lad like that is worth ten of me.'

Jeb grinned at the compliment and his ears turned pink. 'You does all right,' he assured O'Cleary kindly. 'I will do as you bid, my lady, but if I am needed back at the cottage, just send word by one of the lads from the Green Man.'

'I promise I will.'

Ethan looked down at her and wanted to kiss her for her kindness. He rolled his aching shoulders instead. The problem was, how could he trust these feelings he had for her when they were together? He could not.

In his boyhood, love was a gift given and taken without rhyme nor reason. His hurt and betrayal haunted him even now. How could he trust that she would not throw his emotions back in his face as she had his marriage proposal?

'Jeb's help is very welcome, Lady Petra. Thank you for your generosity.' Somehow his thanks sounded grudging.

'What are neighbours for, if not to help?' she said lightly.

Inwardly he sighed. Their dealings in future would always be thus. Formal and stiff and uncomfortable.

'Compton's ploughman will come over next week,' he said by way of changing the topic. 'We should be able to plough all of fields we talked about before the onset of winter.'

'That is excellent.' She turned and glanced at the pile of furniture. 'When did you plan setting light to it?'

More trivial conversation. 'As soon as it is all out of the house, I suppose. Shouldn't be more than a couple of days.'

A thoughtful expression filled her face as she gazed up at him. 'Would you mind waiting until next week? I have had an idea.'

'What idea?' Damn, he sounded suspicious.

'I would sooner not say until I am sure it will work. I need to talk to Marguerite.

'I suppose it can wait a few days. It can't do any harm where it is. As long as we don't get a lot of rain, it will just as well light in a few days from now. However, I am due at the opening of Parliament on the fourth and I have to go a few days before then for the fitting of my robe and to allow time for alterations. It is all arranged.'

'Oh, then perhaps my idea will not work. I think you should be here when the fire is lit.'

'I'm sorry, I am confused.'

'Can you be at Longhurst Park on the fifth, the day after Parliament opens?'

'If you want me here, then I will be here. It isn't much of a journey.'

She nodded. 'Very well. As soon as I am sure it can be managed, I will let you know which day your presence is needed.'

He gazed at her, puzzled. 'You have something in mind for this pile of furniture? It cannot be sold. I will not put someone else's property in danger.'

Her smile warmed slightly. 'I know you would not. No, I have an idea about the fire.'

He glanced around. 'It can't do any damage here. It is far away from the house and the trees. You need not fear that.'

'I would expect no less from you, Lord Longhurst.'

Damn it, she was not going to tell him her idea. Because it might not work. And she didn't trust him enough to know that he wouldn't tease her, if it turned out to be without merit.

The thought made him feel unaccountably sad. He nodded briskly. 'Then I shall wait to hear from you before doing anything with it. But I hope we do not get a downpour before I have a chance to light it. The quicker it burns, the better.'

She winced. 'You are right, of course. Perhaps tarpaulins would be the answer. You must have some about somewhere.'

He closed his eyes briefly. 'Of course. I'll see what we can find.'

He handed her up into the trap and watched her drive off.

Tarpaulins. He heaved a sigh and looked at O'Cleary.

'As it happens, Yer Lordship, there be a pile of tarpaulins in the hayloft. I'm guessing they were used to cover the haystacks in inclement weather.'

He should have known about that. He still had so much to learn. 'Right. See if you and Jeb can cover up the damned bonfire with them after all the stuff is out of the house.'

Chapter Fourteen

'Are you sure His Lordship agrees with all this?' Marguerite asked, looking at the list Petra was working on.

'Yes. I wrote to him shortly before he left for London and he agreed to the plan.'

'Well, it is very generous of him.'

'Not that generous. His only outlay is two or three barrels of beer from the Green Man. Jenks is providing them at an excellent price. Everything else, the ladies from the church are providing.'

'I suppose so.' Marguerite looked doubtful.

'The village needs this, Marguerite. Everyone has been at sixes and sevens since the Beckridges left. Quite a few of them still blame His Lordship for letting the gypsies stay on his land as being the reason for the departure of the Vicar. This will help establish some goodwill.'

Marguerite nodded slowly. 'I can see your reasoning. And free beer will go a long way to smoothing any ruffled feathers. But I can't help asking...' She coloured. 'This thing between you and...'

So that was what bothered her sister. 'It is over. We are friends. Nothing more.'

Sympathy filled her sister's face. 'Oh, my dear Petra—'

Petra's heart clenched. 'No. No. You misunderstand. It is ended at my instigation. It was a fling, nothing more. I made it perfectly clear I did not wish for marriage.'

Marguerite looked at her with an expression of wonder. 'If you are sure?'

'I am sure. We get along famously as friends, but the very idea of marrying again gives me nightmares.' Nightmares of Harry being shot alongside her brother and Marguerite's husband. The letter that had come from the military had been a little too graphic in that regard. Red had tried to stop her from reading it, but she had insisted. She did not want to be imagining the same thing about Ethan. Obviously, now he had the money to hire the bailiff he needed to turn the estate around there was no need for him to stay in England and he could be back to the war, exactly as he wanted.

'I see.' Marguerite cocked her head on one side. 'It is good that you are able to be friendly with him. He seems like a very nice man.' Yet there was still some doubt in her voice.

'He is a very nice man and we are friends. That is all there is to it.'

Marguerite recoiled a fraction. Oh, dear, she had spoken with a little too much force.

'The question is,' Petra added hastily, 'can you put this together in time?' She pointed at the rough picture she had drawn. The picture that had started them off on this tangent.

Marguerite gave a rueful little shake of her head. 'Of course I can. It will make a nice break from what I am working on.' She tilted her head back as if easing a crick in her neck.

Petra threw her arms around her sister's shoulders and kissed her on the cheek. 'Thank you, thank you. I knew you would come through for us. Tell me what you need and I'll find it for you.' She pointed to the bag she'd brought from the church. They were clothes donated for the poor. As far as she knew, not one single person had ever taken anything from the bag in all the time she had lived in Westram.

Marguerite rummaged through the bag and set several items on one side. A shirt. An old coat. A pair of workmen's trousers. 'These will be a good start.'

'Wonderful. Let me know when you are finished and I'll have Jeb take it over to Longhurst. Mr O'Cleary knows what to do with it. Now, if you will excuse me, I need to take this list to the church ladies and this advertisement to Mr Barker. He promised to make sure everyone knows about the change in venue.'

'And the free beer.'

The villagers usually had to pay for their beer at this particular annual event. Feeling extremely satisfied with her efforts, Petra grinned. 'And the free beer.'

The ride down from London had been unusually pleasant. Despite the chill in the air, Ethan could only describe it as a perfect autumn day. Beneath a clear blue sky, the trees displayed their reds, yellows and browns, making the rolling countryside come alive with colour and making his travel all the more enjoyable.

Though, to be honest, he was more interested in seeing Petra again and discovering what surprises she had in store for him this time.

He hadn't expected to enjoy being an earl and running an estate, but she had opened his eyes to the bounty and the beauty of the English countryside. Which was why it was a disappointment that she wanted nothing to do with him as a husband. More than a disappointment. It was a cold lump somewhere in the centre of his chest.

He turned Jack into the driveway. The old lad picked up his pace, no doubt thinking of a manger full of hay or a bucket of corn. Ethan could only think of Petra.

Would she be at Longhurst as she had promised?

He hadn't quibbled about any of the things she had requested for her village festival, as she'd called it, even though it had used up all the money from selling his commission. He still could not believe he had sold out from the army without a qualm. His regiment had been his life, yet the thought of leaving England, of leaving his estate in the hands of another now he had the means to do so, had not sat well in his gut.

The house came into view.

Home at last.

He started. When had he come to think of this place as home? He hadn't even known he wanted one. He'd been perfectly happy moving from camp to camp across Europe. It wasn't always comfortable, but he'd enjoyed the comradeship of his fellow officers, leavened by the occasional excitement of battle. Perhaps he was getting old?

His heart lifted at the sight of the diminutive figure on the lawn beside the tottering heap of furniture now more than ten feet high. She lifted a hand to shield her eyes from the glare of the sun as she watched him ride towards her. He sighed. Maybe she was the reason he thought of this place as home.

Except she wasn't part of it.

That icy weight settled on his chest once again, making him struggle to breathe.

He dismounted the moment he came within a few feet of her. 'Lady Petra. Here I am, as requested.'

'Good day, Longhurst.' She smiled brightly enough, but with less warmth than she used to. He ignored the hurt and beamed back.

He liked it better when she called him Ethan. But, of course, that was all over now.

'How was your first taste of the House of Lords?' she asked, tilting her head as if she really cared about the answer.

He forced himself not to respond like an eager schoolboy to that display of interest and reminded himself she was only being polite.

'Not as bad as I thought, to be honest. I took my seat. Asked my question and met the Prince of Wales, who decided to be charming. Of course, he wanted to talk about my treasure trove of paintings. News of that sort travels fast. It appears he is going to be one of those bidding at the auction, but he was angling for a special price. I was able to make a bargain with him.'

'Then I am glad it all went well.'

She sounded happy for him and that pleased him greatly.

'I see you have been busy also,' he said, looking up at the woodpile. At the very top was one of the armchairs that had graced his study and in it was sitting the effigy of a man. He stepped back to get a better look. 'My word, that looks lifelike. Fortunately, it doesn't look like anyone I know.'

Her laugh was full of delight. 'No, indeed. Marguerite was very careful on that score despite that there were a few models she might have liked to use. She used one of the drawings of the original Mr Guy Fawkes as her inspiration.'

'It is splendid. What can I do to help?'

'The funds were all the help we needed. The ladies from the church have the food well in hand, Mr Jenks will deliver the beer barrels in a short while and Mr O'Cleary will set out the benches and the hay bales for people to sit on before everyone arrives.'

'Benches?'

'O'Cleary and Jeb made them up out of odd bits of your furniture. They will go on the fire after everyone has left.'

'Let us hope they do not collapse beneath anyone in the meantime.'

'Even if they do, I doubt anyone will mind, provided they have quaffed a sufficient amount of the beer you have so generously provided.'

He laughed. 'It is my very great pleasure to assist the village in its celebration of the foiling of the plot to blow up the Houses of Parliament, given that I am now one of those sitting above the barrels of gunpowder. Several tuns of beer is a small price to pay for my safety.'

A thought occurred to him. 'When I was a lad we would light squibs and set them off among the folks gathered around the bonfire. I assume that is not the order of the day?'

'No. It is expressly forbidden. Everyone understands that and those with unruly lads are checking their pockets before they leave home.'

'I think I will check O'Cleary's pockets, as well. He is as unruly as any boy I have ever encountered.' He grinned at the thought of the surprise he had brought with him from London. The villagers should enjoy it. He hoped.

She laughed. 'Mr O'Cleary has been a great help. It was he who climbed up and set the chair and Mr Fawkes on top.'

'As I said, a most unruly lad. I wager he enjoyed himself thoroughly.'

'He did. He made sure to do it when I was here showing some of the women from the church what was required. He basked in their admiration.'

'I presume they included one or more of the lasses from the Green Man.' O'Cleary had been spending a good deal of his free time at the inn recently and came home looking very pleased with himself to boot.

'Naturally.'

He wagged a finger at her. 'A man can be convinced to undertake the most dangerous of tasks when watched by one or more pretty ladies.'

They chuckled together, like old friends. Perhaps they could indeed be friends, but he found the idea didn't help with the ever-present chill in his chest.

'I am glad you made it back in such good time,' she said. 'It will help greatly if you are here when the villagers start arriving. I also asked the constable to come and keep an eye on things, and sent a note to Lord Compton inviting him to attend. Unfortunately, he declined. It seems he doesn't like to leave his children.'

'He has several, I believe. All female. I never met them on any of my visits there, but from the noise I heard, they are an unruly lot.'

'Poor man. He lost his wife not long after the birth of his third girl. I am surprised he hasn't married again. He must need an heir.'

Ethan's heart jolted. Was that why she had turned him down? She was thinking of setting her cap at Compton? His earlier regret that Compton would not attend the fire was replaced by a feeling of relief.

'Is there anything you need me to do?' he asked.

'Just play the part of the lord of the manor and make sure no one gets out of order and all will be well.'

'I can do that.' He couldn't wait to see her face when she saw his surprise. And those of the villagers, too, of course.

'I am on my way home,' she said. 'Marguerite and I will come together later. The ladies of the village will arrive shortly to help Mrs Stone in the kitchen. I hope that is all right.'

'Of course. As I said, do whatever you think is best.'

'Thank you. I will be back in plenty of time.'

'Good. I don't want to face the hordes alone.'

She patted his arm and he basked in that little sign of affection. He gritted his teeth against the foolish emotion.

'You know,' she said musingly, 'it is a good thing the Beckridges left when they did or we would be facing a sermon on the evils of popery instead of a cheerful gathering around the bonfire.'

'A blessing indeed.'

Her pretty laugh rang out. He wanted to capture it and put it in a jar. Oh, hell, what had happened to him that he had become so maudlin?

'Make sure you dress warmly when you come back,' he said. 'It will be chilly tonight.'

She gave him an odd look, a measuring glance that he did not understand, but she nodded. 'I'll make sure and remind Marguerite, too.'

He didn't care about her sister. Only her. 'Good idea.'

He watched her hurry towards her waiting trap, her skirts swaying with every step.

What had that expression on her face meant?

Dress warmly. Did he think she was a child? Or was it something else which had prompted his concern? The look on his face when he had said those words had made her really look at him. He looked lonely. When she first met him, he had seemed perfectly happy. Now there was an expression of longing in the depths of his blue eyes.

She shook her head at her wandering thoughts. She had been seeking some sign that he missed her as much as she missed him and that was nonsense. She glanced over at her sister driving the trap. She, too, was bundled up against the evening chill.

'Hopefully, it will be warm by the fire,' Marguerite said as if guessing at her thoughts. Or at least part of them.

They came up on a group of villagers walking down the lane towards Longhurst. They waved cheerfully as the trap passed. 'See you soon, my ladies,' Mr Barker called out.

'Yes, indeed,' Petra replied turning in her seat to wave back. 'All will be ready for your arrival,' she called out.

'Arr,' said another member of the group. 'We seed the beer cart go by. 'Tis all we need.'

The ladies among them giggled.

Petra felt a sense of pride that she had been instrumental in bringing this evening about, though she could not have done it without everyone's help. Especially Ethan's.

Dress warmly.

Did it mean that despite everything he had said, he really did care about her? And if he did, why did it matter? She had ended their affair. They had both agreed it was for the best. The man needed to marry and set about getting an heir.

Her chest squeezed uncomfortably.

No. She did not want to marry again and risk all that heartache.

Only Ethan was not like Harry.

He was honourable and kind.

But he did not love her any more than Harry had.

They turned into Longhurst's drive. A glow in the distance made her frown. 'Have they started the fire already?' Disappointment filled her.

'I don't think so,' Marguerite said. 'No. Look. There are torches set up around the bonfire and partway down the drive. So we can see our way.'

'Oh, yes, I see now.' Ethan must have done that. How clever of him. And it would help keep an eye on the younger revellers, too.

Ethan was waiting to help them down when the trap drew up at the front door. One of the young men from the village leaped forward to take care of Patch and lead him to the stables at the back of the house.

'My,' Petra commented with approval, 'you have been busy in my absence.'

He grinned down at her with his lovely boyish smile. Her heart gave a little jolt. 'And I have found myself a new groom, provided his family agrees.' He gestured to the lad leading their horse away.

She chuckled. 'You are not one to let the grass grow under your feet.'

He glanced down. 'It can't grow under these enormous boots, so I have to keep moving.'

She shook her head at him. 'I'll go and check on things in the kitchen.'

He grasped her arm before she could move. And Marguerite's, too. 'You ladies have done quite enough. Mrs Stone has everything in hand. Leave her to it. Come and take your place by the fire. It will soon be time to light it.'

He led them to a bench. 'Mind how you sit. I cannot promise it won't give way beneath you.'

'I am not that heavy,' Marguerite said with a teasing note in her voice.

'Oh, no, my lady. You are not heavy at all, but those timbers are as weak as water.'

Marguerite sat down with Petra beside her and within a very short space of time all the benches were filled and the men had their mugs of beer and the ladies were quaffing lemonade or the mulled wine set out on a trestle table.

'Light the fire,' someone shouted.

'I'm freezing,' a woman grumbled.

Ethan came forward with a mug of beer in his hand. 'Before we start the festivities, I want to thank you all for coming this evening. We will raise a glass to our King, if you please.'

When the chatter died down, Ethan raised his mug. 'God bless His Majesty, King George. Long may he reign.'

'Even if he is mad,' Marguerite whispered.

'King George,' the villagers shouted, holding up their mugs before drinking.

'God bless His Lordship!' someone else shouted.

Mr Barker, Petra thought.

'His Lordship,' they all cried and drank again.

Ethan looked pleased. 'And here is to the health of Lady Petra, whose idea it was to have this bonfire.'

More cheering and laughing. Then Mr O'Cleary grabbed one of the torches and went around the fire, lighting the strategically placed paper spills. Smoke wafted up and the people on the windward side coughed, fanned their faces and wiped their eyes. Then a chair caught light and flames shot up, and the fire was soon burning merrily.

The women came out of the kitchen and filled the table with trays of food, roasted meat, breads and cheese. 'Help yourselves, everyone,' Ethan said, gesturing to the bounty. A queue formed instantly, with some good-natured pushing and shoving.

'Enough of that now,' O'Cleary said, shouting like a sergeant major. 'There's plenty for all. And I've put some tatties and chestnuts in the ashes to keep your hands warm later.'

Everyone murmured appreciatively and the queue became orderly.

A few minutes later, Ethan arrived at their bench with two plates, one for her and one for Marguerite.

'Don't tell me you used your title to get to the head of the line,' she teased.

'All right, I won't.'

She and Marguerite laughed.

'There have to be some privileges for all this work, you know,' he said cheerfully. 'Besides, the moment I went to the end, they all moved back, to put me at the head, so what else was I to do?'

She laughed at the puzzlement on his face. 'They like and respect you. This is good.'

'I like them, too.' He still sounded puzzled. He handed them cutlery and wandered away. Petra thought he had gone back for food for himself, but then she realised he was moving from group to group around the fire, talking and laughing, and from their beams of delight, clearly charming them.

She had thought Harry charming. But he was not. His charm was shallow and false, used to get what he wanted. Ethan charmed because he was genuinely kind and listened to what each person had to say to him. He had truly found his feet. He would make a wonderful landlord and an excellent lord.

He filled his new shoes as easily as he drew breath. From here on in, he would manage perfectly well without her help.

A lump rose in her throat. A feeling of loss.

Nonsense. They would remain friends.

Not once he was married. They would become nodding acquaintances only. It had to be that way, she could not bear the idea of being the cause of a wife enduring what she had gone through with Harry.

The food on her plate was like cotton wool in her mouth. She ploughed through it determinedly. She did not want Marguerite questioning her appetite or, worse yet, it coming to Ethan's attention.

Who had not as yet eaten anything himself.

She rose and took their dirty plates back to the table, where they were being stacked and from there carried back to the kitchen. She smiled at Mrs Stone, who was presiding over an enormous sponge cake, and was given two napkins and two large slices of the confection. She leaned over the table and murmured, 'I don't believe His Lordship has as yet had any of the food.'

'Ah,' said the cook, nodding in understanding. 'I'll see about that.'

As Petra walked away, Mrs Stone was directing Mr O'Cleary to see to his master's needs.

Petra smiled. His staff loved him almost as much as she did.

She closed her eyes against a sudden burn in their depths. She really had fallen too far and too fast. How could she have done such a foolish thing?

Fallen for a man who frankly admitted he did not love her. At least he had told her the truth. She had to respect him for his honesty.

She went back to her seat beside Marguerite.

'Mmm, this is delicious,' Marguerite said.

'It is, isn't it?' she said cheerfully.

When the food table was empty and everyone had settled down around the fire to keep warm on the outside and quaffed their chosen libations to warm them on the inside, Ethan joined her and Marguerite on their bench.

The warm glow of the fire danced across his face. 'I have a surprise.'

'You do?'

'I do.'

There was a sudden loud bang and the night sky was filled with a million-coloured stars.

'Fireworks,' Petra squeaked. 'Oh, my, how did you manage it?'

'My bargain with the Prince.'

'I love fireworks,' Petra exclaimed and put an arm around his shoulders and gave him a squeeze.

She gazed up in awe, along with everyone else, until she felt the sensation of someone watching her in the flickering firelight. She glanced at Ethan. His gaze was fixed on her face, not the display.

'Is something wrong?'

'No,' he said slowly. 'Nothing at all is wrong.'

Petra looked confused.

'Or maybe there is one thing.' He tipped her chin up and kissed her mouth. 'I have missed this.'

'Ethan! Do not. Someone may notice.'

He straightened. 'No one is looking at us. Watch the fireworks, Petra.' He got up and went to speak with a group of boys who looked like they were about to get up to mischief. He held out his hand and she very nearly laughed when the ringleader dropped what looked like a couple of squibs in his palm.

The man would make a wonderful father.

Her heart felt like it was breaking.

His front was warm from the fire, but his back was freezing. He was used to it from his army days. He glanced at across the circle at Petra. It was probably one of the last times they would be in each other's company. Even if they were sitting far apart.

He had told her to wrap up warm, but the coat she

wore wasn't nearly thick enough. Ladies always preferred fashion over comfort. Although most of the time Petra seemed a great deal more sensible than most women.

He gestured to O'Cleary, who sauntered over, tossing a tattie from one hand to the other. 'Bring out blankets for all the ladies.'

O'Cleary's jaw dropped. 'All the ladies.'

It wouldn't do to single Petra out. Ethan nodded. 'All who want one. There are enough to cover a regiment in the linen cupboard. Take young Jeb with you. He'll help.'

'At once, my lord.'

It wasn't many minutes before he and Jeb returned with armloads of blankets and Petra and her sister were snuggled up warmly. For once he was glad his cousin had hoarded so many items. He didn't even care if the village women took theirs home as long as Petra was warm.

She looked up at his approach. 'Handing out blankets was a wonderful idea,' she said.

He grinned and handed her one of the hot potatoes. 'Eat it or simply use it to keep your hands warm. It's an old army trick.' Not that soldiers ever didn't eat theirs when they could get them. He gave another to her sister, who took it and got to her feet. 'I will go and see if Mrs Stone needs any help.' She wandered off, tossing her potato from hand to hand, her blanket trailing behind her.

'Your sister doesn't look happy,' he remarked.

'No. She's been unhappy since her husband died.' She wrinkled her nose thoughtfully. 'Even before he died. Sometimes I wonder if she lost a child, she seems so sad. But she always denies anything is wrong.'

'There was no issue from the marriage, then?'

'No, and she was married a great deal longer than I.'

'Perhaps that is why she is not happy.'

'Perhaps.' She smiled at him. 'This has been a wonderful celebration, Lord Longhurst.'

A change of topic. He liked that Petra did not gossip about those closest to her. 'Thanks to you.'

She smiled briefly. 'It was my pleasure. I have enjoyed it enormously, but it's probably better if we do not appear to be too cosy together. You know how people gossip.'

The hard, cold lump in his chest expanded until it was once again almost impossible to draw breath. What was the matter with him? He'd faced all kinds of danger in the army and never once felt such a horrible feeling of dread.

He got to his feet and bowed. 'As you wish, Lady Petra.'

He walked away. But he walked away blind. He saw nothing until a young woman stumbled, putting a hand on his chest to save herself. He grabbed her by the elbows.

'Oops, sorry, Your Lordship,' she slurred. She flung her arms around his neck and he barely avoided her planting her lips on his.

'Who are you?' he asked, frowning. She was obviously inebriated. He steadied her, then set her back on her feet a little distance from him.

'I be Kitty, Your Lordship. I work at the Green Man.'

He didn't recognise her, despite the fact he'd called into the tavern for a pint on a couple of occasions, since the one thing his cousin had not collected was good-quality ale. She looked to be about nineteen or so. 'I think you should sit down, Miss Kitty.'

O'Cleary appeared at his elbow, taking charge of the young woman in a most territorial way. 'Feeling a bit under the weather, are you, Miss Kitty?' he said solicitously, putting an arm around her shoulders. 'I think maybe I should see you home.'

Ethan glared at him. 'Not taking advantage of the young lady, are you, O'Cleary?'

'Not at all, me lord.' O'Cleary gave him a cheerful grin. 'I'm making sure those who gave Miss Kitty here too many swigs from their flasks aren't going to take advantage.'

Ethan frowned, then realisation dawned. 'She's the reason you spend so much time at the Green Man.'

O'Cleary winked.

Well, damn. O'Cleary had never been what Ethan would call a lady's man, but judging by his expression when he looked at Miss Kitty, that might well be about to change. 'Well, go on. Get her home safe and sound.'

O'Cleary saluted and put his arms around the girl's waist, whispering something in her ear as he walked away. Apparently, whatever he said found favour with the girl, for she leaned her head against his shoulder.

Ethan had no doubts that Miss Kitty would be safe. In his own rough way, O'Cleary was also a gentleman.

He glanced over to where Petra was seated. All that remained on the bench was a neatly folded blanket. Had she seen what had happened with Kitty and assumed the worst? He did not want her thinking he was the sort of man who would take advantage of a girl out of her wits with drink.

Marguerite was still chatting with the ladies from

the church so Petra could not have gone far. She'd likely be back in a few minutes. He turned at the postmaster's greeting.

'Good evening, Barker. Mrs Barker.'

The lady dipped a curtsy. He supposed he'd get used to all this bowing and scraping one day. 'Thank you for a lovely evening, Your Lordship,' she said. 'It is getting late. Time I took the little one home.' She gestured to the child clinging to her skirts. 'I don't remember when the village had such a good Guy Fawkes Night, truly I do not.'

'I am delighted you think so.'

She beamed. 'So nice not to be forever starting and jumping at the squibs being thrown. And the fireworks were wonderful. I never saw anything so fine, truly I did not. Let us hope we can make it an annual event.'

Good Lord, it seemed he'd started a tradition. Or Petra had. He glanced back to her seat.

Still not there.

His heart gave a horrible lurch. Had something happened to her?

Chapter Fifteen

Petra lay on the grass looking up at the stars. She'd noticed them on her way back from taking care of a call of nature at the conclusion of the fireworks. And as a way to recover from that soft kiss Ethan had pressed on her lips.

It must never happen again. He'd known it, too. The pain of recognising that brief touch of his lips to hers as the end of their relationship had sent her wandering off the moment he left her side. Soon he would marry and rejoin the army. Perhaps once he was out of the country, she would be able to regain some peace. Her heart twisted painfully. How could she ever do that? She would worry about him every single day he was risking his life. Hopefully, in time, she would be able to put him out of her heart, but seeing him tonight, talking with him as if there had never been anything between them, had been difficult to say the least.

She forced her gaze up into the firmament, tried to focus on the vastness above her as a way to redirect her racing mind. She recalled how she and her siblings had crept out on a clear night just like this one when Red had pointed out the constellations with all the authority of an elder brother. She had been very young and she remembered little of his lecture. She did, however, recognise the Milky Way.

Would it appear the same to Ethan in Portugal? How hard he had worked to learn about the estate these past few weeks. And he had an excellent manner with the villagers. Friendly but firm. They would, in time, come to trust him to be fair with them. He would make an excellent earl. If he returned. A hollowness filled her stomach. So many men did not return from the war. She closed her eyes briefly. She would not think of that.

The patch of sky above her went dark.

'Are you all right?' a worried voice asked.

She came up on her elbows. 'Ethan? Oh, you gave me a start.' Dash it all, she should have guessed he would seek her out when he did not see her at the fire. Being alone with him was the last thing she needed right now.

'Did you fall?' he asked. The concern in his voice caused her heart to clench painfully. Why could he not see she came here to be alone? To get her feelings under control. He could not understand, precisely because he did not have those same feelings as she did.

She blinked away the moisture dimming her vision. She would not cry. Their affair was over and that was that.

'I was on my way back to the fire and stopped to look at the stars.'

He sank down beside her and tipped his head back. 'How clear it is. We will have frost tomorrow morning, I fear.'

She forced a laugh. It sounded brittle even to her

own ears. She had to end this and quickly. 'You sound like a proper farmer now.' She sat up, preparing to rise.

He chuckled. 'Soldiers also keep an eye out for the weather, I can assure you.'

'I suppose they must. It is a hard life, yet you miss it.'

'It is all I have known since I was little more than a lad.' He sounded wistful.

She didn't want to talk about his return to the army. She would end up begging him not to go. She did not want him guessing at the depths of her feelings for him. He might feel under some sort of obligation to offer for her again. She really could not bear another of his cool proposals. She pointed upwards and grabbed for a faint memory. 'Isn't that Ursa Minor? I seem to remember it had a bright star at the top.'

'Yes. Polaris.' He pointed and his finger traced a line. 'And there is the Plough.'

She gazed up. 'The vastness makes one feel quite insignificant.'

He lay back. 'Yes, it does.'

Oh, no, him joining her out here was not what she intended at all. 'Oh, my lord, Marguerite. She will be wondering where I am.' She began to rise.

He touched to her shoulder. 'About just now. That girl.'

She froze. 'What girl?'

'You didn't see her?' He hesitated. 'One of the girls from the Green Man threw herself into my arms a few minutes ago beside the fire. I didn't want you to think there was anything untoward going on.'

A chill travelled outwards from her chest. That was just the sort of excuse she always heard from Harry.

Not my fault. I only stopped to help. She kissed me. It meant nothing.

She shook off his hand and scrambled to her feet. 'I have no idea what you are talking about and whatever happened between you and a tavern girl is certainly none of my business.'

He stood up beside her. 'That wasn't why you left the fire and went wandering in the dark?' He sounded confused.

'What you do and who you do it with is none of my concern.'

He stepped back. 'I— No, of course not. I beg your pardon for thinking it might be.'

His cool response stung. But then she had snapped at him the way she never would have dared snapped at Harry, who would have gone off in a sulk for days. Ethan, on the other hand, simply sounded calm and matter-of-fact. Uninterested.

'The fire is dying and people are leaving. It is time I went home.'

He gazed towards the fire, not looking at her. 'Allow me to send you home in my carriage.'

'That will not be necessary.' She did not want to be under any sort of obligation to him. Men. They were all the same. Why had she thought he was any different? She should have known better than to let him worm his way into her heart. Apparently, she had learned nothing from her marriage. Thank heavens she had turned down his proposal. If only it didn't hurt quite so much, then she could be truly grateful.

'Then at least allow me to escort you back to your sister.' The indifference in his voice sent a shiver down her spine.

'As you wish.'

They walked back in a silence so fraught with tension she wanted to scream.

The Guy was nothing but ashes in a fire that had dwindled to a glowing heap of embers. With the food and the beer all gone, the villagers were drifting away in little groups.

'Thank you for a lovely evening, my lord,' Petra said as good manners dictated and honestly, up until the last half an hour, she had enjoyed it immensely. She wasn't one to deny credit where it was due.

He bowed formally and aided them into the trap. The journey home seemed a great deal longer than usual and the wind had the cold bite of looming winter.

Compton's ploughman, Martin Mudge, arrived ready for work the morning after the bonfire. A quiet man with a straw gripped between his teeth, which waggled in front of his face when he spoke. Most distracting as Mudge happily shared his knowledge about ploughs, horses and how to keep a row straight and at the right depth.

For the next two days, Ethan learned all he could. On the third day Mudge let him handle the reins on his own. His back and arms ached from the efforts of the previous two days, when he'd had a hard time controlling both the horses and the plough, but he was determined to continue. Fortunately today, it seemed he had mastered it, somewhat, and with a feeling of satisfaction, he guided the horses across the width of the field, turned them and started back down under Mudge's watchful gaze.

The work did not keep Ethan's mind off the way Petra had turned from warm to frigid in a heartbeat at the bonfire. It had hurt. Perhaps he should not have mentioned the girl, but how could he not? Even if Petra had not seen the way the girl had hung about his neck, she would have learned of it, eventually. Nothing passed unnoticed or uncommented upon by the village gossips. It was the same in the army. The men loved to talk and whisper about anything and everything. When they were in camp for the winter there was little else to do.

Too bad Miss Kitty hadn't fallen into O'Cleary's arms instead of Ethan's. If she had...

Ah, well. There was no point playing what ifs. Petra had assumed the worst of him, the way his father had always assumed the worst. There would be no pleasing a woman like her and it was as well to discover her true nature before he did something stupid like proposing to her again. God help him, she might have accepted, too, if it were not for little Miss Kitty.

He certainly had not expected her to immediately judge him guilty of some wrongdoing. His father always had and his mother had always taken Father's part. Not that Ethan blamed his mother for that. Father had had a wicked temper. For years, Ethan hadn't stood up to him either. Until that last time Father had lashed out.

His father had not realised just how much Ethan had grown that summer. He'd gone from a weedy fourteen-year-old to a strapping lad of fifteen summers in the blink of an eye.

Tired of the bullying, Ethan had lost his temper and struck back. He'd landed a solid blow. Enough to put

Father on his back. Father had at first looked shocked and then furious.

Ungrateful bastard! his father had yelled at him.

The usual feelings of guilt assailed Ethan. And the wish that he could have found a better way of settling his differences with Father. A way that would have brought them closer together. Instead, he'd lost his temper. He had made sure never to do that again. He'd even apologised. But Father had stormed out of the house and Mother had blamed Ethan for the contretemps.

It had struck Ethan then that the only way to get along with his parents was to do his best never to put a foot wrong, never to have opinions of his own or to be anything but perfect. And perfect was something he could never be. Not in his father's eyes anyway.

He'd retreated into silence. Speaking only when spoken to and doing what he was told, no less, no more. He'd been miserable and confused.

A few days later, his uncle came for a visit. His uncle had been a jolly fellow with lots of stories of high jinks from his army days. Ethan expressed interest in the service and his uncle had offered to buy him a cornetcy in the infantry. Ethan had leaped at the chance to leave home.

Much later he had learned that the offer of a commission was his mother's idea. He never knew if it was because she'd wanted to help Ethan or because she simply didn't want Father upset ever again. He'd never cared enough to ask while she was alive and now it was too late.

He shrugged. He doubted he'd like the answer. The army had been the best thing that ever happened to him, despite the risks. And now the army was no longer an option, he was determined to make a go of managing his lands.

He plodded on, up and down, letting his mind go where it would until they reached the other side of the field. It was done.

He dropped the reins and gave the rump of the nearest shire a good solid pat. The rows of heavy soil, curling like ocean waves spread out before him, gave him a feeling of accomplishment. It reminded him of the first time he'd got a company of raw recruits to finally march in unison.

Compton's ploughman grinned at him around his straw. 'We'll make a farmer of you yet, my lord.'

A band seemed to tighten around his chest. Petra had said something similar when they were looking at stars and he had thought about proposing to her again. And then, like an idiot, he had tried to explain what had happened with little Miss Kitty. Just like his parents, Petra had turned on him as if Kitty's actions had been his fault.

Damn it. He should have known better than to attempt to trust anyone, no matter how close they had once been.

He glanced down the rows. No, they were not perfect. Just like him. 'I need a bit more practice.'

'I ain't never seen anyone get the hang of ploughing as fast as you, my lord.'

That was something, he supposed. 'You'll be heading back to the Compton estate this evening, I gather.'

'Yes, my lord. We also has a couple more fields to turn over and they can't wait.'

'I'll send Lord Compton a note of thanks for his

help, if you would be so good as to deliver it. Having you here has been invaluable.' He gave the man a coin.

The old fellow grinned, touched his forelock and was soon on his way. Ethan bade him farewell and led the horses to their stable.

Entering the house through the kitchen door, intending to scrub some of the filth off himself in the scullery, Ethan found O'Cleary dressed, ready to go out.

'It's cook's day off,' O'Cleary announced. 'She left a cold roast in the pantry and there's soup on the hob. I thought I'd go to the pub for a bite to eat, if that suits you, my lord.'

'Very well. I'll help myself.'

'Yes, sir. By the way, the carter arrived with some of the furniture you selected from the town house. I had him put it in the barn. I'll get a couple of lads from the village to help move it inside tomorrow. Meantime, I put your desk and a sofa in the study. Mail is on the desk.' He rattled the information off at great speed.

Ethan nodded.

'Is there anything else I can get for you, my lord?'

O'Cleary clearly wanted to be off. 'No, thank you. Give my regards to Miss Kitty.'

His friend grinned shyly. 'That I will.' He shot off.

Oh, good lord, the man was besotted. Well, he wished him good luck. He just hoped he wouldn't lose him. He'd lost too many people in his life and O'Cleary was one of the better ones.

Along with Petra. He stilled. Where had that thought come from? She'd shown herself to be like every other woman in his life, hadn't she? Hot one minute, then cold the next and without a scrap of caring for him as a person. She certainly didn't want him for a husband.

Ethan stripped off, washed in the scullery sink and, after putting on his dressing gown, ate his supper at the kitchen table. He was starving after working all day in the fields. He hacked hunks off the loaf of bread and dipped them in the soup. He even polished off most of the roast beef. Thoroughly replete, he wandered into his study.

A pile of mail sat in the centre of his new desk.

Thank heavens there had been no woodworm at the town house. He'd been able to keep the plainest pieces for his own use and still had plenty left to sell.

He sorted through the mail. The duns he put to one side. He would deal with those in the morning. He was left with two. One from his man of business and the other in a feminine hand that looked vaguely familiar.

He opened it.

The more he read, the heavier the food in his belly seemed to become. At the end of reading the missive from Lady Frances, his elderly cousin removed by several degrees, he closed his eyes and leaned back in his chair.

Damn her.

She complained that he hadn't let her know he was planning a visit to London or she would have cut short her visit to Bath to meet him there. However, now she was back in town, she had arranged a party to introduce him to the family and to present him with several choices for a bride. The woman arrogantly stated she intended to see him wed and with an heir and a spare before she died.

Not content with forcing an earldom on him and

having him sent home from the war, she now planned to organise his life to her satisfaction.

Well, the lady would have to learn he was not a man to be shoved around.

'His Lordship's gone off to London again,' Mr Barker announced, handing Petra the mail for Westram Cottage.

Petra's heart gave a painful little squeeze. She hadn't known he was going. But then why should she?

'Has he?' she said vaguely, sorting through the letters as if interested in what they contained, yet waiting on tenterhooks for him to say more.

'Yes. Poor Miss Kitty, she be weeping fit to bust.'

The pain in her chest grew worse. She knew exactly how poor Miss Kitty felt. 'Really?'

'Oh, yes, he got all his furniture delivered from town and off he went. Visiting a relative, Mr O'Cleary said.'

Mr O'Cleary should know better to gossip about his master. 'How nice.'

'Arr. When he comes back they are getting married.'

She blinked.

He gave her a smug look. 'Thought you'd be surprised. Old Jenks couldn't believe it hisself. It is not like his Kitty's been an angel, though she seems a lot steadier now.'

'They are getting married?' she said faintly. Indeed, perhaps she was going to faint she felt so dizzy. She had never fainted before, but this news…it robbed her of breath. Ethan and Kitty?

'Yes, my lady. As soon as His Lordship returns and the new Vicar arrives to read the banns.'

'How…how delightful.' She turned to leave.

'Whoever would have expected Kitty Jenks to catch as fine a fellow as Mr O'Cleary? You would think he would have more sense. But there's no accounting for love, they says.'

The world that had been spinning around Petra's head came to a sudden stop. She grabbed for the nearest object to steady herself. It proved to be a table full of bolts of cloth and she leaned against it gratefully.

Barker rushed around the end of the counter. 'Are you ill, Lady Petra?' he asked. 'You've gone all pale. Can I get you something? Water? Smelling salts?'

Petra looked at him through watery eyes. Great heavens, was she crying? 'I am perfectly fine, Barker.' Oh, goodness, yes. She was perfectly fine.

It was if the world had shifted on its axis, giving her a whole new perspective on things.

She put the letters in her basket and marched for home.

'I need to go up to town,' Marguerite announced, glancing up from one of the letters that had arrived in the post.

Petra put down her pen. She had been trying to write to Ethan, but she hadn't got past the initial greeting. How did one apologise and ask a gentleman to offer for one again? 'You do?' Her heart leaped with gladness, because London was where Ethan was and it would be far easier to talk to him than write a letter. But there was an odd expression on Marguerite's face. Petra looked at her sister. 'Why do you need to go again so soon? It is barely three weeks since we were there last.'

Colour washed up Marguerite's cheeks. 'I need to

deliver these drawings in person, they took longer than I expected and I need the money owing on them.'

Marguerite looked...uncomfortable.

'You aren't in any sort of trouble, are you?'

The colour seemed to deepen. Poor Marguerite with her colouring, she never could hide her embarrassment. 'No. I am not in any trouble, but it is not something I wish to discuss.'

Marguerite and her secrets. She would tell Petra only what she wanted her to know. Besides, why did she care about Marguerite's reason? She also wanted to go to London.

'When do you wish to leave?'

'First thing in the morning. Can you be ready by then?'

'I can. Will the town house be open?'

'We are not staying at the town house. We will go to a hotel.'

'Is Red not to know that we are going, then?' Petra asked.

'I will write and tell him. I expect we shall be home before he receives the letter.'

'I wouldn't bank on it. You would be better to give Briggs two days' notice so he can put the knocker on the door. Then Red won't be annoyed.' Briggs was the caretaker and also served as butler when the family came to town.

Marguerite frowned. 'You are right, but I don't have time to await Briggs's pleasure. Dash it, he can put the knocker on the door the moment we arrive. It is not as if the place has been closed up for months. I certainly don't want Red hotfooting down to London for no reason.'

'I'll get started on my packing.'

With a hopeful heart. Petra went upstairs and pulled her trunk out from beneath her bed.

Her heart dipped a bit when she stared into the bottom of it. What if Ethan wouldn't see her after she'd been so distant towards him?

Chapter Sixteen

To Petra's pleasant surprise, Red had been invited to meet the new Earl of Longhurst at a ball being given by Lady Frances. The invitation had been waiting on the hall stand when Petra and Marguerite arrived. To Petra's disappointment, she and Marguerite were not included in the invitation.

'But there is no need for us to go in Red's place anyway,' Marguerite said. 'We have met him many times. He is our neighbour.'

'He is also our friend,' Petra argued. 'I am sure he would appreciate the sight of a familiar face or two.'

'Lord Longhurst seems perfectly capable of taking care of himself.'

'I am going regardless.'

Marguerite heaved a sigh. 'You always were a spoiled brat.'

Capitulation. Petra smiled. 'You always were an absolute dear.'

Marguerite laughed and gave her a hug. 'So, what are you up to, Petra? Have you decided you want him after all? If so, I pity the poor fellow. He doesn't stand a chance.'

She did want him. She'd realised that after the storm of emotions she had suffered in the post office. She wanted him so badly it hurt. But she wanted all of him, not just his friendship or his duty. She wanted his love. On reflection, she was almost convinced he felt more for her than mere friendship. Or attraction. If only he would admit it.

The way he looked at her, spoke to her, responded to her, said he did, whether they were making love or simply talking about his fields. Except that every time things got to a point when he should be expressing his feelings for her, he seemed to shy away from doing so. Perhaps there was something in his past holding him back? It had taken her a great deal of thinking to come up with this revelation. She just hoped she wasn't fooling herself.

'I am not yet completely sure he wants me. Not as much as I'm certain I want him.' She noticed she was not using the word *love*. She had flung it about with abandon in regard to Harry, but with Ethan it seemed too precious, too vulnerable, too easily broken to be sprinkled hither and yon. When she spoke of it, he would be the first to hear it from her lips.

Marguerite patted her shoulder. 'Did you argue the night of the bonfire?'

'Oh, dear, was it that obvious?'

'Perhaps not to others. I sensed a coolness when you bid each other farewell.'

Petra sighed. 'It was my fault. I jumped to a wrong conclusion.'

Marguerite's expression filled with sympathy. 'And you wish to apologise.'

'Yes.'

'Then we shall go to his introductory ball. I will reply to Lady Frances that while Red is not in town, you and I will be delighted to attend in his place. I doubt she will have the nerve to refuse us admittance.' She winced. 'I have heard that Lady Frances is doing her best to marry him off to her niece.'

Petra felt the blood drain from her face. 'Don't tell me she is an heiress.'

Marguerite frowned. 'Not that I am aware. But she is from a very good family, just out of the schoolroom and quite lovely.'

Petra's heart sank. Perhaps he'd prefer to marry a fresh young miss than a widow who had not trusted him to behave with honour.

Well, there was only one way to find out.

Introductory ball! Ethan ran a glance over the debutantes arrayed before him in their finest silks. It was more like market day in Oxted. He tried not to show his distaste. The young ladies were only doing their parents' bidding after all.

Lady Frances, the woman he thought of as his nemesis, had turned out to be a feisty elderly lady with dropsy who favoured the enormous wigs of the last century. And he liked her a great deal despite her odd ways. He stood beside her where she presided over the ballroom from a golden chair of state near the fireplace. She hated to be cold. Something she had in common with the Prince Regent.

Lady Frances slammed her stick against the floor. Her way of getting his attention. 'All you have to do is pick one. Do your duty and get an heir. I went to a great deal of trouble to find you. Now repay me by playing your part, young man.'

While the words were harsh, the twinkle in her eye was not unfriendly. He'd crossed swords a few times with her since their first meeting and she had been delighted by his spirit, as she called it. Apparently, she liked a man who could stand up for himself.

Good lord, what sort of men was she used to? 'I do not suppose you care that I would have preferred to remain a simple soldier.'

'Nonsense.'

It hadn't been nonsense. But... While he didn't care much about the title, there was that odd sensation that at Longhurst Park he was finally home. Much as he had tried, he could not shake it loose.

He had decided that having someone to share his home with would be a good thing. Provided it was the right person. He did not want to end up in the sort of marriage his parents had endured.

'Lady Marguerite Saxby and Lady Petra Davenport,' the butler announced.

His heart gave a painful thump.

'Widows,' Lady Frances said, grimacing. 'Their husbands, silly fellows, went off to war because of some foolish wager. Died for it, too. Those two gals went off and buried themselves in the country.'

She'd been editorialising every guest as they entered. 'They are my neighbours at Longhurst.'

'Are they, by God?'

Her salty language kept taking him by surprise and making him want to laugh. 'They are.'

She perched her pince-nez on the end of her nose and leaned forward. 'Handsome pair. The older one had a come out. The younger married straight out of the schoolroom. Married a proper rogue, as I hear it. Had a wandering eye. Never let an opportunity pass when it came to an available female. She is far better off without him in my opinion.'

Ethan froze, recalling his last conversation with Petra. He'd been explaining the Miss Kitty event, as he'd come to think of it. He'd been wounded by her lack of trust, but in light of this information, her reaction made far more sense. Somewhat. He remained troubled by how quickly she'd turned chilly towards him.

'Which one takes your fancy?' the old lady asked.

Damnation, he had been staring at Petra like a lovelorn swain. 'Lady Frances, I would be obliged—'

'Fiddle-faddle. What is a mind for, if it is not to speak it? Why not enjoy yourself with a lovely widow? They are both of an age to choose a lover.'

Anger heated his blood. 'The ladies are friends of mine. You will not speak of them with such disrespect.' He forced a smile that was both pleasant and dangerous. 'And you will listen to me. I am, after all, the head of your house.'

Lady Frances reared back. Ran her gaze up and down his length. A smile appeared on her face. 'Proving your mettle, are you? Have at it, then, sirrah.' She nodded. 'You will do. Yes, indeed, you will. Glad I didn't let that totty-headed Prince of Wales put the title into abeyance. Very glad.'

Strangely, he was glad, too. 'Good. I will bring the ladies to meet you.'

He marched across the ballroom. People moved out of his path and for once he did not mind that his height and his bulk tended to make people give way.

Petra was smiling at him.

And he was grinning back like a fool.

She held out a hand as he reached her and he took it, touching his lips to the back of her glove, though he knew he should not have. He turned and greeted Lady Marguerite.

'I did not know you ladies were coming up to town.'

'We arrived two days ago,' Petra said. 'We are here as representatives of our brother.'

That would account for their presence. Lady Frances had insisted on inviting every member of the *ton* to this ball. And all their daughters and nieces.

'I want you to meet my elderly relative, Lady Frances.'

'Good heavens, must we? The woman terrifies me,' Marguerite muttered.

'You know her?' Petra asked.

'She is one of the denizens. I was warned at my come out to make sure I did not annoy her or I would find myself barred from Almack's and all sorts of other horrid fates.'

'Oh, my goodness,' Petra exclaimed. 'She sounds like a tartar.'

'Her bark is worse than her bite,' Ethan explained. 'She likes people who stand their ground.'

'Tally-ho!' Petra said and laughed.

God, he'd missed her sense of humour. And her laughter. He'd missed all of her. 'Will you save a dance for me?' he asked. 'The supper dance?' That way, he would be able to take her into supper and sit with her while she ate. It would be a chance to talk. He also had reacted badly at the bonfire. He had withdrawn from combat when he should have regrouped and counter-attacked.

His dealings with his parents had taught him that in relationships it was better to leave the field, but Petra was not like his mother or his father. On the other hand, she should have trusted him. Still, he should not have pulled back without giving her his side of the story.

He offered the ladies an arm each and walked them to stand before Lady Frances's chair. Both ladies dipped elegant curtsies.

'Lady Frances, may I introduce Lady Petra Davenport and Lady Marguerite Saxby. As I mentioned, they are neighbours of mine in Kent.'

'I know them,' the lady replied. 'The Westram girls. Where's that brother of yours? Westram. He was the one I invited.'

'Our brother finds himself detained in Gloucestershire, my lady,' Marguerite replied. 'As I wrote to you.'

The old lady waved a dismissive hand. 'My secretary takes care of correspondence.'

'Our brother suggested we come in his stead,' Marguerite said. 'I had no idea you were related to Lord Longhurst, Lady Frances.'

'Nor did he,' the old lady replied drily. 'But I winkled him out in the end.'

'You did indeed, my lady,' Ethan said, keeping a straight face. 'You are a force to be reckoned with. Even Wellington bowed to your wishes.'

Lady Frances beamed. She was not in the least averse to a bit of flattery.

'Perhaps you ladies can help me,' she said, lowering her voice. 'I need to get this rapscallion cousin of mine married off so I can die a happy woman. Which of these lovelies—' she gave an all-encompassing glance around the room '—would you see as being ideal for him?'

Petra's eyes widened and Ethen wanted to put his boot in his cousin's mouth. Gently but firmly.

Marguerite gave one of her cool smiles. 'Regretfully, I doubt we can be of much help, my lady. We have been out of society for some considerable time and know nothing of this Season's crop of debutantes.'

'Then you are of no use to me,' Lady Frances said, waving them away.

They curtsied and left.

'That was rather rude of you,' Ethan said, watching Petra's diminutive figure as she crossed the room.

Lady Frances sniffed. 'It was the truth. No one ever likes to hear the truth.' She beckoned another young lady hovering on the sidelines just out of earshot. 'Let me introduce you to Miss Carver. Her family have ironworks in the North. Related to some of the best families in England.'

'Not even you can spike my guns, Lady Frances,' he murmured as the young lady hesitantly moved closer.

Lady Frances cackled. 'Don't tempt me.'

The girl, executing a perfect curtsy, gazed at her in terror.

'My word, she really *is* terrifying,' Petra said as she and Marguerite wandered the length of the ballroom.

'Longhurst is more than a match for her,' Marguerite replied. 'She can't resist a handsome face.'

Petra sighed. 'He truly is handsome, isn't he? But more than that he is a truly honourable man.'

Marguerite made a face. 'He certainly appears so.'

'You think otherwise?'

She shook her head. 'I have no reason to doubt him. But then I had no reason to doubt Neville either. Before I married him.'

Petra stopped walking to look at her sister. Really look at her and what she saw was worrisome. Marguerite looked weary and desperately unhappy. 'I—I thought you loved Neville.'

'I hated him so much I wished him dead.'

'Oh, my goodness, Marguerite. Truly?'

'Truly. And that is all I am going to say about it. But, Petra, unless you think you have a real chance for happiness with Lord Longhurst, I recommend you think very carefully before you jump in with both feet.'

'As I did with Harry. He was certainly no angel.'

'As I believe Red tried to tell you.'

Petra sighed. 'He did. But I am older now and much wiser. Besides, I know Ethan a great deal better than I ever knew Harry before we wed. In Harry's case, I saw only what I wanted to see.' She gave a little shrug. 'To be honest, I may have burned my bridges with Longhurst. I was awful to him the last time we spoke.'

'Whatever you do, don't rush headlong into things. It may have worked for Carrie, but that does not mean it works for everyone.'

Was she rushing headlong into Ethan's arms? If only that were true!

'Marguerite Saxby!' One of Marguerite's friends from her debutante days sailed towards them. 'It is an age since I saw you. How are you?' The two ladies entered into a deep conversation about everyone they recalled from their come out and Petra let her mind and gaze wander. It didn't take but a moment for her to spot Ethan dancing with a young lady. A very pretty young lady.

A pang of jealousy struck savagely behind her breastbone. She ignored it. He was the honoured guest at this party. He had to dance with as many young ladies as were introduced to him, but he had claimed her for the supper dance, the best dance of all. She clung to the hope that thought engendered deep in her heart.

'Lady Petra, may I have this dance?'

The gentleman standing before her looked familiar. One of Harry's friends.

He grinned. 'Nate Weatherby, you may recall.'

'Mr Weatherby. I'm sorry. I was wool-gathering. I would love to dance.'

It certainly wouldn't do to dance only with Ethan. People would see it as marked behaviour and start to gossip. Not for anything would she spoil his introduction to society or his chances of making an advantageous marriage, if that was what he wanted.

No one in their right mind would consider her a good match for him. A widow with no fortune. What if he once more offered for her out of a sense of duty? Could she accept that, when she loved him so much? Could she pin her hopes on him growing to love her? Harry certainly hadn't.

She should not have come here. She was doing what she had done with Harry. Chasing him until he had no choice but to make an offer. A sense of panic filled her. The urge to run.

'Is everything all right, Lady Petra?' Weatherby asked. 'You look worried.'

She smiled the way one did in company. One did not wear one's heart on one's sleeve. It simply was not done. 'Everything is wonderful, Mr Weatherby.'

They joined a set that was not yet full and she

danced with all the liveliness of a lady enjoying herself, while inside her stomach was churning and her head was aching. But the more she thought about it the more she worried that she might be ruining Ethan's life.

You ruined my life. The last words Harry had flung at her before he went off to war and got himself and two other men killed.

She could not do that to Ethan, too.

Chapter Seventeen

All evening, he'd anticipated this dance with Petra, but something had changed. Earlier she'd seemed pleased to see him, but now her smile was too bright, her laughter too brittle. And a waltz was no place to hold a serious discussion.

As the music drew to a close, she glanced up with another forced smile and dipped a curtsy. 'Thank you, my lord.'

For a moment or two, he considered walking away. It was what he'd always done at home when Father was in one of his moods and Mother began to flutter in distress. But not this time. He was going to get to the bottom of this. If Petra was upset, then he wanted to know the reason.

He escorted her into the supper room, helped her fill her plate and then found them a table in the corner. It was not the best place for a serious conversation either, but it would have to do.

A waiter brought them drinks—wine for him, ratafia for her—and finally they were as alone as they could be in a crowded room.

'What is making you unhappy?' he asked.

'What are you talking about?' She sounded wary.

'I believe we know each other well enough to sense each other's moods. I cannot tell what is wrong, but I know something troubles you.'

A softness filled her expression as if he had said something that touched her heart. Then she straightened her shoulders as if steeling herself to say something unpleasant. These contradictory signals were driving him mad.

'I wanted to apologise for doubting your word at the bonfire, about Kitty. I was wrong to react as I did.'

Now, that, he had not expected. And how did he tell her that he understood perfectly why she'd reacted that way, without revealing his knowledge of how her husband had behaved? 'Don't give it another thought.'

She frowned.

Clearly that was not the right thing to say. Dash it all, most of their dealings had been honest and straightforward. He wasn't a politician to be dancing around the truth. 'To be honest, I thought you knew me to be better than that.'

There it was out in the open, the plain truth.

She was staring at him, open-mouthed.

'Eat your supper,' he said sotto voce.

Mechanically, she lifted her fork to her mouth, chewed and swallowed. She gave him a bright fake smile. 'You are right. I should have known better.' The words were spoken with great seriousness, but something about the way she looked did not bode well.

'We really need to talk where we cannot be overheard,' he murmured.

'I agree.' She glanced around. 'Where?'

'My chamber.'

'You are staying here?'

'Yes. The auctioneers are still preparing the items in my town house for sale and they have bidders coming and going all day long so Lady Frances offered me a place to stay in the meantime. I actually think she wants to keep an eye on me, in case I decide to make good my escape.'

At that he got a genuine laugh. He relaxed. Somewhat.

'Do you feel like escaping?' she asked gently.

'From here? Certainly.'

'I meant from the Earldom?'

'Not in the least. Much as I hate to admit it, I believe General Wellington will deal with Napoleon and his generals without the aid of yours truly, whereas Longhurst needs its Earl.'

And he planned to do the best job he could, whatever the outcome of this evening. It would be far better, though, if he managed to convince her to stand by his side.

'Where is your chamber?' she asked quietly.

'On the second floor. I'll meet you at the top of the stairs in an hour.'

When they'd finished their supper, he escorted her back to her sister, danced with the next young lady presented to him by his cousin and then slipped away.

With her heart pounding in her chest and her stomach in knots, Petra felt like a schoolgirl up to no good. What if someone saw her? Marguerite might forgive her, but Red never would. What if all Ethan was going to tell her was that he had offered for another lady? Or that he had not forgiven her for mistrusting him? Twice she almost turned back.

Once, when she made her excuses to Marguerite and again now when she set foot on the bottom stair. But then she had not come all the way from Kent and arrived at this party without being specifically invited, only to creep away quietly. If she did not meet him, she knew she would regret it for the rest of her life. She glanced around. There wasn't a soul to see her, so she took a deep breath and hurried up to the second floor.

As he had promised, he was waiting at the top.

He kissed her, a brief hard kiss full on the lips that shocked and delighted her by turns, then he hurried her a few yards down the corridor and opened the door into his chamber. Or rather a suite of rooms. This first room was a grand sitting room, with a sofa and arm-chairs and beautifully polished wood. The muted dark blues and reds made it seem like a very male domain. An interior door led to another room, which she assumed must be the bedroom.

'How very grand,' she remarked, looking around.

'As Earl, I am entitled to the best bedroom in the house.'

She chuckled. 'I can imagine Lady Frances saying those very words.'

He smiled. 'Please. Have a seat.' He poured them both some brandy and handed her a glass and sat beside her on the sofa. 'We might as well be comfortable.'

Always so thoughtful.

She sipped at her drink. It was the very best brandy. She was glad Lady Frances was taking such good care of him.

He gave her a considering glance. 'Do you want to start?'

Did she? Yes, she must. Because if she did not, she might never say what had to be said. 'I am sorry I jumped to such an awful conclusion about you and Kitty Jenks. I value our friendship too much not to attempt an apology. You are right when you said I should have known better. I do hope you will forgive me.' One thing she knew for certain was that she could not bear it if he now hated or despised her.

His mouth tightened a fraction. 'I, too, value our friendship.' He hesitated. 'To be honest, given that you had already declined my offer of marriage, I did not understand why you would react so strongly to a young inebriated wench making improper overtures towards me as if it was all my fault.'

Somehow, he had managed to give her the perfect opening to explain. To reveal her deepest fear. If she dared take it.

She sipped at her drink, whether to grab some courage or time or a bit of both, she wasn't sure. But if she did not take this chance to explain, how could she ever expect him to understand?

'I was very young when I met Harry, my husband,' she said. 'Thirteen. He was only three years older, though it seemed a great deal more at the time. He was charming and fun and he used to talk to me as if I was the most interesting person in the world, unlike my older brothers, who could not wait to get away from me. To them I was nothing but a nuisance.'

'I never had siblings,' he said, 'so it is hard for me to relate, but I can recall friends who had little sisters. They were much the same.'

'Harry was so different from my brothers. So charming. He always took the time to speak to me. I learned later he could not help himself. There was never a female he met that he did not feel obligated to charm. But back then, I thought I was the only one. And I decided he was the man I was going to marry.'

She hung her head in shame when she thought back to how she had plotted and schemed to be in his company every time he visited their home.

'You are a very determined lady,' he said gently. 'It is not a bad trait.'

She forced a smile. 'I am not so sure. I was a spoiled brat, used to getting everything I wanted. Mama died not long after I was born and it so happened I take after her in looks. My older siblings all said I was Papa's favourite and, truth to tell, I knew it. I used his weakness to get what I wanted.'

'And you wanted Harry.'

'Yes. Unfortunately for him, his father also wanted the match. He was in trade and what better way to lift the family up than by marrying into the nobility. He handed over a handsome sum for the privilege of becoming part of our family. Apparently, Harry was pushed into making me an offer.

'I had no idea whatsoever that it was being forced on him. I was full of romantic dreams and proud of being his wife. Until I caught him kissing one of my friends at a party. Another time I found him flirting with my ladies' maid. He laughed it off. Blamed the lady and the maid and said it would not happen again. But it did. Repeatedly.'

Misery filled her heart. She had never been good enough for Harry.

'Finally, I accused him of not loving me or he wouldn't be tempted to stray. He told me he had never loved me and that he wished we had never met. In fact, he said marrying me had ruined his life. The next day he went to join the army on the Peninsula, taking my brother and my brother-in-law with him. They had made some sort of stupid bet about who would make the better soldier. I should never have objected to his dalliances. He was only doing what fashionable men do. All my friends said so.'

Ethan took her hand and stroked it. Even through two layers of gloves it was a lovely sensation. Comforting. Understanding. 'Are you saying because you confronted him with his infidelities, you somehow caused his death?'

'If I had just let him do as he pleased, he would never have gone off to war and Marguerite and Carrie would not have lost their husbands. I swore then that I would never marry again. I was clearly not cut out to be a conformable wife.'

'The man was a fool not to see the treasure he had won.'

Her heart gave a sweetly painful little thump. She swallowed. 'That is the kind of thing my family used to say. But how can I believe it? I chased the man until he had no option but to offer me marriage. I spent hours in his company on our estate, yet I didn't know him at all. He hated the country. He was only happy when in London attending balls and gambling hells.'

'He should have told you this before you wed.' He made a wry face. 'I have met other men like your husband. Men who need to conquer every woman who cross their path. There are also a great many more of us who are true to their wives, you know.'

'I know. There must be something wrong with me, that I could not keep his attention. That is what makes it so hard. Knowing if I had been a better wife, a more interesting woman, Neville Saxby and my other brother might also be alive today.'

'Nonsense. You did everything a wife was supposed to do, not to mention that you are beautiful and clever and sweet. What more could a man want in a wife?'

It wasn't enough. Not without love.

She shook her head miserably. 'I do not know.'

His heart went out to her. Indeed, it was a most painful feeling in his chest now he realised how badly she had been treated, not just by her husband, who was clearly an ass, but also by her family in allowing her to marry at such a young age.

He had learned that all young people go through what was commonly called calf love. He'd experienced it first-hand with one of his superiors' wives when he was about sixteen. He'd made calf's eyes at her for weeks. Fortunately, she'd been kind and motherly and he had recovered very quickly. And later, as he'd matured, he'd recognised it for what it was when other recruits had gone through similar experiences.

Never had any of them married their objects of utter devotion, but then, most of those ladies had been married.

'Petra, I can imagine Harry being flattered by your adoration and letting it go to his head. But he was three years older and three years wiser, and once he agreed to marry you he should have done his duty and been loyal to his wife.'

'His duty.' She sounded appalled.

Damn.

He closed his eyes briefly. 'Ah, yes, my proposal.'

She pulled her hand from his and clasped her hands in her lap. 'Please do not think I am expecting you to offer for me again. I am not. Nor would I accept—'

He touched a finger to her lips. 'I was an ass.'

She kept her gaze fixed on her hands, but he could tell by the slight straightening of her back that she was listening.

He forced himself to continue. 'I waffled on about friendship and duty and companionship when I should have told you instead what was in my heart. Petra, I grew up in a household where my father used love as a weapon. If you did not do exactly what he wanted, praise him to the skies, devote yourself to pleasing him, then you clearly did not love and respect him as you ought. He cared nothing for anyone's accomplishments or successes unless it added something to his own. And when I fell out of favour, which was often, then I fell out of favour with my mother, too. She would whisper that she loved me, but never ever took my side against my father even when she knew I was right. Not that I was the only one to suffer because of his pride. My mother took her fair share of his temper and accusations. When I joined the army, I thought I had found a haven of peace.' He laughed. 'How ironic is that?'

She was gazing at him now. 'It sounds as if you were never sure you were loved.'

'I was not loved in the true sense of the word,' he

said flatly. 'I also learned to distrust the use of that word. It usually followed some sort of punishment.'

'Oh, Ethan, here I am bemoaning that my family loved me far too much for my own good and you were deprived of even a smidgeon of family closeness. What a selfish person I am.'

He retrieved one of her hands and brought it to his lips. He wasn't sure how he'd managed to say all of that, but her response was just what his poor bruised heart needed. 'No. You are a person who gives love as well as receives it. Whereas I have avoided anything closer than distant friendship, or at most companionship. I thought I was happier that way. But when you told me, and rightly so, that what I offered was not enough for you, well, it made me think that perhaps I was missing something important.

'Petra, dearest, I have been drifting through life feeling reasonably contented, satisfied by my work, sure of my honour until I met you. Then I started feeling uneasy to say the least.'

'Oh, Ethan, I am so sorry. I had no idea I made you uncomfortable.'

Hell. That wasn't exactly what he meant. Not at all close.

'What I am trying to say is that, although it has taken me some time to understand what has changed, I now realise that I love you. Indeed, I am in love.' He realised with a wince that he sounded surprised, when he had intended to sound confident and sure of himself.

She gave him a worried look. 'You are?'

'I am.' He threw caution to the wind and went down on one knee. 'Darling, I love you madly. Marry me, please.'

Her pretty face crumpled as if she was going to cry and a chill ran through his blood. She was going to turn him down. Again. He had said too little too late.

'But I am a widow and I have nothing to bring to a marriage. And what if you tire of me and look elsewhere for companionship? I wouldn't be able to bear it.'

He took her in his arms and held her. 'It cannot happen, because I really, truly love you. You have all my heart, my love. There is nothing left for anyone else. I promise.'

He brushed her lips with his and she looked at him shyly. 'I love you so very much, Ethan. Until now, I was afraid to trust what my heart was telling me. It hurt so badly when I thought I had lost you.'

His heart swelled in his chest at her painful admission. He enfolded her in his arms. 'I will trust in that love to see me through all the years of my life. I will never ever give you cause to doubt me, sweetheart, I promise. Shall we go and announce our engagement to the awaiting world?'

'What? Now?'

'Do you still have doubts, then, my sweet?' He held his breath, but, no, he let his breath go. His Petra was as loyal and true as he was himself. And brave, too. She would never back away from a challenge.

'No doubts at all.' She hesitated. 'Oh, dear, but what about Marguerite? I will be leaving her to manage alone.'

'We will invite her to live with us. There is lots of room at Longhurst. She may have a whole wing to herself if she wishes, my love.'

My love. He would never tire of saying it. Until

now, he hadn't realised it was the one thing he didn't have. Had never had. And it was the one thing he really needed.

Her heart was in her eyes when she gazed back at him. 'Oh, Ethan, thank you. I do love you so much. You are the kindest, sweetest...' She flung her arms around his neck and kissed him.

And he would never ever tire of her kisses. When they finally broke apart, they were both grinning like children. He could never remember feeling as happy as he did at this moment.

He squeezed her hard. 'Then let us not delay, please. Let us announce it to the world. Today. Now.'

'I see you have no sympathy for all those debutantes waiting below in hopes of snagging an earl.'

He laughed out loud. 'Not when I can only think of you.'

She sighed. 'That is the most romantic thing I have ever heard. Let's do it.' She swallowed. 'What will Lady Frances say?'

He grinned. 'She will do what any sensible general does when he is faced with defeat. She will withdraw with good grace and say it was part of her strategy all along.'

'Then lay on, Macduff, for tonight will be ours.'

'And all the nights following.'

Arm in arm they went down to the ballroom to make their announcement.

Epilogue

'Let me take a look at you, gal.' Lady Frances rustled into Petra's chamber at the Westram town house, where Marguerite and Carrie were helping her dress for her wedding. Petra had grown fond of Lady Frances, despite her rather dictatorial manner.

Today, the old dear looked magnificent in a striped-black-and-emerald-green silk gown, though her grey-powdered wig with its stiff curls and elaborate decorations made her look eccentric rather than fashionable. When questioned, Lady Frances had explained her hair was far too thin and white to be worn au naturel and, she had added in lowered tones, she felt naked without her wig.

Carrie and Marguerite stepped back out of Lady Frances's way.

Petra twirled to give her about-to-be relative a full view of her wedding gown of rose silk, decorated with Bruges lace and pale cream ribbons. 'Do I meet with your approval, Lady Frances?' she asked in teasing tones.

Lady Frances stared down her nose, but there was a

twinkle in her eyes. 'Pretty enough. I'll say one thing about this modern-day taste for skimpy skirts—looking at your figure, there will be no talk of a babe.'

Marguerite gasped.

Carrie choked on a laugh.

It was also the reason Lady Frances has insisted on a St George's wedding, with the banns being called and the whole of the *ton* invited to witness. There must be nothing havey-cavey or rushed about a Longhurst wedding, she had declared.

While it had been the longest three weeks of Petra's life, she and Ethan had survived the wait and now, today, she was getting married. Her heart picked up speed at the thought of the eyes that would be watching her as she walked down the aisle. But why would she not want to please an old woman who had been nothing but kind, in her own gruff way?

Petra rose up on her toes and kissed the old woman's powdered cheek, inhaling the scent of attar of roses and brandy. 'I am glad you are pleased.'

Lady Frances cackled. 'I liked your spirit the first time I met you, my gal. Now, enough of your titivating, Westram is pacing the floor downstairs.'

'I will be down in a moment.' Petra had quickly realised that while Lady Frances's bark was worse than her bite, the woman was a shocking bully and would ride roughshod over anyone who did not stand up to her. 'But, my dear cousin Frances, you need to leave for St George's right away if you wish to arrive ahead of me.' Lady Frances was renowned for not letting her carriage move faster than a crawl.

The old lady glanced over at her sisters and frowned.

'Who are you?' she asked, pointing a gnarled finger at Carrie.

'That is my sister-in-law, Lady Avery,' Petra said. 'I told you she and Lord Avery were invited to the wedding.'

Lady Frances grunted. 'The other Westram widow.'

Petra winced. None of them liked to be reminded of their disastrous first marriages. Especially Marguerite.

'That's right, my lady,' Carrie said calmly. 'But I'm a married lady now and a Gilmore besides, but I still consider Marguerite and Petra as my sisters, as I hope they consider me.' She opened her arms wide and Petra and Marguerite moved to each side and tucked an arm around her waist.

'Always,' Petra agreed.

'We suffered a great deal together,' Marguerite explained. She gave them both a warm smile. 'It does my heart good to see them happy.'

'Sentimental claptrap,' Lady Frances declared, but she looked pleased. 'All we need now is to see the last of you married and no doubt your brother will be very satisfied. And relieved.'

Marguerite paled.

'Not every widow needs to re-enter the married state,' Petra said firmly, ushering Lady Frances towards the door. 'Why, you yourself never married again after the death of your husband.'

Another cackle greeted this sally. 'I was already an old woman before my Peter died. Well past my child-bearing years and not once did he chide me for not giving him his heir.' She glanced back over her shoulder at Carrie and Marguerite, grinned and winked. 'Not that we didn't give it our best try.'

Carrie giggled. Marguerite looked pained.

'Well, you can be assured Longhurst and I will also give it our very best effort,' Petra said. She opened the door and shooed the old lady out, closing it before the woman could deliver yet another of her shockingly frank remarks.

Carrie collapsed on the bed with a hand over her mouth and her eyes dancing with merriment.

Marguerite lifted her chin. 'It's a good thing she plans to retire back to Bath after the wedding. She is a handful and no mistake.'

'I know,' Petra said. 'But Longhurst seems to manage her very well. She has accepted that he is head of the family.' She chuckled. 'He just has to smile at her and she turns up sweet.'

'He is an extremely charming man, Petra. You have found yourself a gem,' Carrie declared.

'Not charming enough to convince Marguerite to live with us at Longhurst Park,' Petra said. Both she and Ethan had tried to convince Marguerite it was for the best, without success. She was determined to maintain her independence.

'You are planning to get married today, are you not?' Marguerite gave a significant glance at the ormolu clock on the mantel. 'Your poor bridegroom will start to worry that you have changed your mind.'

'Oh,' Petra said, realising how close to the hour it was. 'Let us go.'

They walked down to the carriage arm in arm and climbed in. Red gave the orders to the coachman, who really didn't need any orders. He knew exactly where they were going.

'Next is your wedding, Red,' Marguerite said when he had settled himself beside Carrie.

'It is,' he said, shoulders stiffening as if the reminder was not exactly pleasant. 'The offer still stands for you to come and live with me at Danesbury, you know, Marguerite.'

'Or with us in Wrendean, my dear,' Carrie offered.

'I wouldn't dream of intruding on newly married couples,' Marguerite said firmly. 'It would make none of us happy. I promise I will not be a stranger to your homes and will visit as often as you would care to invite me, but I am happy in Westram with my drawings for company.'

'And she has said the same to me,' Petra added, 'but you may be assured I will be visiting our sister every other day, so you have no need for worry.' Red did worry about her and Marguerite, and Carrie, too, but Petra wanted her sister to lead the life she wanted.

'Not quite every other day, I hope,' Marguerite said drily.

They all laughed and the tension in Red's shoulders eased.

The coach drew up at the door of St George's. On the steps, Lord Avery was waiting for his wife. He looked so handsome in the weak early-December sunlight and the way Carrie's face lit up when he took her arm and gazed down at her was a delight to see. She knew her own face lit up the same way, whenever she looked at Ethan. She just wished Marguerite could find a similar joy.

That wasn't fair. Marguerite was perfectly happy with her independent state and Petra certainly did not want her sister to lose what she considered her precious freedom.

Once the others had entered the church, Red helped her down. He gave her a cheerful brotherly smile, though there were shadows in his eyes. 'It is not too late to change your mind, you know.'

Her jaw dropped. 'W-what?' she spluttered.

He gave her a look askance and shrugged. 'I have been doing some thinking. I do not want you to feel obliged to wed just to please me.'

'I can assure you, I am marrying to please no one but myself.' And Ethan, of course. Dear Ethan.

Red nodded. 'Then on your head be it.'

He had to be jesting, surely. She shook her head at him. 'Really, Red, you do pick the worst of times to tease me. Really, you do.'

His mouth tightened, but he held out his arm to her and together they walked beneath the imposing portico and through the great doors into the church.

Standing at the altar, Ethan turned to watch her walk towards him. For some reason, while this was exactly the way she had pictured this in her mind for the past three weeks, she suddenly felt terribly nervous. Everything inside her fluttered wildly. This was her second time walking down the aisle after all.

Ethan smiled and held out his hand, taking a few steps towards her as she approached. She calmed. This was Ethan. Her beloved, sweet, dear Ethan, who had been deprived of love as a child, yet love for her still shone in his lovely blue eyes and in his expression.

She smiled back and placed her hand in his and together they walked the last few steps to meet their new life. He leaned close. 'You look beautiful. Have I told you recently how much I love you?' he murmured.

'Every day, for the last three weeks,' she whispered back, hugging the memory of their stolen kisses.

'Every day, except today,' he whispered. 'I do love you, my darling Petra.'

'And I love you,' she murmured, leaning into him.

The Vicar gave them a severe look over his glasses.

They released hands and Ethan nodded at him to begin.

'Dearly beloved,' the Vicar said.

Petra had never felt so happy or beloved in her entire life and she knew she would feel like this for ever.

* * * * *